ALMOST HEAVEN

KEVIN BROPHY

DEDICATION

For Sara, a twenty-first gift

First published in 1997 by
Marino Books
an imprint of Mercier Press
16 Hume Street Dublin 2

Trade enquiries to CMD Distribution
55A Spruce Ave Stillorgan Industrial Park
Blackrock County Dublin

© Kevin Brophy 1997

ISBN 1 86023 051 2

A CIP record for this title is available
from the British Library

Cover design by Penhouse Design
Set by Richard Parfrey in Caslon
Regular 9.5/15
Printed in Ireland by ColourBooks,
Baldoyle Industrial Estate, Dublin 13

The Publishers gratefully
acknowledge the financial assistance
of The Arts Council/An Chomhairle
Ealaíon.

TODAY

ONE

It was a shock to see the name in the obituary page of *The Times*: Esmonde FitzArthur.

It wasn't the main obituary, of course. That distinction belonged to yet another knight general of the British military: you got the impression these days from reading the obituary columns (a favourite section of the newspaper for me) that the braided ranks of the British military could by now muster a strong presence on the parade ground of the next life; hardly a week passed without the tribute of printed honours to some deceased hero of Alamein or fallen warrior of Dunkirk. It sometimes seemed to me that the English valued their generals and admirals more than any race on earth.

Which made it all the more surprising to see that name in bold capitals, in the lower right-hand corner of the section: Esmonde FitzArthur.

You didn't expect to find a once-notorious Irish firebrand tucked in among generals of the British Empire and captains of British industry. The irony would not be lost on the old fraud himself, to be numbered among the CBEs, Knights of the Garter and other clusters of imperial initials. I found myself involuntarily leaning back in my chair – my personal property, an old carver salvaged from Portobello Road before the tourists moved in and prices soared beyond the reach of mere lecturers – to study my ceiling (styroboard, standard issue dropped ceiling, lecturers Grade I for the use of, at the University of West London), as if I might hear from above the distinctive, high-pitched FitzArthur giggle, aroused, as usual, by its owner's appreciation of his own magnificence.

It was over thirty years since I'd heard that almost-feminine voice, seen the rounded shoulders shake with unselfconscious glee at some sally of his own. I could still hear it now as I leaned back in my chair, seeing through my office window the red-and-yellow narrowboat moving with laboured gentleness along the Regent's Canal. Sometimes I'd watch the slow passage of these cumbersome vessels for hours – the demand for Comparative Religion at the University of West London was less than hectic – but this morning the canal might have been a distempered factory wall for all the interest it held for me.

Even the dust-dry words of the brief obituary could not conceal the many unexpected paths which Esmonde FitzArthur had walked.

The few words in bold type at the head of the piece were the usual summary in tombstone *Times* style:

Esmonde FitzArthur, noted Irish lawyer, writer and Republican agitator, died at his home in County Mayo on September 14 aged 81. He was born in Belfast on December 27, 1910.

I read on:

Esmonde FitzArthur was a prominent Irish Protestant solicitor who, for his staunchly Republican views, was interned at the Curragh with hundreds of IRA members by the de Valera government in 1943. FitzArthur,

6

according to IRA custom, neither admitted nor claimed membership of the Irish Republican Army: he simply refused to recognise the court of the Irish Free State.

He was a unique figure in Irish life. His father was a noted Gaelic scholar at the old Queen's College, Belfast (now Queen's University) who, unusually for a Protestant, moved his family south to the fledgeling Irish Free State following partition of the island in 1921. He settled in Dublin, moved from academic life to law and, after taking a law degree at Trinity, became a prosperous and popular solicitor.

From his father, Esmonde FitzArthur inherited a love of the law and of Gaelic scholarship, winning an exhibition to Trinity where he read Gaelic Literature. He also developed into a passionate Republican: his vehement denunciation of de Valera's actions as Taoiseach (Prime Minister) – which the young FitzArthur saw as the betrayal of the Irish Republican movement by its sometime leader – would have earned him rustication from Trinity but for the intervention of some powerful friends. In the event, he was awarded a general degree, a disappointment for a scholar of his undoubted promise, and he turned, like his father, to the practice of solicitor.

Throughout the 1930s and early 1940s he represented many of the leading Republicans who were arraigned by the de Valera government. His vigorous protests against the Offences Against the State Acts, which permitted internment without trial, eventually led to his own arrest and internment. He used his time in the notorious Curragh internment camp to teach Gaelic to his fellow-prisoners and, reputedly, to write his autobiography in

Gaelic. Released in 1945, he returned to his legal practice but maintained his Republican links.

In 1948 he was elected to the Irish Parliament on a Republican ticket but lost his seat in the 1951 General Election. This electoral defeat signalled the end of his brief involvement in national politics.

Thereafter he contributed to many journals, legal and political, but his politics were confined to membership of Mayo County Council: he had settled in that western county after his marriage to a local teacher, Irene Shanahan, who predeceased him. He is survived by his only child, a daughter.

His only child, a daughter. Ella from long ago.

Had old Esmonde FitzArthur, like me, concentrated his hopes and passions on his beautiful daughter? When the voters of his parliamentary constituency had rejected him in 1951, had he turned for comfort and inspiration to Ella's embrace? Ella had been seven then, a year younger than myself: in the photographs she had shown me in our stolen, too-brief moments together in our secret places she was a solemn little child: her unsmiling expression in the glossy black-and-white photographs gave no hint of the slender, beautiful young woman whose finger-touch, accepting the photographs back, could reduce me to trembling adoration.

The door of my office swung open abruptly.

Peggy stood in the doorway, grinning at me as she knocked on the opened door.

'Most people knock first,' I said to her.

The secretary of the Department of Comparative Religion (also of the Departments of Social Engineering and of Political Theory) ignored my remark. 'Are we bored to be back after our little junket to the fleshpots of Amsterdam?'

I untilted my chair so that its four legs rested on the parquet floor. 'I was at a conference,' I said slowly, 'on community living in post–Christian society.'

Peggy winked lewdly. You'd never think she was a governor of her local Church of England school in Pinner. 'Looked more like post-coital recollection,' she said, 'the way you were lounging in that chair.'

'How did you ever get to be a grandmother?'

The cramped den from which Peggy single-handedly serviced three (admittedly small) departments in the university's Faculty of Arts and Communications was wallpapered with pictures of Peggy's twin granddaughters at various, minutely recorded stages of their two-year-old lives.

Peggy laughed. 'It all began with that fig leaf and the apple-in-the-garden story that you don't teach in this Religion department.'

I liked Peggy and we enjoyed joshing each other but I wasn't in the mood for a lecture on the shortcomings of religious education today. Esmonde FitzArthur's name stared up at me from the desk. Memory stirred like the remembered taste of wine the morning after: it wasn't pleasant.

I stood up. 'What can I do for you?' I asked her.

'I just thought you'd come to have coffee with me. Next week the canteen will be full of thugs with rings in their ears and trollops with studs in their noses. At least we could have a slightly civilised chat today before the Visigoths return.'

I laughed. Our distinguished university owed its lack of a canteen or restaurant reserved for staff to its origins in the optimistic and egalitarian late 1960s: like Blake's lion and lamb, we all sat down together at the formica-topped tables which more often resembled troughs awash with aluminium Coke cans, styrofoam coffee cups and overflowing tinfoil ashtrays. An image from the High School floated from my subconscious to the forefront of my mind, encouraged, no doubt, by *The Times*'s passionless prose: the long wooden tables in the refectory, each one guarded by a gowned master or mistress, the crockery neatly, almost geometrically arranged on the bare, scrubbed, wooden tables.

Scrubbed by my mother. Her sleeves rolled above her elbows as she worked the hard-bristled scrubbing brush up and down along the grain of the wood. The sweat beaded on her forehead like liquid pearls. Up, down, up, down, along the grain.

'Are you coming?' I heard Peggy ask. 'Or are you still fantasising about the scarlet ladies of Amsterdam?'

Long trestles that stretched the length of the refectory, with long wooden benches on each side of the tables, ten pupils per bench. Ella among them, her solemn features breaking into that beautiful smile at something said by a girl beside or opposite her. That smile that lighted the day and assured you that the world was a beautiful place after all. How could it be otherwise, the way her eyes lit up and her lips opened like a flower?

Myself at the window, my shoes sinking into the soft clay of the rose bed that my father tended, craning to see her through the small pane in the corner of the window, cowering lest I be seen by any of the pupils or teachers seated inside.

'Michael?'

It wasn't, after all, my mother calling my name, wondering what I was doing half-bent in the rose bed under the refectory window. It wasn't then but now, and Peggy's impish features puckered into a quizzical frown.

'Sorry,' I said. 'Time warp. I was just reading about the death of someone I used to know.'

'A close friend?'

10

I shook my head. 'Just the father of someone I used to be close to.'

'I'm sorry.'

'There's no need to be. He led a long and eventful life.'

'Even so.'

'Even so,' I agreed.

I could feel Peggy's eyes upon me. 'And the someone you used to know?'

I turned away from her towards the window. The stretch of the Regent's Canal that fitted into my aluminium window-frame was free of large traffic and birdlife but there were ghosts on the water. I put my hand to my eyes to ward off the spectres that hung out there like hazy question marks.

'Our paths haven't crossed for over thirty years,' I said to Peggy. I half turned towards her, saw the question forming on her lips. Peggy knew half the secrets of the entire faculty and knew where the other half was buried.

Something in my demeanour must have stayed her next question. She and I were the longest-serving members of staff in the building: we accorded to each other the respect due to survivors from a different world, another age.

'I'll be in the coffee shop,' she said.

'I'll be along in a few minutes, Peggy.'

'Please do,' Peggy said. 'I saw Palmer on the prowl a little while ago looking for something else to cut back.'

I grimaced. Palmer, newly appointed dean of the faculty, considered the study of comparative religion to be irrelevant to the modern pursuit of Arts and Communications and had made no secret of his dislike for my tenure at the university. He could bore you into a state worse than death inside two minutes.

'I won't be long,' I promised.

Peggy closed the door of the office gently.

I stared at the institutional-grey door as if it might offer answers. It did not even suggest the right questions.

That part of my life was a distant territory that I had never revisited. This concrete England had taken me to its stony bosom: this late-twentieth-century Ruth did not sing sad songs amid the alien pylons, the hostile garbage on the unswept streets, the mindless graffiti of the Underground. This Babylonian captivity had been entered into willingly: my Babylonian passport had been earned by years of service and acceptance. The alien corn made the bread that I daily broke.

Why then did the voices, echoes anyway, mutter in the attic of my brain? An egotistical, terrorist fellow-traveller had gone to his eternal reward, whatever that might be, and *The Times* had condescended to mark his passing: and nothing more.

But there was more.

There was Ella, her hand in mine as we walked together on a stolen Saturday afternoon along the path beside the railway line. The wind rose, the sea was on the wind and when we turned awkwardly to each other in the shelter of the dark bridge beneath the military barracks I could taste the salt on her lips.

I could taste it now on my own mouth while the waters of a dirty London canal moved not at all beyond my window.

'Oh, Ella,' I whispered, 'Ella, where are you?'

Peggy had a window table in the cafeteria. It afforded a full-frontal view of the three-storey car park, strangely vulnerable now with its empty spaces exposed. Beyond the car park a magenta tube train of the old Hammersmith line rolled across the cityscape: at this distance you could only smell the noise.

I pushed Peggy's tinfoil ashtray towards her as I sat down. 'I thought you were off those bloody things,' I said, 'or was that just yesterday?'

Peggy's eyebrows arched. 'And I thought it was Palmer I should be avoiding,' she said, drawing deeply on her untipped cigarette.

'There's such a thing as passive smoking,' I snapped, 'or hadn't you heard!'

'Fuck off,' Peggy said mildly. 'It's my table, or hadn't you noticed?'

'Sorry – it's just – ' I shook my head wearily.

In the car park a dirty-blue Citroen 2CV was drawing to a halt against the waist-high wall of the second storey. I watched as a tall, skinny youth got out on the driver's side, carrying a paperback. He put his arm around the girl who had got out on the other side: mini-skirt, black tights on good legs, long hair that fell over the neck of her heavy sweater. They paused, and I watched their lingering kiss and the reluctant way in which their bodies separated. Hip-to-hip they moved into the shadows of the car park and out of sight.

'Love's young dream,' Peggy said quietly, and I knew that my attention to the young couple had not gone unnoticed.

'Sorry I snapped at you.'

'Forget it.' She inhaled deeply again: the smoke swirled from her nostrils. 'What's eating you – or would you prefer I didn't ask?'

I shrugged. 'Maybe it's just trying to settle in after the conference, or maybe it's the thought of the Assyrians coming down like the wolf on the fold again next week.'

Peggy drew back from the table, leaned back in her chair. 'I'm sorry I asked. I didn't mean to intrude.'

I looked at her then, saw the hurt in her eyes. We had served too long in the field together for me to fob her off with candy and chewing-gum. Maybe she shouldn't have asked to see my wounds, but I could at least let her see I was shell-shocked.

'No,' I said, 'I'm the one who should be sorry. The truth is I'm not quite sure what's the matter – ' My words floated amid the clouds of her cigarette smoke.

'Maybe it's the someone whose father just died,' she said.

She saw the question in my eyes. 'I am a grandmother,' she said, 'as I so constantly remind everybody. There isn't much I haven't seen before.'

'It was all along time ago,' I said, 'a very long time ago.'

'And you never go back – you never have gone back, all these years.'

I smiled at her. 'How could I leave all this?' I asked, indicating with a sweep of my hand the enormous emptiness of the cafeteria, the shiny-surfaced tables, the empty ashtrays.

'All the same – '

I shook my head.

'I'd always thought the Irish never cut their umbilical cord to the motherland, no matter how far they went.'

'I cut mine a long time ago.'

Peggy stubbed her cigarette in the ashtray, a black hole in the middle of the golden tinfoil sun. I sipped my tea, anything to wipe away the after-taste of those salt lips long ago. Our closed mouths had not even pushed against each other, only the faintest brushing of flesh on flesh, yet I had died there, under the blackened arch of the stone railway bridge.

'We'll be back to normal next week,' Peggy said, 'or whatever passes for normal in these parts, so I'm never going to say this again – what I mean is, I hope you'll forgive me for saying it now.'

I said nothing. The afternoon train from Dublin rumbled towards us and Ella leaned closer to me: a red-faced fellow leaned out of a carriage waving a Guinness bottle in his hand. He yahooed cheerfully to us in the mangled Irish-Cockney accent of a labourer returning from a London building site. 'Hold on to her, lad!' he'd roared. The train whistled, signalling its approach to the town, choking the rest of his benediction. His red face was superimposed upon Peggy's.

'You ought to be married, or with somebody anyway,' Peggy said. 'You owe it to yourself. You're a good man, for all that crusty exterior you wrap around yourself. You should have somebody to go home to, somebody to bring a cuppa to in the mornings.'

She leaned closer to me, elbows on the table.

'You're a nice-looking man, Michael, and you could be happy with somebody – I've seen the way those girls troop into your office with their big calves' eyes and their mouths open.'

'They're always only First Years,' I said, 'and I always leave the door of my office open.'

'I've noticed your open-door policy,' Peggy said, 'and I don't blame you – some of your Religion students look more like raging Madonnas to me.'

'They're only First Years, Peggy,' I repeated.

'Yes, but they'd be back in Second Year and Third Year if you'd open up and let them get close to you.'

'You've been listening to Palmer, Peggy.'

She laughed. Our dean never failed to raise at faculty meetings the phenomenon of a subject which hadn't been taken by a single student at degree level for the last ten years or more.

'He doesn't close his door when he's interviewing female students.'

It was my turn to laugh. 'He's a happily married man,' I said.

'His wife's a lucky woman.'

We began to laugh and then stopped, embarrassed: at the Christmas faculty drinks get-together in this very room we had

15

all been charmed by Palmer's wife and wondered what she was doing with the likes of him. 'Strike that,' I said.

'I shouldn't have said it.'

'We all say things we don't mean.'

'You don't,' Peggy said, 'not often anyway.'

Oh, but I do, I thought. I told the red-faced fellow hanging out of the train carriage that I'd hold on to Ella forever. He hadn't heard me, whisked noisily away by the train, but I'd told him all right and my fingers had fastened more closely around Ella's hand.

'There's still a touch of the priest about you,' Peggy said to me.

'I was never ordained,' I answered. She knew that anyway, from the files in her office.

'You know what I mean, Michael.'

I passed my hand over my eyes. 'I'm not sure what anything means any more,' I said.

She reached across the table. I felt her fingers resting on my arm. 'Term is still eight days away, Michael.'

'So?'

'So why don't you take a break?'

'I've only just come back from a break – remember? Post-Christian society in Amsterdam?'

'That's not what I meant, Michael.'

I didn't want to look at her. 'I know,' I said.

'So what about it?'

I could meet her gaze only for a second. I looked out the window again. You spend your life looking through windows, I told myself: inside or outside, life is always on the other side.

'It was a long time ago, Peggy – there's nobody back there now.'

'It wouldn't hurt to look.' Peggy stood up. 'Think about it,' she said.

'What about Palmer? There's a pre-term faculty meeting day after tomorrow.'

'Fuck Palmer,' Peggy said. 'I'll tell him you're gone off to be installed as the new Archbishop of Canterbury.'

Neither of us laughed.

'I'll think about it, Peggy.'

'Don't think,' she said, 'just get up and go.' She winked at me before she walked away.

I could see Palmer bearing down upon me, an executive galleon decked out in light-grey double-breasted suit with wide multi-coloured tie above a rigging of pale blue shirt-creation. 'O'Hara!' he boomed. 'Just the chap – I've been wanting to have a word with you!' Palmer spoke in cannonades: you could lose your head if you didn't duck occasionally. 'Item Three on the agenda for our pre-term faculty meeting – I'm sure you'll have noticed it – '

'Actually I hadn't.'

Palmer blinked as if an errant seagull had flashed across the sky. The grey plastic-mould chair shuddered as he lowered himself on to it: a toy dock receiving a leviathan. A fit one too: I recognised my envy of his hard, muscled body.

'I'd have thought it'd be the first item you'd notice, O'Hara – correlative analysis of student performance. Absolutely vital to track and analyse if we're to maximise our resources.'

'It somehow escaped my attention.'

Palmer laid his book on the table, with the title accidentally turned towards me: *A Model for Effective Academic Management* by Robin Palmer. It was the third occasion on which Palmer had managed to leave his latest publication under my nose: for the third time I made no comment about the book.

'You did see my piece,' Palmer asked, 'in last week's *Higher Education Supplement*?'

'Afraid not,' I lied, despising myself for the petty envy or anger or whatever it was that prevented me from uttering the ritual compliments on a colleague's work.

Undaunted, Palmer sailed on. I would never be able to like him but I had to admit that he was an impressive figure. Although his half-dozen books, including the one on the table, had been well received by the academic community, his status was not confined to the narrow academic sphere: he was an acknowledged popular guru of academic management (whatever that was) and had appeared more than once on television news programmes and studio chat shows to interpret educational trends for the masses. His acceptance of the job at our very minor university (only recently upgraded from polytechnic status) was a feather in the institution's cap, but most of us realised (some of us gratefully) that the ambitious messiah of academic management would not long walk among us.

'So what d'you think, O'Hara?'

I realised, with some amazement, that Palmer had interrupted himself for long enough to wait for me to say something. I also realised that I hadn't the faintest idea what he had been talking about. 'Sorry,' I said. 'I'm afraid I haven't been listening.'

I was pleased to see Palmer looking outraged. 'And I'm afraid,' he spluttered, 'that I don't have time to repeat it all for you.'

'Don't trouble yourself, Palmer,' I said. 'I have no intention of listening, no matter how many times you repeat yourself.'

'This – this is outrageous!'

'Not really,' I said, standing up. 'I've just had enough of your opinionated hectoring and lecturing, and I don't intend to take any more of it.'

I stood there, looking down at him, watching his jaw move like a broken concertina that gave out no sound. Three postgrad students (none of them mine) had fallen silent at the next table: I knew that we were being observed. I didn't care: I had not lied when I told Peggy that I didn't know what anything meant any more.

The broken squeeze-box at last made a sound. 'Have you gone mad, O'Hara?'

'I'm fine,' I said, 'never better.'

Palmer had recovered his composure and was leaning back in his chair, studying me as if I were an unusual form of lesser life. Ella's father had looked at me like that – oh, there had been a kind enough twinkle in his owlish eyes but there had been no mistaking his expression of surprise and sympathy for what he saw as foolishness.

'I begin to doubt that,' Palmer said slowly. 'In any case, you might consider the question of tracking and analysis before our faculty meeting.'

'Not much point,' I heard myself say, 'since I won't be at the meeting.'

'I beg your pardon!'

'I won't be at the meeting.'

I could almost feel sorry for Palmer: I felt as astonished by my words as he looked. The postgrads at the next table had given up pretending not to be interested in the exchange between Palmer and myself.

'It's a faculty meeting,' Palmer intoned, at his most regal, 'and your attendance is expected.'

I shook my head. 'Sorry, Palmer,' I said, trying to quell the nervous tremor in my voice. 'Nobody is obliged to attend any meetings except during term – and that doesn't begin till next week.'

I picked up my *Times* from the formica-topped table and turned on my heel. My hands were shaking: as I threaded my way between

19

the tables I began to doubt that I'd be able to make it safely to the exit.

I was almost there when his voice boomed. 'O'Hara!'

I turned to face him. He was relaxed and smiling, right ankle draped languorously across his left knee. The restaurant had fallen silent. The few coffee-drinkers, mainly staff, had turned to face me, drawn by the great boom of Palmer's voice in the empty expanse.

'Why?' he called out. 'Why?'

I felt the eyes upon me, felt the crimson spreading across my face. I was a teenager again, and Ella's schoolmates, spruce and confident in the grey uniforms of the High School, were staring at me in the refectory, an interloper with the wrong accent and the wrong clothes.

Palmer's smile did not wane as he waited for my reply.

I cleared my throat nervously. 'I have to go back to the source,' I said, and my voice sounded hollow in the nearly empty cafeteria.

'What source?' he called out.

'The source of everything – where it all began.'

'It sounds like the Garden of Eden,' Palmer said, and the postgrads sniggered.

I let him have the last word. I was too busy trying to grasp the enormity of what I had said. Eden it was not, but the world had been young then. Now was as good a time as any to go back.

I waved cheerfully to Palmer with my rolled-up *Times* as I left. When his time came, he too would figure in its obituary columns: even from beyond the grave the shadow of his achievements would fall upon us. The irony of it struck me: though alive and kicking (or nearly so) I might not even be recognised back among the faces and streets of my youth.

I left the cafeteria: the automatic door swung shut behind me with a pneumatic hiss.

YESTERDAY

Two

The First Year boarders always started the new year at the High School on the first Sunday in September. From about two o'clock onwards there was a steady procession of cars past the gate lodge where we lived, up the short drive to the gravelled crescent in front of the main entrance to the school.

On this occasion, as on all the other first Sundays that I could recall, my mother was nervous and excited about the imminent arrival of the new boys and girls at the High School.

'Eat up your dinner quickly like a good boy and girl,' she said. 'I want to get cleared up so that I'll have time to check a few things before they start arriving.'

'It's only half-twelve, Mammy!' I protested. 'They won't be here for ages yet!'

I was still resentful about having been shunted out to eight o'clock Mass in St Patrick's on the last Sunday of my own holidays. After Mass we'd been allowed barely enough time to wolf down our Sunday sausages and fried bread before Mammy had whipped the crockery off the table and out to the small scullery for washing up.

At ten o'clock she had disappeared into the school, threatening to give a 'last rub' to the linoleum-covered corridors which, you could be sure, were already shining from the previous day's exertion. It had been after midday when she'd come back to prepare, hastily, the dinner we were now being encouraged to bolt.

'Just eat up like a good lad,' Mammy said mildly. 'I want to give the door brasses another rub just to be on the safe side.'

'But they're all shining like gold, Mammy!' Sadie exclaimed. Sadie was twelve, a year younger than me, and still inclined to juvenile fits of exaggeration. 'Sure, didn't you shine them only this morning!'

My mother smiled at her. She was picking indifferently at her usual dinner of mashed potatoes sprinkled with salt and coloured with a knob of butter. She ate like a bird and she looked like one.

'All the same, Sadie,' she said, 'I'd like to give the knob and the knocker a final rub.'

'I'll help you,' Sadie offered. 'I'll do the wash-up.'

My mother reached across the table to lay her hand upon my sister's arm. 'Thanks, pet,' she said. You could see Sadie fairly squirming with pleasure. What else could you expect from a kid sister? My father paused long enough in his assault upon the heaped plate of bacon and cabbage to wink at my sister.

I think I might have been able to keep my mouth shut if it hadn't been for that wink. He never winked at me, and now here we were all happily united in a frenzied gulping-down of our dinner just so that my Mother could apply a fresh coat of Brasso to knobs and knockers that were already gleaming on the school's front door . . . And all to impress a bunch of snooty Protestants who couldn't care less about us!

'I think it's thick,' I said into my plate, taking care not to catch my father's eye. 'It's just stupid polishing those brasses again.'

Out of the corner of my eye I saw his hands pause in mid-air, knife and fork suddenly frozen above his plate. 'What did you say?' His voice was loud in the sudden stillness of our kitchen.

'He didn't mean anything, Jack,' my mother said quickly.

My father ignored her. I noticed even Sadie had stopped eating.

'What was that you said?' my father asked again.

I looked across at him then. He looked huge, framed against the open doorway of the lodge, blocking out the bright September sun. His hands were clenched around his knife and fork; the purple veins stood out in his powerful forearms, angled against the edge of the table.

I bent my head. 'Nothing,' I said.

'It didn't sound like nothing to me.' Still nobody moved at the table. 'Apologise to your mother.'

'He didn't mean anything, Jack,' my mother said again.

'Apologise.'

'Sorry,' I muttered.

'I didn't hear that.'

'I'm sorry!' I said loudly.

'No need to shout,' my father said. 'Just remember to keep a civil tongue in your head – you still have to have manners here, no matter what secondary school you're getting into.'

He bent to his eating again. His full head of dark hair was lustrous in the midday sunlight spilling through the doorway of the lodge. He ate slowly and methodically, turning his fork over to load it with heaped mounds of the white cabbage that Mammy had cooked in the saucepan along with the piece of bacon from Herterich's butcher's shop beside my old school. I waited until he had cleared his plate to make my reluctant request. In another minute he'd be gone, checking the grounds for litter and the flowerbeds for deadheads and it would be too late for reprieve.

'Can I go to the pictures with Billy?' I asked, adding hastily, 'I have the money myself.'

My father looked across the table at me, frowning. 'Sure how can you go to the pictures? Don't you know the day that's in it?'

'There's a good picture in the Hall,' I said, trying to keep my voice level, 'and Billy and all the lads are going to it.'

'You know full well that you can't go to the pictures.' My father's deep voice filled our kitchen. 'You're wanted here to bring the cases in, the same as always.'

'It's not fair!' I protested. 'I'm starting secondary school myself tomorrow and I don't want to be carrying suitcases for a bunch of oul' Protestant snobs and it's not – '

The table shook under the impact of my father's fist. 'There'll be no more talk of that kind in this house,' he said, and the quietness of his tone was more menacing than his bellow. 'The food on this table comes from this school, the roof over your head belongs to them, and don't you ever forget it!'

How could I? I wanted to protest but the tears in my eyes and the fear in my heart made speech impossible.

'The cars'll be arriving soon,' my father said. 'Make sure you're at the school to help me carry the cases and stuff in.' He stood up from the table. The screech of his chair, pushed back on the stone-flagged floor, was piercing in the hushed kitchen. I was afraid to look up at him.

His Sunday shoes padded on the kitchen floor. 'Look at me when I'm talking to you.'

I forced my glance upwards, saw his bulk filling the doorway. 'Don't start getting too big for your boots just because you're going to the secondary school.' He half turned in the open doorway. 'You didn't even earn it, did you?'

'Jack!' My mother's voice was indignant. I could barely see her through the film of my tears.

'Well, it's true,' my father said, then I heard his step crunching along the drive towards the school.

I felt my mother's fingers closing on mine and I whipped my hand away as if I'd been scorched. 'He didn't mean it, pet,' my mother said. Her voice was almost a whisper.

'He meant it,' I cried, choking on my tears, 'and I hate him.'

'Don't say that about your dad!'

I was on my feet then. 'Well it's not fair!' I bawled. 'It's not my fault if I got sick and I'd have gotten the scholarship if I hadn't been sick – '

My mother stood beside me, reaching her hand up to touch my face. 'Your father doesn't always mean what he says!'

'Then why does he say such rotten things?'

My mother sighed. 'What am I going to do with the pair of ye at all?' She seemed to be talking to herself. She sat down again and you'd wonder at someone so bird-like dropping so heavily. 'You're at each other all the time like two oul' dogs at a bone . . .'

'Well, it wasn't my fault that I got sick the day of the maths exam, was it?' My mother could only shake her head, talking to herself. She had no answer to my logic but my debating triumph was small consolation for the ashes in my mouth.

We could hear the gravel groaning under the car before we saw it. Our eyes were drawn to it as it slid by our door, black body and silver chrome gleaming in the sunlight.

'It's the first car,' Sadie said.

'I'm not going up there, Mammy.'

'Come over here to me,' she said.

I shuffled across the floor until I stood beside her chair. This time, when she took my hand in hers, I did not withdraw it. 'He needs your help with all them cases and bags, Michael – don't you know that?'

'I hate it,' I said to her, 'the way they all look through you when you're carrying their stuff, as if you didn't exist at all.'

'They're not so bad when you get to know them,' she said.

'Why did he have to say that anyway?'

27

Her fingers tightened around my hand. 'Will you do it for me so?' she asked. 'Will you go and wash your face and go up and give him a hand?'

Sadie winked at me, but I refused to wink back at her.

'All right,' I muttered, 'but it's not fair.'

When I was washing my face in our scullery I thought I heard my mother saying, 'Lots of things aren't fair', but I couldn't be sure. I dried my face and combed my hair with extra care before going up to the school to carry the new boarders' suitcases into the dormitories.

When Brother Anthony had appeared at the door of the lodge I knew instinctively that my nightmare had come true.

My mother had spotted him first. She was working at the big brown sink in the scullery when she called out to me. 'Open the door, Michael,' she shouted, 'I see Brother Anthony coming through the gate on his bike.' You could see everything that passed through the gate when you stood in the scullery: the small window over the sink faced directly on to the entrance to the grounds of the High School.

Brother Anthony was propping his bicycle against the wall of the lodge when I stepped outside. He stooped to remove the bicycle clips from the bottoms of his trousers and stuffed them into his jacket pocket. Even when he straightened up he reached no higher than my shoulder.

'Is your Mammy in?' he asked me. He smiled at me but his expression gave nothing away. I had not seen Brother Anthony since the last day of the scholarship examination.

'She's inside, Brother.'

I stood aside to let him enter. You stepped straight from the gravelled driveway on to the stone-flagged floor of our kitchen.

My mother was standing in front of the range drying her hands. She laid the towel aside, patted her hair and moved across the floor to welcome Brother Anthony. I wasn't sure if the nervousness of her movements was dictated by the arrival of the Brother or was simply a reflection of my own unease.

I stood back, leaning against the doorjamb, while the preliminaries unfolded. Although there was no fire lighting (it was late August) my mother placed the good fireside chair (my father's seat) in front of the range and pressed tea upon Brother Anthony three or four times. He declined courteously but firmly. He wasn't a great man for the tea at all, he said: at his age it kept him awake at night if he took too much. And no, he wouldn't have a drop of sherry either – there was a bottle of Cyprus sherry stored on the top shelf of the press in the corner of the kitchen – he never took a drop during daylight hours.

It seemed as if this ritual of welcome and tea-offering would last forever, like a dance in slow motion, but it ended somehow with Mammy sitting on one of the kitchen chairs at a respectful distance from Brother Anthony.

The Brother looked about our kitchen with obvious curiosity. 'I thought I might need a passport to get into this place,' he said, 'I mean, me with a Roman collar and all.' He poked a skinny finger inside the front of his stiff white collar as he spoke but he smiled to show that he wasn't serious.

'Sure aren't they the same as ourselves?' My mother said, smiling back at him. She was at ease with Brother Anthony now, sharing a badge, and anyway she'd met him a few times during the years he'd been teaching me.

'All the same – '

'I know what you mean, Brother, what's strange can be frightening.'

Brother Anthony slowly turned his black hat between his small hands. 'I've never been inside a Protestant school before, you know,' he confessed.

'Sure why would you be?' my mother asked.

'Why, indeed?' Brother Anthony mused, as if to himself. He turned in his chair and looked across at me. I wondered if the sudden thumping of my heart could be heard in the kitchen.

'You have news?' my mother prompted.

'I have news,' Brother Anthony answered. He paused and then added, 'I'm afraid it's not the news you'd like to be hearing.'

From his inside pocket he withdrew a folded sheet of paper and handed it to my mother. I watched her unfold the page, watched the characteristic way in which she bit her bottom lip as she concentrated on the contents of the page.

I felt I couldn't breathe: I wanted to turn my head to gulp for air at the open door but my eyes were locked on my mother. Not a breath stirred in the kitchen. Finally she lowered the page until it rested on her knees. She seemed to sag in the chair, as if the effort of sitting upright were suddenly too much for her. She looked at the Brother, then at me. I saw the pity in her eyes and felt the coldness inside myself.

'It seems a shame,' she said at last. Her voice was small; you had to strain to hear her. 'Ten scholarships,' my mother said, 'and Michael came eleventh.'

'It was the maths,' I said, and I didn't try to keep the misery out of my voice. 'I was sick the day of the maths exam . . . '

'You were, to be sure,' Brother Anthony said.

'You got thirty-four marks,' Mammy said.

I could feel again the cramps knotting my stomach as the superintendent handed out the maths papers. Heads bent over the desks, nibs scratched all round me but the cramps had refused to go away. Sweat beading on my forehead, tears streaming from my eyes, I'd been accompanied to the lavatory by the second superintendent. He'd allowed me to half-close the door of the cubicle while my stomach churned and the diarrhoea splashed noisily into the bowl. I reddened, remembering the shame of the smell, the slow process of cleaning my bottom and the insides of my thighs. Three times more I'd been accompanied to the cubicle, while the nibs of my competitors scratched and the minutes ticked away and my hopes of a scholarship were flushed away with the diarrhoea . . .

'You came first or second in everything else,' Brother Anthony said, 'but it was too much to make up with only thirty-four in the maths.'

'I could do them all,' I said, unable to meet his gaze. On the night of the examination, the poison washed out of me, I'd sat at the kitchen table and worked my way, with infinite sadness, through the entire maths paper.

'I suppose there's nothing for it but the Tech so.' My mother's words gave substance to my nightmare. I leaned my forehead against the distempered wall and felt the anger rising inside my shame. The Tech was where the slow fellows went, fellows who'd become messenger boys on black bicycles with wide baskets in front, shouting cheerful obscenities at each other as they negotiated the narrow streets of the town.

I heard myself groan.

Brother Anthony cleared his throat noisily. 'That's not the way of it at all,' he said. 'I had a word with Brother Cyprian, the headmaster in the secondary school, and I explained the situation to him. Anyway, when I told him about Michael being sick and all for the maths exam, well, he agreed with me that it would be a pity if he didn't go to our secondary school.'

I heard the silence in our kitchen. 'But the fees, Brother – ' My mother stammered. 'Sure we couldn't afford it – '

'That's what I'm trying to tell you, Mrs O'Hara, and a bad job I'm making of it too,' Brother Anthony said. 'There won't be any fees.'

My mother exhaled loudly. 'Thanks be to God,' she said, 'and God bless yourself and the Brothers for your kindness.'

Brother Anthony stood up. 'No thanks are necessary,' he said, 'the lad deserves the chance.'

'Have you anything to say to Brother Anthony?' My mother was also standing, looking directly at me.

'Thanks, Brother,' I managed to mutter.

'I told the Brothers in the secondary that you were special,' he said. 'Don't let me down over there.'

I blushed.

'He won't,' I heard my mother say.

Brother Anthony paused in the doorway, standing close to me. 'Anyway,' he said, dropping his voice conspiratorially, 'if we didn't have you, they might take you in up here and turn you into a nice little Protestant.'

'You're a holy terror, Brother!' my mother laughed.

He said good luck to us, bent to fold his trouser bottoms inside his bicycle clips and swung his leg over the bar of his Raleigh. With a final wave he was gone through the open gateway and out on to College Road.

My mother turned to me, her eyes shining. 'Wait till I tell your father,' she whispered.

Reverend Willoughby was standing on the top step, speaking animatedly to a couple of parents. The headmaster of the High School was well served by his name: he was a tall, lean fellow with long arms that he waved with a willowy grace as he spoke, like elegant branches on a high tree.

His high, fluted voice floated towards me, birdsong from a treetop, as I trudged reluctantly along the drive.

'I have been so looking forward to meeting you,' Reverend Willoughby was saying to the shorter man beside him on the top step. 'I have followed your career with the greatest of interest, Mr FitzArthur.'

I paid no attention to the name: a lot of Proddies had unusual surnames.

'It's very kind of you to say so,' I head Mr FitzArthur say in a reedy voice that seemed too thin for his muscular girth.

'I feel it is absolutely vital,' Reverend Willoughby said earnestly, 'that minorites such as ourselves should be able to make their voices heard in the larger community – don't you think so, Mrs FitzArthur?'

The woman on the top step was probably about my mother's age. Her short dark hair was expensively permed and dark-red lipstick emphasised her full mouth. 'You should know,' she said to the headmaster, smiling at him, 'that the Protestant church in Ireland is not the only minority my husband defends.'

'And loves,' Mr FitzArthur added quickly, 'defends and loves.'

'Quite so,' Reverend Willoughby said, and I noticed, standing on the gravel at the foot of the school steps, that Reverend Willoughby's expression was serious now.

'We are not here to discuss my very chequered career,' Mr FitzArthur said, 'but to launch my daughter on her career at boarding school.'

He half turned and I saw the girl who had been standing between the group of adults and the school door. Her father took her hand and drew her into the group. 'I have no doubt,' he said, looking directly at his daughter, but with his voice raised as if he were addressing a large gathering, 'that it will be a successful voyage of discovery and invention – '

'Dad! Don't start!' The girl's protest interrupted what had promised to be a lengthly paean.

'Your father does tend to get carried away at times,' Mrs FitzArthur said dryly, almost to herself.

I watched, unnoticed, as the girl caught her father's arm and leaned her face into his sleeve, laughing. Her father smiled. With his other hand he drew his daughter's dark head closer to himself. Mrs FitzArthur smiled indulgently.

'We're very happy to have your daughter here,' Reverend Willoughby said, 'and we hope she'll enjoy her time with us.'

At that moment the door of the school swung open and my parents emerged, blinking in the sunshine. My father was wearing his good navy-blue suit; my mother had on the black cardigan and black skirt that she wore on Saturday nights when she helped to serve the evening meal in the refectory. I was surprised to see her. After I'd left the lodge she must have changed hurriedly and entered the school through the rear entrance.

I watched my father and mother hover uncertainly beside the little group, waiting for instructions.

'The real managers of the High School,' the headmaster said, stepping around Mr FitzArthur so that he stood beside my parents. 'Our indispensable caretaker, Jack O'Hara, and the equally indispensable Mrs O'Hara.'

Mr and Mrs FitzArthur smiled and said good afternoon.

'Miss Ella FitzArthur is starting school with us today,' the headmaster said.

My father smiled, his hands lightly clasped in front of him, and inclined his head. My mother smiled and made a little curtsy.

I turned away, happy to escape unnoticed.

'Mrs O'Hara's apple tarts and rhubarb tarts are positively divine,' Reverend Willoughby said. 'I hope you'll have time to sample them later in the afternoon in the refectory with the other parents – Mrs Willoughby will be along, of course – I should like you to meet her.'

Mrs FitzArthur said she looked forward to meeting Mrs Willoughby. Mr FitzArthur smiled at my mother and said he was looking forward to trying some really good rhubarb tart.

I tried to press myself into the low balustrade of the steps. 'Will we bring the bags in now, sir?' I heard my father ask.

'Good idea, Jack,' the headmaster said. 'In the next hour or so you're going to be run off your feet with bags and cases.'

'There's no problem, sir,' my father said. 'Michael is going to give me a hand.'

It was no longer possible to blend invisibly into the stone balustrade. At my father's words the headmaster swung towards me; when I raised my eyes I found myself facing the collective appraisal of the entire group. Even the dark-haired girl was studying me with interest. Under their eyes I felt my face warming with redness.

I hated Reverend Willoughby's elegant stance, one thin branch extended, while he looked from me to the FitzArthurs.

'Young Michael,' he fluted, 'is not only a great help to his parents here, but is also the makings of a scholar of whom great things are expected. In fact, he starts his secondary education tomorrow at St Joseph's on – ' the headmaster paused, looking benignly at my mother ' – on a personal scholarship, I'm told.'

I caught a glimpse of my mother's smile as my eyes sought the safety of the gravel.

'I congratulate you on your good fortune, Michael,' Reverend

Willoughby intoned from his eminence. No matter how hard I studied the gravel, it refused to open up and swallow me. I contented myself with imagining the slow cooking of the head-master over an Apache death-fire. 'Make the most of your opportunity, young man.'

I was so surprised to hear myself addressed by the girl's father that I discovered the use of my tongue. 'Thank you,' I managed to stammer.

'Thank you, *sir*,' my father said from the back of the group.

'Never mind that,' Mr FitzArthur said. He turned to the headmaster. 'This St Joseph's is a good school, then?'

Reverend Willoughby thought for a moment before replying. 'Obviously it's not of our persuasion, but it has an excellent reputation for schooling the boys of the town – quite a number of them go up to the local university.'

'You hear that, young man?' Mr FitzArthur said to me. 'You make very sure that you make the most of your scholarship!' I wondered where the crowd was that he seemed to be addressing from the top of the stone staircase.

'It's not really a scholarship – ' I couldn't believe that I was listening to the words uttered by my father. It was bad enough to be subjected to inspection in the first place, but now to hear my father coming out with this stuff –

'Mrs O'Hara has explained that to me,' the headmaster said smoothly and for once I was grateful to him. 'It seems to me that the boy's opportunity is well deserved.'

The gravel crunched again: not one but two cars were nosing their way along the drive. 'More parents!' Reverend Willoughby exclaimed, and the excitement in his voice seemed genuine. 'The Arnolds and the Darlings, I do believe!' He lowered one long leg to the step below and addressed the FitzArthurs again: 'Jack and his lad will see that Ella's bags are brought to the dormitory – do have a look around the school and then be sure to have tea with us and the rest of the parents in the refectory.' He smiled towards the dark-haired girl. 'Naturally your daughter and the other students will be joining us.'

And he left them with an elegant waving of thin branches, beaming past me as he welcomed the new arrivals who were spilling out of their shining cars in a cascade of hats and handbags and pleated frocks.

My father and the FitzArthurs stood beside me on the driveway. 'We'll take the cases in then, sir,' my father said.

Mr FitzArthur opened the boot of the car. A small brown suitcase rested on top of the usual brown wooden trunk that filled the boot: it seemed as if all the High School boarders bought their trunks in the same shop.

My father removed the suitcase and placed it on the gravel. 'We'll take the trunk up first,' he said. He manoeuvred the trunk inside the boot until we could each get a grip of the brown leather handle at each end. His eyes met mine. 'Ready?'

I nodded. Together we heaved the trunk up out of the interior, and he steadied himself, swinging round so that he carried the trunk behind him. I kept my eyes on his back as we mounted the steps to the front door of the school. I wondered what these boarders put into their trunks. Everything I owned, including my school books, would fit into the suitcase that we had left standing on the ground beside the car. Maybe the stuff that they used in the High School uniform not only looked like grey stone but was made of stone as well.

Our small procession entered the front hall of the school. The dark linoleum gleamed from my mother's elbow-grease; the air was rich with the smell of Johnson's floor polish.

'It must have been a lovely old house to live in,' I heard Mr FitzArthur say behind me.

'Difficult to run,' Mrs FitzArthur said. 'Think of all the servants it must have needed.'

I had never thought of the building as anything other than a school. What family would require such spacious rooms, such high windows, such a wide and spacious entrance hall?

'Even so,' Mr FitzArthur murmured, 'even so.'

We passed the school secretary's office on the left: the sliding, frosted-glass hatch was open and you could see Mrs Curtis's dark mahogany desk and straight-backed chair, both of them strangely diminished by the absence of their large, grey-haired owner. On we panted past the Reverend Willoughby's office on the left and the staff toilets and the common room on the right until we reached the foot of the wide staircase which divided the hallway down the middle. Ahead, on each side of the stairs, were doors leading into classrooms. The division of the hallway was further emphasised by the double bank of grey metal lockers which filled the space under the staircase, the boy's lockers on the right, those of the girls on the left.

My father half turned towards me at the bottom of the staircase. 'Are you OK?'

I nodded but said nothing. They'd be queueing outside the Town Hall now, lining up in the shadow of the high grey wall with the coloured poster promising unheard-of adventure in the big picture. I felt the weight of the trunk press itself upon me as my father began the ascent up the stairs. I could sense the FitzArthurs hovering uncertainly behind me as we began our slow progress upwards. When I glanced sideways I caught the doubtful expression on the girl's face and I squared my shoulders visibly and jerked the trunk higher in my palms with such unexpected and unnecessary force that my father was almost thrown off-balance.

'Take it easy, Mikey,' he said, 'we have plenty of time.' I said nothing. We paused to draw breath on the half-landing. 'D'you want to go in front?' my father asked me.

I could feel the dark-haired girl's eyes upon me as I shook my head. I hoped that the half-smile on her lips was not occasioned by the single bead of sweat that was refusing to dislodge itself from its precarious perch on the tip of my nose. It seemed to take for ever to reach the top of the stairs. A narrow gallery ran around the stairwell: when you looked over the mahogany banister the entrance hall seemed a long way down. There were classrooms up here also, on both sides, for the senior classes. The boys and girls up here had separate folding tables and chairs and they used lockers arranged against the walls between the classroom doors. The lockers in the entrance hall were for the younger students.

The other distinction was registered in Latin above the doors, one on each side of the staircase. The sign above the door to the right read *Pueri*; above the door on the left was the inscription *Puellae*.

'Very impressive,' I heard Mr FitzArthur say while I was drawing my breath. 'Take note, Ella,' he went on, 'that the language of Virgil may well be the vernacular in the High School.'

His daughter laughed. She pushed upon the door marked '*Puellae*' and we followed her inside. Everybody knew that the two Latin words meant 'Boys' and 'Girls': Reverend Willoughby had explained them to me years previously, when I had been young enough and foolish enough to be keen on helping my mother with such chores as polishing stairs and shining newels. I wondered, however, who this fellow Virgil was . . .

The dormitory was bisected by a six-foot-high partition that ran almost the entire length of the rom. At right angles to this partition was a series of shorter partitions, like bookends, dividing the dormitory into cramped cubicles, each barely big enough to house a narrow iron-framed bed and a small wooden locker. The cubicles had neither door nor curtain to provide privacy for the occupants. Just a week previously I'd stood on top of a stepladder replacing bulbs in the dormitory: when I'd looked down from the height the entire room had resembled a cardboard box divided up into flimsy compartments and my small room in the lodge had seemed suddenly desirable.

'Is it all right for us non-females to be in here, Jack?' Mr FitzArthur's voice sounded hollow in the empty dormitory.

'Only girls are allowed in here during term, sir,' my father said, without turning round.

'I should think so too,' Mrs FitzArthur said, and her permed hair bounced at the outer edge of my vision.

We came to a halt at the furthest end of the dormitory. Together my father and I lowered the heavy trunk to the linoleum-covered floor. When he straightened I could see the sweat glistening in the ridges on his forehead. 'Since you're first in,' he said to the girl, 'you may as well have the best spot – you're closest to the showers and you'll have at least one side without somebody snoring beside you.'

'Opposite a window too, Ella,' her father said approvingly. 'It faces east, so you'll have the sun to warm you in the mornings.'

'Don't the radiators work?' There was a hint of laughter in the girl's voice.

'I'm afraid we don't turn them on until the first of October,' my father said. What he didn't add was that it meant an extra burden for him, filling the rusty furnace with forkfuls of turf that left a fine layer of turf-mould on his hair and face for months on end.

For a moment we stood in silence at the open mouth of the cubicle that would be the girl's home for years to come. The brown trunk filled the floor space between the bed and the partition. The bed itself looked cold and inhospitable: the naked mattress and uncovered pillow seemed damp, despite my mother's unceasing turning of them throughout the warm and silent days of the summer holidays.

'Let's get the bedclothes out of the trunk,' Mrs FitzArthur said, as if voicing all our thoughts, 'and make your bed, darling.'

'I can do that myself, Mum!'

All the boys and girls in the High School called their mothers 'Mum', like characters in comics or the Jennings stories that I'd begun reading recently.

'Mrs O'Hara will be glad to give you a hand,' my father said.

'Nonsense!' Mrs FitzArthur said emphatically. 'I've been making beds all my life and anyway I'm sure your poor wife has more than enough to do on a day like this.'

'I'll leave you to it so,' my father said, turning away. 'There'll be others below needing a hand.'

'Thank you for your help, Jack,' the girl's father said, fumbling with a fistful of coins. I saw my father pocket the silver coin – it looked a two-shilling piece – heard him say thank you and wished I were dead when the girl caught my eye. It seemed to me that she was able to tell what I was thinking.

'I'll go down for my case,' the girl said.

'Michael will bring it up,' my father said. He seemed to tip a non-existent cap to the FitzArthurs and then marched away with the rolling swagger that gave away his boxing youth. There would be plenty of trunks to carry upstairs; you could tell from the excited babble of voices coming through the open windows of the dormitory that the trickle of arrivals had swelled to a flood. There would be too much for my father to handle; the boys and their fathers generally helped out.

'I'll come with you,' the girl said. I knew I was blushing. 'To get my suitcase,' she added. 'Come on, slowcoach!'

She gave a small wave to her parents as she propelled me towards the door, along the passageway between the cubicles and the row of washbasins that occupied the wall space between the windows, one basin per cubicle.

A cloud of noise and cigarette smoke rose to meet us when we stepped out of the dormitory on to the landing. When we looked over the banister we could see the crowd of parents milling about in the hall below, the men in suits or blazers, the women mostly in short-sleeved frocks and summer hats. All my life I'd been listening to the braying of these parents, and still I wondered at the loudness of their voices, the ease with which they seemed to colonise whatever space they occupied.

'Your dad's lovely,' the girl said to me. She still had her left hand on my upper arm. She made no move to go down the stairs.

'He's OK.'

'Was he a boxer?'

I looked at her then. 'Yes – how did you know.'

'He moves like a boxer,' she said, 'and – and his nose.'

'It was broken a few times,' I told her. I hated that nose: it made my father look like a gangster. 'The last time he broke it, he won the Irish heavyweight final.'

'He was the Irish champion?'

'Yes,' I said, anxious to impress her further. 'He won it five times altogether.'

'Gosh!' Nobody I knew said 'gosh'. When my pals and I were impressed or excited we said 'Janey Mac' or 'Jeepers Jack'. If you wanted to display how tough you were, you could say 'Jaysus', but you'd get a right clip on the ear from your mother if she heard you. Only in the *School Friend* would you find girls saying 'Gosh!' Or in the High School . . .

'I heard the Head saying you're going to a new school tomorrow?'

'Old Willows,' I murmured, daringly, although I was still unable to look the girl in the face.

'What's it like?'

'What?' I could see my father manoeuvring an enormous trunk through the front door, like a coffin.

'What's your new school like?'

I avoided meeting my father's eye: he was standing beside the upright trunk, waving to me. 'We don't have to wear a uniform,' I said.

'Why not?'

'Dunno.'

'I never heard of a school,' the girl said, 'that didn't have a uniform.'

'Loads of schools don't have uniforms.'

'I never heard of them.'

'Well,' I said, 'you don't know everything.'

I saw the surprised look on her face, as if I had slapped her with my open hand. 'I didn't mean – ' I stammered, unable to get the words out.

'I don't care what kind of silly school you're going to,' she said, and her voice wobbled.

'I only meant – '

'Your father is waving at you,' she interrupted. 'He has an absolutely huge trunk to carry up.'

She started down the stairs ahead of me.

'I'll bring your suitcase up,' I called after her.

She stopped and looked back up at me. Her dark hair fell to her shoulders and the dark-blue eyes were filled with hurt. 'I can manage by myself, thank you,' she said, and she hurried away down the stairs.

I followed twelve-year-old Ella FitzArthur down, but slowly.

THREE

There was a pimple beside the right corner of my mouth. I studied it from various angles in the mirror that stood on the windowsill in the scullery. The mirror was set in a frame of dark wood, arched at the top like one of the small side altars in the Franciscan church. You could tip the mirror backwards and forwards on the hinges which linked it to its outer frame: no matter what angle I adjusted the mirror to, my pimple was still spectacularly visible. It wasn't a whitehead, the kind you could press between two tentative index fingers, and wipe away the tiny prick of blood that welled up in pursuit of the white stuff: this was a hard red-topped article which seemed to have no soft centre and was therefore impervious to pushing or probing finger-tips. It seemed especially cruel that I should be visited by such an unappetising specimen on my first day at St Joseph's.

'Is he up?' My father's voice came clearly to me through the closed kitchen door, deeper and more powerful than the voice of the newsreader on Radio Eireann.

'He's washing himself,' I heard my mother say. She laughed, a clinking sound that seemed an essential part of our kitchen's morning noises — cups and plates ringing on the table, the eight o'clock news on the wireless, the clanging sound of the centre-plate being lifted from the range, the rattling noise that the poker made when Mammy pushed it between the bars of the grate to rouse the fire to redder life.

'He's in the scullery for the last half-hour,' she said, and the laughter tickled in her throat. 'You'd swear it was to the university he was going!'

There was a faint pouring noise: I could imagine her standing at the range, lifting the shiny swan-necked kettle to pour the boiling water on to the three spoons of tea that she'd already scooped into the teapot. I never blushed when Mammy joked about me: it never seemed as if she was laughing at me.

The door from the kitchen opened. 'Are you ready yet?' Sadie asked impatiently.

'Close the door!' I said sharply.

'I have to get washed!'

I looked at her then. Her fair hair was already arranged into two long plaits that hung in front of her shoulders. She had a habit of shaking her head when she was irritated by something: she did so now, and her plaits bounced like fine silken ropes around her fair-skinned face. 'Why don't you go and play with your dolls,' I said to her, turning back to the mirror to begin the business of combing my hair.

'Hurry up!' Sadie hissed, but she closed the door.

I heard my mother telling Sadie that I wouldn't be long, while I parted my hair on the left and then began the tedious process of arranging the front in a quiff. You did it by instinct, an odd mixture of combing to the side and to the back which left you with a kind of sausage roll of hair perched at the front of your head. I surveyed my Brylcreem-shining hair with satisfaction: I had a good quiff and I knew it.

I laboriously knotted my green tie. It was the only tie I owned, purchased two years previously as an essential ingredient in our class's appearance in a school gymnastic display at the sportsground. It made you shudder just to think of it – row upon row of us in green ties and white shirts, with matching white shorts, and all of us waving silly green flags while we chanted childish inanities in Irish. At least that kind of nonsense was behind me, I thought, as I turned the collar of my shirt down over my necktie.

It was my best shirt. My other shirt was also white, bought for my confirmation the previous year: wear on the collar had eventually led to the loss of its status as my best shirt. On a long evening a few months earlier I'd watched my mother remove the collar and then, with infinite care, 'turn' the collar on the shirt. She'd knitted my navy-blue V-necked jumper too. It was new, specially for starting secondary school.

I didn't like to look below my waist-level. My knees stared up at me, naked and accusing lumps shamelessly exposed between my grey knee-socks and my short grey corduroy trousers. My mother had closed her ears against my entreaties for a pair of 'longers'. 'Soon enough you'll be in long trousers,' she'd said, mildly enough. 'And long enough you'll be wearing them.' She was deaf to all pleas of mitigating circumstances – that I was the tallest boy in the class, that I would be the only fellow in the whole school wearing short trousers. 'Sure what if you are, Michael?' she'd demanded. 'Aren't you as good as any of them?' She'd gone on with her knitting while I railed inwardly against the obduracy of parents and the injustice of my bony legs still bared to the world.

I gave myself one last look in the mirror before stepping out into the kitchen. Sadie was half-sitting on the deep sill of the front window of the lodge. 'I thought you fell down the sink!' she said to me, pouting.

'Buzz off,' I said, without any venom.

She stood beside me and looked carefully at my face. 'You have a pimple beside your mouth,' she said, 'a huge big red one.'

'Mind your own business!' I snarled, trying to push past her.

Sadie wrinkled her nose at me in triumph.

'Will ye for God's sake be civil to each other!' my mother said.

My father said nothing. He went on eating his brown soda bread, spooning his boiled egg with deliberation. The empty shell of his first egg lay on the table beside his plate. When I was very young he used to feed me the top of the egg on his own spoon, and I'd often filled the empty shell with clay, topped with blades of grass like fantastic green hair, pencilling in the round eyes and nose and upturned crescent mouth of an imbecile with box-like teeth. I no longer took the top of my father's egg: now I simply wished that he would not so carelessly discard the bruised and empty shells on the table.

I sat down on his left, facing the open door of the lodge. Within a few hours the sun would be shining through our south-facing door but even this early in the morning you could sense the heat in the glistening gravelled drive. They'd be at their breakfast in the refectory now, seated at the long tables with their bowls of porridge and thick slices of the batch loaves that were delivered fresh from the GBC bakery every morning. I surprised myself by remembering the dark-haired girl of the previous day, wondering if she were lonely on this, her first morning at boarding school. It was hard to know about Protestants: their ministers wore grey suits and got married – maybe Proddy boys and girls didn't get homesick.

'I'd say ye'll be getting a half-day today,' my father said, chewing on a slice of fresh soda-bread. 'They'll hardly keep ye for the full day on the first day back.'

'I'm not sure,' I said. Billy's older brother Tommy had already assured us that there was always a half-day at St Joseph's on the first day of term but I had learned that it was sometimes unwise to broadcast such information indiscriminately.

'Whatever time you get off,' my father said, 'you'll be wanted here, so come straight home.'

'What am I wanted for?' I addressed the question to my mug of tea, unable to look at my father.

'Because I said so!'

'But Dad – '

'You know well that the seniors are coming back today,' he interrupted, 'and I'll need you to lend a hand!'

'I'm always lending a hand!'

'A pity about you!'

'It's not fair – '

'Michael!' My mother's softly spoken interruption silenced me. 'Have manners talking to your father,' she said.

I made as if to interrupt but thought better of it, looking at her darkened brow. She turned to my father. 'Will you go easy on him, Jack,' she said quietly. 'He's starting himself today, the same as the boys and girls coming here. He'll be having homework like them too, and he'll be busy. Are you sure you need him today?'

My mother and I waited for his answer. 'I doubt he'll have homework on the first day,' my father said. He stood up from the table. 'Let him come home straight after school to give me a hand.' He lifted his second-best dark-grey jacket from the back of the kitchen chair and drew it on with slow, deliberate movements, settled the chair back neatly under the table and turned towards the door. He paused in the doorway and the kitchen darkened when he turned to face us. 'I'll be expecting you.' The words were said softly but came from his shadowed face. The gravel crunched as he headed towards the school.

'It's not – '

'Don't – ' my mother said, interrupting me. 'Don't spoil your first day in the secondary school. It's just his way – he doesn't mean any harm.' She crossed the kitchen and I felt her hand on

49

my shoulder. 'I'm as proud as punch of you – and so is your father.'

I snorted, bristling with resentment.

'He is,' my mother said, 'even if he's not able to show it. Now, stand up and let me have a look at you.' I felt myself being drawn upwards from the chair.

'Mammy, I'm not a baby any more!'

'Don't I know,' she said, looking up into my face. 'Will you look at the height of you!'

'Skinny-ma-link-melodeon!' Sadie chanted.

'Ratstails and pigtails,' I called back cheerfully.

'Will ye stop calling each other names!'

Sadie and myself laughed. 'I'll have to go,' I said. 'I told Billy I'd call for him.' The clock on the mantelpiece said a quarter past eight. 'We have to be in at nine,' I added.

'Sure you'll be there in ten minutes,' Mammy said.

'We want to be early,' I said, moving towards the door. There were no books to carry on the first day, just two new hard-cover exercise books that I'd bought in Woolworth's.

'Bless yourself – ' my mother began.

' – going out the door,' Sadie completed, and my sister and I laughed again.

'Ye're a right pair of mockers!' my mother said, smiling.

'We're only coddin', Mammy,' Sadie said.

I dipped my finger in the holy water font that hung inside the front door: the font was a silken shell glued to the base of a small picture of St Bernadette at Lourdes. I touched my wet finger to my forehead and blessed myself. 'So long,' I said.

'Good luck,' my mother said.

I was out on the drive, going through the school gate on to College Road when I heard Sadie calling my name. I turned and saw her standing in the doorway of our cottage. 'Good luck in your new school!' she called, waving at me. I waved back before turning down the hill towards Billy's house.

Billy's mother opened the door, drying her hands on her flowered apron. 'I thought it might be yourself, Michael,' she said to me. 'He's nearly ready – go on in to him.'

I knew Billy's house as well as I knew my own. I edged by Mrs Lally into the short, narrow hall. The door of the rarely used front room was, as usual, wide open, displaying the three-piece suite and the china cabinet packed with the tea-service and the dinner-service that Billy had nicknamed the 'Romanoff treasure' after he'd read about the fall of the Russian imperial family. Even his father now used the term to describe the array of gilt-edged crockery.

The only other room downstairs was the kitchen. Billy was standing at the sink under the back window, carefully combing his hair. His ginger hair looked golden in the sunlight shafting through the kitchen window. The small rectangular mirror hung by a length of shoelace from the window catch. Billy stepped backwards from the sink, still stooped so that he could see his face in the mirror.

When he turned round he was smiling. 'Take a look at perfection,' he said to me. 'I'll be fighting them off as usual this morning.'

'You'll be fighting the Brothers off,' his father said, 'if you don't get a move on – will you look at the time.'

Josie Lally was seated at the kitchen table, his enormous stomach extending outwards and upwards so that he was forced to keep his chair well back from the table. His navy-blue CIE jacket hung from the back of his chair; the peaked cap with the silver badge hung on the hook on the kitchen door.

'I'll dazzle them with my wit, Dad,' Billy said, still patting his hair into place, 'and they'll fall at my feet, stunned with admiration.'

'You'll be stunned with a good clip on the ear from Brother Cyprian if you're late.' Mrs Lally had come into the kitchen behind me. She was a diminutive woman with prematurely greying hair. With arms folded she stood beside me, surveying her son. 'You should know from listening to your brothers that they're sticklers for timekeeping down there,' she said to Billy.

'Never fear, mother dear,' Billy crooned. 'The world has moved on since my older brothers laboured in the vineyards at St Joseph's. It's 1956, mother dear! Times are changing, folks.' He struck a pose, standing on his toes, clicking his fingers. 'Aintcha heard of Bill Haley and rock-'n'-roll, folks?'

'Will you for Christ's sake rock-'n'-roll to school!' his father said, laughing. 'You'll be getting Michael into trouble as well for being late!'

Billy came across the kitchen to stand beside me. He had to reach up to put his arm around my shoulder. 'My friend Michael,' he said, 'is a paragon who never gets into trouble.'

'Your friend Michael,' his father said, 'has too much manners to be getting himself into trouble.'

I blushed, feeling the eyes of the kitchen upon me. 'We'd better go,' I said to Billy.

'Onward, Christian soldiers,' Billy said. He was a voracious reader: you never knew what he might say.

'Are them Christian soldiers back at the High School yet?' his father asked me.

'The First Years came yesterday,' I answered, 'and the rest'll be back today.'

'It'll be an ease to us all,' Billy's mother said, 'to have ye back at school and have things back to normal.'

'That fellow there'll never be normal,' Josie Lally said, winking at Billy.

'No man,' Billy said, 'is a prophet in his own land.'

'Will ye for God's sake go!' Mrs Lally exclaimed in exasperation.

'See how they love me,' Billy said in mock-sadness.

'Go!' his father ordered.

'We're going!' Billy said, taking me by the hand. He turned to his mother. 'Try not to forget me,' he said softly.

'Will you get out of here,' she said to him, 'before you have me in Ballinasloe.'

'And we won't forget to bless ourselves going out the door!' Billy laughed. 'Will we, comrade Michael?' We were both laughing as we dashed along the hall. Inside the front door we paused. The Lallys' holy water font was a crucifix, with the water receptacle at the foot of the cross. We tipped our fingers in the holy water and ceremonially sprinkled each other.

'*Sursum corda*,' Billy intoned, 'and *viva Zapata*.' Now that we were starting secondary school we had both decided we were too old to continue serving Mass at St Patrick's. More than once Billy's personalised version of the Latin responses had almost reduced me to a shivering wreck of laughter in the sanctuary.

We stepped outside on to the footpath. It was cool on this side of the street, hidden from the sun. Across the road was the four-storey bulk of the Magdalen laundry; not even the flood of morning sunlight could brighten the grey structure. 'We'd better hightail it,' Billy said.

Together we began to run downhill, past the church, round by the black-railed Square and down through our town towards St Joseph's. Instinctively, as if we had been instructed to do so, we stopped on the footpath outside the entrance to our new school. The iron-barred gates were fully opened so that they rested against the curved, railing-topped wall that flanked the gateway. The small concrete school yard was a moving sea of boys of all shapes and sizes. There was so much movement that you couldn't focus on any one boy or group of boys. Just inside the gate, to the left, a soccer match seemed to be in progress, although how the players could tell team-mates from opponents or from non-participants it was impossible to say. Other boys walked in pairs or in groups of three or four; sometimes a boy pushed or jostled another in the group and then broke loose, hanging back from the bunch of boys, laughing, like a puppy yelping at a pack of dogs.

And the sea was noisy: a swell of sound that rose and rose indiscriminately and fell into deep troughs of hoarseness punctuated by irregular shrieks of laughter and outrage. The waves of noise washed over Billy and me, drowning us. I shook myself like a drenched dog and when I turned on the pavement I saw that Billy was watching me. 'We're in babies again,' he grinned. Like myself, he had noticed the other new boys leaning against the walls, trying to melt into the anonymous stone. There was no easy induction day for beginners as there was at the High School.

'C'mon,' Billy said, flashing a comb through his immaculately groomed golden hair, 'let's case the joint.' I found myself, as always, drawing courage from my diminutive friend. Together we crossed the invisible line in the pavement, stepping into the noisy, heaving sea of boys. I followed Billy, not daring to look at any of the boys who milled about us. It did not occur to me that Billy might not know where he was heading.

'Lally! How's she cuttin'?' Two older fellows, who looked as if they might be Sixth Years, stood in our way. The taller of the two had spoken to Billy.

'Great, Tony!' I could only marvel at Billy's composure. 'How's she cuttin' yourself?'

'Sound,' the tall fellow said, 'dead sound. Tell us,' he asked, leaning over Billy, 'is Tom gone to America?'

Billy nodded. 'Took off straight after the Leaving Cert. The brothers in New York took him out.' You'd never know, listening to Billy's confident speech, how bitterly he had wept at his brother Tom's departure.

The tall fellow looked serious. 'Pity,' he said. 'We'll miss him at the hurling. There's nobody left in town could strike a ball like him.' I recognised the tall lad then: he came from Shantalla and had already played for the county's minor hurling team. 'The way things are,' Tony went on, 'I might be looking for your brother's address next June myself.'

'Any time, Tony! I'll bring the address in tomorrow if you like.'

'Hold your horses!' Tony laughed. 'I'll wait to see how the Leaving Cert goes before I book my passage.'

The sea of boys eddied and swirled around us. Tony was oblivious of the tide, standing secure as a lighthouse. I studied him furtively, noticing the tiny patch of razor blade paper covering the spot on his jaw where he had nicked himself while shaving. I wondered if I would ever stand in the yard with such godlike confidence, pondering aloud my prospects in the Leaving Cert. He caught my eye and I blushed. 'Who's your pal?' he asked Billy.

'Michael O'Hara,' Billy said. 'He lives in the gate lodge up at the High School.'

'Crikey!' Tony's companion whooped. 'With all those gorgeous Proddy birds!' I was powerless to halt the crimson spreading across my face. 'Could I come up to visit you and watch those lovely little Proddies playing hockey in their lovely little gym-slips?'

'I suppose so,' I stammered.

'Ignore him,' Tony said smartly. 'Cotter is just a sex maniac in his imagination – he loses his tongue if a girl so much as speaks to him.'

Cotter laughed – a deep laugh that came from deep down in his substantial stomach. He was a great whale basking in the pale shadow of Tony's elegant lighthouse. 'Jealousy!' he barked. 'Tony is simply jealous of my manly body and the way girls worship it!'

'Charles Atlas isn't in it.' I could hardly believe my ears: Billy was joshing this overweight god from Sixth Year. Tony caught my eye and I looked away. Billy stood nonchalantly beside me, grinning as if unaware that he had just made a seriously personal remark about a fellow in Leaving Cert – and we hadn't even started our first day in the school.

Cotter's laugh broke the silence. 'Because I liked your brother Tom,' Cotter said, 'and because Tony here seems to hold you in some esteem, I won't break your miserable neck for impudence . . .'

'Sorry,' Billy muttered, 'I didn't mean – '

'Don't interrupt your betters,' Cotter said mildly, 'or I might disremember to be gentle with you. I will refrain from breaking your neck – on this occasion.'

Tony was smiling. 'King Kong is merciful,' he said to us, 'so be grateful.'

'Just don't let me catch you in the jacks today,' Cotter grinned. Billy and I exchanged a puzzled glance.

'It's good advice,' Tony explained. 'Some of the older guys have a little ritual of shoving First Years' heads under the tap on the first day, or threatening to flush them down the lavatory.'

A cold current swept the school yard sea, pushing Billy and myself closer together. 'A big fellow in short trousers,' Cotter added, looking at me, 'would be very noticeable if he walked into the jacks today.' I felt the blush spread across my face.

'Be as well if you stayed out of the gym for today as well.' I wanted to ask Tony what the gym was but we were interrupted by the ringing of a bell. A tall Brother in black soutane was standing in the main doorway of the school, vigorously swinging a small brass bell with his right hand. For the first few seconds of the bell-ringing the sea continued to move in the yard; then suddenly it quieted, the footballers grew still, the babble of voices fell to a shorelike murmur of tide.

'First Year boys inside!' The tall brother with the bell had a strong deep voice that rang out across the crowded yard. 'First Years inside!' he called again.

'Is that the Head?' Billy asked quietly.

'That's Cyprian,' Tony answered. 'He's an OK guy.'

'Most of the time he's OK,' Cotter added.

'We'd better go,' I said.

'Good luck to ye,' Tony said to us.

Billy dawdled a moment. 'I was only joking,' he said to Cotter. 'I mean – '

'Forget it, little man.' Cotter punched Billy's upper arm playfully. 'Now push off or Cyprian will have a fit.'

We made our way with the other First Years towards Brother Cyprian. We took care not to touch or bump against the older fellows. Most of them ignored us, studiously continuing their conversations, standing in groups like clusters of rocks that our puny First Year current circled with respectful caution. A few of the bigger boys studied us shamelessly, as if we were curious flotsam washed up on their private shore by some careless tide. I was sure they were all studying my naked knees and my short trousers. We gathered around Brother Cyprian at the arched entrance to the school. Under his dark gaze we fell silent and motionless. 'This,' he said at last, gesturing with the bell towards the arched double doors behind him, 'is the staff entrance to the school.'

A boy behind me began to cough. Brother Cyprian's eyes swept past me, seeking out the boy who had interrupted him. The boy's racking cough continued: the headmaster waited, silent, for it to end. So did we all. After what seemed forever, the coughing behind me subsided into a breathless wheezing. Brother Cyprian's voice seemed even louder now, after the age of waiting. 'That,' he said, pointing with the bell to his right, 'is the students' entrance. Go in quietly and go up the stairs to the very top – the Brother inside will show you where to go.'

For a second nobody moved. Then, as if released from a long bondage, we moved *en masse* towards the corner of the building, chattering excitedly. The bell rang again. We stopped in mid-stride, turning to look back at Brother Cyprian. He held the bell high, on a level with his shoulder. 'School has begun,' the headmaster said. 'Go in quietly.' We looked at one another wonderingly, half-sensing the new world on whose threshold we stood. In silence we filed into the dark hallway of our new school.

FOUR

Short trousers notwithstanding, I settled easily into my new world. Most days I forgot to be embarrassed by my well-weathered knees: there was too much to do, too much to learn. Doors were opening on worlds that some part of me already half-knew, half-remembered echoes of voices I could never have heard from lands I could never have visited. I gathered these echoes into myself, turned and twisted them with puzzlement and love in the silent chambers of my own mind, and heard with wonder and gratitude the juvenile symphonies of my own language come tumbling out of my heart.

So tall that he was stooped, so thin his arms and legs seemed like matchsticks attached to a long broomhandle, Rab created a world of wonder in his English classes. Sometimes he stalked about the room like a circus performer atop his own naturally-given stilts, weaving his crazy spells with words that bewitched me. More often than not he gently pushed the two boys in the front desk of the middle row closer together so that he could perch, birdlike, on the top of the bench; drawing his heron-like legs up on to the seat of the desk, his bony knees bulging against the cloth of his wide, flapping trousers. Rab's curious, tinny voice gave breath to the words of poets long dead, and the dreams and visions of Keats and Shelley and Wordsworth and Hopkins floated into life under the high ceiling of our First Year classroom at the top of the school. His words fluttered like exotic butterflies against the tall windows that overlooked the river behind the school, spicy with the mysteries of Ozymandias, redolent of Fletcher's eastern dawns. His words enchanted me, swept me up in a purple cloud that drifted out across the river, beyond our school, further than the known and unknown reaches of time.

Not everyone in First Year was similarly bewitched. For some, Rab was a figure of fun, his unashamed passion for the precious and the beautiful a ready-made butt for mimicry and mickey-taking. Such unbelievers learned quickly that Rab was not to be trifled with nor his homework exercises ignored.

Sometimes, in the middle of a lesson, he'd break off abruptly from whatever he was saying – the unfinished sentence or incomplete verse that he was quoting would crash-land suddenly into silence. An unnerving silence. One that made you hold your breath as you looked cautiously at Rab, wondering who the inattentive culprit was. Rab would let the silence linger, drawing it out theatrically like a Shakespeare of the classroom intent upon tension.

'Cullinane,' he'd say quietly, or Kennedy or McCarthy or whoever his eagle eye had spotted.

'Yes, sir,' came the mumbled reply.

'What was I just saying?'

Muffled reply, indistinct, like a ghost off-stage.

'I can't hear you,' Rab would say, then, poking the boy closest to him with a long finger, 'Can you tell me what he's saying?'

'No, sir.'

The silence settled deeper but two dozen other boys were breathing now, secure in their innocence.

'You see? Your classmate can't hear you either. What was I saying just now? Speak up!'

'I can't remember, sir.'

Rab would settle himself on his perch, smile at the rest of the class, inviting us to share in the drama. 'He can't remember.' Softly this, to the whole class. Then to the unfortunate on his feet, 'Would you like to explain why you can't remember?'

'I wasn't listening, sir.'

More silence. A titter in the back row stifled by Rab's warning glance. 'You weren't listening?'

'No, sir.'

'Don't you think it's time you did penance for not paying attention?'

'Yes, sir.'

You watched the fellow who hadn't been paying attention make his way between the aisles of desks until he stood in front of Rab. He lowered himself to his knees on to the wooden floor, watched with silent interest by by the rest of us. Penance lasted until the end of the class: you had to kneel upright – letting your bottom back on to your heels was strictly forbidden.

Rab raised his voice sometimes, but no matter how angry he was – and his anger was often great with habitual offenders – he never raised a cane or strap to anybody. The same could not be said of all our teachers at St Joseph's.

With so many new teachers, one for each subject, you had to feel your way gingerly through the first weeks of the year. It reminded me of the storm-lashed night during the Christmas holidays when the electricity had failed and my father and I had palmed our way cautiously along the dark walls of the High School, while he tried to assess the extent of the storm damage with the inadequate point of light from a hand-held torch. With the teachers your torch was silence, broken only by the utter necessity of answering a question. To volunteer unbidden information was to court contempt from the other fellows in the class and to invite dangerous attention from your teacher.

Attention from Brother Silenus was particularly unwelcome. His zeal for the language of ancient Rome was imperial in its passion. His dry jokes posed a problem in survival: laugh, and you faced the accusation of disrespect; fail to laugh, and you were guilty of the treasonable charge of not finding Brother Silenus's jokes funny. Sometimes, with Billy's knuckles buried deep into the small of my back, and his whispered exhortation to laugh or be thrown to the lions assailing the back of my head – sometimes survival seemed uncertain.

A month into the term it was Billy who brought destruction on both our heads. Silenus was examining our grasp of the Latin vocabulary that we had been assigned to learn the previous night from the back of Longman's *Latin Grammar* Book 1, and was diligently establishing that, as was usual, Dominick Leyden knew as much of the Latin vocabulary as the salmon that crowded the river beyond the school.

The painstaking routine of question and failure to answer had got to the word *hasta*. Dominick was on his feet, looking everywhere but at Silenus and mumbling the word *hasta* in every intonation known to the human voice. Silenus, large and red-faced, was getting redder by the second. The rest of us were probably as angry with Dominick as was Silenus: we weren't ten minutes into the lesson and here was the Pro-Consul (as he was known) already in a fine consular rage. Had Dominick been 'thick', he would have been the recipient of universal sympathy; on the contrary, he was clever and quick-witted but studied only horses, handicaps and odds, and had told all of us that he'd be leaving school as soon as possible to work in his dad's betting shop. He was deaf to our entreaties to learn Latin to save us all from the wrath of the Pro-Consul.

'Yes, Leyden,' Silenus was saying quietly, 'I know that the Latin word is *hasta*. What I want to know is what it means.'

While Dominick looked to the ceiling for inspiration, I felt Billy's fingertip poking into my back and then his breath was hot upon the back of my head. '*Hasta la vista*,' he whispered, 'and *dominus vobiscum*.'

Dominick had unfortunately ceased his repetitious mumbling and Billy's whispered words fell loudly into the unexpected silence. The class seemed to freeze. Silenus stiffened and swivelled like a marionette to face our corner of the classroom. 'It appears we have a Spanish scholar in our midst.' Silenus was most dangerous when he smiled. He was smiling now – broadly. 'Stand up, Lally,' he said quietly, 'and enlighten us with further gems from your Spanish studies.' I didn't dare turn around as Billy stood up. He shared the last desk in the row beside the wall, directly behind me. 'What did you just say, Lally?'

'*Hasta la vista*, sir.' It was futile to attempt evasions with the Pro-Consul.

'And where did you learn that expression.'

'In a cowboy comic, Brother.'

'A cowboy comic?'

'Yes, Brother.'

Dominick laughed aloud.

'You find this amusing, Leyden?'

You could see Dominick struggling to keep a straight face. 'No, Brother.'

Silenus bestowed upon him an icy smile. 'Then sit, boy, and learn your vocabulary and be thankful that you have escaped my wrath.' When Silenus turned again towards us I knew full well the direction his wrath could take. 'And after your cowboy comic expression,' Silenus went on, 'what did you say then, Lally?'

'Nothing, Brother.'

'Not only a wit, but a liar as well!'

'I'm not a liar,' Billy protested, stung by Silenus's remark.

'Then repeat what else you said.'

'*Dominus vobiscum*, Brother.'

A few heads in front dared to half turn for a quick look at Billy, spectators at the Colosseum grateful that the lions were feasting on someone else. 'Not only cowboy comics,' Silenus said sadly, 'but blasphemy too.' He turned to the teacher's desk to pick up the bamboo cane with the hooked handle. 'Maybe,' he said pensively, 'they go together, these cowboy comics and blasphemy.' His black soutane swished against the desks as he walked along the narrow aisle towards us. He stopped beside my desk, so close that the green Brother's sash that hung from his waist touched my bare knee. 'With whom were you having this conversation, Lally?'

Still Billy said nothing. I forced myself to my feet. 'It was me, Brother,' I said, trying to quell the wobble in my voice.

Silenus shook his head. 'It was I,' he said. 'Nominative case after the verb to be. Repeat.'

'It was I, Brother,' I said.

Silenus looked from me to Billy and back again. 'Disrespect of any kind,' he said, his voice rising, 'will not be tolerated in this class. Is that understood?'

'Yes, Brother,' Billy and I answered in unison.

'Hold it out,' Silenus commanded. I was glad that I was first. At least I didn't have to suffer the pain of Billy's slogs while waiting for my own. I extended my right hand, palm upwards. Silenus drew himself up to his full height of six feet and I felt his dark eyes measuring my palm for the stroke. He extended the cane, tipping my knuckles underneath so that my hand was better placed, like a hurler fixing the *sliotar* for a free puck, then he swung the cane above his shoulder. Pain screamed through me as bamboo met finger-flesh. Twice more the cane fell on my fingers. Silenus was breathing heavily but he had not yet done with me. 'Now the other one,' he said, pointing with the cane to my left hand. Three times more the cane flashed and three times more the exquisite pain juiced through my screaming fingers.

I sat nursing my palms while Billy was dealt with. I nursed my hatred of Silenus, too, while the lesson drifted towards its conclusion in a fog of pain. I hated Billy only a little less, for dragging me into trouble.

'Hold it out, O'Hara,' Billy was trying manfully to ape Brother Silenus's booming tones, but his voice was breaking and his order ended as a kind of girlish shriek.

I extended my right hand. 'Please, Brother, don't hurt me!' I pleaded. 'I didn't mean it!'

Billy drew himself up to his full height. He still reached only to my shoulder. He clambered on top of the low moss-covered rock that we'd been sitting against in the middle of the big meadow. The tall grass had been cut and stacked but they'd left the grass around the rock. I had to look up at Billy now. He was squinting into the last of the low sunlight. 'Hold it out!' he commanded harshly.

I reached my hand up towards him. 'Disrespect will not be tolerated in my classroom!' he boomed.

He swung the imaginary cane above his head. The evening sun burst unexpectedly from behind the cloudbank and caught him for a second in a fiery pose, like an angry Statue of Liberty. Then he toppled on top of me and we were rolling downwards in a tangled heap across the stubbled, sloping face of the meadow. A rising contour in the shaven ground brought our rolling progress to a halt. We lay beside each other, laughing and panting, warmed by the late sun on our faces and the uncontrollable laughter that had seized us both.

Brother Silenus's writ did not run here. Although only a few minutes' walk from the High, this stubbled field was part of a private fiefdom that had been ours for as long as we could remember. The meadow sloped downwards to a bank of bearded thistles and a soggy ditch topped by a screen of whitethorn bushes and brambles. There was a sheer drop of nine or ten feet to the lakeside road, as if some giant hand had sheared away the edge of the meadow to make way for the road. Across the road was the saltwater lake, dark as a mackerel's skin now in the evening shadows, and above, as always, the scavenging gulls circling and wheeling in ceaseless search for food.

'I'll have to sit up,' I panted, 'I've got grass stuck up my trousers.'

'When are you gettin' the longers?' Billy asked, lifting his own leg to study the sharp crease on his charcoal-grey slacks.

'Dunno. I've given up asking.' I was sorry I had mentioned the trousers. Sometimes you could only bear a terrible cross by pretending you weren't carrying it.

'I could ask my brothers,' Billy said tentatively, 'and they'd bring you a pair for Christmas – you'd have to tell me the size.'

I avoided his glance, staring at the dark waters of the lake. Beyond the lake was the great horseshoe sweep of the bay and, beyond that, the Atlantic Ocean, reaching all the way to the shores of America, where Billy's three older brothers worked. 'Ah sure, don't bother,' I said, embarrassed, although the offer was tempting. All three brothers were due home in a few months for Christmas and they were known to be generous with their money on their rare visits home. If Billy asked for trousers I could count on getting them. 'My mother would have a fit,' I went on, still not looking at him. 'You know the way they go on.'

'Who're you telling?' Billy asked. 'The pair of them at home still treat me like I was a baby in nappies.'

I looked at him then. He had raised himself on to his elbows, a blade of grass dangling from his lips. He was wearing a new check sportscoat over a clean white shirt. Billy had a drawerful of shirts at home. His mother made him change his shirt every morning.

'Do they?' I asked.

He laughed. When he spoke the blade of grass clung to his lower lip, making him look like a tough guy with a cigarette in the pictures. 'They won't even let me go to the pictures at night! You'd swear to God I was still a child, being shunted off to the matinee on a Sunday!'

'Sometimes,' I said bitterly, 'that's not so bad.'

Billy straightened up, wrapping his arms around his knees. 'Are you stuck for next Sunday as well?' he asked.

'I don't know,' I shrugged. 'I never know until the day comes. There's always something on – Parents' Day or a hockey match or something.' The High School seemed to operate under different rules from our own school. St Joseph's had no caretaker, no indispensable Mrs O'Hara. Why couldn't the snotty kids at the High School go to schools in their own towns, just like Billy and I did? I said as much to Billy.

'It's just because they're Prods,' Billy said. 'They think they're different from the rest of us.' He stood up, brushing the grass from his clothes. I lay back, looking up at him, watching him straighten his tie.

'Mike?'

'Yes?' I had to shade my eyes with my hand to look up at him. Billy had his hands pushed into his pockets now, and was rolling backwards and forwards on his feet as if the stubby grass were spearing through his shoes.

'I'm sorry – ' he blurted out ' – about today. I'm sorry I landed you in the shite.'

'It's all right,' I said. My fingers had long since ceased to tingle with fire.

'Honest?' Billy reached his hand down towards me, gripping me around my right wrist. 'Up with you,' he said. 'Time to go back to the Latin grammar.'

I returned his grip, clasping his wrist in my fingers. 'Liar,' I said, laughing, as he hauled me up. 'All you'll go back to is those cinema magazines your brothers send you.'

'I'll leave the Latin to you,' Billy said, joining in the laughter. 'But are you sure about the other thing?'

'What other thing?'

'The longers. Will I ask the brothers to bring them for you?'

'I'm sure,' I said. Were we paupers, my mother would demand, that I had to get the neighbours to bring me home a pair of trousers from America?

The shadows were longer now, and there was a chill in the October evening. We headed up the meadow towards home and the High School.

'I suppose we should go in,' Billy said.

'I know.' I spoke without enthusiasm: for once the prospect of homework seemed more boring than challenging. 'Any minute now Sadie'll be sent out to look for me.'

We'd made our slow way up the meadow and down the big field that adjoined the foot of College Road. A curious lassitude had taken hold of me. It was comfortable sitting on the wall, drumming your heels against the grey stone to remind yourself that something at least was alive in the stillness of the evening. The road was deserted. The church, opposite us, was silent: the doors were still open but the only figure in the landscape was the head-scarved woman kneeling at the grotto in the corner of the churchyard. The high windows of the laundry gave nothing away: that front was, as ever, firmly closed against the street. The doors of the houses on Billy's terrace were open but it seemed that nobody had cause to be abroad: knobs and letter-boxes were shined, bluestone doorsteps cleaned.

The road climbed up to our right, bending away to the unseen entrance to the High School. I looked upwards, half-expecting to see my sister standing in the middle of the road, arms waving, pigtails flailing, as she shouted down the hill that Mammy said it was time to come in home.

'It's only half-seven,' Billy said.

I made no answer. It was pointless trying to explain that my mother was more determined than myself that I should do well at St Joseph's: maths and Latin were an utter mystery to her but she never failed to check that my homework in these – and every other subject – had been completed.

'Look!' Billy nudged me in the ribs. 'Look what's coming now!'

Coming towards us from the Square was a line of High School girls. The grey wave kept coming round the corner until the pavement was filled with two moving lines of grey garberdines topped with grey berets (hats were worn for the Sunday afternoon walk by those girls who had not been 'taken out' by visitors).

'Ooh-la-la!' Billy cooed, as the double line came closer. 'Beautiful chicks from the High School!'

'For God's sake,' I pleaded with him, alarmed, 'don't say anything!'

At the head of the column marched Miss Murchison. When she issued commands inside the school in her rolling Scots accent you could hear her in the lodge. She taught home economics and had a moustache. I tugged at Billy's sleeve. 'Promise you won't say anything!'

Miss Murchison and her column were now so close that it was too late to drop back into the field and out of sight. She marched purposefully towards us on her short muscular legs, swinging her gloved hands like an imperial centurion. Behind her, her troops marched in silence; even Sadie and I knew that Miss Murchinson's bite was worse than her bark.

'Oh, baby, baby!' Billy breathed.

'Please!' I begged him.

I felt Miss Murchinson's eyes lock with mine. She seemed to stiffen with recognition. I fancied that her dark-brown moustache bristled. She raised her hand a pace or two before she came abreast of us, like John Wayne at the head of a cavalry patrol approaching Apache territory. The two columns of uniformed girls came to an unexpected halt. Giggling and tittering broke out in the ranks. Billy smiled at the girls.

'No talking, girls!' It sounded like 'G-I-R-R-L-S', the way it rolled off Miss Murchinson's tongue in the evening air. 'We'll cross here!' A ford in a dangerous river, hostiles upstream, rapids below. Miss Murchinson stood in the middle of the road, diverting her charges across the deserted thoroughfare.

The girls walked by seniority, with First Formers at the front, rising to the seniors at the back. Some of them looked shyly up at us from under bobs escaping from the cover of the grey berets with the navy crest on front. A few looked boldly at us. Most of the faces I knew: I had carted trunks upstairs to the *Puellae* dormitory for quite a few of them on the first Sunday in September. I saw the puzzlement in some eyes and knew they were trying to place me.

The dark-haired FitzArthur girl was marching at the rear of

the First Formers, on the inside of the footpath. A tall girl with long yellow hair marched alongside her. The yellow-haired girl had pale skin and wide blue eyes that met mine but moved quickly on to Billy.

'Hi, babe,' Billy said softly, 'you're looking great.'

Without turning away the yellow-haired girl asked Ella FitzArthur, 'Who is this creep?'

I blushed, feeling the FitzArthur girl's dark eyes focusing upon me. 'I don't know,' Ella FitzArthur said, 'but the other one is the caretaker's boy from the lodge.' Her face was impassive as she stepped off the pavement to where Miss Murchison was still holding up the imaginary traffic.

'Bitches!' I heard Billy say cheerfully. 'Snotty-nosed Proddy bitches!'

For a moment I said nothing. The lines of girls waited on the far footpath until Miss Murchinson resumed her place at the head of the column and then moved off up the hill to the High School. 'You're right,' I said at last, 'bitches.'

But I gave the girls plenty of time to get into the school before I headed up the hill to the gate lodge.

FIVE

My first term at St Joseph's ended with Christmas exams. The challenge they presented was as much one of endurance as of recall: for three days you sat in silence in your desk and covered page after foolscap page with words of English, Irish, Latin, history and geography; you totted vast columns of figures in arithmetic, unravelled algebraic equations and constructed careful diagrams for geometry, physics and chemistry. The silence was disturbed only by the scratching of nibs on paper (pencils and ballpoint pens were forbidden), the throat-clearing and coughing of the other guys, and the sentry-like padding of the supervising teacher up and down between the aisles of desks. Morning seemed to hurry towards eleven o'clock and the short noisy break in the school yard; the lunch-hour bell came too quickly to end the second exam of the day. The frantic dash through the December streets of the town had less to do with getting your dinner than with some last-minute swotting for the afternoon test. That session flew, too: there never seemed to be enough time to put down on the blue-lined sheets all that I knew.

The end of the last paper of the Christmas exams also brought the term to an end. The long corridor on the ground floor of the school where we hung our coats was noisier than usual. Two Third Years fought a duel with wooden rulers, prancing up and down the red-tiled corridor with swords drawn, their left hands imperiously perched on their hips like gallant Zorros. A huddle of

Sixth Year guys commandeered a First Year's schoolbag and conducted a rowdy scrum in the corner of the corridor with extravagant cries of 'Now!', 'Lost!' and 'Won!' The owner of the bag waited patiently for the school's senior rugby pack to tire of their sport.

Rab stuck his head out of the staff room and surveyed the activity with a sardonic air. 'The intellectuals are at it again,' he said, but he was smiling as he closed the door.

Billy and myself were waiting with most of the First Years for the scrum-down to conclude before venturing towards the exit past the heaving Sixth Year huddle. Billy nudged me. 'Look!'

Brother Cyprian was standing in the open doorway of the headmaster's office. 'Break it up, lads!' he called.

The schoolbag-ball was being put in again. 'Now!' We recognised the deep-barrel voice of the squat fellow who played scrum-half on the senior team.

'Lost!' came the muffled shout from the scrum.

'Alleluia!' somebody roared from the depths of the huddle.

The makeshift scrum suddenly began to move towards us as the fellows on the far side pushed harder. The limb-locked huddle gathered momentum, barrelling towards the headmaster's open door. The scrum collapsed, with roars and shouts of laughter, at Brother Cyprian's feet. Seven or eight fellows lay back on the red tiles, pushing and shoving one another noisily as they disentangled themselves.

My eyes moved from the sprawled Sixth Years to the headmaster and back again. I saw the realisation of Brother Cyprian's presence dawn upon the fellows and waited for the awfulness of their plight to show itself in their faces. But the fellows on the floor just laughed. They looked a little sheepish as they stood up, brushing their clothes down.

'Sorry about the noise, Brother,' the scrum-half said. He was short and muscular with fair curly hair and a freckled face. 'We were just getting in a little extra training.'

Brother Cyprian hitched the green sash up around his waist before answering. He looked sternly from the scrum-half to the other Sixth Years clustered about him. 'Save it for the pitch,' he said. 'You'll need to be good against the High School.'

'Don't worry, Brother,' the scrum-half said earnestly, 'we'll get them!' He turned to his classmates and you could see the redness in his freckled face. 'Won't we, lads!' A mumbled chorus of agreement was his answer. 'Let's hear it!' the scrum-half urged, and the chanting began: 'Two-four-six-eight – ' The rest of us in the crowded corridor took up the chant: 'Who do we appreciate?' And then the staccato litany of the initials of the school's nickname: 'B-I-S-H-O-P-S, Bishops!' The corridor was filled with a rousing cheer that seemed to engulf us all. When you opened your lungs and throat and bellowed this tribal chant, you knew where you belonged. We were flushed, crowded together in the corridor, waiting for the headmaster to address us. We felt his gaze upon us, moving along his array of troops.

'Brother?' A small, hesitant voice broke the silence.

Brother Cyprian's gaze moved downward. 'Yes?'

'Can I have my schoolbag back, please?' The owner of the schoolbag-ball had pushed his way through the press of boys. Everybody laughed. The scrum-half did a mock-bow and handed over the bag. The First Year boy blushed as he retreated with his schoolbag into the safety of the anonymous crowd.

'Let ye be off home,' Brother Cyprian said. 'Happy Christmas to ye all.'

'Happy Christmas, Brother,' came the chorus of replies.

Brother Cyprian's gaze once more swept the sea of boys filling the strait of the corridor. A half-smile played upon his lips and for a moment I thought he would say more. He shook his head as if bemused and stepped back into his office. The door closed behind him.

We headed *en masse* towards the exit at the end of the L-shaped corridor. The sense of excitement in the crowded passage-way was palpable. It wasn't just the ending of the enforced silence of the exams and the beginning of the Christmas holidays: the small drama that had just been enacted in the corridor had bound us together in a way that I could sense but could not begin to articulate. At St Joseph's we wore neither school tie nor blazer nor any other semblance of uniform yet, at that moment, pushing our way out of the school, we were branded as no blazer could ever brand us. And for those few moments we had found a new voice – raucous yahooing had given way to a quiet buzz of muted conversation.

'He's not so bad, is he?' Billy said to me.

'No,' I said, 'he's not.' I knew he was referring to the headmaster.

'Not a bad oul' stock at all,' Billy added and there was wonder in his voice.

The press of boys came to a halt as we neared the funnel of the doorway. 'Why was he talking about the High School?'

Billy looked at me. 'We're playing the High in the first round of the Senior Cup – after Christmas. I thought everybody knew?'

I shook my head. 'No, I hadn't heard.'

'Anyway,' Billy said, as we began to move forward again, 'it doesn't matter, sure they always beat us.'

We were out in the school yard now, heading for the gym. The gym at St Joseph's had nothing to do with gymnastics: it was a long shed where we stored our bicycles. 'They always beat us?' I asked Billy.

'I used to hear my brothers on about it,' Billy said. 'I often heard them saying that the Bish could never beat that shower up in the High.'

Our bikes were side by side. All around the walls of the gym were bikes: they hung upside-down, suspended by their front wheels from a row of rusted iron hooks attached to planks that hung in turn from the ceiling of the gym. Billy and I walked our bikes together across the yard. Even on the day of the Christmas holidays it seemed foolhardy to break the rule against cycling in the school yard.

'And the High always beats us in rugby?' I came back to the subject.

Billy shrugged. 'I'll ask the brothers – they'll all be home on Christmas Eve!'

We swung our legs across our bikes and cycled slowly through the narrow streets of our town. Billy talked as we cycled. In the white glow of the street-lights his face was animated as he talked about the homecoming of his three elder brothers from America. I knew I'd meet them, knew also that they'd be pressing money into my palm with a nod and a wink, and I was looking forward to the noisy celebrations in Billy's house. The Romanoff treasure, Billy claimed, was due for its annual showing. But I wanted also to hear more about our rugby matches against the High. It was bad enough, on this day of my own holidays, to be hurrying home to help the blazer-clad pupils of the High School carry their precious belongings into their parents' shiny cars; it was unthinkable that they could also beat my school on the rugby pitch.

You had to pick your way between the suitcases and bags on the top landing of the High School. The owners of the luggage, still wearing their grey uniforms, stood around in small clusters talking in loud animated voices. Some of them lounged or sat on the stairs, careless of the breach of rules: the offence went unremarked on this last day of term.

Nor did they move when Billy and I edged by them, carting suitcases downstairs for the girls.

'I say, chaps,' Billy said loudly in his put-on upper-class English accent, 'do move aside so that we can get the young ladies' baggage down!' I was glad that Billy had volunteered to lend a hand: I envied him his easy confidence among these blazered contemporaries who didn't even bother to look you in the face as you stowed their bags in the boot of the car.

Some of the girls did look up from their conversations – most of which seemed to concern arrangements to meet or visit during the Christmas holidays – and give a half-smile as they made way for us on the staircase. The fellows seemed indifferent: they gave way grudgingly, reluctantly moving a seated thigh or extended foot so that Billy and I might pass by with our load.

Negotiating our passage along this crowded gangway seemed, in the company of Billy, more fun than I could ever have imagined. His response to the indifference of the guys was a display of even more nonchalant indifference; even a half-smile from one of the girls was rewarded with his coolest grin and most knowing walk. I felt his cavalier confidence attach itself to me; I could not join him in his wink-and-smile bravado but I could grow strong in its shadow.

As we ferried the bags and cases downstairs we lined them up neatly against the wall inside the front door of the school. The cases were double-banked, stretching as far back as the lockers under the staircase. The grandfather clock standing sentry between the door of the staff room and that of the secretary's office said ten minutes to six: any minute now the gravel would start to churn

77

up under the wheels of motor cars as parents arrived to take away their offspring. A few of the pupils had already been delivered in Mr Willoughby's car to the railway station, to catch trains and buses home.

Billy lowered the two suitcases he was carrying on to the half-landing and stood for a moment gazing downwards. I dropped my own pair of cases and the two bags I was carrying under my arms. I felt a trickle of sweat slide down my back and shook myself to ease my shirt clear of wet skin. My eyes followed Billy's gaze.

Outside the door of his office Reverend Willoughby was engaged in animated conversation with a group of senior boys. His head bobbed up and down as he spoke, like the little boy's on top of the colllection box for black babies; his arms flapped periodically – his every point seemed to require emphasis. Like all the teachers in the High School he wore a black academic robe, like a professor in a film: when his arms flapped his gown billowed and he looked like a benevolent buzzard with spread wings, waiting for some fortuitous morsel.

'He does rabbit on, doesn't he?' Billy sounded amused.

'He's all right,' I said stung into defence of this bird-like creature who never bothered me.

'Who said he wasn't?' Billy asked, smiling.

I shrugged. Who was I to defend the Rev, as I knew he was nicknamed in the school?

Both Reverend Willoughby's arms were suddenly flung wide; his gown hung extended from his outstretched arms like the rich robe draped across the priest's shoulders at benediction. The group of boys fell back. You could see their mouths open in laughter and their whoops of glee reached up to where we stood on the stairs. 'He's a funny man as well,' Billy said, stooping to pick up his burden.

I stuffed one bag under my left arm and picked up my two suitcases. Billy watched me, grinning, as I tried to wrap my arm around the second bag. 'You'd want to be an octopus,' he said cheerfully. He released one of his suitcases, took the extra bag from me and stuffed it under his arm. 'Ready?' he asked, picking up his second case. I nodded. We set off downwards again, threading our way between bodies that were sprawled across the stairs.

'You'd need to be a mountain goat as well,' Billy called back over his shoulder as he side-stepped two fellows who were jostling each other good-humouredly on the stairs.

'Or an elephant in the summer,' I replied, thinking of the trunks loaded with blankets that had to be carted down for the end of the summer term.

My thoughts of elephantine luggage-handling were brought to an abrupt halt as I stumbled against Billy's back and my burden of suitcases collided with his. Our progress had been brought to a dead stop by a sandy-haired fellow who had managed to block the entire width of the staircase. He was seated on the third step from the bottom with his back against the banister, his long legs stretched right across the stairs, bent at the knee.

'Gangway there!' Billy called loudly. The fellow did not turn around; he went on talking to a boy who was standing in the hallway, one hand on the newel of the staircase, one foot propped on the bottom step as he leaned to hear what the fellow sitting on the stairs was saying. 'Gangway!' Billy called again, more loudly. The long legs across the stairs did not move.

The boy standing in the hall – he was a First Year, I remembered helping him to carry his trunk upstairs in September – caught my eye and I saw him make a face as he tapped the angled knee of his seated companion. 'They need to get past you,

Nick,' he said, interrupting the other fellow.

The boy turned his head then, slowly, to look up at us. It was a superior look, from pale blue eyes that were set wide apart in a handsome face. And slowly the head turned away again. It was a large head with strands of sandy hair falling on to a high brow. He reminded me of the Roman emperor in *Demetrius and the Gladiators*. 'Couldn't the peasants just step over me?' He was addressing the boy who was standing at the foot of the stairs but you felt that Billy and I were intended to hear.

I saw Billy's pale face suffused with redness. 'Who're you calling peasants?' Billy's voice crackled with anger.

'Billy – ' I dropped one case on the step and it collided with our tormentor's shoulder.

He pushed the case away from him with a hand that was bigger than my father's. 'And now the bearers are even dropping the baggage on top of the sahibs!' He still did not look at us as he spoke.

'I asked you – ' Billy's voice was loud ' – who're you calling peasants?'

'My, my, the natives are touchy tonight!' He stood up then, slowly, and towered above us, the tallest fellow in the First Form, as tall and strongly built as the biggest boys in the Sixth Form.

Billy let his baggage down with an air of deliberation. The stairs and surrounding area had grown quiet but you could still hear the Reverend Willoughby's voice rattling on. Although he stood on a step above him, Billy still had to look up at the other fellow. His eyes narrowed as he weighed up his adversary. 'Leave it, Billy!' I pleaded. Any second now the Rev would spot what was going on and I'd be reported to my father.

Billy shook off the hand I laid on his arm. 'I asked you a question, mate,' Billy said, and I knew by the wobble in his voice that he was scared.

The big fellow smirked at Billy. 'Don't you peasants ever learn to say "please" or "excuse me"?'

I heard Billy draw his breath in sharply. He suddenly pushed forward against the big fellow with outstretched hand. His opponent laughed, pushing Billy backwards with one great ham of a hand that landed him on his backside on the step. The big fellow's laughing was loud in the hallway.

'Nicholas Kerr! You are the most obnoxious idiot!' The big fellow turned, still laughing, to see who had the temerity to call him names. The FitzArthur girl had pushed her way through a cluster of girls until she stood at the big fellow's elbow. 'You really are a great oaf, Nicholas!' Her nostrils flared as she spoke and it seemed to me that her eyes were dancing in rhythm with the bouncing mass of her long dark hair. 'Sometimes I think you have a brain the size of a pea inside that gorilla-sized head of yours, Nicholas.'

The girls beside her sniggered; the boy who had been speaking to Kerr turned away to hide his smile. 'Why don't you feck off, Miss Fancypants,' Kerr blustered, 'and swallow another dictionary!'

'Why don't you pick on someone your own size?' Ella FitzArthur said, wrinkling her nose.

Nicholas Kerr snorted. 'Pygmies and peasants,' I heard him mutter under his breath. 'C'mon.' He put an arm around the shoulder of his pal and they walked away from us.

'Just ignore him,' the FitzArthur girl said and I blushed as I realised she was addressing Billy and myself.

'It's a good thing for him that you came along just then,' Billy said. 'I was just about to lay him out.'

She laughed, a deep throaty laugh that made me blush even more deeply. 'I could see that,' she said easily.

A car-horn honked outside; you could hear the tyres crunching in the gravelled drive. 'It's the Elliotts!' somebody yelled, and we felt the blast of December air as the main door was pulled open. Headlights swung outside and the beams played on Ella Fitz-Arthur's smiling face before the driver cut the beam off. 'I'll give you a hand,' she said, picking up a suitcase.

'There's no need – ' I stammered.

'No need at all,' Billy added.

'I know that,' she said, looking at us both.

'Thanks,' I croaked.

'Thank you very much,' Billy said with heavy emphasis. He reached out his hand to her. 'My name is Billy Lally,' he said, and I envied him the coolness with which he spoke, like Alan Ladd in *O.S.S.*

'I'm Ella FitzArthur,' she said, taking his hand. 'How d'you do.'

'I'm doin' really well, ma'am,' Billy drawled. He looked disappointed when Ella dropped his hand.

The girl turned to me. 'I know your name – ' She stopped, as if embarrassed. 'Happy Christmas, Michael,' she said, holding out her hand to me.

I swallowed hard. My throat was dry; words seemed strangely impossible to discover. My fingers touched hers and I knew that my face was on fire. 'Happy Christmas – ' I hesitated ' – Ella.' For a moment our eyes met, then she turned away, carrying the suitcase. She placed it neatly in line beside the other cases, then she moved away from us, giving us a small wave of her hand as she went back to her classmates.

'Some chick!' I heard Billy whisper beside me. 'Some chick!'

I couldn't speak. Perhaps it was the crowded hall or the hauling of bags and cases – whatever it was, as I looked at the retreating figure of Ella FitzArthur, I knew that my heart was pounding as it had never pounded before. I left Billy there in the hallway and pushed past the crowds of High School boys and girls until I stood on the stone steps outside the front door. The cold was welcome on my face. I gulped in great gobs of breath, thankful for the icy touch of the wind. I was oblivious of the excited hustle about me as more and more cars arrived and doors slammed and voices were raised in greeting and farewell.

'Mike?' It was Billy, standing beside me. 'You OK?'

"Course I am.'

'It's that FitzArthur chick, isn't it? She really got to you!' Billy was laughing.

'Don't be stupid. I just needed some air.'

'Oh, yeah,' Billy said, 'and I'm a monkey's uncle.'

We went back inside together and for the next hour we busied ourselves loading cases into boots and on to the back seats of cars. While we worked I kept a watchful eye but I did not see her again that night.

Except in my mind. She was smiling at me, the freckled skin around her blue eyes wrinkled up, her hand raised in a small wave.

I could see her clearly when I sat bolt upright in my bed. It took seconds for me to realise that I was in bed and that I was awake. Or was I only dreaming that I was awake, dreaming that I was sitting up in my bed in the darkness of my room? I had been dreaming of Ella FitzArthur.

'I know your name,' she said in the dream. It was a dream. The darkness was becoming less intense: there was never any light from the window in the wall of my room, which was separated by only a couple of feet from the outer wall that surrounded the High School grounds, but the small, uncurtained skylight was suddenly filled with the light of a thousand winter stars.

The light picked out the furniture in my room: the small chest of drawers, the kitchen chair beside my bed, the shiny chromium rail in the corner which served as a wardrobe, curtained by a floor-length piece of fawn velvet which my mother had salvaged from the headmaster's house. I looked with hunger on these familiar objects, searching for comfort after the peculiar terror of my dream. My school books, neatly stacked on top of the chest of drawers, promised the forgiveness of a new term after Christmas.

I didn't know why I needed forgiveness. I only knew that my thighs and pelvis were soaking wet. For a moment I was terrified that I had wet the bed, like a baby, but the stuff with which my groin was covered was thick and sticky. Reluctantly, in fear of what I might see, I turned back the blankets and drew my nightshirt up.

My skin was pale in the shaft of whiteness from the skylight. The black hair on my groin still had the power to surprise me with its strangeness, as if it were not mine but had attached itself to my body like a thing in a horror film. Now this unfamiliar hair was matted together, sticky with this treacly wetness which had come from within me. I touched it, tentatively, and drew my finger away in recoiled distaste.

She had smiled at me. 'I know your name,' she had laughed.

I covered myself quickly, tenting the long nightshirt around my bent knees to avoid contact with the gummy mess. Who was I now? What had I become, lying here in the sibilant darkness, soiled with shame, frightened of shadows? The sound of my father's snoring reached me from the bedroom at the other end of the lodge, on the far side of our kitchen. The sound, so familiar and ghastly that Sadie and I had mimicked it for years, frightened me. What would he say if he could see me now, lying in this inexplicable gooey mess? Or my mother, asleep in the double bed beside my father?

Morning was long in coming. The room whispered around me: brightness alternated unpredictably with darkness as unseen clouds blacked out the moon and darkened my window on the sky. Sadie's breathy wheezing and my father's rumbling snores punctuated the hours before dawn.

Before the lodge stirred itself to morning life I eased myself quietly out of bed on to the small hard mat that was the room's sole concession to luxury. I stood on the corded mat for a moment, unmoving, hardly daring to breathe, as if at any second my bedroom might be invaded by an accuser who would lift the front of my nightshirt and expose the guilty stuff that had congealed into hardness on my pelvis.

Although I braced myself against the chill, the coldness of the linoleum stung when I stepped off my island-mat. I shivered, crossing the floor to the door into the narrow passage that Sadie and I had christened 'the back hall'. The yellow knob turned noiselessly in my hand; the door swung open in merciful silence.

The back hall connected with the scullery that led to the lavatory on the other side of Sadie's bedroom and mine. A small window in the passage looked on to our vegetable garden: beyond the garden I could just see the white outline of the goalposts at the near end of the hockey pitch, a white scaffold in the early morning light.

Sadie did her whinny-breathing noise and I stood frozen, my shoulder touching against the overcoats that we hung from the black metal hooks in the back hall. In a moment I heard the creaking of her bed as she turned in her sleep and I imagined her face, pale on the pillow, surrounded by the spreading mass of her fair hair. I shivered, not from the cold but from the fear that my sister might see me like this, skulking towards the kitchen in a nightshirt that could not possibly cover the stain on my abdomen.

The kitchen was brightening: Mammy drew the curtains back every night when she was going to bed. The door that led from the kitchen to my parents' bedroom at the other end of the lodge was shut: it was silent too – my father, for once, seemed to be deep in unsnoring sleep.

I crossed the kitchen quickly, in front of the fireless range which would shortly spring to new life under my mother's practised coaxing. The room was strangely silent without the ticking of the alarm clock on the mantelpiece: the round-faced clock, with its little hat-like cover for the alarm mechanism, ticked the nights away on top of the chest of drawers in my parents' room.

The scullery door was ajar. I closed it quietly behind me and picked up the white enamel basin from the scrubbed wooden draining board. I didn't dare to leave the basin in the bottom of the square, earthenware sink while I filled it with water: I held it close under the spout and turned the tap slowly. The copper pipe that poked in under the window-frame shuddered as the water coursed its way to the spout, and I cocked my head, listening, but the lodge remained silent. The water splashed noisily into the basin and I turned the tap, allowing only a trickle through the spout. A span of eternity passed before the basin contained enough water to wash.

I worked hurriedly, coating the face-cloth with a soapy layer that made the fabric shiny in my frozen fingers. I lifted my nightshirt, puckered in my left hand, and worked the cold, soapy cloth over and back across my stomach and the downy triangle of my groin. I bent and soaped myself between my legs and the dirty icy drops dripped on my bare feet like a malediction.

I didn't dare take time to fill the basin with fresh water to rinse my skin properly. I wrung out the face-cloth in the basin of soapy water and wiped the lather from my stomach as well as I could. The morning was brightening: soon the lodge would be awake. Through the scullery window I could see a clear and wintry sky: the air was hard like glass, with crooked trails of grey smoke fingering their way upwards from the chimneys of the nuns' laundry at the bottom of the hill – they worked all night down there, Billy had told me, knowingly, and their fires never went out, forever fuelled by those unseen women who, inexplicably, had contrived to have babies without having husbands.

I turned from the window and grabbed the towel that hung on the back of the scullery door. I towelled myself vigorously, feeling the warmth creep back into my flesh and bones. When I allowed the striped flannel nightshirt to fall over my clean white skin it felt as if I had drawn on a warm overcoat against a winter wind.

When I opened the scullery door I found myself looking across the kitchen into my mother's eyes. 'You're up early,' she said, closing her bedroom door behind her. 'You haven't forgotten there's no school for you today?'

My feet were frozen to the stone floor of the kitchen; my fingers could not unwind themselves from the brass knob of the scullery door. 'I had to go to the lav,' I mumbled.

My mother crossed the room and reached upwards to return the green alarm clock to its spot in the centre of the high mantelpiece. She turned towards me and I felt my face reddening as her gaze moved downwards. 'You'll be perished, standing there like that in your bare feet!'

'I'm all right – '

'Would you not slip your feet into your sandals going out to the lavatory on such a cold morning? For a bright scholar you're often foolish!' My feet unglued themselves from the stone floor and I moved around her towards the back hall.

'Did you not see your dad then?' she asked me. 'He went out a while ago to check on the furnace.'

'I didn't see him.' I flung the words over my shoulder as I hurried along the back hall. Inwardly I prayed that he hadn't seen me washing myself in the scullery. In my bedroom I drew on my clothes and boots as fast as I could. The alarm clock had said a quarter past seven: I would just make it.

My mother looked quizzically at me when I rushed past her to comb my hair in front of the mirror in the scullery. 'Where are you off to?' she asked. I hurried back past her, hair quiffed as well as possible in the time available, to grab my coat from the hanger in the back hall. 'Where are you rushing off to at this hour?' she asked again. 'It's not even half-seven.'

I fussed with the buttons of my overcoat. For some reason I couldn't even look at my mother. 'I just thought I'd go to Mass,' I said. I was already at the door. I dipped my finger in the holy water font before she could tell me to do so. I opened the door and the morning was sharp and bright.

'Michael?' I turned in the doorway to face my mother. Behind her the grate in the range was already glowing with new fire. 'Are you all right, Michael?' The anxiety in her voice was mirrored in her face, in the lines creasing her forehead.

"Course I am.' I shrugged. 'I just took a notion to go to Mass.'

She smiled then. 'Don't forget to say a prayer for your mammy.' I closed the door without answering her. I didn't want to be asked why I had suddenly decided to go to Mass on a weekday for the first time in my life, not counting the mornings when I'd had to serve Mass. I couldn't have explained it even to myself.

The High School was silent. I didn't allow my eyes to linger on the broad stone steps and the mahogany door with the brasses that my mother would keep shining throughout the Christmas holiday. I didn't need to look over there to see Ella FitzArthur's smiling mouth and crinkly eyes: that face still smiled inside me.

I ran out the gate of the High School and down the hill to the early morning Mass. The parish priest was coming out of the sacristy as I was stepping inside the church. The purple chasuble of Advent seemed too small for Canon Folan's rounded body: his protruding stomach marched in front of the rest of him towards the altar. I ducked into a seat near the back of the church. The usual couple of dozen men and women were already on their knees, scattered throughout the church in their seats: I knew all these daily Mass-goers from my own years as an altar boy.

The priest bent over the altar, kissed it, and genuflected before the tabernacle. '*Introibo ad altare Dei.*' Canon Folan began the Mass at his usual breakneck speed but the Latin words were familiar to me.

'*Ad Deum qui laetificat juventutem meam.*' The server was a fellow from Prospect Hill: the canon hardly gave him time to finish before launching into the next line. Priest and boy continued their Latin gallop, and I kept pace with them, mouthing the words without having to refer to the leather-bound missal given me by my mother for my confirmation three years previously. Already my limited grasp of Latin grammar, picked up after a term's work at St Joseph's, made the old words simpler.

Hurried or not, the Latin words soothed me. The half-light above the altar – the Canon allowed all the lights in the church to be switched on only on Sundays – soothed me: the coughing and the throat-clearing, even the creak and groan of polished wood as my fellow worshippers stirred in their seats, comforted with their familiarity, like the static on the wireless when you were trying to tune into Radio Luxembourg.

I heard neither epistle nor gospel. I sat, I stood, I signed the sign of the cross upon forehead and mouth and breast, I knelt on the hard wooden kneeler and I gave myself up to the benediction of the familiar. The church brightened as the white fingers of the winter sun poked through the eastern windows and I thawed inwardly in the pale light and felt the burden of the night's sticky darkness lift from me.

'*Hoc est enim corpus meum.*' This is my body: the white host of communion held high in Canon Folan's pudgy fingers, and I bowed my head. Hard and white, like my stomach washed clean by the cold hard water in the early-morning scullery.

There were only a few responses for the altar boy at this section of the Mass and Canon Folan forged ahead without interruption. He could recite the *Pater Noster* without pause: nouns and verbs ran together in a breathless jumble that ended in a wheezing full stop.

'*Agnus Dei, qui tollis peccata mundi . . .* ' Lamb of God, who takes away the sins of the world . . . I shifted, startled, on my knees. Why did the mention of the sins of the world evoke the nightmare of my bed and Ella's face, ghostly in my dreams? Strange worlds whirled inside everyday words.

The metallic turning of the doorknob roused me from a deep sleep. 'Michael?' It was my mother at the half-opened door of my bedroom. I sat up in the bed blinking against the morning. 'It's only eight o'clock,' Mammy said. 'You're in plenty of time for nine Mass.'

I groaned. 'Why didn't you let me sleep!'

'Michael! It's Christmas morning!'

'Oh, Janey!' I sat up in the bed. 'I just forgot.'

My mother took her hand from the doorknob and stepped into my room. The light from my skylight spilled down on her and I could see more clearly the spreading grey in her hair. 'Happy Christmas, Michael,' she said, reaching out her right hand to me.

It took me a few seconds to realise what was draped across her forearm. 'Mam! You got them after all!' I grabbed the pair of long trousers from her, throwing back the blankets to place my feet on the mat. 'Thanks a million, Mammy,' I said.

I stood barefoot in my nightshirt and held the trousers against me. The long grey legs reached below my ankles, more wonderful than any silk that Marco Polo had ever carted on the long trail from Cathay. I could hardly breathe, savouring the richness of the dark cloth draped against my bare legs. I closed my eyes and I saw myself bestride town and school like a colossus, my long legs mercifully covered in grey longers.

'I'm glad you're pleased,' my mother said.

I opened my eyes, smiling, almost laughing at her. 'Why wouldn't I be pleased! I hated going around in short pants!'

'I'll let you get dressed so,' she said, turning to go. 'I'm only sorry that they're not new but sure you know how hard it is.'

The door closed behind her. Her words hung in my small room like a threat. My body seemed to fold in on itself and I sat down heavily on the edge of the bed. I forced my eyes from the back of the door, forced my gaze downwards to my lap, where my hands, of their own volition, had reduced my new long trousers to a crumpled ball of shapeless grey cloth.

I could see the colour now, knew the provenance of my longers even before I looked inside the waistband. The telltale name in indelible marking ink was there: A. J. Mason. I couldn't remember A. J. Mason, but he'd left the High School without his grey school trousers. Perhaps he didn't want them anyway: when I looked closely I could see where Mammy had stitched the long tear under the right-hand pocket. More than once I'd watched my mother execute emergency needle-and-thread repairs for some pupil who hadn't got a spare pair. Maybe she had done it before for A. J.

Mason. And now she'd done it for me.

I threw the pair of trousers from me and I wept, silently, but all the while I cried and shuddered I knew that I would finally pick up A. J. Mason's discarded longers and smooth the creases I had inflicted on them and draw them on with a resentful gratitude. You could rail against the unfairness of the world but in the end you gave way to it. When I opened the door from the back hall into the kitchen, my mother and Sadie exchanged a conspiratorial glance before turning to me. 'Well wear, big brother!' Sadie said.

'Your new jumper is nice,' I said. Mammy had been knitting it for weeks.

Sadie pirouetted so that I could also admire the back of her new jumper. 'It's lovely, isn't it!' she giggled.

'Show-off,' I said but my heart wasn't in my remonstration.

'What happened to your trousers?' I heard my mother ask. 'They're all creased.'

Sadie stopped to inspect my longers. 'Oh,' my sister said, 'they're all scrumpled up.' Her nose wrinkled in exaggerated distaste. I pushed Sadie away gently.

'There's nothing wrong with them, Michael.' There was a pleading, defensive tone in my mother's voice.

'They're grand,' I said, turning away from her. 'I'm off to Mass now.'

'Wait for me!' Sadie cried.

'No!' I answered, more sharply than I intended. 'I'm calling for Billy,' I added, more gently. I avoided my mother's eyes as I left the lodge. Outside on the gravelled drive I felt the tall windows of the High School narrow upon my departing back as I made my way to Christmas Mass, clad in my scavenged trousers.

Six

The din from our crowd filled the breadth of the road from the church across to the fields; it rose upwards in an excited crescendo, higher than the blue-slated roof of the nuns' laundry, up towards the hard blue January sky, a shapeless cloud of sound, shapeless as our school supporters' army on the march.

At least the senior guys at the front of the crowd maintained some semblance of order. The rest of us spilled along haphazardly. The narrowness of the town's main streets had forced us into a natural kind of cohesive formation as we progressed noisily from the school, but when we met the Square most of our marching shape seemed to dissipate as we spread out across the wider roads. Only the Leaving Cert fellows at the front had stuck together, arms linked, hoarsening voices raised in chanted songs and familiar slogans. A single blue-and-white flag was held high by one of their number; another had somehow purloined the headmaster's hand-held brass bell – every now and then he raised it over his head and shook it to such clanging effect that you'd expect the whole town to turn out looking for a fire. Many of the shopkeepers and shop-assistants did just that: they stood in the doorways of their premises, buttoned up in their white or khaki shop-coats, watching our progress through the town.

'Give 'em timber, lads!' one young fellow shouted, punching the air, and Billy nudged me and shouted above the din that the fellow had left our school just last year to work in his father's bar.

'Show the High School what's what!' I heard the same voice roar, as we moved on, leaving him behind in the doorway of the bar.

There were no onlookers to shout encouragement as we climbed the hill of College Road: here were only the silent façades of the church and the laundry and, on the other side, the short terrace of houses where Billy and his neighbours lived. Billy's door was open: his mother stood on the step, arms folded. I poked Billy in the side and we watched her, giggling to ourselves, as her eyes swept our ragged ranks. She spotted us: recognition flashed happily in her eyes and her hand was waving in greeting.

'I hope ye do well!' Billy's mother cried, and the lads around us smiled too, turning to look at Billy.

'Piece o' cake, Mam!' Billy shouted from the middle of the road. 'We'll murder those High School cissies!'

We couldn't hear what she called back: the crowd swept us on and up the hill with a fresh urgency, sensing the nearness of the High School and, close beyond it, the sportsground.

We were suddenly stopped in our tracks by those in front. 'Quiet down and listen up!' The fellow with the school bell had turned to face us. He waited, standing in the middle of the road, until the stragglers behind had closed ranks upon us. Behind our bell-ringing leader a small Ford Prefect had drawn to a halt and I could only marvel at my schoolmate's composure as he ignored the driver's impatient horn-blowing and went on to address us.

'In a minute we'll be passing the High School – ' A chorus of boos cut him short. The Prefect-driver blew his horn again and our bell-ringer waved his bell good-naturedly at him. 'When we're passing the High School there's to be no language or throwing things!' he roared. 'Just good loud cheering for our crowd! Are you with me?'

'Yes-s-s!' we roared in unison.

'Now stand aside and let this guy get past,' he commanded, 'or we'll all be offside before the match even starts!' And we admired him and cheered him as he waved the red-faced driver on, and because our leader saluted the driver we all saluted him as he drove carefully between us down the hill.

We pushed on with new energy in our step, and the chanting started in earnest. 'Two-four-six-eight!' We were abreast of the High School entrance now. 'Who do we appreciate!' I was relieved that neither my mother nor my father was standing otrside the lodge. I cheered my appreciation all the more lustily for their absence.

In a minute we were at the sportsground, and the crowd milled around the main entrance. 'C'mon,' Billy said, grabbing me by the arm.

I didn't need to be told. The pair of us ran on in the shadow of the high perimeter wall until we came to the rusty iron-barred gate that might once, we guessed, have been the main entrance. It took only moments for us to claw our way to the top of the gate; a few extra seconds of care and we had negotiated the half-hearted strands of bullwire that topped the gate. A couple of hand-grips downwards, then we dropped on to the soft earth inside the gate. 'A tanner saved!' Billy said triumphantly. I laughed but I said nothing: I didn't have the sixpence admission fee.

We dusted ourselves off and headed at a run towards the sounds of sideline cheering. A stony, rutted path circled the bottom end of the pitch, leading back up to the gates where the two white-haired old fellows with bus-conductor satchels were collecting sixpences: Billy and I got a dirty look as we trotted past them, and the dirty look did not disappear in response to our cheerful wave. 'You'd think it was their own feckin' money!' Billy grinned at me.

We hurried on up the slope towards the stand, a stone-terraced structure with a rusting roof of galvanised iron. The steps were crowded, apart from a kind of no-man's land that ran from top to bottom, an uninhabited stairway that separated our school from the other crowd. The guys on the bottom step parted good-humouredly to let us up towards the top. Half-way up we met a pool of space and prepared to take our positions.

'*Festina lente,*' we heard, and realised that the presence of Brother Silenus explained the unexpected elbow-room.

'Just getting our breath, Brother,' Billy gulped, dragging me by the arm and careering even higher up into the stand.

A roar from the crowd stopped us in our tracks. We turned, pushing for space and footing, to see both teams running on to the pitch from the small flat-roofed sheds that served as dressing-rooms. The roaring grew. Our bell-ringer rang his bell. The High School crowd had some kind of clackers that rattled as you swung them in your hand. They had more flags too, big ones in purple-and-yellow that made our lone blue-and-white offering seem almost pathetic.

As the two captains came together in the centre of the pitch, the High started their own two-four-six-eight chant. A few of us started to compete, but a collective, instinctive bout of nudging and shushing made us fall silent. We let them at it, their mixed crew of boys' and girls' voices chanting, and we did not interrupt until they reached their demand, 'Who do we appreciate!' but then we let them have it! Oh, we drowned their response, and the metallic skies heard only the initials of our school as we showed the High School how to cheer and how to chant!

We won the toss. Our captain, the short, fair-haired fellow who had discussed this match on such incredibly equal terms with Brother Cyprian after the Christmas scrummage outside the headmaster's office, pointed authoritatively down the slope. Our side of the stand buzzed appreciatively. 'He's taking the wind,' somebody said. 'And the slope too,' another voice added. 'He'll be hoping for a good lead at half-time and then we'll hold their pack in the second half.'

This last sally was essayed by Billy. I half turned to smile at Billy, standing behind and above me, but I stifled my intended mocking jest when I saw that the older guys were nodding in agreement with Billy's appraisal. Billy caught my eye and winked at me, deadpan.

'We need a couple of scores on the board,' a Fifth Year fellow with an acne-splashed neck said.

The High kicked off into the wind and our forwards smothered the ball, and there followed the first of a series of scrums that took up most of the first half. The game seemed to be confined to the far sideline, mostly in the centre of the pitch. It was mind-bogglingly boring but nobody seemed to care, wrapped up as we were in our private battle in the stand. The High School had the favours – even a banner was unfurled after the kick-off – and every last one of them had a long purple-and-yellow scarf to wave in the air, but the cheering honours were undoubtedly ours. They equalled us in number but some hidden factor gave us the edge in roaring in the stand. Odd, I thought: they can open their mouths indoors and silence a room with a word.

The referee blew for half-time. The prognosis at our end of the stand was gloomy. The score stood at nil-all, and the High would have the advantage of wind and slope in the second half.

'We're in trouble,' Billy said, 'if the High get the ball out to their wingers.' The rest of our huddle, mainly older fellows, murmured their agreement.

'I wouldn't mind getting one of their females out to the wing myself!' It was the guy with the acne-inflamed neck who spoke.

He had black hair and even blacker glasses.

His mates whistled appreciatively. 'Go on then!' one fellow jeered. 'They're all waiting for you just a few feet away!'

Everybody laughed. Half-time seemed even longer than the first half and you could feel the cold seeping into your feet. 'I think I'll go and have a closer look at the talent.' For a split second the hubbub in our section of the stand was silenced by Billy's remark.

'Would you listen to Lally!' Red-neck jeered. 'The hard man himself!'

Billy smiled self-consciously: you could see him drawing himself up to his full height. 'Who's coming for a look?' he asked. 'I'm not afraid to say I've got nothing against Protestant birds.'

His remark unleashed another bout of jeering. 'Let's see you then!' Red-neck laughed.

'Let's go, Mike,' Billy said, taking my arm. His grip was firm, propelling me along the terrace despite my protests. Billy ignored the startled looks of our schoolmates as he pushed and pulled me along.

'If you think I'm going over there – '

"Course we're not going over there!' Billy smiled. 'We're just going to study the talent!'

He stopped on the edge of no-man's land. A narrow strip of cracked cement separated us from the grey blazers and the grey slacks and skirts of the High School. The girls were wearing the hats that were reserved for special occasions: the boys were bare-headed, although you could see rolled-up ridiculous peaked caps sticking out of many blazer pockets. Like us, they were now relatively subdued. Like us, they were stomping feet and rubbing hands to keep warm in the darkening January afternoon.

Both sets of supporters on the edge of no-man's land seemed

determined to ignore each other, facing severely inwards towards their own. Which suited me just fine: I didn't want to be recognised by somebody from the High School. 'Smashing birds!' Unlike the rest of us, Billy was resolutely studying the High School supporters' ranks, and with enthusiasm.

It was the high-pitched girl's voice that made us all turn and look across the unoccupied zone. 'Give me back my hat!' she shrieked, and you knew from the way she screamed, half-cry and half-giggle, that she was enjoying her moment as the centre of attraction. Every head turned on our side of the dividing line to watch the girl twirl and swirl on the terrace step, reaching and grabbing in vain for her hat as the boys from the High passed the soft headgear among themselves like a punctured football. The girl's long yellow hair streamed around her shoulders as she danced and jumped and clutched at the air, and her mouth was open in laughter, and anything that might occur on the pitch seemed impossibly unreal compared with this display of loveliness and humour not ten feet from where we stood, speechless. I caught Billy's eye and I knew that he too recognised the tall, long-haired girl who had asked Ella FitzArthur if she knew the two peasants sitting on the wall below the hill. He winked.

The cries grew louder as the hat was passed even more quickly among the grey-blazered fellows and the girl spun and twitched more frantically in pursuit.

'Let's see how well this flying saucer flies!' I had heard the voice once before, clipped and controlled, when its owner had declined to take his long legs out of our way as Billy and I carted suitcases down the staircase of the High. I watched in fascination as Nicholas Kerr drew himself up to his full height, taller even than myself, and extended his arm above the heads of his pals. His fingers twitched, releasing the soft felt hat into the air above no-man's land. The hat twirled at speed, rising above us, and then it seemed to hang there, suspended above our heads, before starting to drift almost languidly towards us, an unmanned parachute straying beyond its borders.

'I've got it!' Billy's was the first pair of hands to reach for the hat: short as he was, his speed enabled him to clutch it safely before the rest of us had snapped out of our dream.

'Give the hat back!' It was Kerr's voice again, arrogantly loud in the moment of drawn breath.

'With pleasure!' Billy cried, starting to push his way out of our crowd.

A large hand reached out to grab him by the collar. 'Hand it over, sparrowfart!' Billy struggled and snorted, but there was no escaping the heavy hand of Acne-neck, who had obviously decided, like Billy, to take a closer look at the other side. He grinned at Billy, and the grin seemed to deepen the redness on his neck. 'Hand it over, kid,' he said, 'and let a real man return it.'

Billy squirmed: the crowd pulled back around the pair of them. 'It's not fair!' he protested. 'I caught it!'

Acne-neck laughed. 'Life's not fair, Lally,' he said, 'but just wait till you grow up to get your own turn.' He bent over Billy, speaking quietly. 'Now give me the hat, like a good little boy.'

'Give the hat back!' Kerr called out again. 'Or we'll have to come over there and get it!' A chorus of jeers greeted Kerr's threat.

Billy handed the hat to Acne-neck. We watched him turn the hat around, dusting it with his sleeve. He punched it lightly with his fist, restoring the hat's shape. He stepped out of our ranks and stood for a moment in the middle of no-man's land. Right up to the enemy he stepped, and we heard him say 'Excuse me.' The grey ranks parted and the yellow-haired First Year girl from the High stood before him and he handed her the hat and her 'Thank you' was audible to all of us, and then he just stood there, looking at the girl.

'About time too! I was just about – '

'Oh, for Pete's sake, Nicholas Kerr, will you shut up!' Who else could it be but Ella FitzArthur, once more silencing Kerr? Everybody laughed, on both sides.

The owner of the hat blushed and said 'Thank you' again.

'It's a pleasure,' Acne-neck said, and he backed out of the bunch and crossed the line again to join us. We yahooed, and you didn't see the scalded skin above his collar now: you saw the victor on the screen at the Savoy, his jaw hard in the light of the setting sun, and angelic voices echoing his exploits before the lights came up. He winked at Billy. 'What a pair of headlights!' he whispered as he pushed by us to join his own pals. 'I thought I'd pass out!' Billy winked back manfully, growing taller with this unsolicited confidence from the Fifth Year fellow. And we all cheered again.

We hadn't much to cheer about after that. Three minutes after the re-start High School forced the ball over our line for a try, and we could only listen in wretchedness as the other half of the stand threatened to lift the rusty roof off the building with the clamour of their celebrations. Ten minutes later they scored again, and once more the High supporters placed the roof of the stand in jeopardy. Our bell-ringer tried to rally us but we knew our cause was lost and our ranks were depleted as our fellows drifted out of the stand in two and threes. The space around Brother Silenus grew wider until he occupied a terrace all by himself. The bell-ringer roared again and summoned us to stand near him, and we gathered round him, a tattered remnant of a once optimistic host, wishing only for the final whistle.

When at last the referee blew the final blast, the score was 18–0. 'Roll on next year!' the bell-ringer cried, but nobody cheered.

The players were shaking hands with one another as they left the pitch. We were on the bottom step of the stand now, watching the two teams pass by on their way to the dressing-rooms. You could see the splashes of mud on their faces and limbs; their hot breath travelled above them in steaming clouds. Our fellows looked diminished beside the exultant High School players. Their supporters thronged about them, shaking hands, clapping backs. From our step we watched them, silent. There was nothing to say, no cause for bell-ringing.

I felt Billy's elbow pushing against me, urgently. Nicholas Kerr and two other fellows were standing on the tarmac, looking up at us. 'You need to know who your betters are!' he taunted.

'Feck off,' Billy said, but amiably.

'Come on, Nick,' one of the other fellows said, 'we have to get back.'

'Yes,' Kerr said, looking at me, 'back to our little gate lodge.'

'Nick! That's not fair!' one of his pals remonstrated.

It was the pity that infuriated me most. I jumped off the step, my hands clawing the air to get at my tormentor. A pair of strong arms clasped me from behind about the chest. 'None of that!' It was our bell-ringer, bell still gripped in his right hand, its metal edge digging into my chest. 'None of that!' he repeated.

He released me then, and I stood there fuming, close to Kerr. His two friends tried to drag him away, but he shook them off. Our eyes met. 'Nice pair of trousers,' he said into the silence. 'Very nice indeed.' He smirked, and turned away with his pals.

'What was that about?' Billy asked.

'Nothing,' I said, unable to look at him, 'nothing at all.'

We headed home disconsolately, in the wake of the celebrating High School supporters.

When we heard the uncertain footsteps on the gravel outside the lodge I caught my mother looking at the clock on the mantelpiece. It was just after nine o'clock. My father hadn't come in for his tea. Throughout the evening, as I bent over my homework on the kitchen table and Sadie's knitting needles clicked erratically at a jumper, my mother had often looked at the clock, her forehead creasing, but she said nothing.

Now her worried glance said everything. The fumbling with the latch of the front door told a tale too: you had to turn the knob at the same time as you lifted the latch to open the door, a feat which seemed to be presenting some difficulty to my father. We heard him swear and my mother winced.

'Sadie,' Mammy said quickly, 'you go off to bed.'

'Mammy, it's only nine o'clock – '

The front door was suddenly pushed in, slamming against the wall, and my father stood in the doorway, blinking in the light. I watched his Adam's apple heave as he swallowed; he shook his head like a horse, up and down, and he extended both palms as if to balance himself against the air.

My mother stood up from her chair beside the fire. 'You're late,' she said.

He swallowed again before turning his head ponderously to look at my mother. 'Amn't I entitled to be late?' he asked slowly, every syllable spoken with laboured precision.

My mother stepped behind him and closed the door gently. 'Come up to the fire,' my mother said, taking him by the arm, 'you must be famished.'

He shook her off. I stole a glance at the bent knuckles resting on the table near my books, as he steadied himself.

'What do I need to go up to the fire for?' he asked, and I hated and feared the truculence in his voice. 'Haven't I good whiskey inside me to warm me! Haven't I!'

'Come up to the fire anyway – '

'The boys had fire in their bellies today!' he interrupted. 'Oh, such fire as they had!'

I kept my head down. I saw the bent knuckles lift from the table, watched them reshape themselves into a fist and saw the fist descend upon the table. My pile of books jumped on the shuddering table.

'Good-night, Mammy, g'night, Daddy.' Sadie had gathered her knitting and disappeared into the back hall almost before we realised it.

My father swayed on his feet, his unfocused eyes moving with difficulty from the door of the back hall to the kitchen. He hiccupped, his shoulders jerking inside his unbuttoned overcoat. My mother led him to the fire but he refused to sit in the armchair. He gripped the mantelpiece for support and lifted his drooping chin from his chest.

His eyes were on me. I could feel them, even without looking. 'There wasn't much fire in that oul' team of yours today, was there?'

I had my elbows on the table, my hands cupped around my ears.

'Are ye deaf as well as useless in that excuse of a school?'

'Jack!' my mother interrupted hastily. 'Leave him alone – he's at his homework!'

From the corner of my eye I watched my father sway and steady himself again, his hand resting on the mantelpiece. 'Homework is probably all they're good for in that place! Eighteen – nothin'! Sure they wouldn't score against a bunch of oul' women!'

'For God's sake, Jack, leave him be!'

'By God, our fellas showed them!' My father ignored her. 'Our fellas played like men! The High School is a school for real men, not excuses for men! That's why old Reverend Sweetman gave me the job here years ago when nobody else'd look sideways at me! They know what makes a man in the High School and they treat a man with respect here – and don't let ye forget it!'

I stood up suddenly, my chair scraping on the stone floor. I gathered the pile of books under my arm.

'Where d'you think you're going?'

I looked quickly at him. He was getting into full flow now: I could tell by the way he stood, his coat hanging open, arm outstretched like an orator. In a moment he'd be launched again upon the interminable story of how the previous headmaster of the High School had given him the job of caretaker.

'I'm going to bed,' I said. Every time he got drunk he told the same story.

'You'll go to no bed till I say so! I'm your father!'

'In God's name, Jack,' my mother said quietly, 'will you let Michael go to bed!'

'He'll go to no bed – ' he swayed again ' – until I tell him about the Reverend Sweetman! What that fellow needs is to have some respect for this school! The High School gives us – '

I didn't wait to hear any more. I dropped my books on the table and ran headlong for the front door. I pulled the door shut behind me, ignoring my mother's cry to come back. Along the gravelled drive I ran, my feet slithering in the loose stones. My face was wet with tears. My head seemed about to explode with pounding.

Past the main door of the school I ran, hurtling gratefully into the darkness. The sight of the headmaster's house, its square bulk confronting me in the darkness, brought me to a sudden halt. I drew back, gulping in great lumps of air, and wiped my face with my hands. The shadow of the school itself drew me into the lee of its walls, and I rested there, leaning against the grey stone, my mind a turmoil.

What did I care about his stupid job? Did all of us have to go on genuflecting forever because a Protestant minister gave my father a job as a caretaker?

'I wasn't right after that last final,' he'd say, whenever he had drink taken. 'I won all right – national champion for the fifth time in a row, sure it's never been done before or since – but I caught a couple of hard blows on the head and I wasn't right after it – I couldn't remember the names of people or streets or anything, and they let me go out of the hardware, out on the street and me with them since I was fourteen, and not just myself any more, but two of us now, and the first child on the way.'

I leaned back into the shadows and I could hear the choke in his voice as he told the story. How Reverend Sweetman had come to the rescue, Reverend Sweetman who had actually founded the boxing club for the poorer boys of the town –

'A gentleman he was,' my father would go on. 'A real gent. What did he need with the likes of us ruffians from the streets of the town and him the headmaster of the High School! And you never heard one of the lads at the club say a bad word about the Reverend, not even behind his back for a joke! We had respect for him – and he had respect for us!'

In the darkness I could hear his voice, with that over-emphatic drunken precision, droning on and on. Once or twice a year we had to listen to the tale of Sweetman to the rescue and the lovely little lodge where I was born and we'd all live happily ever after.

The lodge was hidden from my view here. I could imagine my mother helping him into their bedroom and getting him into bed, and the snoring would be worse than ever, and then some time in the middle of the night I'd waken to the sound of doors opening and you'd know he was urinating in the lav, and you'd hear the coughing as he made his way back to his bed, and you'd lie there, unable to sleep, wondering why you had to be so grateful to the deceased Reverend Sweetman for allowing you to live in the gate lodge of the High School.

The sudden burst of loud singing startled me. The noise came from behind the tall, uncurtained windows of the refectory, at the far end of the wall against which I was sheltering. I edged along the wall towards the lighted windows, taking care to skirt the shrubs and rose bushes in the long flowerbed that ran the length of the wall, facing west. The frozen earth crackled under my cautious feet.

The singing grew louder as I got closer to the window. I bent towards the window and cupped my hand above my eyes, peering into the lighted dining-room. There was no need to worry about detection: everybody inside was looking inwards.

I recognised some of the fellows at the seniors' table and knew that the rugby team was gathered there this evening. And I knew from my mother that Miss Henry, the school cook, had laid on chips and sausages and extra buns as a special treat. The long tables had been cleared of plates and dishes; tall jugs of orange crush stood along the tables and many of those inside were waving their glasses above their heads as they sang:

'The High School stripes are here, are here,

The High School stripes are here . . . '

It had the same air as our own song, and almost the same words. 'The blues, the blues, the blues are here,' we had sung at the match. A foreigner might have thought, listening to our unrehearsed singing, that we were all members of the same tribe, yet my father could praise these fellows inside the windows and count my own school for nothing. He tended the flowerbed in which I stood, and my mother scrubbed the long tables in the ref, yet he prized their shilling more than the free schooling that the

Brothers in St Joseph's had handed me.

I shivered. I was wearing only my fairisle pullover over my school shirt and new long trousers, and the night was still and freezing. It was too risky to go home: my father might not yet have been persuaded and cajoled to his bed – he might still be standing at the fireplace, recounting the heroic saga of the Reverend Sweetman's charge to the rescue.

Inside the volume rose steadily as the singers galloped to the conclusion of their battle-song.

'All we know is there's going to be a show,
And the High School stripes will be there!'

They cheered then and pounded the tables with their fists and stomped on the wooden floors with their feet and the noise echoed beyond the walls of the lighted refectory and rang against the white stars in the January night.

Then I saw Ella FitzArthur, a little to the left of the window, half turned from me. She was on her feet, laughing, and she waved her empty glass triumphantly above her head of shining dark hair, and the other First Years at her table stood up too, all cheering madly, and the fellow beside her took her free hand in his and she turned to him, and went on laughing as their joined hands paddled together in the bright yellow air.

The sight of her hand in Nicholas Kerr's made me draw back suddenly into the refuge of the shadow. Their shared laughter seemed a betrayal: how could she bear to laugh and cheer with such a creep? What kind of person was she, that one moment she could upbraid him for his stupidity and the next she could let him hold her hand?

It was no mirage. I pressed my face again to the cold glass and they were still cheering, their hands still joined. I could look no more. I clasped my shirt-sleeved arms about my chest but my heart seemed as frozen as the distant stars. I turned from the window and slowly moved away from the noise and the light towards the lodge.

It had by now become routine for me to go to the 7.30 am Mass. When I arrived back home the following morning from the church at the foot of the hill, I pushed the door in somewhat gingerly. I was relieved to see that my father wasn't there: our kitchen was its normal self, the eight o'clock Radio Eireann newsreader competing with my mother's regular encouragement to Sadie to 'get a move on'. Any moment now the hairbrushing would begin: the sponsored programme presenters were invariably drowned out by Sadie's screeched protests. Sometimes, to provoke her, I asked why, if the brushing was so painful, she didn't have her hair cut short. The unvarying reply, preceeded by a snorted 'Huh!' was 'That's the why!'

I had no thought of provoking Sadie this morning. My immediate aim was to get out of the house before my father came back from his first visit of the day to the school furnace. My mother clucked at first when I grabbed my schoolbag and made as if to leave without eating; the clucking tone hardened towards anger, however, to such an extent that it seemed politic to sit at the table and eat the bowl of porridge that was placed before me.

I was getting ready to make my escape, the bowl almost emptied, when the door opened and my father entered our kitchen. I risked lifting my eyes from the porridge bowl to look at him and was surprised by the way in which, as our eyes met, he looked guiltily away. He was unshaven, and you could see the sickly paleness of his face under the stubbled growth and the inflamed blotchy patches under his eyes. He always looked like that on the morning after his once-or-twice-a-year heavy nights of drinking.

An uneasy silence settled upon our kitchen as he moved towards the fire. He shuffled more than walked; when he stooped over the fire to warm his outstretched palms he seemed suddenly older, more fragile than I had known him. Sadie neither screeched nor protested against Mammy's brushing of her hair while my father stood beside her, warming his hands and rubbing them together. The soft strokes of the hairbrush and the fleshy sound of my father rubbing his hands together seemed louder than the wireless.

He straightened slowly and opened the door into the scullery. I waited till I heard the lavatory door being closed: it took only seconds to bolt down the remainder of my porridge.

'Wait till your father comes back.' My mother's unexpected command stayed me, just as I was pushing my chair back.

'But – '

'No "buts". Just wait till your Dad comes back.'

'I don't want to wait!' I protested. 'I'm sick of him always getting at me – '

'That's enough of that kind of talk!' my mother said sharply. 'Just do what you're told!' When Mammy was like this, she could be just as unreasonable as my father.

I caught Sadie's eye. She neither grinned nor winked nor stuck her tongue out. Although she had left the kitchen hurriedly the night before, she would certainly have overheard my father's ranting. For all our bickering we were, on occasions such as this, allies in adversity. She returned my glance mournfully and I sighed, waiting for my father to come out of the lavatory.

Waiting was agony: you wanted him to come back so that you could make your exit, yet his absence seemed kinder than his sullen presence. When he did at last appear again from the scullery, the lavatory flushing behind him, I didn't know whether to be relieved or frightened. He took his place wordlessly at the head of the table. His movements were stiff and slow, as if more than the bridge of his nose were broken. He sat with shoulders slumped, turned in upon himself; his hands between his thighs, fingers interlocked. He shook his head when my mother placed in front of him the usual pair of boiled eggs. 'I'll just have a drop of tea,' he said, and you could see him avoiding Mammy's eyes.

Mammy took the eggs away quietly. 'Would ye like an egg?' she said to us. Sadie made a face; I shook my head.

'I'll put them on again so,' she said. 'They'll do again hard-boiled.' For a few moments she busied herself at the cooker, gently lowering the eggs into the saucepan of water. I watched her uneasily, wondering if retreat was still forbidden.

My mother turned from the cooker and came to stand beside the range. She stood with arms folded, looking directly at my father and myself. The silence deepened in the kitchen. My father slurped his tea noisily and when he lowered his cup it rattled noisily on the saucer. My mother cleared her throat. 'Your Dad has something to say to you,' she said.

It was my father's turn to clear his throat. 'About last night – ' he began, and I looked quickly at him, but his gaze was fixed upon the table ' – don't mind what I said,' he went on, 'don't mind me at all.' And he gulped hastily at his tea.

'Jack!' There was an unusually remonstrative tone in my mother's voice. 'Jack! You promised!'

'You don't need to worry about what I said,' he continued. 'It was only oul' talk – '

'Jack!' my mother said again. 'You know you promised me!'

'Promised you what?' he said angrily. 'That I'd go down on my knees? Is that what you want? To see me on my knees again?'

'I only meant – ' My mother spread her hands helplessly, shaking her head. 'You know what you promised me,' she added quietly.

The brief flash of spirit seemed to have left my father. 'Sure I'm sorry,' he said bitterly, eyes still fixed on the table. 'I'm sorry for last night and I'm sorry for loads of things. I'm sorry I got my brains beaten out of me in the ring and I'm sorry I lost my job. But I'm not sorry that I have some respect for the people who took me in and gave us a job when our own crowd of gombeen priests and craw-thumpers wouldn't give us a pot to piss in – '

'Jack! Don't talk like that! – '

'It's true!' he replied quietly. 'And well you know it!'

He turned to me then but looked quickly away again. 'I didn't mean to give you a hard time last night, Mikey,' he said, 'but just remember that all the Brothers are giving you is a bit of schooling – it's the people here that are putting a roof over your head, don't ever forget that.'

He stood up then and slowly crossed the kitchen to take his overcoat from the peg on the back of the door. His fingers seemed to have difficulty with the buttons; an eternity seemed to pass before he was ready to leave. 'I have to go to work,' he said.

An icy blast of wind whipped into the kitchen when he opened the door and then he was gone, the door closing behind him. Nobody spoke. Sadie tied the ribbon in her hair without her usual medley of sighs. My mother stood with folded arms, staring through the window with unseeing eyes.

In my mind's eye I could see him shuffling along the gravel towards the school, setting out on his daily round of chores, a bent figure in a long dark overcoat, a caretaker who wore a white shirt and tie even as he shovelled turf into the school furnace. This morning he seemed less menacing, as if overnight the years had come to burden him and bend him, and leave him looking, almost, like any old man you might pass in the town.

TODAY

SEVEN

The babel that was the departures floor of Terminal 1 almost made me turn back again into the tiled tunnels that led to the tube and the safety of my flat in Maida Vale. It was over twenty years since I had got on an aeroplane: every summer since my appointment to the Department of Comparative Religion at the University (formerly the Polytechnic) of West London, I had religiously journeyed to the great cathedrals of continental Europe – and always by rail, bus and boat. Not for me the computerised anonymity of air travel, the plastic food that matched the plastic cutlery, passenger-cyphers shuttled from one indifferent airport to another. I shuddered, surveying the sprawling mayhem of the departures area from the top of the escalator, and renewed my pledge to avoid air travel like a medieval plague: when your destination was the dark coolness of Girona Cathedral or the soaring magnificence of Notre Dame, then it behoved the modern pilgrim to travel by more traditional means than the aeroplane . . . even if that pilgrim travelled only to admire and wonder, rather than to revere and pray, at such relics of religious magnificence.

There was no magnificence in this hangar-like concourse, just trolleys and creatures attached, some with offspring at heel, and enormous rucksacks that urged on tee-shirted teenagers in jeans and runners, and automatons, male and female, in various military-style uniforms, marching in pairs or trios with a purposeful air; those of their number who were not marching across the concourse were standing behind various counters waiting to smile their synthetic smiles at the pushers of trolleys and owners of rucksacks.

I confronted one of them, a blonde with a red mouth, clad in shades of green, standing under a plastic green shamrock crowned with the words Aer Lingus. 'My name is O'Hara,' I said to her. 'I have a reservation for Dublin.' When Peggy said she would attend to something, you didn't need to worry about it being done.

'You'll have to pick up your ticket at the Reservations Desk, sir,' the blonde red-mouth chirped, pointing over my shoulder, 'and then come back to us to check in.'

I scowled at her, mentally filing yet another bureaucratic irritant that served to confirm my distaste for airports. Standing in the queue at the Reservations Desk provided time to reflect upon my hasty decision. A too-hasty decision, it now seemed to me. What on earth had gotten into me, raising my voice to Palmer like that? The fellow was an idiot but I didn't have to let him know that I was aware of his idiocy, did I? And what was all that sweaty rushing-about for – chasing back to the flat like a lunatic, hurriedly packing shirts and toiletries and books into my battered bag, enduring the discomfort of a seatless journey on the Piccadilly line to Heathrow . . . what was it all for, all this perspiration and irritation on a sticky evening in London? Who cared if some pseudo-patriot-cum-terrorist had been canonised by an obituary in *The Times*? All that High School stuff was a long time ago, and besides, it was a different country . . .

Somebody was poking me in the back.

I turned round, ready to be angry, and found myself looking at a tall, ponytailed young man in a white T-shirt.

'You're next,' he said, smiling. I stared at him, not moving. 'It's your turn,' he went on, as if to a child. 'She's ready for you,' he added, pointing towards the counter.

I mumbled an apology and shuffled away from the square sign that said 'Q-HERE' towards the Aer Lingus clerk, who had by now turned away to talk to her colleague. The ponytailed young man's voice had stunned me: I hadn't heard the accent and intonations of my home town for more than two decades.

In a kind of daze the Aer Lingus girl and I negotiated the ritual of sale and purchase. My name; her fingers on the computer keyboard; her smile of reassurance when the great computer-god admits to knowledge of my existence and, better still, of my booking; my hand extending into hers the plastic wafer of my credit card; a communion of digits and signature; the mouth of the machine spews forth my ticket and I depart, bound now for the check-in desk, and my eyes linger on the black ponytail swinging animatedly at the pretty assistant further along the counter. He's just in from Greece, he's telling her, from the islands, but it's not the narrow streets of Grecian villages I hear in his voice – only the singsong tones of the streets of home and schoolboys shouting at one another across the narrow road. Ponytail does not look round as I pass by him to the end of the green rope that says 'EXIT'. When he's finished chatting up the girl, I know, he'll go back along the line and leave by the spot carefully marked 'NO EXIT' . . . Billy would have done the same.

And I was sour now, tired of always obeying the signs and going where the marshals marshalled: perhaps it was this sour tiredness of conforming that had driven me to this madness on a September evening. Whatever it was I didn't like it. You could get tired of following the signs but life was easier when you followed them, and anyway middle-aged lecturers in comparative religion had no business suddenly deciding to march past signs that said 'NO EXIT'.

I suffered myself to be fed through the system. Shuffling

forward in a long line towards a doorless portal, like sheep to the entrance to a sheep-dip; looking – sheepishly – from one blue-shirted airport official to another when the sheep-dip refuses me entry, with flashing of red light and intermittent beeping of electronic alarm; sensing, woolly-headed, the relief of release when one blue-shirt relieves me of my ring of keys and, thus keyless, the sheep-dip portal allows me through without further alarums or excursions.

Watching, indignant but resigned, the gloved hands of a stranger expertly rifling through my hundred-per-cent cotton underpants and vests and speculating (still sourly) on the connection between the departed Esmonde FitzArthur and the invasion of my shoulder-bag by British security-hands: the aspirations of terrorists seemed trite when some stranger was rummaging among your socks. Along endless corridors then, watched always by television screens purporting to advise you of flight numbers and departure gates, further interception by Aer Lingus clerks and examination of your ticket, followed by more waiting in the plastic lounge, and you stand as you are told when rows 10 to 16 may board, and once more you shuffle towards you know not what. Towards a carpeted tunnel leading to a Boeing 727 or towards a yesterday which would be better left alone?

They're all gone now, and there's nothing more they can do to you. All gone, like Ella's father, the last of the Mohicans who scalped you of your chance of happiness. Her father's shoulders shook, tickled by his own flight of fancy, and you knew, pimples and all, that you were a mere groundling strayed on to a superior stage, and in a moment you would be consigned again to the proper obscurity of your place.

Belted and buckled, I waited for take-off in my non-smoking window seat. Ponytail was seated three rows ahead: I could not explain, even to myself, my relief that he was not sitting beside me. The sensibly dressed, middle-aged woman beside me was reassuringly English: her modulated tones, thanking the hostess for stowing her bag in the overhead compartment, were pure Home Counties. I was ill-prepared for another encounter with the voices of yesterday.

We were airborne, somewhere over Wales, I reckoned, before she broke the blessed peace that had so far been disturbed only by the delivery of plastic tea and sandwiches of dubious provenance. I sensed her shifting towards me in her seat and I looked with great deliberation out the small window at the puffs of cottonwool cloud that surrounded us. I could hear the small swallowing noise that presaged conversation and I willed her into silence by the intensity of my study of the passing cloud formations – but to no avail. This Home Counties matron had decided to speak.

There was no mistaking the firmness with which she cleared her throat – none of your apologetic half-coughing, but a definitive barking noise that was unused to contradiction. 'Have you been over quite often,' I heard her ask, 'or is it your first visit to Ireland?'

I longed to ignore her but I had walked too long in the genteel avenues of English class-life. I turned, reluctantly, to face her. 'I'm not a visitor,' I heard myself say. 'I come from Ireland.'

'Really?' The one word registered surprise that bordered on incredulity.

'Yes,' I went on, surprising myself now, 'it's my first trip back for some time – I was brought up in the west of Ireland.'

'You certainly don't sound Irish,' she said doubtfully. 'You don't have the slightest trace of an accent.'

Doesn't put a tooth in it, my mother would have said: just comes straight out with it – you can't be from over there, since you sound just like one of us. 'I've been away for rather a long time,' I said. I was listening to myself speaking, recalling the long years of practice, of trial and error, that had gone to transform the careless singsong voice of my youth into the standard professional tones of today.

'A very long time, I should think,' my companion commented. Her strong voice brought Miss Murchison to mind, the Scottish teacher of home economics in the High School, famous, Ella had told me laughingly, for her conviction that 'scones' should be pronounced as 'scoons'. 'A very long time indeed,' Home Counties added, when I made no comment. 'Not even the teeniest trace of an accent.' She spoke encouragingly, as if I had somehow improved myself by remaking myself in her image. She was not easily rebuffed: my continuing failure to reply did not silence her. 'It must be very exciting for you, going back home again after such a long absence?'

'Not really,' I answered. I looked her in the eye, then glanced away quickly, feigning embarrassment. 'It's rather a sudden trip – a death, don't you know – '

You could always count on death or its proximity to stop any Englishman or Englishwoman dead in their tracks. Death was something that, like halitosis, they hoped never to experience personally.

'I'm so terribly sorry – ' I felt no sympathy for her confused distress ' – I didn't mean to intrude – '

'That's quite all right,' I said, turning firmly towards the window, confident now that the unwelcome interruption was ended.

The captain's stilted voice told us that we were about to begin our descent. Far below I could see the white waves of the Irish Sea, like suds in my mother's basin of washing long ago. I closed my eyes and the wetness of tears surprised me. My mother had always attacked the washing with a grim cheerfulness, sleeves rolled above her elbows, her knuckled fists working the corrugated washboard like some demented masseuse. Whence then the tears for the recollection of a sinkful of washing in the lodge of the High School?

Eyes still closed, I composed myself, aided by the droning rhythm of the jet-engines. The past had never seemed so vibrantly present as here in this aluminium fuselage, suspended above sudsy waters between my two worlds. It was a comfortless visitation, more accusing finger than welcoming hand: the backhanded compliment of Home Counties woman conspired with the untutored accent of ponytail to accuse me of – of what? I wasn't sure, but my discomfort was not caused solely by the narrow confines of the Aer Lingus economy seat.

I was conscious of the scent of disloyalty, a whiff of infidelity, like turning your back on your pals and feeling their accusing eyes like knives in your fleeing back. The irony of it did not escape me: on that distant January evening after the rugby match I had hated my father's betrayal of what we were, his cap-in-hand acceptance of a braying caste's right to rule, to command him to stoke their furnaces and to be polite to their arrogant offspring. I had raged against his self-effacement, his espousal of alien banners, yet in my own way I too had defected to the same cause. I could intone and modulate with the best of them now, a camouflaged interloper whose disguise could baffle even the twinsetted matron beside me.

I had not known, raging in the darkness against my treacherous father, that I too would willingly abandon my beginnings. The knowledge – the recognition of what I had done, in this moment of epiphany between past and present, between Ireland and England – was both poignant and painful. I wondered, with a sudden insight, if the knowledge of his self-deception had pained my father also, bending his back a little lower, diminishing him before our very eyes, Sadie and Mammy and myself, from that very day. I kept my eyes shut as we came in to land, but my father's sad, broken-nosed face refused to leave me.

YESTERDAY

EIGHT

You didn't notice the months and the terms drifting by. One moment you were a First Year in short trousers peering timidly through the school railings, leaning on Billy for support and encouragement, and a moment later – or so it seemed – you were one of the Second Year guys chasing a red sponge-ball around the yard, seemingly indifferent to but blissfully aware of the open-mouthed awe of a new set of First Years. The open mouths of these new fellows were a measure of your own progress from timid newcomer to confident resident: and it was reassuring to realise that you were no longer at the bottom of the pile, that you had moved to a noticeably higher step.

By the time Third Year came around, the next crop of newcomers held no importance for anybody in our class. We no longer needed another bunch of fellows against whom to measure ourselves. We were all of us over fifteen now, not an unbroken voice among us – although unplanned yelps and girlish screeches from a disobedient larynx could still embarrass you – and our pimpled jaws were beginning to harden into manhood. We tested ourselves against one another now – in the classroom, in exams and in umpteen training sessions on the rugby pitch. In the classroom I led; on the playing pitch I trailed, never one of the first to be chosen for either team in our own practice matches, nor yet one of the last.

Crowded days blurred into an energy-sapping continuum of

school and games and homework that left you exhausted when the handbell was rung at one o'clock every Saturday to toll the end of yet another week. It was a good Saturday when I had a shilling to go to the afternoon show in the Savoy with Billy (and sometimes with one or two other guys from school), but I didn't even mind very much those Saturdays that I had to spend helping my father in the High School. Sometimes he looked at me as if he would reprimand me for being too slow or too sloppy or too fast or too something at whatever task engaged us but always now he seemed to think better of it, and the noise in his throat was like a growl dying. I would ignore his eye and we would just get on with it.

It was like that in St Joseph's too: you just got on with it. You could object – and sometimes we did – to the injustice of being set compositions in both English and Irish for the same night's homework, but if neither Rab, for English, nor Brother Clement, for Irish, was prepared to concede a point to the other, then you were burdened with the two essays and not all the complaints in the world would change things one whit.

'Be sure to put the light out when you're finished,' Mammy would say, standing in the doorway of the bedroom, winding the green alarm clock as she spoke.

'I won't forget, Mammy. Goodnight.'

A pursing of her lips, an infinitesimal adjustment to the small hand that set the alarm to seven o'clock. 'Ten past eleven,' she'd cluck, 'and you're still at the books. Sure they're finished their study inside every night at a quarter to ten.'

'The Bish is different, Mam.' We had this exchange at least once a week. 'We just get more homework than they do in there.'

'But what's it all for?' she'd say. 'What's it all for, all this reading and writing? Sure you'll have your eyes destroyed with all the strain.'

'I'll be all right, Mam.' You had to look at her directly before she'd finally quit the kitchen and close the bedroom door behind her. 'Goodnight, Mam.'

'Goodnight, Michael, and God bless you.' The almost closed door swinging open again, her pale face peering at me. 'You won't forget the lights now – '

'Mam!'

'All right, all right,' hastily now, the door closing hurriedly. A last 'goodnight' from within the bedroom.

Even on those nights when I did not have to study so late, sleep came easily after the long day at school and the regular rugby sessions in the sportsground, where we were allowed to train. I was still vividly aware of Ella FitzArthur's presence whenever we chanced to pass each other in the grounds of the High School, but her long dark hair no longer tumbled across her laughing face in my wet dreams. Whenever we met she smiled and said hello but she never lingered and I could never think of anything to say to her until she had passed by. Sometimes, lying abed under the skylight in the minutes before sleep claimed me, I would compose a dialogue between us in which I charmed her into admiring laughter but our imagined conversations were never completed and in the mornings, hurrying between bedroom and scullery to get myself out on time for half-seven Mass, I could never recall the witticisms with which I had won Ella's smiles.

At Mass I prayed for her conversion. At that supreme moment of consecration, when the priest raised the white wafer of bread above the candle-lighted altar, when the entire and almost empty chapel was enveloped in a whispering stillness, sometimes, in that very moment, her smile flashed through my mind, and I transformed the memory into a prayer by interceding for her: such loveliness as Ella's should not be damned to eternal perdition simply

127

because she was unfortunate enough to be born to Protestant parents.

Sometimes whole weeks passed when I did not set eyes on her. Life in the High School seemed as activity-crammed as my own. I knew enough about the place to know that house exams were a less frequent occurrence here than in my own school, and I knew too that, as my mother so often and so plaintively pointed out to me, their study period lasted for only two hours every night. Yet High School days were full in other ways: the lives of these grey-clad Protestants were organised to the minute from the first morning bell to lights out at half past ten. Every afternoon you could see them on the school's playing fields – the fellows, all in the same grey-and-black strip that was compulsory for rugby practice, the girls in grey gym-slips for hockey – a few times a week (always on separate days for boys or girls) they took off for their walks around the perimeter of our town, marching two abreast, the girls always the subject of close inspection and daring comment by the lads from the town.

'Mike's harem,' Billy would say, elbowing whoever was in the vicinity watching the grey crocodile wind past. 'He tucks them all in every night, the lucky hound.' Once or twice Billy razzed me about 'that FitzArthur chick' but we were best pals and he never took the mickey about her in front of the other guys. We shared a desk in our high-ceilinged classroom and as one term faded into another I became increasingly conscious of how little Billy cared for school. He seemed always to be in trouble with one or more of the teachers for failing to present homework or for lack of attention in class. Matchstick Rab, who was not noted among us for 'getting a set' on individual pupils, developed an obvious dislike of Billy.

'Lally,' he would intone, when Billy had failed yet again to produce an English comp on time, 'you're going to finish up among the hewers of wood and the drawers of water.'

Even Billy's crew cut became an object of Rab's wrath. 'The mark of the Visigoth,' Rab declared on one occasion when he looked up from a poem by Gerard Manley Hopkins to catch Billy stroking his crew cut with his pink finger-hole-grip hairbrush. For weeks afterwards Billy was known as 'the Visigoth.'

Billy took it all in good part, immune both to Rab's barbs and Brother Silenus's slogs. He had 'stretched', as my mother phrased it, and his body was wiry and muscular: on the rugby pitch – which was the only school activity he admitted to loving – he was a powerful and speedy winger, as I discovered during one practice match when I tackled him in full flight, close to the line.

'Feck you, Mike!' he shouted cheerfully at me, as we lay entangled on the muddy sod of the sportsground on a freezing February afternoon. 'Feck you anyway! I was nearly in for the try of the century!'

I tackled him again on the way home after that training session. 'When are you going to start doing a bit of study?' I asked. 'The Inter Cert is only a few months away!' We were in Third Year then; the Inter Cert was the first state examination of secondary school.

'The Inter Cert!' Billy laughed. 'Who gives a feck about the Inter Cert? D'you think I'll be going back to that dump of a school next summer?' He stopped in mid-stride and turned to face me, shoulders back, one hand in his pocket, the other nonchalantly thumbing the duffle bag that was hooked around his shoulder.

'What d'you mean you're not going back after the summer?' But even as I asked the question, I knew the answer.

'Aw, c'mon, Mike!' Billy laughed. 'Sure you know well I'm just dying to go to America, and the brothers will take me out, and I'm working on the old lady about it but she does a lot of whingeing because I'm the youngest and the only one left – '

I turned away from him, away from the bright eyes and impish features that I had come to know as well as my own.

'Mike! What's the matter with you?' I felt his hand on my elbow, hauling me around to face him. 'What's the matter?' he asked again.

I shook myself free of his restraining hand and walked rapidly away from him.

'Mike!' His chasing footsteps were loud in the lee of the high grey wall that surrounded the High School grounds. I tried to shake off his clutching hands but his strong grip forced me to stand still. 'I suppose I should have told you – ' he was panting after his dash along the street to overtake me ' – but I just didn't know how to say it – '

'You don't have to leave!' I protested, and the catch in my voice embarrassed me. 'Why can't you go back after the Inter Cert like the rest of us?'

'Mike,' he said softly, 'you know yourself that I'm not cut out for school – it's just not much good for guys like me.'

'But I'll help you, you know I will! If you don't want to study in my house, then I'll come down to yours! Every night – honest!'

A solitary car rumbled by, and in the yellow light I saw the smile on his face – not the sardonic smile he employed in his frequent homilies on the attractions of various 'chicks' of street or screen, but a small sad smile that made him look, strangely, older, more a grown-up than a sixteen-year-old in Third Year.

'School's all right for you, Mike,' he said. 'You love it and all the teachers think the sun shines out of your tail-end – everybody knows you're going to be a professor or something.' He laughed and shook his head. 'But I'm not interested in school – d'you think I want to stay on for two more years just so's I can get a job pushing a pen up in the railway station? Not a chance, Mike!' he said emphatically. 'Not a chance!'

'But what'll you do?' I could not conceal the misery in my voice.

'I don't know, Mike.' He looked away from me. 'It's the land of opportunity, you know, full of openings for a fellow like me, full of bullshit and blarney – sure my brothers tell me America is the best place in the world for an Irishman to be. I'll come back a millionaire and the two of us will smoke big cigars and drink champagne till the cows come home!'

The small sad smile was gone now; his face was alight with the promise of a future that he could see beyond the grey wall and the station, beyond the town and the school and the pavement beneath our feet. 'Mike? Are you still mad at me for not telling you?'

I shook my head.

'Promise you won't say anything to your old lady about it?'

I looked at him questioningly.

'You know how mothers go on,' Billy said. 'They get each other wound up. Don't say anything yet until I have it all squared up with my old lady. Promise?'

'OK,' I said.

'Onward, Christian soldiers,' Billy said.

We walked on in silence. Ahead lay the lighted entrance to the High School and, opposite, the downward-sloping terrace where Billy lived. I saw nothing of the street: I saw only an unlighted landscape of loss, my best pal lost in America, a future that seemed suddenly cheerless and pointless. We parted at the gateway, and I watched Billy heading downhill for a moment, his step quickening as he crossed the road to his house. I turned away towards the gate lodge. It all seemed empty now – to be nearly sixteen, to be top of the class, to be no longer merely hopeful but rather confident that next year I might sneak on to the senior rugby team – who was there to talk to about anything if Billy fecked off to his brothers in America?

I didn't know then, on that wintry evening, that Rosie would be joining us in September.

Rosie had apple-red cheeks, laughing brown eyes and dark wavy hair. He stood almost six foot tall, with broad shoulders and a powerful chest. Rosie's proper name was Patrick Rose. Within a single day of starting at St Joseph's as a new boy in Fifth Year, Rosie not only knew everybody but was liked by everybody in our class. By the end of that first day back after the long summer break I was experiencing a sense of wonder and gratitude that it was with me that Rosie was sharing a desk.

Rab was at his most entertaining, telling us about his summer excursion to Stratford, when there came a knock on our classroom door and Brother Cyprian, the headmaster, walked in, followed by a tall fellow of our own age in brown trousers and tweed jacket.

We got to our feet but in leisurely fashion: we were, after all, seniors now, with the Inter Cert behind us and, besides, it was the very first class of the very first day of a new school year. Rab's rising was as languorous as our own: he had been interrupted in full flow about the peculiarities of American tourists he had encountered on literary pilgrimage to the home of Shakespeare, and we had learned over the three previous years just how much Rab disliked interruptions to his discourses.

Brother Cyprian motioned us to be seated and we did so, noisily, turning to our neighbour to wonder aloud about the stranger who was standing beside Rab and the headmaster with a smile on his face. 'This is the new arrival I was telling you about,'

Brother Cyprian said to Rab, gesturing offhandedly towards the stranger.

Rab's thin frame seemed to stretch itself even higher towards the ceiling as he turned to look down at the new fellow. We waited for some cutting quotation from Rab which would convey: (a) to Brother Cyprian, Rab's displeasure at the disruption not only of his class but also of our group, whose literary aspirations Rab had been moulding to his own satisfaction for over three years now; and (b) to the newcomer, that his English education to date would count for nil and that he was fortunate to be admitted to Rab's Fifth Year A-stream.

Our new classmate, however, had his own ideas. He stepped briskly past the headmaster, right hand outstretched towards Rab. 'How do you do, sir,' we heard the new fellow say. 'Patrick Rose, sir,' he went on, beaming his rosy-cheeked smile at Rab.

Rab allowed his hand to be grasped in Patrick Rose's beefy paw. He said nothing. We watched the frown deepen on his brow as he studied the new arrival.

'I'm very grateful to you,' Patrick Rose went on, 'for letting me come into your class like this, sir, half-way through school an' all, sir.'

'Perhaps,' said Rab, liberating his right hand, 'you won't be so grateful after you've been in my class for a little while.'

Patrick Rose's smile deepened, and we could all admire his beautiful, even white teeth. 'I don't think so, sir,' he said. 'Everybody says you're the best English teacher for miles.'

Rab's eyebrows were heading towards the ceiling now. 'For an adolescent,' he said, 'you have a dangerous line in flattery.'

Patrick Rose put up his left hand like a fellow in a film taking the oath in a court. 'On my word, sir,' he said, 'not flattery – only what I've heard from everybody.'

We should have hated him for sucking up but his bright eyes and red cheeks and white teeth held us spellbound.

Rab's eyebrows had resumed their normal position. 'I think,' he said to Brother Cyprian, 'that you can safely leave Master Rose in our care.'

Brother Cyprian merely nodded to Rab before turning to go: school rumour had it that there was no love lost between these two. Once more we stood with a noisy upending of desk seats while the headmaster left the room.

'Now,' said Rab, when we were once more seated and a kind of silence had again settled on the room, 'where can our new arrival pitch his tent?'

'There's room here, sir,' I heard myself say, my hand half-raised, half-gesturing in embarrassment at the empty space in my desk.

'I noticed that our Master Lally hadn't returned,' Rab said, looking at me. A few others had also chosen not to come back after the summer holidays, but various new pairings in our desks meant that mine was the only bench with a spare place in it.

Rab turned to Patrick Rose. 'You'll be in good hands with Michael,' he said. 'He's able to do joined-up talking and writing like yourself.'

'Thank you sir,' the new boy said. All eyes were riveted upon him as he manoeuvred his bulky frame almost daintily down the aisle towards my desk.

His hand was stretched out to me and his brown eyes were dancing above those rosy cheeks. 'Patrick Rose,' he said to me, 'but call me Rosie – everyone else does.'

Everything about Rosie was large and untidy. His moss-green tweed jacket hung askew on his large frame: the breast pocket was crammed with a plantation of pencils and fountain pens surrounding a long shiny brown comb; the side-pockets of the jacket bulged and drooped as if they housed an arsenal of grenades that were liable to explode at any moment. In a way, Rosie himself was like that too; there was a restless energy about him, hands never still, forever thrusting briefly among his crowded pockets or flailing in the air to demonstrate yet another inescapable point.

Those large hands were flailing now, as they had been flailing between lessons right through the first morning. We were standing on the bridge at the end of the school lane, perhaps half an hour after school had ended at lunch-hour for the customary half-day on the first day back. Three kids, obviously new First Years, were playing boat races with scraps of paper in the river: I half watched them, with a superior indulgence, as they dropped their paper boats into the brown, weedy water and then raced across the road to see whose craft first appeared on the other side from under the bridge. They gave Rosie and me a wide berth as they galloped across the road.

It seemed like a lifetime since Billy and I had played the same childish game on our first day at St Joseph's. Now I was standing on the bridge with yet another new boy, but in the presence of Rosie's galloping confidence I was the one who felt like a newcomer. 'After three years of Clongowes,' Rosie was saying, 'this place is outstanding.' He was telling me about being at boarding school.

'What kind of place was it?' I felt diffident, as if I were talking to Nicholas Kerr at the High – except that I didn't want Rosie to go on his way and leave me to head back alone to the gate lodge. 'Was it priests or brothers you had teaching there?'

'Priests,' Rosie said, giving me an odd look. 'Clongowes is a Jesuit outfit, like the Jes here.' He was referring to the town's other secondary school: the boys wore wine-coloured blazers and peaked caps, and were always contemptuously referred to in the Bish as 'mugs'.

Rosie answered my unspoken question: 'I had a bit of a job persuading the mater to let me come here,' he said, 'but I kept picking away at her defences until she gave in at last – I finally convinced the old lady that I'd do better in the exams here but really I was just sick of wearing a school uniform and anyway – ' the gleam in his eyes intensified and the grenades in his pockets rattled ' – anyway they don't play rugby in the Jes and I'm absolutely determined to go on playing.'

We watched a solitary black car with spoked wheels trundle by: it was the middle of lunch-hour and the streets were almost deserted. By ten to two the shop owners and their assistants would be back on the streets in their cars and on their bicycles, getting ready to open up again for the afternoon. Rosie waved at the driver of the car, an older man in an overcoat and soft grey hat, and the driver signalled with an index finger as he negotiated the narrow turn into Nun's Island. 'D'you know that oul' fellow?' I asked.

Rosie laughed. 'No, but it doesn't hurt to be friendly, does it?' He didn't wait for an answer, hurrying on in his breathless manner. 'Tell you the truth, the mater isn't a bit pleased that I want to go on playing rugby. Since the pater died she's gone all protective on me, like she wants to wrap me up in swaddling clothes and keep me in her private manger. I keep telling her it's only a game, for God's sake, and I'm a big boy now, I'm well able to take care of myself.' During the morning break he'd told me how his father had died suddenly of a heart attack near the end of the summer term: Rosie had been whisked home for the funeral and had then gone straight back to school for the Inter Cert exams.

'Did you like your father – I mean, did you get on OK with him?' I couldn't bring myself to say pater; I'd only ever seen it used in English comics and in the Jennings books I used to read when I was young.

'Of course I liked him! Sure wasn't he my oul' fella!' Rosie's hands flapped even more energetically, as if to emphasise the daftness of my question. 'Don't you like your father? What does he do anyway?'

I studied Rosie's bike, a dark-green Raleigh with a chain guard and shiny, black-leather saddlebag dangling on top of the carrier. Another fellow would take care to lean such a new machine carefully against the wall of the bridge but even on brief acquaintanceship you weren't surprised that Rosie simply dropped the bike on the ground; it leaned unsteadily on the pavement, handlebars askew, its front wheel angled crazily upwards. I idled my shoe against the tyre, watching the wheel spin slowly in the air.

'What does your oul' fella do?' Rosie asked again. 'Or is he a secret agent and I shouldn't ask?'

'He's a caretaker,' I said, without taking my eyes off the turning wheel.

Rosie had told me his father had been a solicitor with his own offices. 'Where? In some factory?' Rosie was only half-interested. He was flicking small pellets of paper at the First Year flotilla sweeping underneath the bridge.

'He's the caretaker in the High School – we live in the lodge.'

Rosie paused in mid-flick, index finger poised for propulsion on top of the fleshy part of his thumb. 'The High!' he yelped. 'You lucky old son-of-a-gun!' He flicked the paper pellet skywards in delight. 'All those lovely ladies all to yourself up there – you're going to have to invite me home so I can meet them! Yippee!' Rosie reached out his foot and pushed repeatedly against the bell of his bicycle. Ring-ring-ring! 'Tell you what,' he demanded, taking my arm, 'why don't you invite me up right now so I can introduce myself to those Protestant fillies!'

'Rosie, I can't! I've got jobs to do – '

'Oh, I'm only kidding!' he said. 'The mater will have a fit anyway, if I'm not home soon – she's probably been on to the Super already, come to think of it.' He glanced quickly at his gold-braceleted watch. 'Christ, it's after half-one, I'll have to be off!' He bent over the bicycle and awkwardly raised and aligned it. 'I'm glad I'm sitting beside you,' he said. 'I think we're going to be good friends.'

I felt myself blushing as I grunted agreement.

He swung the bicycle around, pointing it towards the other side of the town. 'By the way, Mike,' he said, 'I have a very shapely cousin at the High. You might know her, she's in the same year as ourselves.'

'I don't really know the students,' I said, reddening once more.

'She's my first cousin actually,' Rosie said. 'The mater was a left-footer until she married my father, and now you can't keep her out of the church, Mass every morning and the rosary every evening.'

He was buttoning his flapping sports-jacket in preparation for take-off.

'What's your cousin's name?' I asked, curiosity getting the better of my diffidence.

'FitzArthur,' he said, 'Ella FitzArthur.'

He was pushing off across the road now, throwing his brown-trousered leg over his bike, bound for the western edge of our town. 'So long, Mike,' he called over his shoulder, 'see you tomorrow.'

'So long,' I said to the receding back of Ella FitzArthur's first cousin.

My mother turned to look at me when I came out of the bedroom. She was replacing the dinner plates and cups in the dresser. Her features softened into a smile.

'You look nice, Michael,' she said.

'He ought to look nice!' Sadie was leaning on the sweeping brush, eyeing me critically. 'He's been dollin' himself up for the last hour while the rest of us have to go clearing up after the dinner.'

I wrinkled my nose at her: Sadie was out of sorts with the world because she had been refused permission to go to the Savoy with her pals.

'Sadie,' my mother said, 'why don't you finish sweeping the floor, like a good girl, and then you can go off to play with your friends.'

'Mam, I'm fifteen! I don't want to go out to play with my friends any more – anyway you must know that all my friends are going to the pictures today!'

'That's enough,' my mother said sharply. 'You don't have to be doin' the same thing as the rest of the world all the time. You can read a book or go for a walk.'

'Go for a walk!' my sister scoffed. 'That'd be really interesting, I'm sure! I don't hear you telling my big brother there to go for a walk – oh no, he's off to the Estoria with his high-and-mighty friend and then he's going to tea, if you please, out in Thread-the-Needle Road, no less!'

Sadie attacked the stone floor of our kitchen venomously. Her pale cheeks were flushed with rage and her long, thick plait of blonde hair swung angrily against her back. 'There's no need for that, Sadie,' my mother said.

'Give me the brush,' I said, moving towards her, 'and I'll do the floor for you.'

Sadie straightened from her sweeping. The long handle of the sweeping brush reached as far as the curve of her chin. 'Honest?' Sadie was eyeing me suspiciously. 'No kidding?'

'Honest,' I said, holding out my hand for the brush.

'In that case,' Sadie said, 'I'll finish it myself, thanks.' She was smiling at me. I couldn't remember Sadie and myself ever having a serious row, although she'd become less predictable during the last year or so.

'That's better,' my mother said. 'I don't know why ye always have to be arguing about something or other.'

'Not arguing, Mother dear,' Sadie said archly. 'More in the nature of a discussion.'

These days Sadie was often a surprise to me. She was in the top half-dozen of her class in the Mercy Secondary and sometimes you could see her breasts straining against the stuff of her white school blouse. 'What's this new fellow like anyway?' she asked suddenly. 'Is he nice?'

'Who?'

'The new guy in your class – don't be pretending you don't know who I'm talking about.' Sadie was leaning on the sweeping brush again. 'Rosie – I mean it's such a soft name, what's he really like?'

'He's OK, I suppose.'

'He's OK, I suppose!' Sadie mimicked my reply. 'What kind of an answer is that! Is he OK, or is he like a girl or something, with a name like Rosie?'

I thought of Rosie's broad shoulders and rounded chest and the pockets of his jacket loaded with unidentified missiles. 'No,' I told her, 'he's OK, he's not like a girl.'

'Well, what's he like then?'

'He's all right.'

Sadie tut-tutted: her expression showed her disgust with my answer.

'I'd better go,' I said, looking at the clock.

My mother came to stand beside me. Her hands reached out to adjust my tie inside the new V-neck jumper she had knitted for me. 'I hope you don't get cold cycling all that way out there,' she said.

I drew back from her. I knew what was coming next.

'I wish you'd wear that blazer that I got from Matron – '

'Mam!' I interrupted. 'I told you I'm not going to wear a High School blazer – it's bad enough havin' to wear their trousers!'

'Sure who'd notice,' my mother pleaded, 'when I'd pick the crest out of the pocket and dye it navy? Sure nobody would be a bit the wiser and you'd be warmer with a jacket on you cycling all the way out to that boy's house.'

'I don't want a blazer,' I insisted, 'especially a hand-me-down High School blazer!'

I dipped my finger in the holy water font before she could tell me what to do and stepped out quickly on to the gravelled drive. The new bike was leaning against the front wall under the kitchen window. It wasn't really new: my mother had bought it second-hand from a family further out College Road. I bent over the machine, resting each foot in turn in the fork of the frame to tuck my trouser ends inside my socks.

When I straightened up, ready to go, my mother was standing in the doorway looking at me.

'It's OK,' I said, 'I have the money for the pictures.'

'Take it, you can buy a few sweets for yourself.'

I took the small English sixpenny bit from her and pocketed it. I was ashamed now of my truculence in the kitchen. 'Mam – '

'It's all right, Michael,' she said, 'go off and enjoy yourself.'

I swung the bike out from the wall of the house, eager to be away.

'Good luck, Michael!' Sadie shouted from the kitchen. 'Say hello to Rosie for me!'

'That one!' my mother laughed. 'Always something to say!'

The curved driveway up to the school was deserted. From the playing fields behind the building came the intermittent shouts of the High School at rugby and hockey practice. My father would be there, patrolling the sideline with his increasingly stooped gait, available as always to fetch and carry for the games master and the pupils of the High. Tomorrow, the first Sunday of term, the drive would be choked with cars, the gravel ploughed into wheel-tracks by High School parents on their first visit of the year. There was always something to be done on these visiting Sundays: I'd spent one such afternoon trying to work out how to change a wheel for a half-blind old lady who was visiting her First Year grand-daughter.

'Michael?' I turned again to face my mother. 'At your friend's house,' she said, 'mind your manners at your tea.'

'Mam!' I reddened. 'I'm not a baby!'

'Bye-bye, baby Michael!' Sadie was standing alongside my mother now, grinning at me.

I snorted, throwing my leg over the saddle of the BSA. Without a further backward glance I pedalled through the gateway out on to the hill. The September sun was warm on my face and I was freewheeling down the steep incline but my mother's parting words had unloosed again the faint tremors of disquiet in my insides. Going to tea in Rosie's house had a ring about it that was different from having a cup of tea in the kitchen with Billy's mother. Meeting Rosie's mother was different: she used to be a Protestant before she married Rosie's father, and she and Ella FitzArthur's mother were sisters.

Despite the freewheeling I was in a sweat by the time I rounded

Sammon's corner on the Square, and pushed up the hill, past the Jersey Bar and Egan's grocery, where my mother did her weekly shopping. And then it was downhill again, along Williamsgate Street and Shop Street, past O'Gorman's bookshop, and over O'Brien's Bridge, skirting the lane to St Joseph's, and out through Dominick Street towards the Estoria. The lads at school from around here called the area 'back the west': although I had been to the pictures in the Estoria a few times the territory remained for me a relatively unknown land.

The cinema was a flat-roofed building with two pairs of glass double doors fronted by wide stone steps. Rosie waved to me from the top step as I rounded the corner on my bike. 'C'mon, Mike,' he yelled, 'I've got the tickets.'

Heads turned in the queue to look from Rosie to me. It was a long queue, snaking back down from the steps on to the footpath: they made a gap to let me through into the clay-surfaced yard at the side of the cinema. Dozens of bicycles, two and three deep, were piled against the unpainted side wall of the cinema. I rested my own machine against the furthest end of the wall, unloosed my trousers from my sock-tops and hurried back to meet Rosie on the steps.

Rosie seemed always to have a smile on his face. He was smiling now, waiting for me, the pink skin crinkling with humour around the corners of his eyes. Tiny freckles, darker than brown, flecked his smooth unpimpled face like dark diamonds. You couldn't help smiling yourself when he talked at you. 'Let's go!' he said. His loosely clenched fist waved us onwards through the foyer.

'Wait,' I said, digging into my pocket, 'I have to pay you.'

'Don't mind it,' Rosie said, 'sure you can get me again.'

I was heading for the door into the stalls when I felt his fingers gripping my upper arm. 'You can see it better upstairs,' he said, steering me towards the marbled steps that led to the balcony.

'I haven't enough, Rosie,' I blushed. It was one and tenpence for the balcony, compared with a shilling for downstairs.

'Didn't I tell you I have the tickets?'

'But I won't be able to pay you back.'

'Then it's my treat,' he said, 'now come on.'

NINE

'You'll get drenched,' my mother said, 'cycling all that way out to Salthill.' I stood behind her in the open doorway of the lodge.

'You're always fussin', Mammy,' I said to her, half-laughing. 'Anyone'd think I was going to melt in a shower.'

She half turned to face me. 'All the same – '

'All the same, nothing, Mammy!' I cried. 'Look over there!'

I pointed with outstretched arm towards the skies above the perimeter wall of the High School. West and south the light was shining, breaking through the leaden clouds.

'All the same – ' my mother began again.

'All the same!' I laughed. 'All the same!'

'I don't want you catching a chill!' she remonstrated. She glared fiercely up at me, arms folded across her thin chest. 'You were in bed a week last March with that flu and Dr Powell said your chest isn't all that strong – '

'Dr Powell is an old fusspot, Mother,' I cried gaily, 'and there's two of ye in it.'

Her eyes narrowed, measuring me. 'You're in a great humour altogether,' she said quietly.

I couldn't stop myself smiling at her, she looked so small and vulnerable, framed in our doorway, worrying about me. 'It's not a crime to be in a good humour, is it?' My words mocked her concern, but gently. The falling rain was gentle too, pattering softly on the gravelled drive. The school wore its usual Saturday afternoon air

145

of relaxation, as if it had removed its school tie and opened its obligatory white shirt at the neck: classrooms empty, girls at hockey, boys on the rugger pitches. Sometimes, like now, the place overtook me stealthily: something stirred inside me, confusing me, as if there could be any real attachment between me and these alien buildings that housed us.

'You've changed, Michael, these last few weeks.' My mother's words were soft as the dying rain. 'Ever since you started going out to this lad's house in Thread-the-Needle Road you're – I don't know – ' I watched her in amazement, flailing for words ' – you're just different, that's all.'

I couldn't let go of it. The rain had ceased to fall now, the sky was pale blue all over, blue like the stripes on the everyday cups and saucers in the kitchen dresser. 'It's not a crime, is it,' I asked again, 'to be in good humour?'

She shook herself as if she were cold, although the November afternoon held a hint of warmth in the watery sun. 'And the lad's mother doesn't mind you spending so much time in her house? Sure we hardly see you at all now at the weekends, you're out there so much!'

'Mam! I only go out on a Saturday!'

My mother ignored my protest. 'And she doesn't mind you being under her feet so much?' she persisted.

'I'm not under anybody's feet, Mam! You couldn't be under anybody's feet in Rosie's house – it's a big place with a separate dining-room and a sitting-room and loads of rooms – it's not like – ' I gestured helplessly at our kitchen.

'It's not like here,' my mother finished. I said nothing. 'And they're not like us, Michael.'

'That's ridiculous, Mam!' I exploded. 'Rosie and myself are pals.'

'There's pals and pals, Michael – '

'What does that mean!' I was angry now. 'There's pals and pals!' I mimicked. 'What kind of talk is that?'

I saw the wounded look in her eyes before she turned away from me and went back into the kitchen. She bent over the fire, poking needlessly at the red coals with the iron poker. She kept her face hidden from me. 'Mammy, I didn't mean anything – ' And I was the one who was flailing now: the anger still burned in me and yet I could not bear the thought of wounding her. 'Why d'you keep going on at me about Rosie – he's just a guy at school like myself.'

She hung the black poker on its hook above the hob and straightened to face me. 'I just don't want you getting hurt, Michael, that's all,' she said.

'Why would I get hurt, Mam?' I said from the doorway. I longed to cross the kitchen and touch her hurt face, but such intimacies had ended when I graduated to long trousers.

She lowered herself on to the armchair beside the fire. She sat on the edge of the chair, her roughened hands resting on her knees. 'I don't know, Michael,' she said, without looking at me. 'Just mind yourself.'

'There's nothing for you to be worrying about, Mam.'

I passed by her into the back hall to get my new navy-blue overcoat. She'd taken me with her to the Blackrock Drapery in Shop Street one afternoon the previous week and I had tried on nine or ten coats until she pronounced herself satisfied. I had watched her hand over the big five-pound note and I had tried to look away, embarrassed, as if I were not with her, when she studied the receipt, pursing her mouth in concentration, before carefully stowing the folded paper and the penny change in her black purse.

'The coat looks grand on you,' she said, when I came back into the kitchen.

'It's fine, Mam,' I said shortly.

I was tired of admiring my coat, bored with the endless debates about colour and single-breasted and the comparative prices in the Blackrock and Frank McDonagh's: in a moment my mother would begin to expound for the umpteenth time on the merits of buying a coat that was over-large for a growing young fellow like myself.

'It's still a bit big for you – '

' – but I'll grow into it, Mam, I know, you've told me a hundred times!'

She grew smaller, shrivelled into herself on the edge of the chair. And inwardly I raged at us both: why did she force me to say such hateful things to her? I could not bear to see her suffer and yet her repetitive silliness left me no choice.

'What's his mother like?' There was no need to ask whose mother.

'She's OK – a bit strange maybe.' I laughed nervously. 'She seems to pray an awful lot, there're statues and holy pictures all over the house – and she wears little rubber gloves when she's washing the dishes.'

'Rubber gloves?'

'There's a maid comes in in the daytime, but Mrs Rose is forever cleaning and polishing herself.' I laughed nervously again. 'Rosie drives her mad, always leaving his books and stuff lying around everywhere.'

'Polishing and praying!' My mother was smiling now, and I smiled back at her.

'She used to be a Protestant,' I went on, 'until she got married.'

'A convert!' my mother said in a whisper. 'They often put the rest of us to shame, they're so devoted to their prayers.'

'There's something else, Mam.' For weeks I had been longing

to tell her of how Rosie linked in himself my two worlds, my two schools.

'What else, Michael?'

'Rosie's first cousin goes to school here – Ella FitzArthur.' I felt my face flush red, but inwardly I warmed also with the pleasure of saying her name aloud in the lodge for the first time. 'D'you remember her, Mam? The first day she came here with her mother and father, we were all standing outside the front door of the school and Reverend Willoughby was there and – and he introduced us all – don't you remember, Mam? – she was starting here the same year I started in St Joseph's – '

My tongue was tripping over itself. I felt my cheeks flush redder under my mother's direct gaze. In the silence that followed my tumbling words, my heart thumped loudly, drowning the ticking of the alarm clock on the mantelpiece and the soft hissing of the coal fire.

'Oh Michael!' was all she said, but I turned away from her, knowing she could read my pounding heart in my crimson face. The chair creaked as she stood up, and I felt her fingers touch my shoulder. 'Michael, *a ghrá*,' she said timidly, 'just be careful, that's all – I don't want you to get hurt.'

'How could I get hurt, Mam?' I faced her with a lopsided smile. 'All I'm telling you is that myself and Rosie are good pals, and that his cousin goes to school here.'

She smiled at me, a small sad smile. 'And you remember her first day at school here, years ago.'

'That's nothing, Mam – sure I remember loads of things.'

'All the same – '

'Mam!' I exclaimed, and we both laughed.

I tried to go. The rain had stopped, and the grey gravel was washed in the pale sunlight. 'Does the lassie get out sometimes to visit the family in Thread-the-Needle Road?' My mother's question stayed me.

'Not yet,' I said.

'And today?'

'Yes,' I told her. 'Rosie said she was allowed out for a visit today.'

Neither of us spoke. A single heavy drop of rain plopped noisily from the laden eave-chute on to the doorstep.

'Remember what I said to you, Michael.'

'I will,' I said. I dipped my finger into the holy water font before she could remind me.

My father had rigged up a tarpaulin-covered lean-to against the gable end of the lodge, to shelter my bicycle. I stuffed my trouser ends inside my socks and threw my leg over the bike.

'Take care, Michael.' My mother was standing in the doorway of the lodge. I waved to her over my shoulder as I pedalled through the gateway of the High.

The entrance porch to Rosie's house was floored with pale red tiles. My shoes were clean but I wiped them again on the hard-bristled fawn mat that covered most of the red tiles in the small porch. I hesitated, unsure whether I should ring the bell or use the knocker. On my previous visits I had always arrived in company with Rosie or he had spotted me from his bedroom window and would be there in the open doorway, words and arms flying in noisy welcome, so that there was no need to confront the question of bell versus knocker.

I gingerly lifted the heavy black iron knocker between my thumb and forefinger and pondered the consequences of drumming it on the black iron stopper in the centre of the door. It was the added presence of the bell that was confusing. How was I to know what I was supposed to do? The bell looked the more modern, a white delph bubble set into a shiny brass circle on the right hand door-frame, with the word 'PRESS' commandingly printed in small black capitals . . . I lowered the knocker gently back into its resting place, careful not to make a noise, and deliberately raised my right thumb into a pressing position, opposite the white bell.

I hesitated, wishing that the heavy brown door would swing open and Rosie's boisterous greeting would resolve my dilemma. The door was flanked by two vertical panels of stained glass, but the darkness of the glass made it impossible to see into the hall, peer as I might. I listened closely, my ear pressed against the door, but from inside the big white house came only waves of silence. I didn't know if Ella FitzArthur had arrived yet. Whoever was at home must be in the sitting-room at the back of the house.

I was trying vainly to peer through the glass panel when I heard a car drawing up outside the gate. I swung round guiltily, my thumb still poised for bell-pushing, to see Ella getting out of the back door of Reverend Willoughby's car. I watched her swing the door shut with a neat economical movement. 'Thank you very much, Mrs Willoughby,' I heard her say. 'Thank you, sir!'

I had a glimpse of Reverend Willoughby's patrician features, focused firmly forwards, as the car pulled away from the gate. Instinctively I withdrew into the recess of the porch, but she saw me anyway, and came striding towards me across the cement drive, her face lighting up into a smile.

'Michael!' Was it my imagination or was she really pleased to see me?

'Hello,' I said, not daring to speak her name.

'Did you ring the bell?' She didn't wait for an answer. 'It's temperamental, the same bell, and even when it works they wouldn't hear it half the time, especially if Aunt Frances is out the back.'

I felt her fingers touch my elbow and I knew I was being steered around the side of the house to the back door, but I was not at all aware of the afternoon sky or the green lawns and still-wet hedges or the shadows cast by the tall trees that surrounded the Roses' back garden. It was as if my senses were suspended – or rather not suspended at all, but focused in a dreamy, filmy way upon Ella FitzArthur. As we moved together she spoke but I was only half-aware of what she was saying; she was close to me and yet, had I closed my eyes, I should have been unable to describe how her hair was arranged or what clothes she wore. Her fingers had touched my arm and yet I could not have said whether or not her hands were gloved. The few paces that took us from the front door to the back door of Rosie's house belonged not in the afternoon on Threadneedle Road but in some different time zone on the borderlands between sleeping and waking.

'Ella! We were expecting you!' Mrs Rose's effusive greeting restored me to consciousness. Ella had steered us through the back door and kitchen and into the sitting-room, where Rosie's mother was on her feet in front of a glowing coal fire, bending forward to be kissed by her niece.

'I collected this stray outside,' Ella said, gesturing towards me with a smile.

'Hello, Mrs Rose,' I managed to say, managing also to drag my eyes away from Ella.

'Hello, Michael.' Her greeting was restrained, her glance moving from Ella to me and back again.

'I forgot,' Mrs Rose said. Rosie had told me that his mother had become very forgetful. 'Naturally you and Michael know each other.'

'We see each other all the time, Aunt Frances,' Ella replied, smiling. 'If it weren't for Mr O'Hara, the entire High School would come to a full stop in no time at all!'

'Who is Mr O'Hara?' Rosie's mother was frowning.

'Michael's father, of course!' Ella said. 'Sure he practically runs the High School!'

'He's the caretaker,' I said quietly.

'Oh.' I felt Mrs Rose's eyes upon me as she attempted to digest this information. 'Patrick never told me that.'

'Never told you what, Mother?' The room was suddenly smaller as Rosie burst in upon us. 'What did I never tell you?'

'You didn't tell me that Michael's father is the caretaker in Ella's school.'

'Is that all?' Rosie was across the room by now, taking both of Ella's hands in his, his eyes crinkling with delight as he looked at her. 'Who cares what Michael's dad does? I just forgot. D'you care, Ella?'

She tossed her head then, and her dark rich hair swung about her smiling face. 'Everybody likes Mr O'Hara,' she said, looking at me. 'He just – he just gets things done.'

It was strange to hear my father spoken of in this affectionate manner: insofar as I had ever wondered about the attitude of the students in the High School to my father, I had only ever been conscious of a mixture of shame and resentment for the way in which he was expected to run and fetch like a paid retriever. And not the least cause of my resentment was the formal willingness with which my father conducted his fetching and carrying.

'Mr O'Hara is always so polite,' Ella was saying, 'and he never loses his temper, no matter what has to be done.'

'Just like Michael!' Rosie laughed.

'I don't know about that, since I don't really know Michael,' Ella said, 'but I can assure you that every single one of the girls in my class thinks that Mr O'Hara is an absolute pet!'

Rosie rolled his eyes and pretended to swoon. I blushed and tried unsuccessfully to stop staring at Ella. Mrs Rose coughed and said she was sure that we all needed tea and sandwiches.

Throughout the afternoon I perched on the edge of my chair in Mrs Rose's back sitting-room – the front sitting-room with the baby grand piano in the bay window was reserved, according to Rosie, for the parish priest and other visitors of similar importance – and spoke only when spoken to. Once, lifting the cup to my lips, my hand shook unaccountably and the tea slopped into the saucer, and when I tried to lower my cup into the brimming saucer, my hand refused to stop shaking and the tinkling noise of cup against saucer sounded to my reddening ears like the tolling of an unforgiving bell and the brown tea dripped heedlessly from the trembling saucer on to Mrs Rose's fireside rug. I felt myself drowning in waves of panic until Ella's cool hands removed from mine the impossible cup and saucer and set them on the coffee table beside me and once more I was beached and safe and I felt her pressing a dry paper napkin into my soaking, shaking hands. In another moment she had washed the stained section of the rug with a clean cloth and cold water and she had assured her Aunt Frances that all would be well and there wouldn't be even the faintest trace of a stain since Michael had this curious habit of drinking tea without milk and everybody knew it was the milk, not the tea, that caused the stains . . .

The truth was that I had forgotten to add the milk and had been drinking the tea without even noticing that I had forgotten. When I returned from my hasty, furniture-bumping retreat to Mrs Rose's immaculate bathroom, none of the trio seated around the fire said a word about my clumsiness with the tea. Rosie winked at me and Ella gave me a flash of a smile, but she was smiling anyway at Rosie's mother as she went on describing the lights-out procedure in the girls' dormitory at the High School.

She was a good mimic and if you closed your eyes you could imagine it really was the rolling Scots voice of Miss Murchison that filled the sitting-room with the command of 'Lights out, gir-r-r-rls!' Miss Murchison's room adjoined the dormitory; at eleven o'clock sharp, Ella said, half an hour after lights out, Miss Murchison conducted her nightly patrol, slipper-footed and torch-lighted.

'She thinks we're all asleep,' Ella laughed, 'but everybody is wide awake. Sometimes when she's flashing the torch it shines across herself and we get a glimpse of her with her hair all done up in curlers and she looks just like – like some sort of golliwog with the curlers sticking up out of her head!'

Rosie laughed and his mother gave a small smile.

'Promise me you won't repeat a word of this back at the High, Michael O'Hara!' Ella had turned to me; her hand was resting on mine on the arm of the chair.

I stammered a protestation and she took her hand away, still talking, still smiling. I drew back into the armchair, watching her. Outside the day was fading but the curtains were still open and the fire gave the only light in the room. Ella's face softened into repose in the firelight. It was curious: the more animated her words, the more the firelight danced around her. When her words danced, the shadows danced too, flickering across the walls of the room: when her words came low and soft, imitating the sleepiness that somehow settled each night on the dorm, the shadows lengthened too and seemed to settle into stillness. The darkening room, heavy with flowered wallpaper and dark-brown furniture, became Ella's chameleon, changing in tone and texture with the weight of her words and mood.

'I know we have to economise in our changed circumstances,

Mother,' Rosie said suddenly, interrupting another yarn of Ella's, 'but don't you think we can afford to have the light on?' His dry, ironic delivery belied his age. To me he seemed grown-up, like a man who owned his own house.

Ella poked him in the ribs. 'But it's much more romantic,' she cried, 'sitting like this in the firelight!'

'I'm only teasing the mater, Ella.' Rosie was smiling. 'She's been on an economy drive ever since you-know-what.'

'Patrick!' His mother's voice was indignant. 'That's no way to talk about – about you-know-what!'

I had to suppress a laugh, but Ella leaned across me and took Mrs Rose's hand in hers. 'He's just an impossible tease, Mrs Rose,' Ella said, 'but I think he means well.'

'He means,' Rosie said with great deliberation, 'that we ought to turn the lights on and not sit here in the dark like paupers.'

'You should spend a month in the High School, Patrick,' Ella laughed, 'and then you'd know all about lights out!'

'You must be joking!' Rosie's large untidy frame was fairly shaking with laughter. 'Me in the High School – with a bunch of Proddy perverts!'

His mother gave a little cry. She opened her mouth as if to speak, and then shut it again, her face shapeless with dismay.

'Patrick! Why d'you try so hard to shock your mother!' There was no doubting the anger in Ella's voice.

Rosie was contrite. 'I'm so sorry, Mum,' he said. 'It was just a silly joke.'

You could see his mother struggling to regain her composure. She looked sadly at her son, seated beside the fireplace on her right, then turned slowly to face Ella, sitting on the other side of the hearth. I had the sensation of being invisible as Mrs Rose sat staring at Ella. 'I pray for you every day, Ella, morning and night.'

The words came out in a hoarse whisper. 'It's such a comfort to me, knowing that your Uncle Jack was given time at the end to receive the sacraments of the Holy Mother Church.'

Ella got up from her chair and stood in front of Mrs Rose. She placed her hands lightly on her aunt's shoulders, then she bent slowly to kiss the older woman on the cheek. 'I know, Aunt Frances, I know,' she said quietly, 'and thank you.'

Ella's long dark hair was bathed in golden light from the fire. Her gentle face grew even softer in the shadows, pressing its sweetness against the white, papery skin of her aunt's cheek.

'Every day,' Mrs Rose repeated, 'morning and night.'

Rosie stood up and crossed the room. In a second the room was filled with light. I heard the rattle-and-swish of the curtains being drawn but I had eyes only for Ella, still bent over Mrs Rose's slumped figure. Her face glowed with serenity, I thought, like the picture of the Little Flower that my mother had given me for my First Communion and which still hung on the wall beside my bed.

'It's after five,' I heard Rosie say, 'and you know the Gestapo will be on the trail if Ella isn't back for tea.'

'Yes,' Ella said, 'I'd better be getting back.' Her hands briefly touched her aunt's face, and when she stepped out of the arc of chairs around the hearth it was as if a spell had been broken. What had been an enchanted place was now just another fireside around which some chairs were loosely arranged.

Mrs Rose stood up. 'I'll get my hat and coat,' she said, leaving the room.

We avoided looking at one another when the door had closed behind her. We heard another door opening and closing, and then the hurried sound of her feet upon the stairs. 'She can never find the car keys,' Rosie said. 'She tidies everything away and then she can't remember where anything is.' There was an edge of humour to his voice but neither Ella nor I smiled.

'Will she be all right?' Ella asked. 'I mean, is she OK to drive the car?'

'It's no bother to her,' Rosie said. 'Honestly,' he went on, in response to Ella's doubtful expression, 'she could drive a bus right now. She gets these moments, like now, and then she just seems to snap out of them.'

'I hope you're right, Patrick,' Ella said.

Rosie looked uncomfortable. He pushed his hands into the bulging pockets of his jacket and played with the contents for a moment before withdrawing them just as hastily. I had never seen Rosie unsure of himself before and I watched with curiosity as he shoved his hands now into his trouser pockets and then abruptly took them out again. Finally he folded his arms across his chest and stood, swaying slightly backwards and forwards.

'I hope you can understand when she goes on with all that stuff about religion.' His words, I felt, were addressed to me as much as to his cousin. 'She thinks it's great that Dad had time to get the priest when he got the heart attack and got Extreme Unction and all that. It – it comforts her,' he said, echoing his mother's own phrase. 'Don't mind her going on with that old codology about praying for you every day – it's probably just the way she is because of – you know – being a convert and all that – '

He didn't seem any longer like the owner of a house, just a guy like myself, shuffling from foot to foot, unsure of the ground beneath him. His apple-red cheeks glowed redder, and not from the heat of the fire. 'I don't mind, Patrick,' Ella said. 'I think your mother is great.'

Just then the door opened and Mrs Rose entered, shaking a ring of keys in front of her face. 'I must have put these into the drawer with my handkerchiefs,' she said, 'but for the life of me I can't remember when or why!'

Rosie looked from Ella to me and the three of us exchanged a conspiratorial smile.

'All set?' There was a forced gaiety about Mrs Rose's smile.

'Bye, Michael,' Ella said to me. 'Bye, Patrick. Maybe I'll see you next weekend – it depends on the humour at the penitentiary.'

Rosie's mother was dropping Ella back to the High. Now that she was engaged in a definite activity, Mrs Rose moved with purposeful speed; it was as if she feared she might forget what she was doing if she paused, even for a moment, to draw breath. She handed Ella her school beret and then helped her into her grey school gaberdine. We were in the wide hallway of the house by then, and Mrs Rose was dipping her hand into the holy water font beside the door and showering all three of us with holy water. Behind his mother's back, Rosie spread his hands in a helpless gesture of apology to Ella, but she just smiled and mouthed the words, 'It's OK.'

With a last wave Ella left us and hurried after Mrs Rose. I stood with Rosie outside the porch, watching Ella and Rosie's mother settle themselves in the front of the Wolsley car. It was only a few minutes after five, but the December darkness had fallen quickly. I felt a pang of loss, looking at the car: I could hardly see Ella's face in the shadowy interior of the vehicle. Her face, barely seen, was ghost-like; already the afternoon, so golden with the pealing of her voice and laughter, seemed but the shadowy stuff of a dream.

It was taking Mrs Rose rather a long time to get the car started,

'That feckin' battery,' Rosie said, beside me. 'I told her she needed a new one!'

The ignition coughed hoarsely, then glugged itself into silence.

Mrs Rose was again forcing the ignition into even more reluctant life when Rosie hurried across the cement drive and flung the door of the car open. 'Mum!' Rosie's voice was peremptory. 'You know it's no good! You'll just have to get a new battery fitted!'

His mother looked panic-stricken. 'But what are we going to do?' she cried. 'Poor Ella will get into all kinds of trouble if she gets back late! What are we going to do?'

'There's no need to panic, Mum,' Rosie soothed, as if he were addressing a child. He put his arm around her shoulder and shepherded her towards the porch of the house.

'But what about Ella!' Mrs Rose wailed. 'We'll have to phone – '

'We'll have to phone nobody, Mum,' Rosie said, more sternly now. 'Michael will give Ella a lift on the bike, won't you, Mike?'

'Yes – ' I stammered.

'But – '

'No "buts", Mum,' Rosie interrupted his mother. He turned to me. 'Better get your coat, Mike, and hit the road – Ella will be in trouble if she's late.'

I looked at Ella but she merely smiled and shrugged her shoulders. I hurried indoors to retrieve my long black coat. When I came out again Rosie was in full flow, extolling the many virtues of my second-hand BSA. 'Two good tyres,' he was saying, 'a lamp in front and a reflector on the rear mudguard and – best of all – a fabulous crossbar to give my cousin a lift to the High School!'

I covered my confusion by bending over to tuck my trousers inside my socks. When I straightened up, there was no place to hide: I was the focus of their attention. Rosie pushed the bicycle towards me. My hands wouldn't stop trembling as I took hold of the handlebars. I threw my leg over the bar and sat on the saddle. I looked hesitantly at Ella. She smiled and came to stand beside the bike. I lifted my left hand and angled the frame of the machine towards her. Without hesitation she reversed herself inside my arm and levered herself on to the bar of the bike. Her hair brushed against my chin and of a sudden the chilly air was warm with the smell of her. She took hold of the centre of the handlebars with her gloved hands and my fingers fastened around the left handlebar, encasing her in my arms. The nearness of her almost overwhelmed me; for a moment I was lightheaded.

'What're you waiting for?' Rosie laughed. 'A starter gun?'

Mrs Rose was starting to protest again. I pushed down on the pedal with my right foot and we moved off shakily.

'See you Monday!' I heard Rosie shout as I pedalled out of the driveway and on to Threadneedle Road. It was the beginning of a journey that would live forever in my memory. The road home was transformed by Ella's nearness into a journey along an enchanted way. It was the same black tarmac road but now its blackness was encrusted not with pebbles of stone but with shards of glinting diamond. I freewheeled down the slope of Threadneedle Road towards the sea: when I turned left on to the prom it was as if the wind changed direction to push us towards town. The tide was coming in: the white wintry waves that rolled noisily along the sand were crowned with a creamy whiteness.

She turned her head towards me, her face dreamy in the dusk, and said to me: 'Isn't it just perfect?'

One gloved hand she raised from the handlebars to indicate the sea and the sand, but my words were murmured into the dark softness of her hair, inches from my lips. 'Yes,' I whispered, 'it's perfect, just perfect.'

And it was. Nowhere in this world, or in any other world among the pale stars that littered the early evening sky – nowhere could there exist a time and a place of such perfection as this. This sea and sky. This dark, almost deserted road. This second-hand bike whose wheels turned without effort. This friendly wind at my back. This girl with dark hair enfolded between my arms, and the smell of her so rich that I could taste her sweetness in the core of my heart.

We sped past the gloomy bulk of the Hangar Ballroom on our left, on towards the end of the prom at Seapoint. I pushed harder, uphill now, past Salthill Church.

Ella shifted on the bar of the bike. The soft grey stuff of her school beret brushed against my nose as she half turned her head back to me. 'Let me off, Michael,' she said. 'We can walk up the hill.'

I shook my head. I knew that, at that moment, I could cycle straight up any hill or mountain in the whole wide, wonderful world, just so long as this girl with the freckles around her eyes was there on the crossbar of my bike. I bent to my task, and the touch of her hair against my forehead was at once a benediction and a fire in my veins, and the ascent seemed almost effortless and then once more we were cruising downhill, down past the Warwick Hotel and on towards the Estoria cinema.

'Will you take me to the pictures some Saturday, Michael,' she asked, 'if I can manage to get out?'

'Oh God, yes,' I said into her hair. I couldn't believe what was happening to me. I took my right hand from the bicycle and began to wave at the cinema. 'See you soon, cinema!' I shouted as we passed the Estoria. An elderly couple walking on the footpath stopped in their tracks to stare at me.

'Michael!' Ella protested, but she was laughing.

I didn't care. I wanted to shout at the stars in the sky. 'Bye-bye, Estoria!' I roared as we rounded the corner of The Crescent.

I felt Ella shifting once more on the bar and then she was leaning backwards into my chest. I gasped, burning with the touch of her. Her gloved fingers touched my left hand and she spoke without turning round. 'You should have gloves,' Ella said. 'Your hands will be frozen.'

I laughed out loud. The fire had spread within me to the very tips of my fingers. She left her hand there, resting on mine.

The shops in Dominick Street spilled white and yellow gold from their windows, lighting our way into the town. Overhead the streetlamps on their wooden poles shone with a brightness that I had never known before. And always, wherever we turned, the kindly wind turned with us, lending wings to my pedals.

Beyond O'Brien's Bridge the white face of the clock shone like another moon on top of the dark spire of the Protestant church. 'Ella – '

'Yes,' she responded, leaning her head back towards me.

The dark tower of the church was stark against the December sky.

'Does it bother you when – when Rosie's mother goes on about praying for you and – and all that?'

I had to strain to hear her answer above the tumbling noise of the river. 'She doesn't mean any harm,' Ella said. 'Everybody knows that poor Aunt Frances is obsessed by all that nonsense about Protestants and Catholics. She irritates Mum sometimes but Dad just laughs at her and asks her to say an extra decade of the rosary for him.'

'And does your aunt get mad about that?'

'I don't really know, Michael. I don't think that kind of stuff is important. Do you?'

We were in the shadow of the church tower then. Once, when I had been in primary school, Billy and I had ventured inside the door of that dark-grey church but the sight of a tall, thin man in a black soutane – for all the world like a Brother without his green sash tied around his waist – had frightened us into flight.

'That kind of stuff isn't important to you, Michael, is it?'

Just for a moment the singing stars of the evening were silenced by the remembered clattering of our fleeing boots on the stone floor of the church and the angry exclamation of the thin, soutane-clad figure.

'No,' I said at last, and then more firmly I said it again: 'It doesn't matter at all.'

And we left the shadow of the church behind us. Shop Street had never seemed so magical, shop windows ablaze with light, pedestrians' faces animated with their discovery of this bright new world in this bright new day.

Three Leaving Cert fellows from my school were standing on the footpath outside the Marian Café and they all three waved as we approached. One of them shouted something unintelligible and I saw the faces of the other two break into laughter and knew that some remark had been passed about Ella and me but I didn't care. I was glad that these three fellows, all of them in Final Year and all of them on the school rugby team, had noticed our progress along Shop Street. I waved and rang my bell as we cycled past.

We were swinging around the corner of Eyre Square, the dark railings on our right, when I felt her fingers pressing urgently on mine. 'Let me off at the bottom, Michael,' she said. 'It's better if we don't go in together.'

'We'll be OK as far as the church.' I had been expecting this. 'You can go up the hill by yourself.'

I turned into Forster Street, pedalling more slowly now, and then, reluctantly, I drew to a halt beside the stone cattle-trough outside the church gates. Ella got down off the bar stiffly and began shaking her hips from side to side. 'My bottom is as stiff as a board!' she laughed.

I blushed, and the dark bulk of the home for the unmarried mothers seemed to grow even darker.

'I'll have to hurry,' Ella said. But she stayed where she was on the pavement, still swaying lightly on the balls of her feet.

'Will you be going out again to Rosie's house?' I couldn't look at her as I asked the question: her shimmering reflection stared up at me from the still water of the stone trough.

'Oh Michael!'

I looked at her then. She was softer than her reflection in the dark water, standing under the streetlight, her pale face framed by the long dark hair that tumbled to her shoulders from under her beret. 'Of course I'll be going out again to Rosie's house,' Ella said. 'I don't have any choice any more, do I?' And then she was gone, half-running up the hill past the gloom of the convent building. Near the top she stopped and turned to wave and I waved back at her and then she had turned the bend in the road and was lost from view.

I didn't want to move. I felt as if I had been journeying alone for a long time and had stumbled at last into an enchanted place where the wind was always at your back and stars swam in streetside troughs of water.

The door of the lodge opened inward before I could take hold of the latch. I blinked into the light. My father stood in front of me, as startled as myself. I stepped back on to the gravel to allow him to come forward out of the kitchen. I caught a glimpse of his worried expression as he hurried away, wordlessly, along the drive towards the school, and I wanted to tell him that there was no need for frowning any more, that I had carried Ella FitzArthur back to the school on the bar of my bike and that henceforth frowns were banished in the dawning light of a beautiful new world.

I could say nothing. I watched his departing back with an unexpected taste of sadness in my bursting heart. Over the last couple of years I had watched his broad shoulders sag lower, had heard him puff and pant more loudly with the never-ending school routine of lifting and carrying. My eyes followed him as he passed the school, headed in the direction of the headmaster's house. I shrugged. It took no great effort to forget him as I stepped into our kitchen and closed the door behind me.

My mother was seated on the armchair beside the open fireplace. She glanced up when I closed the door and for a second our eyes met, then she returned to resume her examination of the fire. Her look was troubled and I wondered if she and my father had had words about something.

Sadie was sitting at the kitchen table, idly tapping a teaspoon against her cup.

'For God's sake, Sadie!' The sharpness in my mother's voice startled me.

Sadie made a face, but she laid the spoon obediently on the saucer. I looked from her to my mother, perched nervously on the edge of the armchair, then back to Sadie. 'What's up?' I mouthed the words silently at her.

She shook her head and refused to meet my gaze. I watched her fold her arms tightly together and then she shook her head again, but whether to me, or in denial of some greater problem, I could not tell. The table was set but I noticed that the cups and plates had not been used and that the brown cake lay unsliced on the bread-board on my mother's side of the table.

And all of a sudden I felt ravenous with hunger. 'I could eat a horse,' I said. 'A huge big fat horse.' Neither Sadie nor my mother said anything. 'I could eat two large elephants,' I said, 'and a partridge in a pear tree.'

The clock went on ticking loudly on the mantelpiece and my mother went on staring vacantly into the fire.

'It's that long cycle from Threadneedle Road,' I pressed on. 'All that sea air gives you such an appetite that you could eat a whole zoo-ful of elephants and crocodiles!' My daft words hung uselessly in the charged silence of our kitchen. I crossed the stone floor of the kitchen to stand beside my mother's chair, and I laid my hand on her slouched shoulder. 'What's up, Mam?' I asked.

I could sense the effort with which she lifted her head and looked up at me. She opened her mouth to speak but only a gulping, swallowing noise came out and she dropped her gaze to the stone floor.

'Tell me what's wrong, Mam!' I said.

'It's the school,' Sadie said quietly. 'They're closing it down.'

I heard myself laugh out loud. 'That's ridiculous!' I snorted. 'Sure why would they be closing the school?'

'You're a great swot at school, Michael, but d'you ever see anything that's happening in front of your nose?' Sadie was staring into my face now, half-smiling as if she were addressing a backward child. 'Didn't you even notice that there's only eleven First Years in the High School this year? And that they have only two or three more than that in Second Year?'

'So what!' I said. 'So what!'

'So there's no point in going on, big brother,' Sadie said with mock-patience. 'You can't have a school without pupils.'

'But – but – '

'You can "but" all you like,' Sadie said, 'but the High School is closing.'

'I don't know what to think!' I said peevishly. I was nonplussed by Sadie's assumed air of seniority, as if she were older than me. 'Anyway, how d'you know?'

My mother stirred in her chair. 'They had a board meeting today,' she said. 'I didn't say anything to you because I didn't want to be worrying you. And it's all in God's hands now – there's nothing we can do about it. The place will close down and the boys and girls who are here will be going off to boarding schools in Sligo and the like.'

It hit me then, the prospect of losing her as soon as I had found her. 'When?' I gasped. 'When will they be closing the place?'

'Your father is gone up to talk to Reverend Willoughby now,' my mother said. 'The Reverend was nice to us about it – he took me aside when I was up at the house doing the sandwiches and tea for the gentlemen at the board meeting, you know the kitchen staff in the school are off on Saturday afternoon, and Mrs Willoughby asked me to help her out, the meeting was a kind of emergency, she said to me – '

'Mam!' I interrupted. 'When will the school be closing?'

'That's what I'm telling you,' my mother went on with exasperating slowness. 'Reverend Willoughby said they'd be trying to keep it open for another eighteen months but he's not sure, and anyway the board meeting is only just over and your father is gone up there now to see if the Reverend might be able to tell him anything else.'

'Eighteen months!' Relief flooded over me. 'I'll be finished the Leaving Cert by then!'

'They're going to let the Fourth Formers come back next September,' Sadie said, 'so that they can finish off their Leaving Cert here, but all the Juniors will be finishing up here next summer.'

'Then what are all the long faces for?' The exuberance of the long bicycle ride home welled up in me again. 'Eighteen months is ages away – and anything can happen between now and then.'

'Sometimes – ' Sadie paused, as if measuring her words ' –

sometimes I can't tell if you're just a little stupid, Michael, or if you're just a completely selfish bastard.'

'Sadie!' my mother roused herself to snap the words out. 'Mind your tongue – or you'll feel the flat of my hand!'

I was strong now, the taste of Ella's hair like roses in my mouth, my fingers still glowing with the touch of her hand. 'What would *you* know about anything – little schoolgirl!'

'That'll do you, Michael!' my mother said. 'We have enough trouble coming here without making more for ourselves.'

'What trouble, Mam?' I protested. In a year-and-a-half Ella and I would both be finished school, and with any kind of luck I'd have the university scholarship that Rab said was mine for the taking, with just an extra bit of study. 'Sure what trouble is it if the school closes?'

My mother shook her head but said nothing.

'Are you just pure thick or what?' Sadie cried in exasperation. 'Where are we going to live if the High School closes down?'

I couldn't stop the smile spreading all over my face. It hadn't occurred to me: an end to this living in the gate lodge of the High School. 'The change will do us all good,' I beamed. 'It'll be a new beginning for us – making a new start somewhere else.'

'What new start?' I had to strain to hear my mother's softly spoken words. 'What start will your father get at his age? D'you think there's another Reverend Sweetman out there in the streets who'll give another chance to a man like your father?'

'Maybe they'll let us stay on, Mammy.' Sadie's tone was soothing. 'Reverend Willoughby likes Dad – he won't let them just throw us all out on the street – maybe they'll need a caretaker to look after the place, you never know.'

'You make it sound like we're paupers depending on a hand-out from the gentry!' I protested. 'We're just as good as they are!

Why couldn't we make a new start somewhere?'

Sadie turned on me. 'We all know you're not just as good as anybody else – oh no, you're better than anybody else!'

'You have to believe in yourself!' If Ella believed in you, nothing was impossible.

'Michael – ' my mother began in a choking voice.

'Go and believe in yourself somewhere else for a while?' Sadie stormed. 'You're upsetting Mammy!'

I watched her move purposefully towards my mother. When she bent over my mother it seemed as if it were Sadie's kitchen, as if my mother were an injured toddler in need of pampering. 'I'll get you a cup of tea, Mam,' Sadie cooed, 'and maybe Dad will have better news for us when he comes back from seeing the Reverend.'

I didn't want to be there any more, watching my mother's wet, red eyes and Sadie clucking over her as if she were an invalid. Neither of them noticed when I let myself out of our kitchen and closed the front door quietly behind me.

I padded my way across the familiar lawns between the lodge and the school towards the playing fields. The wide, eerie silence of the deserted pitches was welcome after the raw exchanges in our kitchen. Here, under the big, starry sky, I could again taste the salty wind that had blown us homeward just an hour ago. That wind sang in the bare, wintry trees at the back of the school and in its singing I could hear only her name. What did it matter if the school closed? My father would find some other work and he and my mother would live in another house, freed from their servile labour. I couldn't see myself in that other house, wherever it might be. She was there with me, beside the bare trees, and in some not so distant future she and I rode together up over the goalposts and out over the walls of the High, beyond the sweep of the bay and up among the stars. I looked back at the school through the trees and its lighted windows were beckoning with yellow warmth, filled with the wonder of her presence.

I saw Ella only once more before the schools closed for the Christmas break. Even then it was for only a brief interval, during which I was never alone with her. Ella arrived late at Rosie's house on that Saturday afternoon and there was only a short time before Rosie's mother was obliged to deliver her back to the High. Throughout the hour or so in which we sat in front of Mrs Rose's fire, it seemed to me that Mrs Rose watched Ella and me with a special alertness. She bade Ella go to the kitchen with her to help her carry in the tray and later, when it was time for her to leave with Ella, Rosie was commanded to fetch his mother's coat and car keys.

When he came back, juggling the keys, Rosie turned to me, laughing, and said: 'Sorry, Michael, but there's a new battery in the car at last, so there's no chance of having my lovely cousin on the bar of your bike this evening!'

Ella laughed at him and I tried to smile. His mother frowned but said nothing.

'Bye, Michael,' Ella said. She held out her hand to me. 'Happy Christmas, Michael,' she went on. 'It'll be the new year before we meet again.'

'Happy Christmas, Ella.' The touch of her hand was a gift, not just for Christmas, but for all the days of my life.

'Come along, Ella.' Mrs Rose's tone was sharp. 'We don't want to have you back late.'

Her hand lingered in mine and our eyes met and the smile in her eyes was food enough for me for the long journey through the empty spaces of the Christmas holidays until I should see her again.

'You seem to have clicked with cousin Ella,' Rosie said to me as we watched his mother drive the black Wolsley out on to Threadneedle Road. I didn't answer him. I was too busy trying to commit to memory the precise pattern of the tiny black freckles that clustered around Ella's eyes.

Sometimes, during the end-of-term examinations which took up the following week at school, I used to recall those eyes and freckles like some pagan worshipper fingering his talisman. All around me, in the long room at the top of the school where I had now been sitting regular exams for almost four years, were bent heads and scratching nibs and − in a few cases − expressions of puzzlement and the uneasy postures of ignorance: sometimes, after completing one answer and before attempting the next, I would shut my eyes to recall, however briefly, the tiny crinkled creases at the corners of her eyes, the exact paleness of their blue, like a winter sea, and the way her dark lashes curled upwards, like a prayer. I opened my eyes refreshed, ready to go on dredging the bed of memory and pushing the pen across the foolscap pages.

Rosie's allocated bench for these end-of-term tests was beside a window that overlooked the river at the back of the school. I caught his eye sometimes across the bent heads and he'd grin or wink and then go back to his study of the river below. Watching the careless, even languorous manner in which he lounged in the desk and stared out through the window, you'd think that Rosie was a dosser who had nothing to write, yet somehow he filled page after page with his untidy, scrawled writing. After just one term I knew that Rosie was my only competition in the class. In maths and the science subjects he was at least my equal; in English and Irish and Latin I held a slight advantage over him. The rivalry between us served only to cement our friendship: we regularly helped each other with the more difficult geometry cuts and algebra problems. Once, looking across the room at his wavy hair and rosy cheeks and the nonchalant way in which, yet again, he seemed to be engrossed in the view from the window, it occurred to me that, if I'd ever had a brother, I'd have wanted him to be like Rosie. I envied him his easy confidence and effortless masterfulness: his was the success of a cheerful bumble bee compared with my own incessant, repetitive, ant-like efforts.

We had a half-day on the last day of the exams. Christmas was three days away. The High School was finishing up on the same day but the barrenness of the days ahead, when she would not even be in the same town as myself, was lightened by the prospect of having a whole afternoon in the town with Rosie. I had a half-crown, and I was fingering the big, silver coin in my pocket as Rosie and I made our way down the rickety wooden stairs of St Joseph's after the final test. In Rosie's company I felt strong enough – and rich enough – to venture for the first time into the Marian Café, where the 'hards' hung out, drinking coffee and studying the talent from the convent schools in the town.

'I have some money,' I said to Rosie. 'Just for once I'd like to be able to treat you.'

'Christ, Michael, I can't meet you at all today.'

My disappointment must have shown in my face: Rosie stopped on the small landing outside the office that served as the school bookshop. 'It's the mater,' he said apologetically. 'She insisted that we do the Christmas shopping together after lunch today. Not only that, but the old folks are coming down from Castlebar and we're all having lunch together in the Great Southern.'

'The old folks?'

'Ella's mother and father – Uncle Esmonde and Aunt Irene, to be precise.'

A bunch of First Years, conducting a noisy post-mortem on

their maths test, swirled around us on the landing.

'Hi, Rosie!'

'How're you, Rosie!'

Even these Juniors, who would be wary of addressing any senior fellow by his nickname, cheerfully and confidently hailed him. He greeted each of them by name and they passed down the stairs in front of us, maths problems temporarily forgotten, glowing in Rosie's personal recognition of their existence.

'Ella is coming with us,' Rosie went on as we started down the stairs again. 'Her old man is probably up at the High now, collecting her.'

I tried to swallow my disappointment. 'Maybe we can meet up tomorrow?'

Rosie shook his head. 'I'm really sorry, Michael. We're having a state visit in the morning from the bishop himself and I'm under orders to be on my best behaviour in His Lordship's presence in the front parlour and after that we're driving straight up to Ella's place. I'd much prefer not to go but I've no choice. It's the first Christmas since "you-know-what" – ' Rosie grinned ' – and I suppose they don't want my mother to be on her own.'

The business of collecting and putting on my long black overcoat helped to conceal the emptiness I felt within. Rosie took his time with his fawn duffle coat, tying the wooden toggles with absentminded slowness. 'I can't invite you to lunch, Michael,' Rosie said apologetically. 'You never know what Ella's parents might make of it – and anyway my mother is already watching the pair of you like a hawk, as if you were up to something.'

We made our way along the red-tiled hallway towards the pupils' exit. 'By the way,' Rosie asked in a mock-serious voice, '*are* you up to something with my beautiful cousin?'

The school-yard had been emptied of idlers by the driving

rain that was lashing in from the bay. 'I will tell you,' I said, 'honest. But don't ask me now.'

Rosie laughed. 'I suppose that'll have to do me for now – but I hope your intentions are honourable, Michael O'Hara!'

Rosie chattered on in his usual cheerful fashion as we collected our bikes from the gym. Little of what he said got through to me. The school break, for which I had longed so deeply, seemed suddenly a mere stretch of emptiness. Whereas most of the boys had coasted through the first term of our penultimate year – universally recognised as a 'doss' year, before the rigours of the final year that led to the Leaving Cert – I had allowed myself no easing of my efforts, but continued to pore over my books every night in the kitchen of the lodge. Ella's intimation of interest – nothing had been said between us, and yet everything had been promised between us – had driven me to intensify my efforts. I felt that only through excelling would I come close to being worthy of her interest, and perhaps, too, I was searching for a visa that would take me out of the lodge and all that went with it.

We drew to a halt, as was our custom, on the bridge where our roads parted. Rosie spurned the protection of his duffle coat hood, and his thick wavy hair glistened in the falling rain. 'Happy Christmas, Michael.' He held out his hand and I took it shyly: nobody I knew was as frank and uncomplicated in his emotions as Rosie. 'Thanks for looking after the new boy in his first term.'

'Happy Christmas, Rosie.'

'We're just spending a few days up in Ella's house – we'll have to get together when I get back.' He gave my hand a last vigorous shake and then he pushed away abruptly across the road towards Dominick Street. With one last wave of his hand he disappeared around the corner, oblivious of the startled motorist who had to brake and was now beating out an angry tattoo on his car horn.

Despite my mood, and despite the unrelenting rain, I had to smile.

The afternoon dragged. I sat in the kitchen of the lodge staring with unseeing eyes at the same page of a book whose title I could not recall. The rain went on falling, cars came and went, ferrying the pupils of the High to homes scattered across the west of Ireland. My father left me alone and I was grateful but my relief was tempered by guilt for not volunteering to help him with the carrying and the loading. Throughout the long dark afternoon my mother worked her way through a pile of ironing, the silence of our kitchen periodically interrupted by the hissing noise of the iron when she spat on its bottom to test the temperature. Sadie arrived, noisily dumped her schoolbag on the table, made tea for us, then enquired sarcastically if the cat had got my tongue. My mother told her to leave me alone, that I was tired.

I went to bed early and slept quickly and without dreams. In the morning I arose before seven. My mother smiled at me in the kitchen and told me she'd boil an egg for my breakfast when I got back from Mass. Outside the world seemed shiny and clean after all the rain. The morning was hard and bright and the air had a taste of freshness in it.

The priest galloped his way through the Mass and I lingered a while afterwards in the church to savour the Latin words that I had come to love. *Ave Maria, gratia plena, Dominus tecum* . . . I no longer prayed the Hail Mary in English when I prayed in silence: the prayer itself was invested with an extra grace in the Latin tongue, with its echoes of other lands and older centuries . . . *Benedicta tu in mulieribus* . . . Blessed art thou amongst women . . . and truly was Ella blessed amongst women . . .

I tried to shake myself free of the sacrilegious prayer but found myself unable to concentrate. I got up from my knees, genuflected in the aisle and hurried outside.

The sharp, tangy air was welcome. I climbed the hill briskly, noting that Billy's door was shut. He'd been gone for over four months and, although one of his older brothers was expected home on Christmas Eve, Billy himself would not be coming.

'Sure her heart is broken,' my mother had said wistfully, relating the words of Billy's mother in our own kitchen. I didn't miss him as much as I had feared: the gap in my life had been filled by Rosie.

In the lodge I pulled the armchair up close to the range and I toasted two slices of the pan loaf on the long toasting fork while the egg was boiling. Sadie was still in bed and my father had gone out to stack a fresh lorryload of turf that had been delivered while I was at Mass.

'I was hoping they'd put in the oil system,' my mother said, 'and save him all that dirty work, but sure they won't be doing that now.' It was the first time she had referred to the closure of the school since the day of the board meeting. I said nothing but went on eating. Despite the disappointment of the previous day, a kind of joy was stirring within me. The morning had about it a sense of privilege – the quietness of the kitchen, the boiled egg with a small knob of butter melting into the golden yolk, the unhurried toasting of the shop loaf against the bars of the range.

'We'll be all right, Mam,' I said slowly.

'I hope to God we will, Michael.'

I blessed myself and stood up from the table. 'I'll go and help him with the turf,' I said.

A look of surprise flashed across her face and then she smiled. 'Your father would like that.'

'I'll go and put on my old pants and jumper.'

Sadie heard me when I was passing through the back hall to my bedroom. 'Michael!' she shouted at me. 'Bring us a cuppa tea and I'll adore you for ever!'

I changed out of my good trousers and put on the old pair with the patch on the seat. My old jumper, the navy-blue one, had been darned on both elbows but it was good enough for the job. It didn't matter today: Ella, like the rest of the school, was gone home.

My mother looked up from washing the breakfast things when I went back into the kitchen. 'I haven't seen you wearing those old things for a while, Michael,' she said.

'Sadie is shouting for tea,' I said. 'I'll bring her down a cup.'

'That one thinks she's Lady Muck,' my mother said, but she was laughing. 'I'll make her a fresh drop – you go on and help your father.'

The school seemed to shine in the December sun and the tall windows gleamed like mirrors. It was empty but only like a house whose family had gone away for a little while. Soon the children would return and once more the house would ring with noise. I couldn't figure out how I felt about this particular house being empty.

My father was in his shirtsleeves, building the reek of turf outside the boiler house. He looked up when I came round the far corner of the school, and I felt his eyes take in my old trousers and jumper. 'I'll give you a hand,' I said.

My father nodded. 'You build,' he said, 'and I'll fill.'

You had to construct the outside of the turf reek with care. You laid the black sods alongside one another, like sleeping soldiers, for the length of your reek, and then you put down another row on top. A finished reek was like a mighty black beetle, legless, stranded outside the boiler house, awaiting immolation. Building the four walls required care, but the inside demanded less attention.

I knew from the huge pile of turf that the delivery had come in the great side-railed lorry that was taller than our house. We had the makings of two big reeks here and at least one small one.

After a few minutes I could feel the sweat coming and I peeled off my navy jumper and rolled up my sleeves. Already my hands were brown as tea-stains and I knew that my hair was matted with turf-dust. We didn't speak but the silence was companionable. Soon we had rounded off the top of the first reek and we exchanged roles for the construction of the next one.

'D'you want to stop for a while, Mikey?'

I looked at my father. There were black streaks on his face where he had wiped away the sweat with his dusty hands. 'I'm OK,' I said. 'You go on back to the house for a cuppa.'

'I could use a mouthful of tea,' my father said. 'It's thirsty work.' He took his jacket from the peg on the door of the boiler house and draped it neatly across his arm. I watched him make his way along the gravelled path at the side of the school. He still walked with that distinctive boxer's roll but his step was slower now. When he'd come back from the headmaster's house on that night of the board meeting, he'd looked empty, like a deflated punchbag. Reverend Willoughby would do his best but he could promise nothing. We would be allowed to stay in the lodge until a buyer had been found, but after that our situation would be in the hands of the new owner. 'Old Reverend Sweetman would never have allowed this to happen,' my father kept saying, and long after my mother led him into their bedroom I could hear their hushed voices go on talking, sometimes with lengthy silences, until at last the fire went out and I felt the cold and went to my own bed.

My father went around the corner of the school and I bent again to my task, but now with a kind of anger. What right had they to do this to him, after all his years and all his blind allegiance?

'Michael!' The sound of that voice would dispel any amount of anger. I had to shade my eyes against the pale sun to see him striding towards me with that long ungainly gait of his. His unbuttoned duffle coat flapped around him and he was waving both hands above his head.

'Rosie! I wasn't expecting to see you!'

'Your mother told me I'd find you here at the turf – '

'You met my mother?'

'And your sister!' Rosie's smile broadened. 'You never told me you had a smasher of a sister – I think she'd have shown me the way but just then your father arrived and pointed it out to me. I've just met your entire family, Michael!'

I blushed, suddenly becoming aware of my filthy hands and my dust-matted hair. 'I thought you were going up to – to your uncle's house,' I stammered. 'And wasn't the bishop supposed to visit you?'

'I'll have you know,' Rosie said sternly, 'that I had breakfast with His Lordship, Dr Browne himself! Poor mother! She put out the best silver and napkins so crisp and white you could say Mass with them! But His Lordship said grace before and after, so the mater was satisfied – nothing like a personal word from the bishop to guarantee a higher place in heaven.' Rosie's blasphemy always amused and frightened me.

'And aren't you going away for Christmas?' I asked.

'Thanks for reminding me,' Rosie said. 'My mother's sitting outside in the car, all packed and ready to go. I'm just doing messenger boy here.' He drew out of his duffle coat pocket a slim package wrapped in coloured paper and held it out to me. I wiped my hands hastily on my trousers before gingerly accepting the packet from him. 'It's a present from Ella,' Rosie said. 'She and I slipped away by ourselves for a while yesterday when we were shopping with the old folks. I had to beg Mum to call up here – she thinks I'm just dropping in a little something from myself and that's the truth anyway because I'm doing that as well.'

From his other pocket he took out a second package, wrapped in a brown paper bag. I took it from him with embarrassment. 'I haven't anything to give to you, Rosie.'

'So what!' Rosie laughed. 'Just promise me you'll introduce me to your lovely sister at the first possible chance!'

'To Sadie?'

'Sadie! Is that her name? Sadie! I suppose if I had a sister that looked like her, I'd be keeping quiet about her at school as well.' Rosie didn't seem to be joking – or, rather, he was joking but was also serious.

'Come on, Michael,' he said, laying a hand on my shoulder, 'I'd better get a move on or the mater will be having a canary.'

It felt strange to be walking beside Rosie in the grounds of the High School. He stopped on the gravel in front of the main school entrance and looked up at the building. 'It's not very impressive – not like Clongowes, anyway, although maybe the food is better.' He turned to me and asked: 'Is it true about the school closing? Ella's parents were talking about it.'

'There was a board meeting a while ago – the day I had to give Ella a lift back.' I stopped, remembering. 'I think it's true, Rosie.'

'And what will you do – about your house, I mean?'

'The mother and father are worried about it.' I shrugged. 'I don't know what's going to happen, Rosie.'

'As Christians we must never underestimate the power of divine providence,' Rosie intoned, imitating the unctuous, nasal tones of our bishop.

I laughed and we went on together towards the gate of the school. I could see Sadie looking out at us through the window of the lodge and I hurried Rosie to the exit. The Wolsley was parked just past the entrance to the school: I could see Mrs Rose's black

181

hat through the rear windscreen of the car.

When Rosie opened the door I stooped on the footpath to peer in at his mother. She was wearing a black coat and I wondered idly if it was difficult to see through the black lace trim of her hat when she was driving. 'Happy Christmas, Mrs Rose.'

'Many happy returns, Michael.' She adjusted the black veil of her hat and looked up at Rosie, standing beside me on the pavement. 'Now come along, Patrick – you know that your Aunt Irene is expecting us for lunch.'

Rosie climbed in. The door slammed shut. There was a grinding noise of gears and then the vehicle pulled jerkily away from the cab. I stood there watching until I could no longer see Rosie's hand waving through the open window.

Only then did I dare to look at the coloured package in my hand. Ella had sworn him to secrecy, Rosie had joked. The bright wrapping paper seemed suddenly too bright, too obvious a declaration of the intimacy that Ella and I shared. I had no doubt at all now that she also had felt something special on that shared bicycle ride. Why else would she put Rosie to the trouble of delivering the package? And even as she had sworn him to secrecy, I wanted to treasure our intimacy to myself, away from the eyes of the day. I pushed the slim package inside my turf-stained shirt.

Rosie's gift was a book, a Penguin paperback of *The Grapes of Wrath* by John Steinbeck. On the inside of the cover Rosie had written: 'Happy Christmas, Michael, from your new friend, Patrick Rose.' I felt warm, standing on the footpath outside the High, reading the simple inscription. My entire life was not confined by the walls of this school: beyond its confines was another world, where I was known for myself alone, a world in which somebody bothered to buy me a book for Christmas and write my name inside the cover.

I longed to open the package from Ella but I couldn't do it there on the street, under the sun, with an occasional car passing by. I went back into the school grounds, hurrying past the lodge. Our front door was closed and nobody hailed me from within. The boiler house was at the far end of the school but I turned off on the little path between our house and the main school building. The path twisted its way among the trees and I stopped under the largest of them, an old chestnut with voluminous arms, a few yards from the cropped surfaces of the playing fields. Under the trees the knee-high grass was still wet from the night's rain. The spreading branches of the trees were bare and skeletal but there was a taste of freshness there, looking out on the deserted pitches, as if the spring had already come.

The paper crackled so loudly in my trembling fingers that I half expected to see my parents and Sadie come rushing along the path to examine Ella's present, yet when I looked up guiltily I could see only the bare trees and the wet grass and I could hear only my own heart thumping in the silence.

The paper contained a pair of black leather gloves and an unsealed white envelope. From the envelope, with fingers that refused to stop trembling, I drew out a Christmas card that showed a robin perched on a branch of holly laden with berries as red as the robin's breast. I fumbled the card open and read what she had written on the blank inside page:

Dear Michael,

I promised myself that day on your bicycle that I was going to buy you these for Christmas! Your hands were just frozen that day! I hope you like them!

I wish I could see you before going home but it's just impossible! It's the first time ever that I'm not really looking forward to leaving the High for the hols! But it's also the first time ever that I've been looking forward to coming back! See you in 1960!

Love,

Ella

The earth seemed to move beneath me and the pale blue sky began to spin about my head. I leaned against the horse-chestnut to balance myself. The card shook in my hands as my eyes greedily drank in her words: 'Love, Ella.' I felt dizzy but it was a glorious, triumphant kind of dizziness that I could not keep to myself. I raised my head and through the leafless branches of the tree I could see the vast expanse of the December sky, but that sky was not so distant now and I could reach up and touch its velvety blueness at any time I wanted to.

And then I heard myself roaring: 'YAHOO!'

It was a long roar, hurled out of my chest, beyond the bare trees, ending beyond the skies. Or perhaps never-ending. It would never end inside me, reverberating for light years like a star bursting in my brain. 'Love, Ella.'

There was a printed verse on the opposite page:

Wishing you the Compliments of the Season
for Christmas and throughout the New Year.

Below the printed verse Ella had written:

To Michael O'Hara
From Ella FitzArthur xxxx

She had written four x's after her name. Four kisses. When we were small I'd written such xs with chalk on the footpath to tease my sister: SADIE xxx BILLY. Sometimes I'd done it to tease Billy. Afterwards you'd have a friendly fight and go off to play cowboys together. This was different. These x-kisses were written by the loveliest girl in the world, and she had sent them to me, Michael O'Hara from the gate lodge.

And the gloves – they were like nothing I had ever owned, made of soft black leather with a lining of white fleece. I flexed my fingers inside the soft material, loving the feel of them, thinking of her hands wrapping them for me. Those same hands had written the letter to me. I had never seen so many exclamation marks on a single page. They made the letter seem like Ella's voice – frank and decisive and good-humoured. And I could read what she had not written – that she was looking forward to seeing me at the start of the next term.

Never had Christmas seemed so wonderful, so rich with possibilities. I pocketed the gloves and card carefully and went, with the lightest step of my life, to help my father with the turf.

TEN

We went back to school after that Christmas not just at the beginning of a new year but of a new decade. We were conscious of the change of decade, although none of us, Rosie and myself and the other guys in our class, could have explained what made it different. 'Happy nineteen-sixties,' we said to one another, laughing without knowing why we laughed. Maybe it was because there remained only one more Christmas at school, although nobody said so. In a way, the end was in sight – a year-and-a-half to go – although nobody said that either.

We had already lived through one complete decade but we had been too young to realise when the fifties were beginning. Now it was different. Some of the fellows were shaving. Rosie was playing wing forward on the senior team – and he still wasn't in the Leaving Cert class. A quiet boy who excelled at science had already let it be known that he intended joining the Franciscans, the brown-robed monks who lived in the Abbey Church just past the police station. Like myself, he was only on the fringes of the senior team; like me, he was pretty sure of his place on the side the following year.

And there was Ella. We met often at Rosie's house on Saturdays, and sometimes we walked together along the prom or rambled out past the men's bathing area, past the diving tower and along the stony shore that bounded the golf club. Always Rosie came with us. Ella and I couldn't have left the house in

Threadneedle Road without him, since Mrs Rose was becoming increasingly vigilant and now never left us alone together, but I think that we both wanted him along with us anyway. His liveliness took us out of ourselves. Sometimes the intensity of my feeling for Ella left me tight-chested, unable to breathe: Rosie's irreverent laughter took away that tightness and helped me to see the honest humour that was in Ella herself.

There were Saturdays when we couldn't meet – afternoons when she was tied up with a game or practice for hockey, or when my father needed me to help him in the High. Once her parents arrived to take her out on Saturday afternoon to compensate for the fact that they couldn't come the next day. I happened to be seated at the window that Saturday afternoon, idly turning the pages of *The Grapes of Wrath*, when I saw the new Mercedes turn in through the gateway. It was a shock to see the FitzArthurs' new car arrive unexpectedly, but it was as nothing to the disappointment I felt on seeing Ella in the back seat of the departing car a half-hour later.

I went as planned to Rosie's house that afternoon and the two of us walked together out as far as the headland beyond the golf course, but neither Rosie's inventive chatter nor the changing colours of the hills across the bay interested me very much, and I took my leave early and cycled home in the gathering dusk, seeing and hearing nothing.

The kitchen was quiet. The alarm clock on the mantelpiece said almost half past eight. Only its ticking disturbed the silence – that, and the occasional whoosh! of the fire in the grate when the wind above the chimney turned suddenly and sucked the flames into a momentary incandescent dancing. I was relaxing into Yeats's notion of the grey Connemara fisherman – I had finished the maths, always the first and most demanding part of the daily homework. In the quietness of our kitchen it was easy to imagine the stony greyness of the fisherman's vision and the flick of his expert wrist as he cast the line into the dark pool.

Only Sadie and I were there. One of the kitchen girls was out sick and my mother had been called up to the school to help out. My father was out – as usual – searching for something that needed to be done around the school. I sometimes thought that he was working harder than ever since we'd heard about the coming closure, as if, by his personal efforts, he could keep the place open.

I could sense Sadie looking at me. She was sitting at right-angles to me, with her back to the fire. Out of the corner of my eye, without looking up, I could see that for the last few minutes she had been staring into space, her books forgotten. Sadie, I knew, had something to say and, reluctantly, I lifted my head from Yeats's grey poem and looked at my sister.

'Promise you won't tell Mam,' Sadie said.

'Won't tell her what?'

'What I'm going to tell you,' Sadie laughed. She had a light breathy laugh, a result of the wheeziness that still afflicted her.

'Which is what?' I asked.

'Which is what!' Sadie mimicked my question. 'Honestly, Michael, sometimes you sound like a fellow in a book! I don't know what that FitzArthur one sees in you!'

I didn't answer, but I couldn't stop the warm redness spreading over my face and neck.

Sadie laughed again. 'There's no need to start blushing, big brother,' she said. 'Do you think I'm an eejit or something, that I didn't know why you go rushing out to Threadneedle Road every Saturday?'

'I go out to see Rosie – '

'Oh, yes, and I'm Bill Haley dressed up in a gym-slip! And of course I believed you when you told us that your friend Rosie gave you that lovely pair of leather gloves for Christmas!'

I found myself looking into the dancing pools of Sadie's green eyes and wished that I had stayed where I was, safe in the contemplation of the fisherman's still waters.

'Oh, don't look so worried, Michael!' Sadie said with a smile. 'I don't think Mammy suspects anything – and anyway she's really lovely, the same Ella FitzArthur, although what she sees in my big brother I don't know. Now if it was your friend, Rosie – mmmm!'

She leaned back in her chair and licked her lips as if she were relishing an ice-cream cone. Rosie's words came back to me, and when I looked at Sadie's shoulder-length fair hair and her green eyes and wide mouth, I could see why he thought that my sister was 'a smasher'. She was a year younger but she seemed more like a woman now than Ella: I found myself staring at her breasts, straining against her blouse, and I had to force my eyes away from her.

'Is that what you don't want me to tell Mam?' I asked her.

'What?'

'Before you got side-tracked by your vivid imagination – ' she laughed at that, but said nothing ' – you were going to give me some information which you didn't want passed on to our mother.'

'Michael!' Sadie laughed. 'You're a hoot! Definitely the only professor I know!'

'If you're incapable of communicating in anything more than a street-urchin's vocabulary – '

'Michael!' She couldn't help laughing. 'Shut up!' I watched her force her pale face into seriousness, the wide mouth straight, the green eyes still as my fisherman's pool. 'I'm packing school in this summer,' Sadie said at last.

'You're not serious!' I'd have been less astonished had she told me she was taking up rugby.

'Books and all this stuff – ' Sadie grimaced, indicating with a dismissive wave of her hand the various school books spread across the table ' – I've had enough of them. I want to get a job and get some money of my own. I'm fed up never having a bob and always having to ask for money.'

'But it's stupid giving up after the Inter Cert!' I protested. 'You always do well in the exams and you're easily in the top ten or so in your class!'

'Poor Michael.' There was a kind of sadness in Sadie's little laugh. 'You think there's nothing more important in the whole world than coming first in some exam. Out there – ' the sweep of her hand embraced the world beyond the school walls ' – exams aren't that important. People get jobs and make money and they get their own house and start their own family.'

As so often these days, I had the sensation of listening to an older person who knew more of the world's ways than I did. It was an absurd sensation, one which angered me: again I had to remind myself that I was a year older than Sadie. 'You're only sixteen, Sadie!'

'You can leave school at fourteen, Michael – as if you didn't know.'

For a little while we were silent. The irritation drained away from me, to be replaced by a sadness, as if I had lost something.

'I don't know,' I said at last, searching for words. 'Billy said the same things about leaving school, and he hasn't written once to me since he went to America.'

'People change,' Sadie said. 'He probably has new friends out there – you know, like yourself and Rosie,' she added gently. She stood up and tidied her books. 'Anyway,' she said, 'Don't let on to Mam yet.'

'They mightn't let you leave,' I said. 'What'll you do then?'

'They can't stop me,' Sadie answered, 'but I honestly don't think they'll try. The way things are going around here, we don't know where we're going to be in a year or two and Mam might be delighted about having an extra wage coming in.'

Her words held an inexorable logic. I watched her stack her books on top of the small press beside the dresser, ready for the morning, and in the sureness and economy of her actions there was a sense of purpose that unsettled me. Sadie said she'd make a pot of tea and I told her I'd be back in a minute, that I was just stepping outside to clear my head and get a breath of air. She laughed and said she thought it would take more than a breath of air to clear my head, it was so cluttered up with books and study.

The wind had died down, nothing was stirring outside. The school was anchored solidly in the night, its lighted windows shining like beacons that would go on forever. Standing outside the lodge it was hard to believe that soon these lamps would go out forever. Billy's lamp had gone out, as if he and I had never been best pals, as if he had never sat beside me on the wall and shouted smart-aleck remarks at the marching girls from the High. I thought of Ella then and I knew that I longed for change myself, for a time and place that would be different. I shivered, sensing in some way that change did not walk alone, but came accompanied always by its own peculiar pains of body and soul.

That summer Sadie went to work in Forkan's chemist's shop. She made the announcement casually, as if it were no more than saying she had bumped into Mrs Lally coming up the hill from school.

'I'll be starting work in Forkan's chemist's on Monday week,' she said, taking the cup of tea from my mother and sitting down in the armchair beside the fire.

'What are you saying, Sadie?' my mother asked sharply. 'It's a summer job you're talking about?'

'Not a summer job, Mam,' Sadie said, 'a real job. One of the girls at school was talking about her sister giving up the job and going off to England, so I called in today and spoke to Mr Forkan himself and – and he liked me and I'm starting on Monday week!' My sister's voice was firm but I noticed the forced brightness of her tone and I saw how her hand trembled as she left the cup down on the hob.

In the silence that followed it seemed as if my mother would never speak. She was standing beside the table, setting out the things for tea. In her left hand she held two forgotten side-plates: the knuckles of her right rested on the table as if she needed support.

'But you're in the middle of your Inter Cert, Sadie!' she said at last. 'Haven't you an exam tomorrow morning! Aren't you just after coming home from doing another one this minute! How can you be talking about working in Forkan's when you're in the middle of exams?'

'It's very simple, Mam,' Sadie answered. She stood up and crossed the room to where my mother stood. She took the plates from my mother's unresisting hands and set them on the table. She went on talking as she opened the drawer of the dresser and took out the knives and spoons for tea. 'I called in to see Mr Forkan after I finished the exam today and I'm going to finish the rest of these famous Inter Cert exams next week, and once I've seen the back of them I'm going to start my new job on Monday week.'

'And is that all you want,' my mother asked, 'after all your schooling – to be a shop-girl in a chemist's and hand out lipsticks and Aspros?'

'I'm sixteen, Mam, and I'm finished with school as soon as these exams are over.' There was an unshakable conviction in Sadie's words. 'It's a good job and the money is OK.'

'How much?' My mother seemed reluctant to ask.

'Three pounds,' Sadie said, 'and I'll get an extra ten bob a week after a year.'

'Well,' my mother said slowly, 'the extra bit of money won't go astray, but all the same – '

Once you heard my mother saying 'all the same' in that resigned tone, you knew the deed was done. Sadie looked up from laying the table and flashed me a winning smile, and I smiled back at her but I took care, as yet, not to interrupt the exchange between her and my mother.

'What are we going to say to your father?' My mother's question was more a thought spoken aloud.

'Just leave Dad to me, Mam,' Sadie said.

'No, Sadie,' my mother told her, 'your father isn't himself these days and I don't want to worry him any more.' Her eyes moved to the closed door of their bedroom and her voice dropped. 'Your poor father has enough on his mind. Leave him to me, and I'll tell him myself, in my own way.' We were silent then, all three of us, all of us looking at that bedroom door. I had never known my father to be ill or to complain of being unwell or to fail to get up for work in the morning. This was the second day he had remained in his bed and our kitchen seemed empty without his presence.

'Why don't you get Dr Powell up for him, Mam?'

'Sure I want to get the doctor,' my mother answered Sadie, 'but you know what your father is like when he doesn't want to give in about something.'

'He's like all the men, Mammy,' Sadie said, 'you have to get him to give in without letting him know that he's giving in.'

'Maybe you *are* ready to start work,' my mother said, and I felt as if I was an intruder, noticing the private look that passed between my mother and my sister. She turned towards me then, abruptly, as if she had suddenly remembered me. 'Are you sure you're able to manage the work, Michael?'

'Don't worry, Mam,' I reassured her. 'I can manage.'

I had hoped to get a summer job myself and maybe save a little money each week, so that in my last year at St Joseph's I might have the wherewithal to bring Ella to the pictures or even to the Marian Café. My father's uncharacteristic lying abed had put these plans on hold. I didn't mind: my father's pale, haunted face seemed a good enough reason for foregoing the chance of some pocket money. On the previous evening, when I'd brought a mug of thin soup into the bedroom for him, I'd been almost frightened by the whiteness of his face and the damp dishevelment of his thinning, greying hair. I'd felt a stranger in his presence: he'd mumbled a thank you but made no effort to sit up in the bed and take the soup.

'It's a pity though,' Sadie said. 'It'd be nice if you could get a job for the summer and have your own few bob.'

'I'll manage,' I said again, although I was struck by the increasingly adult tone of my sister's conversation.

'I might be able to lend you a few shillings,' Sadie laughed, 'if you promise to behave yourself.'

I blushed, for that very thought had occurred to me. 'Just remember who's the younger kid around here,' I joked.

'No,' Sadie replied, 'what you have to remember is who's the working girl around here.'

'Everybody works here,' my mother cut in sharply. 'It's a good thing you can help out, Michael – I don't know what we'd do without you.'

'It's no bother, Mam,' I said, embarrassed. 'Like I told you, there's not much to do.'

There wasn't. In the weeks that followed, only the students taking the exams for Inter Cert and Leaving Cert remained on the premises, the rest – including Ella – having gone home for the long summer break. Every morning and afternoon I had to arrange the desks for the examination candidates according to a plan supplied by Reverend Willoughby; the rest of the time I spent mowing the lawns and pitches according to my own whim. My father seemed, unusually, to have no inclination to direct my work or to enquire about its progress. For these fine days, at least, I was content with my role of lawnmower-operator. Already I could see my arms and shoulders darkening from the summer sun and, more importantly, I could sense my muscles hardening and growing – as they must, if I was to make the school senior team for my last year.

'Tea's ready,' Sadie said.

For a moment I sat where I was, staring at the patch of blue through the window of the lodge. I remembered suddenly why I had knocked off work early today. 'Sadie?'

'Yes, Michael?' My sister was busy pouring the tea.

'What was the Irish paper like today? Can I have a look?'

Sadie paused in the act of filling a cup of tea and fixed me with a look of puzzled amusement.

'The exam paper,' I said. 'Can I see it?'

Sadie shook her head, as if in wonder. I saw her glance at my mother and they smiled at each other like equals.

'Our Michael,' Sadie said softly, as she drew the exam paper from the pocket of her gym-slip, 'our Michael.'

Before my eyes my sister grew into a woman that summer. It wasn't merely the use of lipstick or the application of powder from the compact on her cheeks, nor was it simply the brushing of her long, curling lashes with the dark stuff from the slim brass cylinder, although all this make-up did make her look different, and excited, at first, raised eyebrows from my mother and growls from my father. Cosmetics alone could not explain the change in Sadie: it was as if some inner forces, inexorable and irresistible, were transforming her from a teenage girl into a young woman.

You could see it in her skin. Sometimes, when she wasn't looking, I'd sneak a glance at her, and I wanted to touch her face to see if the glow of her skin was real. As the chubbiness fell from her cheeks and her face took on a rare oval beauty, her lips became fuller, lending her an unusual combination of grace and sensuality. Her hair grew thicker: she rose early most mornings and you could hear her, before half past seven, humming to herself amid the pouring and splashing of water into the scullery sink, as she washed the long, long hair that seemed to become fairer by the day. Once, hurrying to the lavatory in the early morning, I had to squeeze past her in the narrow scullery, when she was in the process of emptying the white enamel jugful of cold water over her head, and she laughed and pushed the jug into my hand and commanded me to rinse her hair. I marvelled at the sheer magnificence of those long tresses and I could smell Ella's head pushed back against my chin and I quickly emptied the jug and hurried on into the lavatory, heedless of her requests for another jugful of cold water. When I came out of the lavatory Sadie was still there, drying her hair, and she shook herself like a wet puppy and laughed when I raised a hand against the flying water. I tried not to look, but I could see her full breasts against her slip as I pushed past her into the sanctuary of the kitchen.

She went cheerfully to work each morning, her hair swinging in a ponytail that reached almost to her waist. She came back each lunch-hour and every evening, panting from her brisk walk through the town and up the hill but bubbling with yarns of corncaps and bunions and an ancient, moustached widow who insisted on trying every perfume and lipstick in the shop. The word 'piles' entered our vocabulary: the first time Sadie used the word I reached for my dictionary – its explanation was unsatisfactory, unlike Sadie's own, given later in muffled tones and with much laughter.

When she laughed like that, giggling and bright-eyed, she seeemed still like my kid sister; then she might shrug, or shake that long ponytail with an imperious swing of her head, and you were once again in the presence of a woman. In the woman's presence I felt uneasy and awkward and I wished again for the sister who shrieked agreeably when you pulled her hair and then threw her arms around you to demonstrate that the shrieks themselves were part of the game.

Now that she was indoors at work all day, Sadie seemed determined to spend as much of her free time as possible in the open air. Most evenings after work she tied her hair into a long plait, swung her leg over the bar of my man's bike and took off for Ballyloughane beach, beyond the military barracks, or for Salthill, her towel neatly gripped on the carrier at the back of the bicycle. As the long sunny summer continued, Sadie's skin darkened to the colour of honey and her hair bleached blonder in the sun.

'C'mon, Michael,' she said to me one evening as she was gulping down a cup of tea after work. 'Why don't you come with me for a swim?'

'Go on,' my mother said, 'it'll do you good – you've been hard at it all day.'

'That's for sure,' my father added. 'I'm not much good to anybody these days.'

'That's enough of that kind of talk,' my mother said quickly. 'You know that Dr Powell said you'll have to take it easy for a while.' She turned to me then. 'Go on and get your togs – the porter cake will be ready when you get back.'

It seemed like too much of an effort at first – the day had been long and heavy, chopping and sawing old dead trees in the far corner of the school grounds, and my father had been unable to help much with the work – but in minutes I was ready, and Sadie and I were leaving behind us the yellow lodge and its open door and the porter cake and the brown soda cooling on the windowsill.

'Full steam ahead, big brother!' Sadie grinned as I pedalled out the gateway of the High School.

'You asked for it!' I shouted, and I let the bike go, no brakes, hurtling downhill, past the laundry and the church, careering at full tilt towards the Square, losing momentum only as we passed the steps of the Great Southern Hotel.

Sadie shifted on the bar of the bicycle, and when she turned towards me, her eyes were dancing in her head. 'Oh, Michael,' she said to me, 'isn't it just great to be alive!'

'You ain't seen nuthin' yet, baby sister!' I cried, and I swung left, downhill again, past the Astaire and on pell-mell towards the docks. The smell of the docks met us, sweaty and salty, and I settled down to the long push towards Salthill.

The sun was low over the bay when we arrived but there were still a few bathers in the blue, inviting sea. The tide was ebbing, the wet sand shone slickly in the yellow light. A quietness had settled upon the sea and the land, as if the day were holding its breath.

Sadie changed in the long shelter that backed up against the wall of the prom. I stood on the sand in the lee of the prom and quickly got into my togs. I walked slowly across the grey sand, waiting for Sadie.

In the water she moved like a creature of the sea. Her breast-stroke was an effortless rhythm of arms and legs that carried her easily past me, and soon I contented myself with floating on my back and turning my head occasionally to watch her unhurried progress through the evening sea. She had set a course beyond where I rested out on my back, swimming back and forth parallel with the shore. Her pace seemed unvaried, like that of an animal that knows its own strength.

Afterwards, refreshed and towelled and dressed, we ambled slowly homewards along the prom. Sadie seemed pensive; now and again she turned to smile at me across the bike but she said nothing. She walked with her arms folded across under her breasts, and she had combed her hair out so that it hung loose and rich behind her. She was wearing a new Aran jumper, and its off-white made her honey-coloured skin seem darker. She looked like a visiting Italian, I thought, and I was pleased to be strolling on the prom with my kid sister. Her gaze swept from me to the hills across the bay, as if she were searching for something but didn't know what, then she half-skipped along in front of me and, just as suddenly, turned and faced me. 'Michael,' she said, 'can't you just feel it all around us?'

'Feel what?'

'I don't know, just – just something!' Sadie spread her arms wide, encompassing the prom and the sea and the passing traffic. 'I just feel like I'm waiting for something to happen – something that's just – just great!' She broke off, searching for words. 'I can't explain it – I just feel that I'm waiting for the rest of my life to begin and I can hardly wait, I just know it's going to be great!'

I was surprised by Sadie's outburst. 'You've started already,' I said slowly. 'You've got your new job – '

'Oh, sugar on that job, Michael,' Sadie cried, 'I'm not talking about a job! I'm talking about − about my life! It's like there's a song I'm humming − I don't know it all − but I know it's all going to come to me and it's a lovely song, I just know it!'

I rang the bell of the bike, jangling it over and over. 'You're a poet, Sadie,' I said, 'and I never knew it!'

'Oh, Michael,' she said, frowning at me, 'don't take the mickey when I try to tell you something.'

'No,' I said, contrite, 'I won't.'

She smiled then, with her eyes and her mouth, and two fellows passing by looked at her with ill-concealed interest. One of them blushed and said 'Hello there!' before hurrying by, as if he had exhausted his store of courage, and Sadie laughed and said to me, good-naturedly, 'Kids!'

'They're already finished their Leaving Cert in the Jes,' I said, looking after the two fellows. 'I know them to see.'

'What's that to me?' Sadie responded gaily. 'You're talking to a working girl now who earns her keep.'

'Is there any chance that the working girl has the price of two bags of chips?'

'Sponger!' Sadie said, but she was already crossing the road towards the Park Café.

I followed more slowly, pondering the strangeness of my newly-grown-up sister and the half-heard songs she was humming in her head.

Rosie was away for all of June and July. He called to the lodge when he came home in late August, not long before we were due back at school for our final year. I was at the far corner of the second rugger pitch, the smaller one used by the First Form, when I saw him loping along the path beneath the trees. I waved and dropped the lawnmower and ran towards him.

We shook hands, awkwardly, in the centre of the pitch. I had missed him more than I had expected but it was difficult to know what to say. 'It's great to see you back,' I ventured.

'You don't know how good it feels to be back,' Rosie said. He gestured nervously with his big hands. 'I thought we'd never get back home again. Every week Auntie Irene kept finding some new excuse to keep me up there – always a minor variation on the theme that the mater mustn't be left alone in that big house on Threadneedle Road, full of sad memories since you-know-what and what reason could there be for going back since Patrick had no school anyway – ' Rosie broke off, laughing. 'I even offered to come home alone and leave the mater there behind me but Uncle Arthur was worse than Auntie Irene, pointing out that I was "a mere lad of seventeen" and would be vulnerable to all kinds of immoral influences – you know how it is, Michael!'

I didn't, but I nodded anyway.

'You're a terrible man, Michael!' Rosie said with mock softness. 'You just won't ask, will you?'

'Ask what?'

'How Ella is, of course! For the last ten weeks I've been listening to my cousin talking about you non-stop, and now you don't even bother to ask me how she is – Ella wouldn't be flattered, you know! I'm not even sure she'd want me to pass this epistle on to you,' he went on, taking a folded letter from his inside pocket, 'now that you have apparently forgotten all about my lovely cousin.'

'Is that for me?' I asked, eyeing the letter.

'Is it for you?' Rosie asked with heavy irony. 'I had to use all my powers of persuasion to get her to accept that it would be very inadvisable to write to you here at the High!'

I felt myself tremble, visualising Ella's letter arriving at the lodge and the myriad questions it would excite.

Rosie put the letter gently into my hands. 'I imagine you're dying to read it,' he said, smiling, 'so I'll leave you to it. Will you call out to the house on Saturday and we can have a right chat?'

I made no move to go with him. I watched him cross the pitch on to the path beneath the trees. He turned to wave before the path took him out of view and I waved back to him with the folded envelope that carried my name and address in Ella's large, confident hand. I found a quiet spot in the most distant corner of the grounds, sheltered from sun and prying eyes, and I settled myself comfortably on the mossy ground to read Ella's letter.

It was written on unlined paper. It was the first time I had ever seen printed stationery for a private address, and my eyes lingered on the embossed words at the top of the page:

Grove House
Castlebar
County Mayo
14th August '60

Dear Michael,
I've been longing so much to write to you!

I started to write you five or six letters for Rosie to bring back to you, and then Mum or Dad would persuade Aunt Frances to stay another week, and I never got a single letter to you finished . . . I really love my Aunt Frances but I just wish she could have gone home even for a few days just so that I could have managed to get a letter to you!!

It's been a terrible drag up here for the whole summer – whose fault is that?! – so in some ways it's been great having Rosie around. (Don't think it's easy being an only child!) He's always good fun and we've played a lot of tennis. You won't be surprised to learn that my cousin Rosie is a big hit with the girls at the tennis club, altho' nobody managed to lift him at the club hop last Saturday week! Cousin Rosie seems a bit reluctant to give all his attention to one person in particular. I can't say the same for Nicholas Kerr! He lives around the corner and has been pestering me the whole summer, so Rosie has been really useful in keeping him at a distance. I'm not so sure that Nicholas is at all happy about the competition, having Rosie here for the whole summer!

Michael, you'll have to excuse this rambling nonsense about stuff that's not important! I'm not like you, able to organise my thoughts and my letters like a good exam answer! Sometimes I just go on and on about things and I have to pinch myself to come back to the point!!! Like now!!!

What I'm really trying to tell you is that I'm just so glad that Rosie is going home because he can bring you this letter! I've missed you so much! Isn't it just silly that you and I are seventeen years old and we can't even write to each other? Thank goodness there's only another year left for both of us and then there won't be any need for Rosie to carry our messages – we can do whatever we like then, what do we care what so-called 'grown-ups' think!!

Honestly, Michael, for the first time ever I'm looking forward to going back to the High!

Guess why?!

I really miss you! Honest I do!

Love,

Ella xxxx

Ella's bold, sprawling hand had covered both sides of three sheets of the foolscap paper. I read and reread the letter until I knew it by heart. The references to Nicholas Kerr were a torture – I had not forgotten the sarcastic exchange on the school stairs a lifetime ago, when Billy was still at school and we were both just kids – but there seemed no need to be jealous: how many times, I asked myself, did she have to repeat that she missed me until I believed her? The sun dipped in the afternoon sky and the world was rich with promise, and Sadie's was not the only head humming with a song of good things coming.

ELEVEN

Those first few weeks of my last year at St Joseph's drifted by like the leaves falling in the High School grounds. There was a new urgency in our teachers' approach, as if hitherto we had merely been reserve troops billeted at a safe distance from the front but were now being primed and honed to engage the enemy in mortal combat. Even Rab, whose gentleness had grown gentler as we made our way from First to Final Year, was visibly affected by the nearness of the Leaving Cert examinations.

'So much for English literature,' Rab announced on our first lesson that September. 'From now on we have to treat *Hamlet* and Yeats and everyone else simply as sources of exam questions.' He was as good as his word. Like the other teachers he fed us a relentless diet of exam questions, notes, model answers and yet more questions.

Homework took longer every night. Nor was there any let-up at the weekend in our inexorable march towards the examinations the following June: the shorter classes of Saturday morning afforded an opportunity to scramble through work given the previous day and to load us with new assignments for Monday morning. There were rumblings of fatigue and whispers of discontent as September turned to October and the new regime began to bite.

I was not among the discontented. I revelled in the harshness of the new dispensation. Sometimes the light in the kitchen of the lodge burned past midnight and my mother came out of her bedroom and shook her head, wordlessly, but then she'd make a pot of tea and leave a steaming mug at my elbow and I'd feel the touch of her fingers brushing my hair before she went back to bed. She always said the same thing. 'Goodnight and God bless,' she'd say, 'and don't forget to put the light out.'

'Goodnight, Mam,' I'd say, lifting my head from the book to look at her, standing in the doorway of her bedroom, wrapped in the old fawn gaberdine coat she used as a dressing-gown. I could almost love the lodge on such nights, with the household sleeping around me, the fire glowing in the range and the wind sighing in the trees of the High School.

Ella's presence made the whole world lovable. She was the fire that glowed at the centre of my life, warming all the hours and tasks of the day, lighting up all the corners of the lodge and the Bish. Sometimes in the quietness of the sleeping lodge, I'd pause from my learning and sit listening to the silence and I could imagine her asleep in the darkened, half-empty school and her nearness was spur enough to drive me on to greater efforts.

Ella was also preparing for the Leaving Cert and, however much less pressurised the preparations for High School students, her outside visits were now reduced to one Saturday afternoon each month. Ella and I were alone together only once, for a few minutes, on the opening day of term.

The first Sunday of that last year in the life of the High School was a muted affair. 'It's so queer,' my mother said, patting her hair as she stood looking out the window of the lodge, 'to be having so few of them arriving on the first Sunday of the year.'

'It could be worse,' my father said. 'Sure didn't we think first we'd have only the Sixth Formers this year.'

'I know,' my mother said, still nervously fussing with her hair, 'but all the same – ' She broke off as the wheels of the first car of the afternoon could be heard crunching across the gravel.

'It's the Kerrs,' my mother said. 'Would you believe it, young Nicholas is driving the car! And I can remember the first day the same Nicholas arrived here like it was only yesterday!'

My father was pulling on his jacket as he moved towards the door. 'I'd better be getting up there,' he said.

'I'll come,' I said quickly. 'You'll need a hand.'

He said nothing but my mother flashed me a covert, grateful smile as I followed my father out of the lodge.

The Kerrs' car, a blue Rover, had drawn up at the steps of the school and Nicholas Kerr and his father were studying the contents of the opened boot as my father and I approached. 'Hello, Mr Kerr,' my father said. 'Hello, Mrs Kerr. You're all welcome back.'

'Jack!' Mr Kerr pumped my father's hand as if he were truly glad to see him. 'Lord, but it's good to see that some things don't change around here!'

'There's change coming for us all, sir,' my father said. 'We'll all have to learn to live with it.'

'Amen to that,' Mr Kerr said. He was a thin man of medium height and you could only wonder at the provenance of the height and girth of his son, Nicholas. 'But it's sad all the same, isn't it?' he asked, unconsciously echoing my mother's sentiments.

For a moment there was an awkward silence, then Mr Kerr turned hesitantly to the brown trunk in the boot of the car.

'I'll take that, sir,' my father said, starting forward.

'Jack, are you sure?' Mr Kerr was looking doubtfully at my father, and I could see, with sadness, what he saw: a small man who had grown old and weak.

'I'll do it, Dad.' I stepped between my father and Mr Kerr and I levered the trunk on to the edge of the boot. 'Just give me a hand to get it up on my shoulder,' I said to my father.

'Mikey, we'll do it together.'

'Just get it up on my shoulder!' I said angrily.

Without a word, he helped to ease the trunk upwards on to my left shoulder. I stood for a moment, flexing the muscles of my shoulder, securing my left-hand grip upon the trunk. I could feel the perspiration forming on my forehead as I began to pick my way carefully up the front steps of the school. The sweat didn't matter: I was exultant in my new strength and muscles, born of the months of physical labour throughout the summer. Nicholas Kerr, fair-haired and blazered, raised an eyebrow as I passed him, but I felt neither anger nor shame now in my porter's role. I was stronger than him and I wanted him to know it.

My father shuffled ahead of me to hold the doors open. As I was starting up the stairs I could hear the excited voice of the Reverend Willoughby, breathlessly apologising to the Kerrs for not being there to greet them and assuring them that Mrs Willoughby would be along shortly and that my mother's rhubarb tart had grown better with the years. Even at the top of the stairs I could hear that fluted voice rabbiting on about good wine and passing years. I couldn't resist the childish satisfaction of dumping Nicholas Kerr's trunk upside-down on the dormitory floor. I could hear the sound of car doors slamming and voices raised in greeting as I made my way back down the stairs of the school.

I had been steeling myself to meet her in the company of her family but it was still a shock to see her there on the drive in the afternoon sunlight. The summer months had changed her. Her skin seemed golden, her hair darker and shorter. She was standing beside the car, glancing about her with a distracted look, as if she were searching for somebody or something. I waited, motionless on the top step, until she turned and our eyes met, then she smiled that crinkly smile of hers and, to my surprise, it wasn't the heat of blushing that filled my face. I felt myself tremble, looking at her, and the colour drained from my face and I was suddenly cold in the heat of the day.

I eased my way through the knots of parents and students towards Ella. I saw her lay her head upon her father's arm and heard her say, 'Father, here's Michael.'

Esmonde FitzArthur turned away from the group he had been addressing to face me. He seemed smaller and stouter than on the first day I had seen him and Ella, on this very spot. He was losing his hair, and what remained hung wispily almost to his collar. 'I've heard a lot about you from my daughter, young man!' I felt that Mr FitzArthur's words were addressed as much to the group as to myself. 'I'm told you're a friend of my nephew, Patrick Rose.'

I mumbled agreement while I took Mr FitzArthur's extended hand in mine. 'This young fellow is from the gate lodge,' Ella's father went on, no longer pretending that his words were not spoken to the little group. 'We actually met here on the day our Ella started at the High. This young man had just won a scholarship to a local day school and, by an extraordinary coincidence, he's starting his final year in the same class as Irene's nephew!'

The trembling cold had left me now; in its place was a burning embarrassment that I felt must suffocate me.

'Mrs O'Hara keeps me informed of Michael's progress,' the Reverent Willoughby sang smoothly. 'He is consistently at the top of his class and his school has great expectations of him.'

'Make the most of your opportunities, young man,' Mr FitzArthur intoned magnanimously. 'Make the most of them!'

'I think the young man is doing precisely that.' Ella's mother's words were spoken drily. When I forced myself to look at her I felt that she could see into the heart of me. I dropped my gaze, more intimidated by her sardonic dryness than by her husband's pompous speechifying.

Ella's intervention rescued me. 'Come on, Michael,' she said brightly. 'Give me a hand with my stuff!'

'Let me do that, Ella.' I had spotted Nicholas Kerr hovering on the edge of the group, grinning at my discomfiture. 'I'll be only too glad to help you.'

I half pushed my way through the group to stand beside Ella at the open boot of the car. 'If you weren't man enough to carry your own bloody trunk,' I hissed at my rival, not caring who heard me, 'then you're not bloody fit to carry Ella's!'

Anger gave me added strength. In one movement I bent and jerked the trunk upwards and on to my shoulder. The group parted hastily to let me pass with my burden. Mr FitzArthur's mouth hung open and the Reverend Willoughby looked slightly shocked. I saw Ella's mother narrow her eyes at me as I hurried forward towards the school entrance.

'My hero!' I heard Ella whisper behind me. She skipped ahead to hold the door for me. 'I've missed you, Michael,' she said quietly, as I brushed past her into the school hallway.

'Bloody phoneys!' I was still angry. 'Do they think I'm a circus pony or a performing seal?'

'Michael, they don't mean any harm, really they don't!' There was a note of pleading in Ella's whisper. 'I want you so much to like my parents, don't you know that?'

I didn't answer. I pushed ahead of her up the staircase. Once more she hurried past me. On the landing above she waited with her back turned to me. Even in the shadows her dark hair shone. 'Michael,' she began when I finally reached the landing, 'didn't you miss me at all during the summer?'

'More than you know,' I whispered to her shining hair. 'More than you know.'

She turned to face me then, and her eyes were wet. 'Then let's not quarrel,' Ella said. 'I've been waiting the whole summer long just for this day.'

'I'm sorry,' I said.

'Come on,' Ella said, smiling again. 'If we're lucky we'll have a few minutes to ourselves before anybody else comes.'

We didn't have long to ourselves in the dormitory, but the little time we had was precious. We sat on the uncovered grey-striped mattress side by side and she slipped her hand into mine. Words seemed redundant. The sunlight poured through the high windows of the dormitory and framed her face in a beam of brightness. I looked at the face I had dreamed of all summer long and I started to say something but the words died in a gulping noise in my throat and Ella's fingers pressed upon mine, brushing against the canvassy stuff of the mattress and her eyes crinkled at me and I knew there was no need for words. All the world was here in this high-ceilinged room of tall, glinting windows and dust dancing in the shafts of September sun and our hands joined on the school mattress. The world moved to a different rhythm here in this institutional room, and the beat went on playing in my heart even when we heard footsteps and voices on the stairs and we stood up and left the dormitory together.

The music didn't stop as September became October and the leaves fell in the High School and our mid-term exams at Hallowe'en drew closer. Sometimes the music was so loud inside me that I was surprised that others couldn't hear it. It wasn't always the same music, nor was it always a song. When the red and brown and rusty leaves fell in October, they waltzed gracefully through the autumnal air to the violin-strains of 'The Blue Danube'; Yeats's magic words were not sung to his beloved but to mine, and Roy Orbison told the secrets of my soul when he sang 'Only the Lonely'.

Not that there was sadness inside me but there was a new softness at the heart of me, and I could tell the sorrow of every crooner who told his tale of lost love on Radio Luxembourg or Radio Éireann. The sureness of Ella's interest made my heart big enough to embrace the whole world and all its lonesome love songs. Ella Fitzgerald's haunting song was Ella's song for me, and mine for her:

> *Every time we say goodbye*
> *I die a little*
> *Every time we say goodbye*
> *I wonder why a little*

The singer was a negress, and I had no idea what she looked like, but that detail was unimportant: she shared a name with my Ella, and her singing was all the sweeter for it.

I was humming the song to myself one evening in the boiler house when I heard someone trying to push in the door. My father frequently threatened to adjust the misshapen door but his spirits seemed lower than ever in these darkening days, and his body frailer and more stooped, which was why I was in the boiler house, filling the furnace with forkfuls of brown turf. I leaned the sprong against the wall and crossed the stone floor. You had to lift and pull the heavy door simultaneously to force it open.

I was astonished to see Ella, wearing only her gym-slip and cardigan, hopping from foot to foot in the cold evening. Her eyes lighted up but she put her finger to her lips and slipped past me into the gloom of the boiler house. 'I saw you coming in, Michael,' she said, 'and I managed to slip out for a minute.'

'You'll get into trouble if they catch you, Ella.' Like her, I was whispering, although we were alone.

'They won't.' Ella smiled. 'But I have only a minute.'

She moved closer and made as if to take my hand but I stepped back, holding up my blackened palms.

'My bogman,' Ella said, and she made the words sound special. 'I just wanted to let you know,' she went on, 'about Saturday. Can we meet for the afternoon?'

'But how?'

'I'll have to tell a fib,' Ella said. 'Aunt Frances is going to be away, but it's a Saturday and we're allowed out and I don't want to be stuck in here when I could be with you.'

'But won't you get found out?' Our whispering voices sounded eerie in the confines of the dusty boiler house.

'I don't think so, Michael!' There was a lilt in her voice now. 'Three o'clock in front of the station?'

'OK.'

She wet the tip of her index finger and reached up to rub my nose gently. 'My black-nosed bogman,' she whispered. 'I'm gone.'

And she was. For a long moment I stood there, wondering if I had dreamed her presence in the boiler house. I stirred myself and moved to look out from the open doorway. She was nowhere to be seen amid the darkening trees and shrubs, but I could still feel her fingertip on my turf-blackened nose.

Frightened of being seen at the station, I circled Eyre Square repeatedly on my bike. The big clock on top of the bank looking down on the Square said it was just after three o'clock but there was still no sign of Ella. The town was its usual busy self on a Saturday afternoon, and the flow of traffic in both directions clogged the roads around the black railings of the Square. I weaved my way between the cars and vans, skirting the erratically parked vehicles, overtaking the occasional donkey and cart, always keeping an eye on the uphill approach to the station from Sammon's Corner.

Every eye on the Square was focused on me, I was sure of that. Any moment now Rab or Silenus or even the Reverend Willoughby would step off the footpath and demand to know why I was waiting for Ella FitzArthur, a High School boarder who was attempting to lie her way off the premises. Could I offer any explanation for my despicable behaviour in causing the young lady to tell untruths and to jeopardise her school career by associating with the likes of me? My hands grew hot and sweaty in the gloves she had given me, as I contemplated the inevitable confrontation.

And then I spotted her. She was rounding the corner of Forster Street, her back towards me as she faced uphill towards the station. She was walking quickly, her shoulders purposefully back, her dark hair swinging under her school beret. I was idling past Egan's Bar and Grocery when I saw her, but I let the bike go then, full tilt downhill, past the Jersey Bar and Gill's shop, cutting across the flow of traffic at the corner of the Railway Hotel, heedless of protesting car horns. Then I was pedalling uphill past the row of buses whose destinations told a litany of the small towns of the county, north and south, east and west.

Ella was ahead of me, walking in the lee of the dark wall that separated the station road from an old stone warehouse. She seemed to sense my nearness: she turned and her face broke into a smile that was for me exclusively. The waiting buses and the straggling lines of laden passengers and the jokey, wise-cracking drivers and conductors faded into insignificance beyond the pale of Ella's smile.

'Michael! I thought I'd never get away. The Rev waylaid me and kept on and on about nothing at all!'

'I was afraid you weren't coming,' I said.

'Wild horses wouldn't stop me!' Ella said breezily. 'It's four weeks since we were allowed out!'

'We could go to the pictures or to the Marian,' I told her.

'Sadie gave me half-a-crown.'

Ella looked at the clear, hard sky and shook herself like a puppy. A bus-driver trying to negotiate a passage past us gave a long irritable blast on his horn and Ella smiled and gave him an expansive wave. I watched with delight as the driver's sour expression broke into a broad grin and he waved back as he manoeuvred the vehicle round us.

'He has a nice smile,' Ella said, looking after the bus.

'It's easy to smile at you,' I said haltingly.

'Michael!' Her eyes fastened on mine and I felt the slow blush spreading across my face. 'Thank you,' she said slowly.

'What'll it be?' I asked, looking away to mask my confusion. 'The pictures or the Marian?'

'Let's just go for a walk,' Ella said. 'It's too nice a day to be inside, and it's the only day we've got.' Impulsively she took hold of one of the handlebars and we continued on past the station, wheeling the bike between us. 'I've always noticed this path when I've been on the train,' Ella said. 'It looks like a nice walk.'

The path began at one end of the turning area for buses. Bounded by waist-high stone walls, it ran parallel with the railway tracks until it reached the military barracks on the edge of our town. Locally the path was known simply as 'the line'. It was a walk that I knew well: years previously Billy and I had often walked the line together on our way to the beach beside the barracks.

The town's brass band had a bandroom just inside the wall of the line, close to the station. While Ella waited on the path, I lifted my bicycle over the wall and stowed it at the back of the bandroom. When I came back her eyebrows were raised in a smiling question. 'It'll be safe,' I said, 'and we don't need it.'

She took my hand in hers and we walked on together up the bandroom hill. From the top of the hill you could see clear across

215

the bay to the hills of Clare. Sunshine and cloud mottled the hills and scooped valleys with light and shadow. Below us the half past-three train to Dublin was belching steam and smoke in readiness for departure. Even as we stood there we heard the guard's shrill whistle, piercing through the afternoon, and the great dark beast of an engine lumbered into life, clanking its way below us on shining rails that led east across the country.

'I've never been on the train,' I said. 'I've never been to Dublin.'

'We'll soon be out of school, Michael.' I felt Ella's fingers tighten round mine. 'We can go to Dublin together – we can see the whole world together.'

You could believe it, up there on top of the bandroom hill: that the bay and the hills and all the towns and cities that lay east along the ribbon of track were within reach, that all you had to do was reach out and touch them with your hand.

We walked on, past the railway workers' cottages and the signal-man's box, across the wooden bridge that straddled the saltwater lake. I pointed out the meadow that overlooked the lake, sloping down towards the lakeshore road. 'Billy and I used to play cowboys and Indians there.' We were standing in the middle of the bridge: you could see the water below through the gaps between the planks. 'We were just kids then,' I added lamely.

'Billy?'

'A little guy – he was my best pal.' I looked at her then. 'You might remember him – we were sitting together on a wall one time when a whole line of you went marching past.'

'I remember him!' Ella laughed. 'A cheeky little article too! What became of him?'

'He's in America,' I said, turning away. 'He went out to his brothers after the Inter Cert.'

'D'you miss him?' she asked gently.

I was looking the other way now, out across the bay. 'Sometimes I do,' I admitted. America was beyond the bay, across the width of the Atlantic Ocean.

'We'll go to America as well!' Ella laughed. It didn't seem so distant after all, not when Ella leaned her head against your shoulder and you sauntered together across the wooden planks of the bridge.

Beyond the bridge, out of the shelter of its metal wall, we were exposed to the sharp wind that cut in from the bay. Instinctively we picked up our pace. Within I felt a burgeoning sense of wonder at our presence together on this lonely pathway, and with that sense of wonder came an exhilarating sensation of power: our closeness was unique, allowing us to share a common tomorrow that was divulged only in phrases and implicit under-standing. The words we spoke were precious, but there was no need for every word to be spoken: between us there existed a secret language whose alphabet was smiles and touching fingers and just knowing that you understood and were understood.

When we came to the hill on the path that led up to the soldiers' chapel and the barracks, I held the strands of wire apart to allow Ella to duck inside on to the narrow cinder track beside the railway itself. The line now rose high above us, making it seem as if we had become smaller. When we walked under the black arch of the stone railway bridge Ella's small laugh sounded hollow, as if we had stepped into another dimension. Beyond the bridge the land opened out into flatter, grassier fields: you could imagine the steam engine snorting its way from the station as far as the bridge and then, scenting space and freedom, hurling itself forward across the open spaces of the land.

We walked for miles along the narrow track beside the shining rails. We talked intermittently, content for the most part with the comfort of our silence. The evening grew darker and the track narrower, but we kept on, more slowly but closer together.

'D'you know what you want to do, Michael?' she asked me. 'After school, I mean.'

'Rab says I'm sure of a scholarship, but I'm not sure what to do in college.' I was silent a while, measuring words I had never spoken aloud to anyone. 'I thought maybe I could be a lawyer, like your father, but I don't know if the scholarship money would be enough for that. I think you have to go to Dublin for it.'

'You do have to go to Dublin,' Ella said. 'That's what Daddy wants me to do! Wouldn't it be wonderful if we could study together!' Her excited words spun in the darkened air and she seized my arm with both her hands. 'Just think of it, Michael!'

'But I'm not sure,' I said. 'I love English and writing and I think – ' I stopped, looking shyly at her ' – I think I want to be a writer as well, I mean, I want to write books and novels and things.'

'Oh Michael!' Her eyes were smiling but they were deeper than forever. 'You can be everything you want to be!' She leaned closer against me and buried her face in the black stuff of my long overcoat, not so long now for me, but shiny and threadbare. I felt my heart must burst, pressed close against her in the windy darkness. 'We should go back,' Ella whispered. 'I have to be in by seven.'

Her words brought back the other, closer world, the one we still lived our everyday lives in, at the town end of the shining railway tracks. And yet tomorrow was no mirage: that tomorrow was as real as her hand in mine.

'And you,' I said quietly, as we began to retrace our footsteps. 'Is that what you really want – to be a solicitor, like your father?'

'It's something to do!' Ella laughed. 'Don't look so shocked, Michael! I've seen Daddy in his office, surrounded by paper and bundles of files! It's an OK job but I don't want to be just a solicitor for the rest of my life! I'm like every other girl, Michael O'Hara – I want a home and a family and children of my own!'

She stopped abruptly, staring into my eyes. 'Don't you want the same thing?' Ella asked.

I wasn't able to answer at once. I was astonished anew by the loveliness of her face, the pleading gentleness of her eyes. 'Yes,' I heard myself whisper. 'Yes.'

'Well, I'm glad that's settled then!' Ella said lightly.

For a moment longer we held each other's eyes and then we hurried on towards town. I was grateful for the silence and the darkness. I felt naked, as if Ella's words had uncovered the heart of me and revealed a core that I had not known myself. My long coat was suddenly too tight and too heavy, enclosing me with a sweaty stickiness that brought back the memory of those distant nights before I really knew her, when her face swam in my hot dreams and I awoke to find my thighs and pelvis covered in semen. I unbuttoned the coat and it trailed behind me in the oncoming wind. 'I'm too hot!' I said, avoiding her eyes.

The chilly air was cool on my face and the darkness cloaked my confusion. The miles fell behind us; ahead loomed the arched bulk of the railway bridge beside the barracks. We stopped together under the bridge and turned to each other. In the shadows Ella's face seemed lovelier and more dreamlike than ever. Above the thumping of my heart I could hear the humming of distant train wheels on the tracks. 'Ella,' I whispered.

'Yes.'

'I want to – to kiss you.' I thought she wouldn't hear my timid whisper above the rumble of the approaching train.

'Yes,' Ella said, 'I know.'

The train whistled. The tracks were no longer merely humming: they were alive with the clacking of the approaching train. We drew back against the stone wall of the bridge and Ella raised her face to mine. I felt her lips against my mouth and they were fire and silk, and for a moment time stopped in the arched darkness, pressed like petals between our timid mouths. Then the beam of the engine light caught us, pinned like flies against the grey stone and suddenly there was a vision of a large, florid-faced passenger almost hanging out of one window, his coarse features broken into laughter, and as he flashed by us, I heard him shout, 'Hold on to her, lad, hold on to her!'

The train was gone, but his raucous cry echoed in the vaulted gloom of the bridge. Ella tilted her face back from me, leaning on my arm. 'Are you going to?' she whispered, and I knew what she meant.

'Yes,' I answered.

'Come on then,' she said, taking my arm and almost bustling me along the track in front of her.

I couldn't speak. My mouth was afire with an undreamed-of sensation, as if the wings of butterflies trailed against my lips. The world around me was made new, bathed in a sacramental light that washed the bay and the far hills and the humming rail tracks with grace and love. The world had been asleep and was slowly wakening into a newness that was itself a dream. Her fingers pressed gently on mine and I felt we must both blend and melt as one into the night.

Where the cinder track ran out we ducked between the wires on to the line. The lights of the town were white in the near distance. The wind carried the belching noises of the train back to us from the station but they were magical noises now, blessed by the kiss we had shared under the bridge.

'Michael, we've got time, we don't need to run!' Ella's words, half-gasped, brought me back to the pot-holed path and the sour smell of the foreshore. 'I can't keep up with you!' she laughed.

I slowed, half turning to look at her. Her smiling face was lit up in an erratic ray of slanted moonlight, glancing off the windows of the line of silent railway carriages parked on the shunting line. A movement or a noise, or maybe both, caught my attention and I glanced past Ella at the dark bulk of the carriages that stood between us and the sea. Just for a moment I saw my sister's pale face behind the carriage window, and then a face that I knew swam into the frame of the window beside Sadie's. Then both heads were gone and I was staring open-mouthed at the window of the carriage.

'First full speed and now full stop!' Ella was laughing. 'Come on, Michael!'

I looked again at the row of railway carriages, dark and bulky against the silvery sky. I shook my head as if to clear it but neither white face nor fair head was framed in any window. I felt myself led along the rough path by Ella. Now and then she swung our joined hands upwards, high as our shoulders, like a pair of children at play, and sometimes her fingers clenched mine with a kind of bruising fierceness, and for a few paces she skipped along the line with a high-stepping action and she took me with her like a marionette. I had neither words nor rational thoughts.

We were crossing the saltwater bridge near the town end of the line before I could speak. 'I thought I saw Sadie back there,' I said in a whisper. 'My sister, in one of the railway carriages.'

Ella stopped. The tide stirred beneath the wooden bridge like a hoarse voice. 'Don't be daft, Michael,' she said. 'What would your sister be doing out there in a railway carriage?'

'I don't know. I only got a glimpse.' I couldn't meet her eyes. 'I think Nicholas Kerr was along with her.'

She didn't speak at once. Even the tide below was momentarily silent, gathering its breath between gasps. 'You can't be sure, Michael.'

'No,' I said, 'but I'm almost sure.'

'Don't say anything to her,' Ella said, 'not yet. I'll find out for you if – if you like.'

The tide was stirring again, soughing with keening voice. 'OK,' I said, 'OK.'

'It'll soon be seven,' Ella said.

The old world was still there, ticking away; the new world that she had wrought with the touch of her hand and lip was slipping away like a dream that you can only try to recall. This time we didn't pause on top of the bandroom hill. The bike was still there, at the back of the bandroom, and I lifted it quickly out over the stone wall on to the footpath. I pulled hard on the brakes to steady the machine on the slope, and Ella eased herself up on to the bar. I let the brakes out then and we sped downhill, past the station entrance, and I pedalled my way around the corner as far as the church.

Neither of us had spoken on the downhill spin. 'Wait a few minutes,' Ella said.

I nodded, still unable to speak.

'Michael –' Ella fumbled for words. 'Try not to worry – and keep thinking about us – about you and me. Nothing can change that.'

'Yes,' I said.

'I'll manage some way to see you next week. Maybe we could have afternoon tea in the boiler house!' Her fingers lingered a moment on mine, and then she turned away, hurrying past the laundry, up the hill towards the High School. I waited beside the old water trough, watching her go, remembering with a strange sadness the first time I had carried her home on the bar of my bike, on the road by the sea from Rosie's house. I had seen stars shining in the trough that long-ago night, but when I looked now I could see only my sister's pale face, mirrored ghostlike in the dark water.

I waited beside the old stone trough until I was sure that no prying eyes would link my arrival with Ella's, then I began to walk slowly up the hill, pushing the bike alongside me on the edge of the road. The familiar hill seemed strange, even unfriendly, as if I had not walked it all my life. The well known streetscape of houses and the dark road and the stone wall had been altered by the last few hours — by a kiss, and by two faces glimpsed in an empty railway carriage. Whatever Ella might say, I knew that it was Sadie's face I had seen, and as I went on slowly up the hill I felt the anger grow inside me, anger that she should interfere in my new and wonderful world and shame me in front of Ella. And why should she disgrace me with Kerr, of all people? I despised him as an arrogant twit who was too dim to notice his own limitations. As my anger hardened, I resolved to have it out with Sadie and to put a stop to whatever nonsense had begun.

The car headlights on the school drive temporarily blinded me as I was turning in at the gate of the High. I stepped back, blinking against the beams of light. In the moment of passing, I recognised the FitzArthur car. In the seconds it took for the car to slide out on to the road, Ella's father glared up at me from the driver's seat and I registered the anger on his stony face. I realised that the other occupant of the car was Ella and our eyes met for a single, frozen moment, but it was long enough for me to read the pain and bewilderment in her face. And the fear.

The fear rose inside myself. Sadie was forgotten now in the rush of terror. Something had gone wrong: Ella's father had turned up unexpectedly — perhaps for no other reason than that he doted on her and wanted to take her out for her free afternoon — and her small subterfuge had been revealed. In the darkness I shivered. The lighted window of the lodge looked out accusingly at me: our kiss under the railway bridge had been observed by more than that red-faced fellow hanging out the window.

For a long time I hung back in the shadows, as if the darkness might protect me against the storm that must break over my head. In the end, fearful of what awaited me, I stowed the bike under the lean-to at the gable end and and stepped inside the lodge.

I felt their eyes upon me as I closed the front door. My father opened his mouth as if to speak, but my mother silenced him with a peremptory gesture. I turned away from her to hang my coat on the back door, but it was no more than a momentary reprieve. I made no move towards the fire, but stood with my back to the door, facing her. My mother's expression was unforgiving.

'Your father has already been called up to Reverend Willoughby's house,' she said, and I knew then that not even a faint hope of concealment existed, that all was known. I kept my eyes on the stone floor of our kitchen.

'Have you nothing to say for yourself?' my mother demanded.

'What d'you want me to say?'

'You young pup!' My mumbled words seemed to galvanise my father into action. He tried to rise from the armchair beside the range but my mother, standing beside him, laid a restraining hand on his shoulder and he fell back into the chair without protest.

'I'm surprised at you, Michael.' My mother's voice was low. 'Your father and myself deserve better than this of you, landing us in a position where we can't hold our heads up like we always have. Surely to God you know that?'

'Why can't you hold your heads up?' I flared. 'What have I done that's so awful?'

'What have you done!' my father spluttered.

'Leave this to me,' my mother said to him, before she turned to me again. 'You know well what you have done, Michael,' she went on. 'After all our time here Reverend Willoughby doubts if he can trust us – and all because you've been lying to us and that FitzArthur girl has been lying the same as you to the headmaster.'

I was silent, refusing to meet her gaze.

'Glory be to God, Michael,' my mother said, exasperated, 'but you're old enough to know your place and to know that you and that lassie can't be keeping company. It just can't be – it's just not allowed!'

'Is it any wonder I wouldn't mention it?' I said bitterly. 'I knew you wouldn't understand. The days of "knowing your place" are long gone, but they'll never be gone in this morgue – '

'That's enough!' My father hissed the words at me. 'You'll have respect for your mother as long as you live in this house – '

'Don't – ' my mother began, but my father would not be silenced now. His face was pinched and drawn as he glared at me across the kitchen.

'You've shamed your mother and you've shamed me,' he said, 'and I know you've shamed Reverend Willoughby too. Imagine how he must have felt in front of Mr FitzArthur when all the lying came out in the wash.'

'We didn't do anything!' I protested, unable to stop the hot tears pricking at my eyes. 'We only went for a walk together out the line, that's all, honest!'

'Michael, Michael,' my mother said, 'it cannot be, don't you see that? They're up there – ' she gestured vaguely in the direction of the school ' – and we're down here, and that's all there is to it.'

I rubbed at my wet eyes, gulping back tears.

'There's to be no more of it,' my father said.

'He knows that,' my mother said. 'Don't you, Michael?'

'I don't know anything any more.'

'Come up to the fire,' my mother said, more gently. 'I'll get you something to eat.'

I shook my head. 'I'll just go down to my room,' I mumbled. 'I'm not hungry.'

I didn't look at either of them as I crossed the kitchen. I was at the door into the back hall when my mother spoke. 'I'll bring you down a cup of tea and a bit of toast in a few minutes,' she said.

I couldn't answer her. I pushed open the door and stumbled towards the sanctuary of my room.

Twelve

Ella was brought back to the High School the next day. It was after four when the car turned in at the gate on that Sunday afternoon. My mother looked up from her knitting when she heard the car passing by, and, like me, she recognised the FitzArthurs' car. Our eyes met but she went back to her knitting without a word. I felt uneasy, watching through the lodge window as the car headed on towards the school. Both Ella and her father were staring stonily ahead and it wasn't hard to imagine that the atmosphere in the car was strained.

As it was in the lodge. I'd wanted to go out after the Sunday dinner but my mother's tone as she ordered me to stay where I was had an edge to it that brooked no argument. I stayed put, staring vacantly at the patch of cloudy sky framed by our kitchen window and listening idly to the clock ticking. Inwardly I burned at the injustice of it all. Sadie had gone out without so much as a by-your-leave, breezily announcing that she wouldn't be back for tea. I hated her lipsticked smile and her painted eyes – eyes that looked boldly back at me and dared me to challenge her about Nicholas Kerr.

In the back hall, when we'd been hanging up our coats after Mass, she'd tried to whisper a few words of commiseration to me – increasingly she spoke to my mother on level terms and had probably learned the depth of my ignominy the previous night when I'd remained in my room – but I had listened with a stony face that invited no intimacy. When she'd said Ella's name, I'd been stung into venom. 'Don't even mention her name,' I'd hissed, 'not after you've been out with that – that – ' I couldn't find words venomous enough to convey my contempt for Nicholas Kerr.

Sadie had drawn back, eyes wide with hurt, but then her expression hardened into determination. 'Suit yourself, my high-and-mighty brother,' she whispered, 'but Nicholas is just as good as you any day and he's a lot kinder too.' She left me beside the row of old coats and jackets hanging in the back hall and in a moment I heard her treacherous voice raised in cheerful chatter with my mother.

All that week I felt that eyes followed me wherever I went. My every move was watched; every minute between school and home had to be accounted for. We had rugby practice twice that week, and I could have sworn that my mother had been waiting by the door when I turned in through the gate both evenings at half past five. On the Wednesday I was late, and my explanation of a trip to the library was accepted only when I waved the two borrowed books under my mother's face.

'Why don't you read the bloody books!' I demanded. 'Or would that be too difficult for you!' My mother's shocked, wounded face shamed me. 'I'm sorry, Mam,' I mumbled, and I hurried from the kitchen to my room, blinded by hot tears of rage.

She brought me a mug of tea a little later and laid it carefully on top of the chest of drawers, and I sat on the edge of my bed and slowly raised my head to look at her. I met her hurt look and I tried to speak, but all I could do was mumble thank you and, when she left, my room was heavy with pain and pride.

And an aching that would not be still. I longed to see Ella, to hear her voice, to feel her hand tucked trustingly into mine. How could they ever understand that what Ella and I shared was too precious and holy to be bound within the walls of this or any other High School? The world was on the march: I had glimpsed those new horizons beyond the visible limits of the bay that bounded the town; I had felt the new tomorrow stirring inside me, in my own strength and my own heart. At school Rab had gloried in the result of the American Elections: the following January, John F. Kennedy, a descendant of Irish Famine emigrants, would be installed as the first-ever Catholic President of the United States. 'The world is on the move,' Rab had told us, in a brief diversion from examining the entrails of *Hamlet*. 'It's a Catholic coming-of-age. Remember it: Irish and Catholic and brilliant.'

I wanted to tell Ella what Rab had said, although I would omit – or at least tone down – the Catholic references. I wanted to tell her that the same strength and optimism were mine so long as she was with me. To contemplate life without her was to look down a long vista of emptiness, days without joy, nights without sleep. Such an existence was too awful to contemplate, and yet contemplate it I did, mostly at night, watching the darkness deepen above my skylight and then realising with a bleak despair that the light was stirring in the blackness and that yet another school day was upon me after yet another sleepless night.

At school, Rab looked strangely at me when I was unable to offer any meaning for a couple of less obscure lines in one of Browning's dramatic monologues. Silenus raged at me for my inability to translate a paragraph of Livy. Our maths teacher, a sarcastic fellow who was feared and revered in equal measure by the entire class, merely raised an eyebrow when I confessed for the third or fourth consecutive day that I had been unable to solve the geometry cuts set for homework. Rosie offered assistance once or twice but I rebuffed him sulkily, sure that he knew more than he was pretending to, and he smiled his rosy-cheeked smile and left me alone.

Morning and evening I watched for Ella, but to no avail. The High School seemed almost empty, having only the Third Form and the senior class, but its very emptiness made it more difficult to search unseen for her. Each evening I headed for the boiler house, ostensibly to top up the furnace, but each time I did so, my father mysteriously materialised beside me within minutes. On one occasion I came face-to-face on the path with Reverend Willoughby and I blushed, but he merely wished me 'Good evening' and went on his way beneath the bare trees, talking quietly to himself.

On the Thursday of that second week I was shovelling turf into the furnace when I heard the door of the boiler house creak open. Bang on time, I thought wearily, checking up on me. I didn't turn around, but went on chucking sods of turf into the furnace. In a moment, I thought, I'll hear my father's voice enquire, 'Everything OK, Mikey?'

'Michael?' Ella was standing beside me, a frightened look on her face.

I stood, speechless, still gripping the big fork.

'I was dying,' Ella said. 'I was afraid I'd never see you again.' She glanced nervously towards the door. 'Nobody is saying anything but they're watching me like hawks.'

'I know,' I said. 'I thought you were my father – he comes in here every time I do.'

'I know,' Ella said, half-smiling. 'I've been trying to slip away to see you. I've seen you coming round here, and I've noticed your dad going along after you.'

'There'll be murder,' I said, 'if you're caught here.'

'Or something like it,' Ella smiled. 'But your dad will be busy for a while – the Rev has him stacking tables and chairs in the ref – God knows why – they'll have to be unstacked again for supper.'

She laughed then and I couldn't help joining in. The so-called adult world had more than its share of daftness. The rules and regulations they invoked against us were just more of it.

'Ella – ' I laid the fork against the mound of black turf ' – what did your father say?'

Ella shivered, although the furnace door was open and the boiler house was sweaty with heat. 'He ranted a lot. Mostly he was angry because I had lied to the Rev and because I had dragged Aunt Frances into the lie.' She folded her arms, hugging herself against the recollection. 'I don't like lying, Michael, I hate it. I don't want to have to do it again.'

'But – ' I wasn't sure how to ask the question ' – what did he say about – about me?'

'Dad's always going on about family stuff,' Ella answered. 'He was brought up in the North, you know, in Belfast, and sometimes he goes on about dissenters and traditions and – and half the time, Michael, he's making a speech to himself – he was in some kind of trouble during the war, I think – I asked him about it once and he just said that there comes a time when you have to stand up for your beliefs – ' Ella broke off, confused.

'Me,' I prompted her, 'me and you.'

'Michael!' she teased. 'You and I!'

The light of the flames danced on her face and I felt the life stirring in me again, bathed in the glow of her smile.

'He didn't say much,' Ella said. 'He didn't forbid me to see you – just went on and on that I knew what was right and that I had to do what was right. I think he's afraid to come straight out and tell me not to see you – '

'Afraid?' I asked in the silence.

'He's afraid that I'll defy him straight up,' Ella said, almost to herself. She looked at me then and said firmly: 'I couldn't do that,

Michael. I – I wouldn't do anything to hurt him, he doesn't deserve that.'

I was alarmed by the turn of the conversation. 'But it doesn't arise,' I said, pleadingly. 'He didn't say that we couldn't meet.'

'No,' Ella said, 'He didn't, and in a way I'm taking advantage of him for that. He wants to give me everything I want and he knows I want to see you, Michael.' There was sadness in her voice. 'But no more lying, Michael, I can't bear it. We might be able to meet for a few minutes like this but I'm grounded for the rest of the term, so there's no more visits to Patrick's house.'

'It doesn't matter,' I said, 'so long as I know that you want to see me.'

'I do,' she whispered. 'I do.'

'We can write,' I said to her. 'Look – just here, over the door.' I moved around her towards the door of the boiler house. 'There's a loose brick up here, and a space behind it.' I reached up over the lintel of the low door of the boiler house and carefully removed one of the red bricks. 'The whole place is falling apart,' I said to Ella, pointing at the exposed space, like a gaping cavity in a mouth. The small building seemed of higgledy-piggledy construction, part brick, part stone and cement, a continuing effort to keep time and decay at bay. The mortar had crumbled in places, and the brickwork was loose.

'Will it be safe?' Ella asked, eyeing the small space dubiously.

'Nobody comes here,' I said, 'except me and my father, and he wouldn't notice it in a thousand years.'

'I'll try,' Ella smiled, 'but you're the one who's good with the pen.' She pulled her cardigan closer about her. 'I'd better run or somebody will notice that I'm missing.'

'Wait!' I said. 'Did you find out anything about Sadie and – and that fellow?'

'I asked him straight up,' Ella said simply. 'He just asked me was I jealous and walked away from me.'

'The bastard – '

'Michael!' She laid her fingers on my lips, silencing me. 'Nicholas can be a bit much sometimes, but he's OK. Forget about him. Just think about you and me – and post me a lovely letter in our private letter box.'

Her fingers pressed lightly on my mouth and then she opened the door of the boiler house. A quick look in either direction, a last backward wave at me, and she was gone, hurrying through the darkness. Long after she had gone I realised that I was still holding in my hands the brick from the boiler house wall. I replaced it carefully and bent again to the business of feeding the furnace. I was whistling as I worked.

Silenus had organised a practice match on Saturday afternoon against a team from the local boys' club. The club could muster only thirteen players – they were mostly messenger boys, apprentices and shop assistants, many of whom had to work on Saturdays – so we loaned them two of our subs and played a half-hour each way on the boggy pitch that was universally known as 'the Swamp'. The boys' club players were smaller than us, but work had lent them harder muscles and an edge of cunning: at close quarters, out of sight of Silenus's refereeing eye, you were liable to be on the receiving end of an elbow in the ribs or an indiscriminate raking of boot studs across your back – and these were the more polite misdemeanours. At the end of an hour of battling, however, our more obvious casualties numbered only one black eye and one badly bitten ear. Blue shins and bruised ribs didn't count.

Silenus seemed as pleased with the casualty-count as with the score – and so was the team: it was no small achievement to hold such opposition to a scoreless draw.

'Roll on the Cup,' Rosie intoned, and we grunted with comradely satisfaction. Silenus made no comment but he crossed the stone-floored dressing-room to convey his thanks for 'a splendid contest' to the boys' club fellows at the other end. One of them muttered 'Prick' in an audible voice and Silenus coloured but he made no comment. Or perhaps he did and it was drowned by the ripple of giggling laughter at the boys' club end of the dressing-room.

The windy expanse of the Swamp was no place for hanging about. The dressing-room was cleared within minutes of Silenus's departure. A few of the guys were going home; most were going up town. 'Are you coming, Michael?' Rosie asked me. 'A few of us are going to the Marian.'

'I don't think I can,' I said. 'I have to go home.'

His features settled slowly into their habitual smiling expression. 'It's OK,' Rosie said. 'I understand.'

It was more than I did. I couldn't understand even myself. On the way back up through town, cycling along Shop Street, I mused unhappily about the way I had rebuffed Rosie. He was my best friend and yet I felt uneasy in his presence since the business with Ella. I couldn't say why. I had no reason to doubt that Rosie would be on my side, that he would bolster my diffidence with his considerable charm and self-belief. And yet it was that very confidence of his that frightened me now: his adult poise and easy manner made him part of that world of FitzArthurs and Willoughbys which would exclude me from the company of Ella. In some way I was afraid of Rosie and the realisation of my timidity served only to intensify my feelings of failure and shame.

I had to get off the bike to get past a confusion of traffic that was defying the arm-waving efforts of a garda at the town-centre crossroads that we called 'the four corners'. This Saturday afternoon, traffic seemed to be coming and going in both directions on all four roads that led into these four corners. The crux of the problem was a donkey and cart, no doubt left over from the Saturday morning market, which was strategically so positioned at the heart of the crossroads that nothing at all could get past. The grizzled donkey was indifferent to the half-hearted encouragement of its master, still seated on the front edge of the dirty blue-and-orange cart; motorists and onlookers alike seemed amused less by the inactivity of ass and owner than by the increasingly choleric energy of the large garda who was trying to unravel the knot of traffic.

'Send for Gordon Richards!' a fellow standing in the doorway of Gleeson's drapery advised.

'Useless!' his companion told him cheerfully. 'You'd want Vincent O'Brien to train that fella!'

'Sure he knows feck-all about trainin' guards!' the first fellow said, much to the delight of the gathering bunch of onlookers and the irritation of the guard.

I was smiling to myself as I edged my bike between the vehicles, and up the street towards the Square.

'It's a nice change to see you smiling!'

I looked up guiltily. Sadie was standing in the open doorway of the chemist's shop, across the road from the Marian Café. She made the blue nylon shop-coat seem elegant, standing there like a star from some film in the Savoy, her blonde hair swept back around her perfect oval face.

'The way you're going on,' I said, 'there isn't much to be smiling about.'

'Oh Michael, can't you give it a rest?' She glanced nervously over her shoulder into the interior of the shop. 'I'm not doing anything that you're not doing yourself.'

'Aren't you!' I flung back at her. 'You're only seventeen and you're skulking around in railway carriages with that so-and-so – ' I broke off, cooled by my anger.

'Jesus Christ!' Sadie said at last. 'Would you listen to grandad!'

'You just haven't a clue about people!' I said heatedly.

'I must remember that,' Sadie said calmly, 'the next time you're asking me for the loan of a half-a-crown.'

I flushed. 'That's got nothing to do with it.'

'Hasn't it?' Sadie asked, arching a pencilled eyebrow. She stepped aside to let a pair of middle-aged women with shopping bags into the shop, smiling as the did so. From behind her came the deep voice of Mr Forkan, calling her name softly and without impatience. 'Some of us have jobs to do,' Sadie said, with a certain primness, and she went back into the lighted interior of the chemist's with a toss of her long blonde hair.

I got back on my bike, and pushed off disconsolately up the sloping street past the Blackrock shop where, so many years previously, my mother had carefully chosen my long-serving overcoat. The encounter with Sadie, coming so quickly after my difficulty with Rosie, had added an edge of anger to my earlier feelings of shame. Convinced as I was that my sister's behaviour was stupid, I was also suddenly sure that her only motive was to embarrass me further. Any chance that Ella and I had of being able to meet without attracting attention was seriously diminished by Sadie's absurd posturing with Nicholas Kerr. The fellow was such an idiot that there couldn't be any other reason for my sister's carry-on with him. The anger grew in me as I turned the corner of the Square at Newell's pub and allowed the bike to freewheel downhill past the Skeffington Arms Hotel. The black iron bars of the Square whizzed by on the other side, mute witnesses to my confusion. By the time I checked at the bottom of the hill to swing left past the superior façade of the Great Southern, my anger had turned to despair.

Whatever I did was wrong; whatever I said caused offence. Nobody liked me, not even my best friend: a fat chance I had of ever getting Ella FitzArthur, not with the Rev and her parents lined up in opposition – not to mention my own parents. The Nicholas Kerrs of the High Schools of the world would always have an edge over the Michaels of the gate lodge.

I was crying as I turned into the entrance of the High School, and I was grateful for the Saturday quietness of the place, grateful that no one was there to witness my wet nose and my face streaked with tears. I dumped the bike under the lean-to and stood for a moment, uncertain of what to do. The thought of my mother's fussing concern and the inevitable mug of tea was a further irritant. I turned on my heel and took off aimlessly along the path under the trees.

The High School seemed deserted. There were no lights in the great barracks of the main building. Nowadays it seemed often so, with just the two exam classes in the school: more than once I had heard both my parents comment sadly on the sepulchral appearance of the place. This afternoon, I knew, both the boys' rugby teams and the girls' hockey teams were away visiting some school in the midlands. If anyone had opted to stay behind, he or she was burning no electricity in the school study hall or dormitories.

Inevitably my aimless route took me to the boiler house. I took hold of the latch-handle, half lifting and at the same time pushing the old door. The boiler house was heavy with the warm smell of dry turf. There was enough dim light to see the particles of turf dust floating in the air – they were always there, tiny organisms of black and brown, intent on getting up your nose and into your eyes and settling deeply into your hair.

I tipped up the metal catch on the furnace door and swung the door back. The fire was low – you economised when the school was away on a trip – but there was glow enough to fill the boiler house with a flickering orange light. I took off the gloves that Ella had given me and held my hands against the heat of the furnace. I found no comfort in the fire. It was dying, as everything died, everything in the whole world. Doors fell off their rusting hinges and boarding schools that had been there forever suddenly announced that they were closing down. The silken fire of a first kiss under a railway bridge could no more endure than the dying fire in this old cast-iron furnace.

I had asked Ella to write, but what should I write to her? Two days previously, standing together in this dusty old boiler house, it had seemed such a good idea, a metaphorical touching of hands, a convergence of hearts that would prevail against all the restrictions of school and parents. But what could I write to her that was worth the writing or the reading? Sunlight danced around the laughing corners of her lovely eyes: of what possible interest to Ella would be my gloomy prognostications of failure and mortality? Ella walked on the same side of the street as the Nicholas Kerrs of the world, and in the finish she would raise her mouth to be kissed by one of her own kind.

You have to know your place. Perhaps my mother was right.

I began listlessly to feed the fire with turf. I should have raked it first, pushing the ashes between the bars into the box below, but I didn't care any more. One by one I cast the sods through the open door of the furnace, watching each one land with a splash of sparks and ashes before finding its place in the rearranged fire. Everything was consumed and died. Nothing lasted. A small puff of ashes made a new world and what had been no longer existed.

I was reaching idly for another sod of turf when my glance wandered in the direction of the loose brick over the boiler house door. It looked slightly askew, as if I hadn't pushed it home properly after showing it to Ella. I reached up, pushing gently at the red brick with my fingertips, but it refused to budge. With both hands I removed the brick. Behind it was a black pouch, barely visible in the recess of the wall. My fingers were trembling as I took the pouch from its place. It was a slim pencil case, envelope-style, with a flap that snapped shut with a metal button. The flap opened with a single click that sounded loudly in the silence of the boiler house. Inside, folded lengthways to suit the shape of the pouch, was a wad of foolscap pages and, along with them, a smaller sheet of paper, folded separately, as if it were an afterthought.

I opened this single page first. On it Ella had written: 'I don't want my letter to get cold and lonely, stuck between two old bricks, so I'm leaving it snug and cosy in its own little leather bag! It's our own special post bag!! Love, E.'

I carried the letter towards the furnace with reverence. In the light of the fire I opened the wad of pages, torn from a school notebook, and began to read:

Dearest Michael,
I couldn't sleep the last two nights – I kept going over and over what we said in the boiler house. I kept remembering how sad you looked when I was leaving! I don't have your gift for words and things come out the wrong way! I don't want to lie again to anybody – certainly not to Mum or Dad! – not even to the Rev!! That doesn't mean I don't want you. I've never known anyone like you

– you're kind and gentle and you make me feel special!

Don't worry about my parents!! All will be well!! In time they'll get to know you like I do and they'll be glad to know you. Just leave all that to me!! Mum takes a little longer to get around, but Dad's a dote – I always work on him first and get him to handle Mum for me! Us scheming women! Aren't we awful!

Just don't be in such a hurry, Michael! We have less than a year to go now. Get your scholarship – I know you can do it!! You'll become a famous lawyer and write books that will make you more famous and my Dad will go around boasting and making speeches to his friends about you!!

Give it time, Michael. Give us time. We'll have plenty of days to be together! Sometimes I hug myself and think about that lovely day walking by the railway line – and all the lovely things that happened on that walk!!!

Excuse my writing. It's never very good but this is worse than usual because I'm scribbling it in bed. It's just after six in the morning, and the rest of the dorm is still sound asleep. I should be too!! Instead of lying here thinking and worrying about you!!! I can't see your house from the window of the dorm, but I know you're near and that's good enough!! We're going off to play a match today – I wish you were coming with us! – but I'm going to sneak out first and post this letter to you in our own private letter box!!!

I wonder if you've written to me yet? It would be wonderful to find a letter there, waiting for me.

Must finish! Any minute now Sgt. Mjr. Murchison

will come in shouting, etc. etc. And I don't want any of the girls to see me writing this!

Your own Ella

xxx

Over and over I read her letter by the light of the furnace. The evening darkened and the shadows deepened but still the world was brighter. Her words held the promise of a new tomorrow and a new world, and in that new world there might after all be a place for me. I carefully cleaned out the fragments of stone and rubble from our hiding place and stowed the now empty pouch in the dark recess. The brick slid neatly into its place like a door closing on a tabernacle. With a lighter step I headed for home.

My step was not always so light over the ensuing weeks. Sometimes the music of the day seemed to burst inside me and I would suddenly realise that I was singing as I washed and towelled myself in the scullery and then, minutes later, a careless word – or even a look – from Sadie or my mother would set me snarling like a rabid cur. Once, in the run-up to the Christmas exams – always, now, it was exams: getting ready, sitting them and then inspecting the entrails – I suddenly became aware of a deep silence in Rab's class, and realised that Rab himself, together with the entire class, was waiting patiently for an answer to a question I had not heard. Blushing, I admitted as much to Rab. He cocked a sardonic eyebrow and I braced myself for a tide of irony. What came was only a mild wave. 'Be a poet by all means, Michael,' Rab said to me, 'but first get your exams and get yourself qualified to do something. Understand?'

Strangely enough, I had no difficulty understanding Rab's cynical remark. What was difficult to understand was his uncanny ability to see to the heart of things. More than once I had attempted to put into verse my feelings for Ella: every time I tried I was engulfed by the sheer enormity of those feelings. Vast waves of music swelled within me but I lacked the power to tame these waves into tidy rhythms and rhymes. I could hear the song in my heart but had not the voice to give it life. I went back to Ella Fitzgerald and mythical Yeatsian ladies who carried tall white candles in their long, pale hands.

Ella was close, tantalisingly so, but like the music in my heart she was beyond touch and taste. Her letters, sprawled over foolscap pages, were her authentic voice, and I trembled each time I heard it in the boiler house and later in my bedroom: yet as often as not, minutes after reading a letter of hers, I would feel the anger rising in me and rail against the iniquity of a world which forbade me to see her. For all her nearness, Ella was as remote as one of Yeats's dreamlike ladies.

I spilled it all out to Rosie one evening after rugby practice in the sportsground. He listened without interruption, standing in the lee of the high sportsground wall, the streetlamp lighting up his handsome face. Even in repose, Rosie looked as if he were smiling at the world. When I had finished, he looked at me and said, 'I heard about it, but I didn't want to say anything until you told me yourself.'

I looked away from him, up the hill to where the sportsground met the boundary of the High School. 'I couldn't,' I said, unable to look him in the eye. 'I didn't know what you'd say – ' I was fumbling for words ' – you know, Ella is your first cousin – '

'And you're my best friend,' Rosie said, 'aren't you?'

I looked at him then, and he was smiling. 'I wish I'd told you,' I said to him. 'It's awful, never seeing her. I won't even see her for Christmas,' I finished miserably.

'Maybe you will,' Rosie said.

'How?' I asked bitterly. 'Her father will whisk her out of there the minute the school closes.'

'He nearly did just that the day she went walking with you,' Rosie laughed. 'Uncle Esmonde in full flow is a sight to behold! I almost wish I'd been there to see it. He took off like a bat out of hell straight back to Castlebar, threatening to sue the High School for negligence and promising to have Ella in a new school before the week was out. Ella's mother had a right old time pointing out to him that it wouldn't be very wise to change schools half-way through her final year and that they'd be a laughing stock if he took the school to court.'

Rosie's words held me spellbound, affording me a glimpse into Ella's personal world. When he was finished, I shrugged bitterly. 'Well, there you are,' I said lamely, 'there's no chance of seeing Ella for Christmas.'

'I can't promise anything,' Rosie said, 'but I'll do my best.'

I hardly dared to hope but Rosie's smile was beguiling and the evening traffic purred by with a soft and comforting murmur.

Christmas Day fell on a Sunday: like our own school, the High was breaking for the holidays at lunch-hour on Wednesday.

Rosie came sauntering towards me between the rows of desks after the last exam papers had been collected by a couple of Second Year fellows. He looked as careless and certain of himself as ever. The knot of his dark tie hung askew beneath the unbuttoned neck of his shirt and the pockets of his sports jacket bulged with the unseen grenades. He was, without doubt, the most popular guy in the school and I, noticed – if at all – only as a 'swot' and a fellow you could rely on for the right answer, had grown taller in his generous shadow. His very optimism made most things possible:

perhaps, I thought, watching his smiling progress, perhaps after all I'll get to see Ella before she goes home.

'How'd it go?' Rosie asked.

'OK,' I nodded.

'Modesty forbids.' Rosie laughed.

'I don't know,' I said. 'It hasn't been going so well for me lately.'

'I know – I've noticed.' He seemed to weigh his words. 'Don't worry about it – it'll come back to you.'

I waited, saying nothing.

'All right,' Rosie said, finally. 'I can't guarantee anything, but I think it'll be OK. Be in the Mar about half-four.'

'Are you serious?'

'Perfectly,' Rosie said smoothly. 'My uncle phoned very early this morning in a flap – something about a late sitting of the court that would go on all day and he couldn't get down in time to pick Ella up. Of course the mater told him not to worry – she's probably picking Ella up – ' Rosie looked at his watch ' – just about now.'

'You're a right fecker,' I said to him. 'You could have told me this earlier!'

'And distract you,' Rosie drawled, 'from your chemistry exam?'

I threw a mock-punch at him and he danced away, laughing, with surprising lightness.

'It's a relief to see you laughing, Michael.' Rab, who had been supervising the last exam, had materialised silently beside us. 'I've been a bit worried about you lately.'

'I know, sir,' I managed to answer. I wanted to please Rab more than any of my teachers and yet, even for him, my work had of late been frustratingly inadequate.

'Rest up over Christmas, Michael,' Rab said kindly. 'Get some fresh air, go for plenty of long walks.'

'Yes, sir,' I said. Rab's concern embarrassed me no less than the restrained comments he wrote at the end of essays which – I knew myself – were less than my best.

'Are your parents fixed up yet? I mean, after the High School closes?'

'Not yet,' I answered, looking closely at Rab. It was the first time he had ever mentioned the school and I was surprised that he even knew where I lived. 'There's nothing decided as yet.'

'Try not to worry about it.' Rab's voice was gentle. 'Your job is to get a good Leaving Cert and get yourself a scholarship, remember that.'

'Yes, sir.' In the face of Rab's kindness, I felt a fraud. My parents' situation was none of my concern.

'And your mother, Patrick,' Rab asked, turning to Rosie, 'how is she getting along?'

'Pretty well, sir,' Rosie answered. 'She gets a bit down sometimes, but generally she's getting better all the time.' He spoke as an adult might about a troubled child.

'I'm glad to hear it, Patrick. Give her my regards.'

'Yes, sir, thank you.'

Rab measured us both with a glance and gave us a rare smile. 'Happy Christmas, boys.'

'Happy Christmas, sir,' we answered together.

We watched Rab move away, his tall, angular figure marching jerkily between the rows of desks.

'Old Rab doesn't miss much,' I said wonderingly.

'Maybe he'll turn up at the Marian Café at half past four.' Rosie was laughing.

'One of these days . . . ' I began, scowling at him, but I couldn't imagine what might or might not happen to Rosie one of these days and I joined him in laughter as we left the exam hall together.

Heads turned when I pushed open the swing door of the Marian Café. I felt the eyes of strangers flick over me and then, satisfied that I was uninteresting, return to their own companions and their own tables. The large, square room was on the first floor of the building; Rosie was sitting, as I expected, at one of the window tables that he preferred, overlooking Shop Street. He gave me an expansive wave and I raised my hand, diffidently, for some of the watching eyes might yet be trained upon me, and I felt exposed, standing there in my Blackrock overcoat with my fingers in the air. Ella had her back to me, but Rosie leaned towards her now and I saw his lips move and his head nod in my direction, then Ella turned her head, pushing her chair back, and her face became bright as the sun, welcoming me as I began to move awkwardly between the tables.

'Can I help you?' A young waitress, dressed in the Marian uniform of black dress and fitted white apron, was standing in front of me.

'It's OK – ' I pointed towards Rosie, fumbling for words. 'I'm with – '

'Oh!' she smiled suddenly. 'You're with our Rosie then.'

I nodded, squeezing past her, registering without surprise that 'our Rosie' had yet another admirer.

Ella was on her feet when I got to the table. 'Michael,' she said, and then she said my name again: 'Michael.'

'Hello, Ella.' I felt her take my hand in hers but I had seen classmates of mine at other tables and I knew their eyes were upon us, on my long black coat and Ella's snowy linen blouse and soft blue cardigan, and I drew my hand from hers and just stood there, looking at her.

'I can see I'm not wanted here.' Rosie's words were heavily ironic but there was an easy laughter in his tone. He stood up then, picking up his fawn duffle coat and scarf from where they lay clumsily balled together on a chair.

'Patrick – '

'Don't try to stop me, Ella,' Rosie grinned. 'You have – ' he made a great show of looking at his watch ' – a little over half an hour while my mother helps me to pick presents for Ella and her Mum. OK?'

'Patrick, you're just a dote – '

'Yes, I know, Ella,' Rosie laughed, 'but just don't land me in it. Be ready to leave the minute I come back to get you.'

'You're sure Aunt Frances won't come up here with you?'

Rosie laughed again. 'You must be joking!' he said good-humouredly. 'She wouldn't be seen dead in this dive!' With a last farewell, a friendly half-puck on my upper arm and an admonition to enjoy ourselves, he was gone. I watched him move easily between the tables, smiling and bantering with strangers and acquaintances alike, stopping briefly to hand a bill and some coins to the young waitress who had called him 'our Rosie'. The door swung noisily shut behind him, as if a great wind had passed through it.

'He's great,' I said, finally returning my gaze from the swinging door to Ella. 'I don't know anyone like him.'

'Neither do I,' Ella said.

'When he told me at school today that he might be able to fix it up – I mean, us meeting, I didn't know how to thank him.'

'Michael O'Hara,' Ella said sternly, 'did you drag me in here just to sing the praises of my cousin, Patrick?'

'I didn't mean – ' I blushed ' – I mean – '

'Do you realise it's eight weeks since we met?' Ella asked.

'Nine,' I said. 'Or it will be tomorrow. It was a Thursday when we last met – remember, in the boiler house?'

'Do I remember?' Ella laughed then and she laid her hand on top of mine on the white tablecloth. 'Do I remember!'

And I looked into her blue eyes then, saw how they were flecked with tiny traces of grey, saw the nine weeks that were gone slowly dissolve in that limpid blue, and saw again the promise of a tomorrow rise from their never-ending depths. The clinking of cups died, and the babble of conversation, and there remained only us, looking at each other, our hands together on the tablecloth.

'Two coffees, compliments of Rosie!' The young waitress was placing cups in front of us and we started guiltily, our hands parting. 'Carry on!' the waitress said breezily. 'Don't mind me! I'm only doing my job!' But she lingered for a moment and I sensed a kind of hunger in her look as she stood there, smiling at us. 'It's great, isn't it,' she asked, 'being in love? Enjoy it while you can!' For a moment her gaze swept the busy street below, ablaze with lighted windows and chains of red and yellow lights strung high across the streets. She was no older than we were, yet the smile she flashed us was full of years beyond ours. 'Remember what I said,' she told us. 'Happy Christmas.'

'She's so nice,' Ella said, when the waitress had gone.

'A bit sad,' I said, wonderingly.

'You noticed it too,' Ella said slowly. 'That's why you're different, Michael. Patrick wouldn't notice that in a hundred years.'

'Don't be so sure,' I said, recalling his reticence and his reluctance to intrude upon my sulkiness throughout the term just ended. 'Anyway,' I laughed, 'now who's talking about Rosie?'

She laughed again, and shook her head, a cascade of dark hair swirling in the smoky café. 'I got you a present,' she said, reaching to retrieve her duffle bag from the floor. She loosened the white cord and took out a small package wrapped in silvery paper. 'Open it,' she said handing it to me.

'No.' I shook my head. 'I had nothing for you last year but I got you something this time.'

I had the long slim package in my inside pocket. My hands shook as I gave it to her. I loved the energy with which she took it and the joyous curiosity with which she tore the wrapping open. Just for a moment the slim grey box rested in her hands and then she snapped it open and the fountain pen was there, nestling in its scooped-out bed in the velvety stuff of the box.

'Is it OK?' I asked tentatively.

Her fingers sought mine again on the tablecloth. 'It's perfect,' Ella said. 'Thank you.'

The pen looked so prosaic yet she turned it in her fingers as if it were precious. I'd wanted to spend the twelve-and-sixpence on a brooch in Dillon's, but I hadn't been able to screw up my courage to do so. Another time Sadie would have bought the lady's brooch for me, but now I was barely on speaking terms with my sister.

'It's perfect,' Ella repeated. 'I'm going to write you dozens and dozens of letters with it!' She glanced quickly at her watch. 'We haven't much time, Michael,' she said, 'before Patrick comes back.'

I opened her present then, conscious that the noise of tearing paper was drawing glances from the neighbouring tables. Inside was a pocket-sized hardback book. I turned the book with nervous fingers to read the gold-lettered title on the dark blue spine: *Love Poems of W. B. Yeats*. Faded, almost sepia-coloured ink on the fly-leaf told the name of the original owner. Under that fading inscription Ella had written: 'To Michael, with all my love, Ella'. She had added, in letters smaller than her usual bold script, 'Christmas 1960'.

'It's not new,' Ella said, 'but I thought you'd like it.'

'You know me so well,' I said, wonderingly.

'I want to know you better,' she said lightly. A trick of the streetlights, shaking in the December wind, bathed her face briefly in a golden glow.

'He had the words,' I said, with an awkward, jerking movement of the book. 'I wish I had – I'm not able – '

'You have more words than anyone I know,' Ella said intensely, 'and you have all the time in the world. Now stop giving out to yourself!'

'Thank you,' I said. I felt foolish and ungrateful. 'For everything.' I spotted Rosie bursting his way through the small-paned swing door. He wasn't alone. 'What's he doing here?' I demanded of Ella.

'Oh Michael, please don't make a scene!' Ella pleaded.

Nicholas Kerr, taller and larger than Rosie, was shunting along in his wake. I watched, angry and confused, as the pair of them bore down upon us between the tables.

'Why?' I demanded again. They were almost upon us now, Kerr was smiling broadly, his oddly effeminate creamy skin a striking contrast to Rosie's apple-red cheeks.

'Please, Michael,' Ella said again. 'Daddy is giving him a lift home tonight from Patrick's house – Nicholas's father had a heart-attack yesterday.'

'Why didn't you tell me?' I whispered fiercely.

'Because I didn't want to upset you, Michael!' Ella's voice was edged with tears. 'Patrick's mother collected the two of us today, but I was afraid you'd be unhappy if I told you. Nicholas is a neighbour at home, Michael, and his dad's in hospital!'

I hated the sleek sureness of him. Rosie had paused in his passage towards us to chat to the young waitress and I saw Nicholas's features break into a grin as he nodded casually to her. And the more the waitress smiled back at him, the more I despised him.

I stood up suddenly. 'I have to go,' I said, picking up my overcoat.

'Michael!' Rosie's greeting boomed at me like a friendly cannon.

'You're not going! Stay and say hello to this riff-raff from the High School — my mother was tired of him and insisted that I take him off her hands for a while!'

Nicholas had hove to alongside Rosie, on the opposite side of the table. Facing them both, I felt small and overwhelmed. Nicholas's smile was tight and uncomfortable but he stretched his hand across the table towards me. 'Hello, Michael,' he said.

His fingers hung there, sausages dwarfing the plate of pastries. I wanted to break those flabby fingers. I turned to Ella. 'I have to go,' I said again.

'It's Christmas, Michael,' Ella said in a small voice.

'Stay for a minute,' Rosie said quietly. 'My mother won't leave without us.'

I looked at Rosie then, not trusting myself to meet Nicholas's eye. 'I'd like this fellow to stay away from my sister,' I said.

'Michael!' I felt my hand taken lightly in Ella's.

'What have you got against me, O'Hara?' Nicholas spoke without anger.

'I want you to leave Sadie alone,' I said.

'That's for Sadie to decide.' Nicholas was smiling thinly at me now. 'Isn't it?'

'She's too good for the likes of you,' I snarled, hardly knowing what I said.

'What's wrong with you, O'Hara?' Nicholas laughed. 'It's not my fault that you're living in the gate lodge and I'm not.'

'Cut it out, Nick!' Rosie remonstrated.

'Well, it isn't my fault!' Nicholas exploded. 'I can't help this guy's pathetic hang-ups just because his sister likes me!'

Something snapped in me. I made a dive for Nicholas but Rosie's two hands clamped my arms tightly. Nicholas was white-faced, bracing himself for an onslaught.

'No, Michael!' Rosie's voice was low and urgent.

I was aware of a sudden lull in the conversational babel of the café, of heads turning towards us. I didn't care. I struggled in Rosie's grip.

'For God's sake, Michael!' Rosie whispered.

'Michael, Michael!' It was Ella's pleading that stayed me. My shoulders slumped in Rosie's grip and the tension left me.

'OK,' I mumbled, 'OK.'

Around me the indistinct voices began re-building babel.

'Shake hands,' Rosie said.

I shook my head. 'Let him stay away from my sister,' I said, looking directly at Nicholas now, 'or else it'll be the worse for him.'

Nicholas gave a little laugh. 'You're all talk.'

'Nicholas, shut up!' Ella flared. 'The pair of you are worse than children!'

For a moment silence settled upon us, broken only by my own heavy breathing. 'I'm going now,' I said. 'Happy Christmas, Ella. Happy Christmas, Rosie.'

Nobody answered me. I stumbled among the tables towards the exit. The young waitress paused in the act of clearing a table and smiled at me. 'Don't forget what I told you!' She smiled at me conspiratorially, and I had a fleeting impression of her hurt face as I pushed wordlessly past her.

Outside on the crowded street the wind hit me. The sudden icy cold wakened in me a sense of what had been said and done. The crowds crushing past me on the narrow pavement spelled out my aloneness. In the yellow glow of the Christmas streetlights I felt alien and restless. There were voices raised on the street in cheerful salutation and farewell, but none for me.

'Michael!' I turned, hearing that voice that filled my dreams.

She was running towards me along the footpath, her hand held high above her head. 'You forgot your book!' Ella said, panting.

I gulped back tears, unable to speak.

'Happy Christmas, Michael.'

Our fingers touched as I took the book from her. 'Happy Christmas, Ella.'

'Don't look now,' Ella said, 'but Aunt Frances is right across the road looking into Moon's window.'

I did look. Even with her back turned to us, Rosie's mother, in her dark widow's coat, was unmistakable. Ella shivered in her cardigan and blouse.

'You'll catch your death,' I said to her.

'I just rushed out without thinking,' Ella said. 'I couldn't bear you to go off like that.'

'I couldn't bear to look at him any more,' I said.

'Nicholas was trying to be friendly.'

I shook my head. 'I can't,' I said. 'Not with him.'

The crowd eddied around us, pushing Ella off balance. I reached out my hand to steady her. 'You'll catch your death,' I said again, feeling the cold skin through the cardigan.

'I'd better go,' she said.

'I know.'

'The last thing we need is for Patrick's mother to turn around and see us.'

'I know.'

'I'll go, so,' she said.

'All right.'

She had her arms folded tightly across her body against the biting wind. It might have been the wind that stirred the wetness in her blue eyes. 'See you next year,' she said.

'Yes,' I whispered.

'Happy Christmas, Michael.'

She backed away from me for a step or two. She bumped into a woman coming out of the Odeon Bakery and I watched her flash the bag-laden woman an apologetic smile, then she turned away from me. Her head of dark hair, haloed by the golden lights, bobbed among the hurrying throng. At the entrance to the Marian she stopped and turned again to wave at me. I waved back and then in a moment she was gone. The crowded street seemed empty without her.

Throughout that last Christmas in the lodge it seemed as if our lives had stopped. Like boxers warily circling each other in a tiny ring, we moved around one another with excessive politeness, saying no more than was necessary, avoiding any contact that was not essential. Christmas dinner was like that – eaten quickly, accompanied by the usual comments on the turkey, then the table cleared and dishes stacked as if the day were nothing more than your common-or-garden Sunday. Afterwards my father went alone for a walk and my mother sat in silence before the range. Sadie and I did the washing-up in the scullery. We exchanged a few words but I could tell that her relief was no less than mine when the task was done and we could escape each other's presence.

When Sadie went back to work on the Wednesday after Christmas Day I almost envied her: going to the chemist's shop every morning gave, at least, some purpose to the day. I went to daily Mass at ten o' clock myself and I tried to study for a few hours each day, but the exercise seemed sterile. The last days of the old year tasted like the dregs of a mug of cold tea: it seemed always to be raining and Rosie was away with his mother in Ella's house.

Without Ella the days seemed pointless. Even through the

long weeks of term, when we could not meet, there was a kind of bitter-sweetness about knowing that there might be a letter behind the loose brick in the boiler house; about knowing that, even if unseen, she was close by, like a guardian angel that you never can see but you know is there, always a hovering presence at your shoulder. There was no presence now in the great bulky school building: grey and gaunt in the dying days of the year, it promised only a final emptying, an ultimate silence.

My parents would not have understood *Hamlet*. They neither raged against the forces that had brought them to their present pass nor speculated about what the new year might herald. In my mother's face I could read only a stoical acceptance of God's will, the certainty that 'God is good'. My father's face, broken nose and all, still seemed eager to please, eager to show his gratitude to old Reverend Willoughby and his predecessors for allocating him a place in life. They were two of a kind, I decided, my father and mother – bending the knee to forces greater than themselves, utterly reliant on some other providence.

Perhaps Hamlet would have understood. I didn't.

On New Year's Eve I left the house at about nine o'clock. A cold, sleety rain was falling and I had my collar turned up under my chin. Outside Billy's house, half-way down the hill, I stood for a moment, listening. The sounds of laughter and raised voices came from behind the drawn curtain of the front room: I recognised the American drawl of Billy's eldest brother, who had come home alone for Christmas. Inwardly I debated whether to knock and enter: inside there would be jokes and teasing of Mrs Lally and news of Billy and maybe a dollar bill or two stuffed into my breast pocket. My courage failed me and I mooched on slowly along the dimly lighted footpath, my hands pushed deep into my overcoat pockets.

I met nobody I knew – nor expected to – on the streets of the town. On the corner where you turned into the street leading to our school, I paused, but for a moment only: I felt embarrassed, fearful lest anyone I knew, especially a teacher or fellow student, should happen by and demand to know what I was doing there alone, on New Year's Eve, within sight of the school. Had I been asked, I would not have known how to answer. I turned hurriedly away, confused, the echo of voices from the school yard faint in my mind, and quickened my step across the bridge towards the Protestant church. They'd be gathering there before midnight, I knew, a bunch of young fellows and girls, with bottles of beer and stout, to ring in the New Year in the lee of the old church while the bells overhead heralded the new beginning.

My footsteps led me home again. Céili music was playing on the wireless but neither my father nor my mother, sitting in the armchairs on either side of the range, appeared to be paying any attention to it. I didn't really want any tea, but I let my mother make it for me, just to please her, and I was sitting at the table, trying to gulp it down, when Sadie arrived in. She was short with my mother – 'the picture wasn't great, just OK' – and she didn't want tea. She took off her coat and stood for a little while in front of the fire, warming herself. When she half turned to answer some question of my mother's, I could see the big silver-and-diamond butterfly brooch on her lemon jumper shining in the firelight: Sadie claimed to have bought it herself but I didn't need telling that it was a Christmas gift from Nicholas Kerr. She said goodnight a few minutes later: the scent of her perfume lingered in the kitchen after she had closed the door of the back hall.

Not long after that I stood up from the table and said goodnight. My mother asked if I wouldn't wait until it was midnight, to see the New Year in, but I pleaded tiredness and said goodnight again. She said goodnight, and *The Irish Independent* shook in my father's hand as he also wished me goodnight. I was glad to shut the back-hall door behind me. The light was shining under the bottom of Sadie's door. In the old days – or in what now seemed like the 'old days' – I would have gone in to chat a while with her. Now I passed by on tiptoe, anxious only for the privacy of my own room.

I threw an old coat of my father's on top of the blankets against the cold of the night. I lay on my back, waiting for my body heat to warm the space I lay in. Through the skylight there came only the faintest light: the night was still misty and the sky was hidden by clouds.

I knew it was midnight when I heard the sounds of the ship sirens, faint but clear, from the docks and the bay. In the darkness I thought I heard the bells pealing in the Protestant church, but I couldn't be sure. I shut my eyes, hugging myself in the night, and I could hear Ella's gurgled laughter. She was standing beside a white marble fireplace and all the eyes of a crowded room were directed upon her. Tall flames danced in the fireplace, bathing her face in a golden light. In another time, on another New Year's Eve, I wanted to be there beside her, warmed by her golden smile.

THIRTEEN

The High School didn't reopen until the twenty-third of January; by then we had been back at school for almost a fortnight. The days, short and grey though they were, seemed less pointless: I had plenty of homework, Rosie was back and Silenus was putting us through tougher workouts twice a week on the near-frozen surface of the rugby pitch . . . ways to fill the days until Ella returned.

I caught a glimpse of her that Sunday evening, seated in the back, behind her parents, as their car shunted across the gravel past the lodge: for a moment she turned her head towards me but I knew she couldn't see me in the evening shadows of our kitchen, hidden behind the patterned lace curtain. Knowing it was futile, but hoping against all outrageous hope, I slunk beneath the bare trees to the boiler house later that night, but my hopeful fingers encountered only my own letter in the pouch behind the bare brick, lovingly folded and deposited there earlier that day after Mass. My letter was still uncollected on Monday night. On Tuesday I placed a second letter alongside it in the black pouch. On Thursday evening both letters were still there. And likewise on Friday night.

Before class on Saturday morning, Rosie was sympathetic but unable to help. He shook his head when I asked if Ella had phoned his mother during the week.

'She never does,' he said. 'They're not allowed to use the phone except in emergencies – you know, the school's on fire or Matron is giving birth to twins.'

'I've a good mind,' I said, 'to go and ask the Rev if Ella is OK – something might have happened to her.'

'Brilliant idea,' Rosie said, stony-faced. 'One simple hint like that and my uncle will have Ella out of the High School quicker than you can say I-was-only-asking.'

The school bell was ringing for the start of class, and under the watchful gaze of Brother Cyprian we sauntered with studied seniority towards the school door, shepherding ahead of us First Years and other lesser mortals. Despite myself, I was laughing.

My letters were gone when I pulled back the brick that afternoon. In their place the leather pencil case held Ella's breathless letter.

Friday

Michael –

I'm going out of my mind! We all are! Old Murchison seems to have made a New Year resolution to turn the High into Mountjoy!! She never lets us out of her sight – everywhere you look, she's there watching you! Last thing at night and first thing in the morning!

She's really lost her marbles. Yesterday she insisted on going through one girl's locker and looked at all her stuff! What on earth can she have been looking for? The mind boggles!

Anyway, I had to tear up the letters I had written to you and flush the little pieces away in the toilet. Old Murchy would have had 15 kinds of canaries if she'd found them!

I'm writing this in prep – behind a wall of books to

keep out prying eyes! Just pray old Hawkeye doesn't come swooping! And pray that I can get to our postbox tomorrow – she'll have to close her eyes sometime! Or will she?

I'm dying to see you, Michael, and I'm dying to get your letter. If there isn't a letter waiting for me, Michael, I'll never speak to you again!!

Happy New Year, Michael – our last one here!!!

Love

Ella XXXX

I could breathe again, holding her letter, hearing her voice in every exuberant exclamation mark. That night, for the first time in many weeks, my sleep was deep and dreamless.

I thought at first that I was dreaming. My room was filled with the brightness of stars flooding through the skylight. And then I heard it again: the distinct clicking noise of a latch being loosened gently. For a moment I thought it might be Sadie at the door of the back hall on a trip to the lavatory, but then came the faintly sawing sound of a knob being turned, hoarse and metallic, and I knew that our front door was being eased shut: we had often teased my mother about what treasures she must have hidden away in the chest of drawers to justify securing our front door with knob and latch and heavy, black iron key.

I swung my legs out over the side of the bed, searching for the comfort of the small mat that took the sting out of the cold brown linoleum. I reached out for my navy school trousers – the good pair were left for Sundays – and drew them on over the long shirt I wore in bed. There was no need to switch on the light, so bright was the night sky above my skylight. Barefooted, I made no sound as I stepped into the back hall. Gingerly, but clutching the knob as tightly as I could, I opened the door of Sadie's room.

The sight of her empty bed, neatly made, woke me properly. The luminous face on the small alarm clock that she had bought out of her own money said ten past one. At eleven Sadie had said goodnight to me in the kitchen, formal and faintly hostile as were most words that now passed between us. After midnight, when at last I had finished my homework, there had been no crack of white light beneath her door in the back hall and I had clearly heard her familiar breathing, rhythmic and, as always, slightly wheezing.

I stood in the doorway of her room, suddenly alert, the tumblers of my brain falling reluctantly into place at this unaccustomed hour. The room, more tomb-like than my own, windowless save for the skylight, seemed to echo with the wheezing pattern of Sadie's breathing over the years – no more than a reminder now of the often panicky nights when I'd hear her gulping for breath as a small child and then, in the darkness, I'd hear my mother's voice, encouraging and comforting, and it was a comfort also to me to know that she was there, on the other side of the partition, seated on the edge of Sadie's bed, cradling her, massaging her back. I shook myself, angry with the unbidden memory.

No more than seconds had passed. I left the door ajar, pushed open the door into the kitchen. The door was unlatched, as if Sadie had left it so. After the brightness of the bedroom, the kitchen was dark, filled with the leftover whisperings of a room that is busy and bright by day. Still in bare feet, I crossed to the window of the kitchen. The night outside seemed bright as day, filled with the hard light of stars and a March moon. The bare branches of the tree opposite the lodge glistened in the night, and the pebbles of the drive glinted like diamond shards.

I heard the faintest whisper. Nothing distinct, a murmur in

the bright night. And then I saw them. Nicholas Kerr was padding along on the grass margin of the drive, planting each foot carefully ahead of the other as if he were negotiating a minefield. My sister was taking equal care, as if she were parodying Nicholas's exaggerated caution. It was the bicycle that Kerr was carrying on his shoulder that enraged me. In the moonlight I could see clearly that it was mine. In my fury I raised my fist to hammer on the small window panes, to accuse him of theft and anything else I could think of.

Afterwards I would recollect that moment, would wonder what stayed my hand in that split second of time. I might have changed much – perhaps everything – had I pounded on our kitchen window. I'd have roused the house – perhaps it was the instinctive realisation of that which stopped me – and possibly the school too. The consequences would have been disastrous: my father furious, my mother tearful and Sadie in the sulks. And Nicholas Kerr perhaps expelled.

There is a divinity that shapes our ends: only hours previously I had read and memorised the words of Hamlet. And afterwards, when it was all over, I would recall that frozen moment and wonder what malevolent deity had stayed my furious hand.

I saw Nicholas Kerr turn suddenly, one leg in mid-air, a deliberate self-caricature, mocking his own caution. He was grinning broadly as he turned to Sadie. I watched as her face broke into a smile and she put her hand to her mouth, as if she were stifling laughter. The front wheel of the bike started to turn with a whirring noise that I could detect from my hiding place, and my sister reached out her hand to touch it into stillness. All the while their eyes locked, and I knew I could lurk there forever behind the curtained window and neither would ever think to look towards me.

In the cold, fireless kitchen I felt my body grow warm with an emotion I did not care to name. When Nicholas and Sadie had passed out of sight, through the gateway and on to the road, I stood for a moment watching the night. I saw nothing. I heard nothing. My father suddenly began to snore, a rumbling noise that filled the house. I started guiltily and hurried back to my room. My anger gave me speed. Within seconds I had put on my shoes and the heavy jumper that my mother had knitted me for Christmas. My bedroom window was useless for light, but it opened easily and I was able to drop down into the narrow space between the wall and the lodge. On the mossy soil my feet made no sound as I made my way around the house towards the school gates.

It felt strange to be out on the road in the middle of the night. The world seemed washed in light, as if it were not night but day. On my left the long vista of College Road stretched downwards, silent and empty. They had not gone that way. I started to run in the opposite direction, downhill towards the laundry and the fair green. I almost stumbled on them.

My bicycle lay askew against the dark railings that guarded the laundry for unmarried mothers. Sadie and Nicholas, careless of who might be watching from the tall and silent windows of the laundry, were embracing on the footpath. I drew back into the shadow of the stone wall at the top of the hill, my heart hammering inside me. I watched them separate, then Sadie climbed on to the bar of the bike and Nicholas pushed off along the road towards the Square. I could no longer see my sister: it was as if she had disappeared into Nicholas's embracing bulk.

Once more I began to run. My shoes pounded on the pavement, but they were too far ahead to hear me. I was afraid I might lose them at the corner of the Square but they moved slowly, as if they knew where they were going, as if there were no need to hurry through the sleeping town. I ran easily, grateful for the long and sometimes lung-burning sessions on the rugby pitch under the eye of Silenus. At the corner of the Square, beside Fox's bar, they swung left, uphill towards the station. I loped along the empty footpath, confident now that they were headed for the line. When I rounded the corner myself I could see no sign of them, but I moved more carefully now: it was uphill here, and they were probably walking.

They were. I stopped at the station entrance and climbed the grey steps to duck out of sight. I could see Nicholas and Sadie up ahead, their heads close together as they made their way up the line. Their pace was unhurried, two people out for a stroll in the middle of a Sunday afternoon.

After they had passed out of sight I hurried on again. The untarred surface of the line was quiet after the pounding surface of the streets. At the top of the bandroom hill I stopped, panting, my hot hands resting gratefully on the cold metal of the railway bridge. Below me the station was silent, the tracks gleaming like silver in the night. The sea shone silvery too, still and silent in the windless night. My eyes followed the curving tracks, ahead and below, curving through the silent landscape like a twisted scissors.

I knew it was them, too distant now to make out their faces, close together on the bike, but it was them all right careering along the pathway, so that at this distance you thought they might be sailing along on the silver tracks. I watched, angry and perhaps envious too, remembering how I had walked this way with Ella on a stolen Saturday. They were beyond the middle bridge on the path now, the faintest of silhouettes. I couldn't see them any more – and yet I could. Sadie climbed down from the bar of the bicycle, then Nicholas propped the machine against the grey stone wall that guarded one side of the path and he held apart the wires of the fence on the other side of the path for my sister to climb between them on to the strong bed of the railway. Nicholas followed her across the tracks to where the empty carriages awaited them, dark and blind, on the shunting line, silent above the wide expanse of the bay.

How long I stood there on the hilltop, watching the dark carriages and the shiny sea, I didn't know. Perhaps it was the chill of the night that brought me back to myself, to the cold metal of the bridge, to the sleeping town and silent sea spread out below me. I retraced my steps along the empty streets, past the locked doors of station and shops and houses and laundry. The world was heedless of the railway carriages above the bay and my bike leaning against the stone wall, waiting for my sister and Nicholas Kerr.

Nobody heard me as I climbed through the window into my bedroom. I was still awake some time later, staring up at the skylight, when I heard the click of the latch and the hoarse turn of the knob and the muffled thud of the key. I drifted into an uneasy sleep and woke, frightened, my mind still hot and fresh with the terror that I was alone in a cushioned room with Sadie, and my arms were about her. I sat on the edge of my bed, trembling, and allowed the morning sounds of the kitchen-poker against grate, cups on the table, the kettle whistling, to still the shivering that racked me.

'You're late,' my mother said cheerfully, when I ventured into the kitchen.

'Sweet dreams,' Sadie said, looking up, laughing, from her toast. 'Our Michael is having too many sweet dreams these nights.'

I looked at her, sitting there as bright as the day, her skin glowing and her hair shining as if – as if she had been at home all night. At that moment I could have choked her.

A few days later I was standing shoulder-to-shoulder beside Nicholas Kerr, frozen to death and wondering would the match never end. I was half-way down the line-out. In front and behind stood the rest of our pack, caked with mud, panting heavily, waiting for our hooker to throw the ball in.

'Double-four!' the call came from the hooker, our code for a ball thrown towards me in the middle of the line-out. I braced myself, ready to spring. Out of the corner of my eye I caught sight of Nicholas tensing himself in readiness. On the sideline our hooker, small and wire-haired like a terrier, prepared to launch the ball. I watched his fingers, saw his arm frozen in the split second before releasing the ball.

Behind him, in the stand, the crowd − mostly our crowd − bayed for a score. Our terrier-hooker threw the oval ball. Kerr gathered himself to spring for it. In that moment I lifted my right foot and drove it down, hard, on Kerr's instep. He gasped in pain. The ball dropped neatly into my waiting hands and I gathered it to my chest, as Silenus had coached us, backing into the enemy, my pack gathering around me before I passed the ball back to Kelly, our other wire-haired terrier, this one our scrum-half. His boot connected with the ball with a satisfying smack as he kicked over our heads into touch, driving the High back towards their line.

The crowd roared. It was no contest in the stand: the High supporters huddled together like a ragged bunch of refugees fearful of contact with our monstrous horde of baying schoolfellows. The roar drove us on. Getting ready for the next line-out gave us a chance to draw breath. Behind us, in the three-quarter line, strung out in attacking formation across the pitch, Rosie urged us on. 'Keep it going!' he urged us. 'We have them on the run.'

And in truth it seemed we did. Although the match was scoreless, and half-time could only be minutes away, you could sense that the High School fellows were wilting. We waited in the line-out, inside the High School's twenty-five.

'Bastard!'

I looked sideways at Nicholas Kerr and smiled at him. He'd limped his way towards the line-out and he grimaced in pain as he spat the words at me. 'Play the game fair, you prick!' he snarled.

This time I dug my elbow hard into his ribs as he prepared to jump. Once more the referee's attention was elsewhere, and once more I gathered the greasy ball against my mud-caked jersey. When I gave it back to Kelly he jinked outside, then inside, side-stepping one opponent after-another as he made for the line. When he put the ball down under the posts for a try the stand erupted: it was all blue and white now, and not even a hint of the purple-and-yellow favours of the High. Kelly took the conversion kick himself and tapped it nonchalantly over the bar. Another mighty roar: the blue-and-white sea waved again. Kelly was cool. He trotted back to take his place again without a hint of histrionics: it was the way you played the game.

The whistle blew for half-time just after the High School kicked off. We huddled together in the centre of the pitch, sucking on our orange segments, listening to our captain's exhortations. Alone among us, his knicks and jersey were unsoiled by mud. He played on the wing and hadn't touched the ball during the first half. 'Keep it tight, lads,' he said to us. He was tall and lean and looked like a greyhound with a crew cut. 'We've waited too long to throw it away now.' He had no need to explain further. Throughout my years at school we had never beaten the High; neither had we ever won against Sligo Grammar, the only other school in our three-cornered championship.

'Jesus, but I could use a fag.' Kelly's words made us laugh, although our greyhound-captain frowned at such frivolity.

'I'll buy you a bloody cigar,' he told Kelly, 'if you manage another try for us.'

The referee blew his whistle, three sharp blasts that told us it was time to begin again. Rosie took me by the arm. 'You're not playing fair with Nicholas,' he said to me.

I shrugged. 'You'll get caught,' he said. 'You'll be sent off.'

The three-quarters were lining up in their usual position to face the kick-off. Our greyhound shouted angrily at Rosie to get back. 'You'll be sent off,' Rosie said again. 'Everybody can see you at it – it's some kind of miracle the way the ref hasn't – so far.'

Our captain shouted at him again and he trotted off to take his place. I looked over at the stand. It wasn't hard to pick out Ella, tall and slim, in the middle of the High School few. I wondered idly whether she had noticed my offences – and what she thought of me for them. There was no need to speculate about Sadie's reaction. I'd spotted her on the far touchline, among the small scattering of neutrals and parents who always came to watch these school matches. Maybe that was why the games were always held on Thursday afternoons, the town's half-day, to allow these few shopkeepers and past pupils the chance to freeze on the sideline for an hour and a half of schoolboy rugby.

High School began the second half in desultory manner. The peculiar combination of spirit and technique which had always enabled then to beat us – although we had a much bigger pick of boys in our school – seemed to have deserted them. You could see it in the lethargic way in which they got down into set scrums and you could feel it in their half-hearted tackling. Midway through the half we knew the game was ours: by then we were ahead by eleven points to nil. Our supporters took to raising a derisory cheer whenever the High managed to put even a simple passing movement together. We were too engrossed in our own performance to notice it but the High was dying on the pitch, just as surely as the school itself would die in June.

I took Rosie's advice and refrained from kicking or elbowing Nicholas Kerr. In loose play he stayed out of my way and I made no attempt to seek him out. In the line-outs, when I was obliged to stand beside him, I studiously avoided looking at him, content twice over in the knowledge that we were not only winning but that I was out-jumping Nicholas for every ball.

We were into the last five minutes of the match when it happened. The icy rain had started to fall again, whipped diagonally across the pitch by a northerly wind that felt as if it came directly from the Arctic. By then all of us were heavy with mud and weariness, going through the motions like sodden neanderthal creatures bent on some senseless battle of attrition. High School had the throw for a line-out on the far touchline. As Nicholas and I went up for the ball together, I felt his elbow slam into my shoulder. Knocked off balance, I fell heavily on the greasy pitch. The ball squirted out of Nicholas's clutching hands as he, in turn, was bundled aside by my team-mates. Nicholas fell beside me. There was no mistaking the hatred in his eyes, squinting at me through the driving rain.

'Peasant!' He spat the word at me. The other players were around us now, as High School unexpectedly forced the play back towards us. The ball, an ugly black oval of mucky leather, was suddenly loose beside us. Nicholas, on his knees, grabbed at it. So did I. I grabbed only Nicholas's fingers. He tried to pull his hand away, but I tightened my grip, forcing his hand down towards the mud. The play surged about us as our two packs went through their slow-motion, heavy-limbed ballet in the rain. On the mucky sod, hidden from view by our drenched team-mates, Nicholas and I played out our private *pas-de-deux*. I could see the pain in his blue eyes as I levered his hand down and down. His palm squelched against the greasy sod and still I tightened my grip on his fingers. Our eyes were locked together like our hands and I sensed the pleasure in myself as I saw the pleading there in the frightened depths. The other players moved wraithlike in the rain about us, separated from us by our private bond of pain.

I began to force his fingers backwards and upwards, still grinding the palm of his hand into the sod. I could see the white tears of sweat beading on his brow. He shook his upper body frantically to break free and I applied the last ounce of vice-like pressure on his fingers.

I heard the sudden snap of breaking bones.

I heard Nicholas scream.

The referee blew his whistle.

I looked towards the referee, not caring if I were sent to the line. I needn't have worried: the whistle had been blown only for a scrum-down. I could have stayed there a long time on the mucky pitch, studying the splayed angles of Nicholas's fingers, but I thought it prudent to get to my feet and lumber through the sleeting rain towards the scrum.

The High School fellows shouted for Nicholas to get a move on. Someone said he must be hurt, the way he was just lying there. Our fellows looked over at him, not terribly interested, wishing he'd get up and on with it and then we could all get in out of this bloody rain. Someone said that Nicholas had passed out. Kelly said that he'd bloody well pass out soon himself if he didn't get a bloody fag. Our captain, still immaculate in unmuddied togs and jersey, shushed him with a withering glance. It was bad form to take the mickey when one of the other crowd was down injured.

Nicholas must have recovered. We watched him get to his feet, surrounded by his solicitous team-mates. He must have fallen awkwardly, one of them said: at least two of his fingers seemed to be broken. His team-mates helped him, white-faced and stooped, towards the sideline. Our supporters in the stand, generous now with victory assured, refrained from jeering. A couple of minutes later the referee blew the final whistle to put us all out of our sodden, frozen misery. Our gang surged towards us from the stand, ringing the headmaster's hand-bell, trying vainly to wave our single, sodden flag.

Nobody looked accusingly at me. The rain and the mud had cloaked my assault on Nicholas's white fingers. Eager, jubilant supporters slapped my drenched back, whooping with exultation. I could recall the feel of his fingers, vulnerable and fragile as twigs that you'd snap to light the fire with. Across the heads of the milling crowd of supporters I could see Rosie, surrounded by a bunch of excited First Years. His handsome face, rosy even in the freezing rain, was wreathed in a happy smile. Above the drenched heads he caught my eye and I saw the smile fade from his face. I knew that one person, at least, was wondering how Nicholas Kerr's fingers had been broken.

FOURTEEN

Day followed day, week followed week, in a seamless continuum of school, study and sleep. June and the exams were the shrine at the end of our pilgrim way. Nothing else mattered: every teacher in the school beat the same drum. It didn't matter, after all, that we lost the final by a few points – the game was no more than a light-hearted diversion from the serious pursuit of honours and scholarships.

Easter came and went; Ella went and came. There was no chance to meet, but on one occasion she smiled and waved discreetly when I passed her in the school corridors, manhandling school desks from now deserted classrooms. The High School had, apparently, found a buyer for some of its redundant furniture: a flat-backed lorry ploughed its way along the gravelled drive, its cargo of graffiti-gouged desks caped, hearse-like, by a blanket of black tarpaulin that glistened with pearls of April rain. My father stalked away, wordless, as if he had bidden goodbye to an emigrant boat.

And the letters came and went, two or three times a week, secured in our secret postbox in the boiler house. Time after time I told her of my longing for her and always, in her breathless rush of exclamation marks, she reminded me that the days of our 'Babylonian captivity', as she blithely termed it, were drawing to a close. Her optimism was fresh and tangible: I could see it in the green shoots of the High School trees and in the dwindling days of April crossed off the Egan's Bar and Grocery calendar that hung on the back of my bedroom door. I read her letters in my room, hugging her words to myself, and then I would look towards the calendar on the headless nail on the door and know that she was right, that our separation, like everything else, must one day end. Best of all, despite my forebodings, Ella made no reference in her letters to Nicholas Kerr's broken fingers.

At first I made nothing of it, that last Friday night, when Sadie didn't come home after work. I was trying to unravel an applied maths problem at about nine o'clock, when I heard my mother's gentle tap on the door. She came in carrying a mug of tea which she placed beside me on the table. 'Would you come up to the kitchen for a while?' Her voice had that tentative edge with which she often spoke to me now, as if she were wondering who I was. 'It's warmer there,' she added.

'It's easier to study here, Mam,' I said, taking the blue-and-white striped mug in both my hands. 'You know, it's quieter.'

'Quieter!' My mother laughed, a small, sad sound. 'Sure it's like the grave up there it's that quiet, with only myself to talk to. I don't know what's happened to this house at all.'

'You used to give out to us,' I said, sipping at the hot sweet tea, 'when we wouldn't be quiet.'

'Sometimes,' my mother said, 'we don't know when we're well off.'

I said nothing. I stretched in my chair, easing the stiffness out of my back and shoulders. Part of my mind was tracking the maths problem and I felt I could see the solution. I took another contented mouthful of the warming tea.

'Sadie didn't come home from work tonight.' My mother seemed disinclined to return to the empty kitchen. 'Did she say anything to you?'

I half-laughed. 'Sadie says hardly anything to me these days, Mam.'

'So I've noticed,' she said. 'And ye used to be thick as thieves. Did you have a row or something?'

'It's only Sadie's moods,' I said evasively. I was sure I had the answer to the maths problem now, and I was anxious to get back to it.

'That's just it,' my mother said. 'She's so moody these days you can't even look at her. She'd snap the head off you if you look sideways at her.'

'She's probably gone to the pictures, Mam,' I said, finishing off the tea and lowering the mug with a conclusive flourish. At least she couldn't be with Kerr: he was locked up inside with the others for what they called 'prep'.

'It's Friday night, Mam,' I went on briskly. 'It's payday – she's just gone off with one of her pals.'

'All the same – '

'Hasn't she done it before, Mam? Beans and chips in the Odeon, then off to the Savoy afterwards.'

'I suppose you're right,' my mother said uncertainly.

'Sure I'm right,' I said. 'She'll be home shortly giving out to the lot of us again, the same old Sadie. You know she will.'

She wasn't.

I had decided to call it a day just before midnight, and I was making my way along the back hall towards the kitchen, when I heard the knocking on our front door. I wondered who it might be at this late hour, but without much interest – my mind was still engaged in the memorising of dates and battles of the Second Punic War.

'Who can that be at such an hour?' I could detect the seriousness in my mother's voice.

'Answer the door,' I heard my father say, 'and then you'll know.' It was a long time since he had been up so late.

'I'll get it, Mam,' I said, pushing open the door of the back hall. My mother looked apprehensive, as if were were still worried about Sadie not coming home.

There was no light outside the door of the lodge. For a moment, peering into the dripping darkness, I thought I was mistaken – but there could be no mistaking the tall, spare figure under the big black umbrella. 'Reverend Willoughby!'

'Ah – Michael – I'm deeply sorry to be so late – I wonder if your father – '

But my father was already on his feet, brushing me aside, cutting off the headmaster's strangely hesitant speech. 'Come in, sir, for God's sake, out of the rain – I don't know what kind of manners they're learning them in some schools,' he added, looking meaningfully at me. 'Sure it's a terrible night for you to be out in. Come in, sir.'

My mother, too, had risen to her feet. She quietly took the umbrella from the headmaster, closed it and led him to the fire. 'Would you like a cup of tea, sir?' she asked him.

Reverend Willoughby shook his head. 'I'm sorry to disturb you at this late hour. Do forgive me, Mrs O'Hara.' The headmaster seemed to have lost his hesitancy. 'Jack,' he said, turning to my father, 'one of the boys is missing – Kerr, from the Sixth Form.'

'Sure maybe – ' my father seemed reluctant to answer ' – maybe he's just gone out over the wall for a mineral or – or a bag of sweets or – '

'Or a smoke, you mean?' The Rev cocked a thin eyebrow at my father. 'Not this time, Jack. Mr Harrison didn't miss him until lights out, but he's questioned all the boys and it appears nobody has seen Kerr since tea.'

'You know how the lads are, sir,' my father said, tentatively, 'when they're trying to cover up or something.'

'Mr Harrison assures me,' the headmaster said dryly, 'that his questioning was thorough.' You could expect nothing less of Harrison: thin-faced and bald, his science classes, according to Ella, were conducted with Gestapo-like efficiency.

Nobody spoke for a moment. The kitchen was darkened by Reverend Willoughby's gangling presence, as he stood with his back to the range. 'Young Kerr is a good lad,' my father said at length. 'He'll be back soon, sir, with some foolish excuse or other. Wait till you see.'

I looked at my father in astonishment. He spoke with a tenderness that was rare in him, as if referring to one of his own.

The headmaster was not reassured. 'I don't know, Jack,' he said at last. 'It seems to be past the time for silly excuses and silly pranks.' He half turned to look at the alarm clock on the mantelpiece. 'It's after midnight, for God's sake!' The branch-like arms waved in frustration. 'I'm at my wit's end to know whether I should telephone the police or his parents.'

I caught the quick glance exchanged between my parents. 'Wait a while, sir,' my father said, 'sure he'll be back.'

'And take a cup of tea, sir,' my mother added. 'Sure you could use it to calm you.'

Reverend Willoughby looked as if he needed calming. His face was white, his high brow puckered into a deep frown. Watching him, it suddenly occurred to me that the headmaster was frightened, that he, like my father, had to give an account of his stewardship to somebody above him. He visibly gathered himself together, like some loose-limbed automaton locking his working parts into place. 'I'd better get back to my wife,' he said. 'She's just as worried as I am.' His words were addressed to the kitchen in general but he turned now to address my father directly. 'I know that the boys come to you sometimes, Jack, if they're in a scrape, and I thought that perhaps you knew something of Kerr's . . . of his absence.' He waited but my father shook his head. 'Anyway, if you do hear anything – or even if Kerr turns up here looking for any kind of assistance – let me know at once. And assure him, of course,' he added, with a bleak smile, 'that while the consequences of his excursion may be painful, they will not be fatal.'

'I will of course, sir,' my father said.

'Goodnight, Jack, goodnight, Mrs O'Hara.' He turned to me then. 'Studies going well, Michael?'

'Yes, sir.'

'We all have great hopes of you.' He spoke offhandedly, as if I were not there. 'Goodnight then.'

We chorused goodnight to him. My father opened the door and the kitchen was filled with the noise of rain spilling on the gravelled drive. The falling rain drowned the sound of the headmaster's departing footsteps. When my father closed the door, the silence seemed abrupt, as if someone had suddenly switched off the wireless. I watched him leaning against the coats that hung on the back of the door. His head was bent and I could see the mottled skin of his bald patch. He looked older than even the headmaster.

'Jack?' My mother's voice was timid, frightened. 'You don't think . . . I mean, with Sadie gone as well . . . you don't think that the two of them . . . I mean . . . '

'What're you taking about? And who said anything about Sadie being missing? Sure the child is only out a bit late – although God knows she'll get a good talking-to when she comes in, worrying her mother like this.'

'I just meant . . . I mean, the two of them are missing, and I'm just wondering, Jack, if there's anything in it . . . '

'There's nothing in it!' my father exploded, yet in his anger I could read his fear. 'Sure Sadie and young Kerr don't even know each other!'

I had been standing beside the table, caught between their fire. Now I turned away towards the back hall. 'Do they know one another, Michael?'

'You know Sadie,' I said, 'she talks to everybody.' I opened the door, anxious to be gone from the overheated kitchen. 'Don't be worrying about Sadie, Mam – she'll be back.'

More's the pity, I thought to myself, as I said goodnight and closed the door behind me. In the early morning will come the telltale sounds of locks gingerly turning and her bedroom door squeaking open and shut while I lie beneath my skylight and wish that I had broken Nicholas Kerr's arms and legs and not just two of his bloody fingers. At least, I thought with some satisfaction, at least this particular escapade might put a stop to their carry-on. I could imagine my mother sitting white-faced by the fire, waiting to confront a startled Sadie as she sneaked in home in the small hours. With luck, Mr Gestapo-Harrison would interrupt Nicholas Kerr at the portals of '*Pueri*' at about the same moment. Perhaps, after all, there was a divinity that dished out just desserts in this vale of tears. The neatness of it did not displease me – and it would reveal to my father a home truth or two about these boys of whom he spoke in such tender and protective terms. Sadie and Kerr would just have to take their medicine like everybody else who got found out.

The rain still hammering on my skylight could not keep me from quick and welcome sleep.

Yet when I awoke a few hours later I was filled with a sense of unease. The rain had ceased but the sky was heavy with clouds and the familiar pieces of furniture in my room were shrouded in grey, as if the dampness of the dawn had penetrated the distempered walls. I sensed, even before I looked, that Sadie hadn't come back. The clock beside her bed said five past four and I wondered if some trick of the mind had wakened me. Twice in the last few weeks the stealthy, clicking noises of her return had wakened me in the uncertain hours between night and dawn.

I stood a moment in the back hall, listening to my pounding heart and the night-time noises of the lodge. The familiar sibilances of the sleeping house seemed unfamiliar; the line of old coats hanging in the back hall were alien presences, ill-defined shapes that were strangely threatening. Standing there, listening to my own breathing, I remembered how I had lain awake as a child, frightened of the brooding bulk of the coats on the back of my door. There was an extra sound, another's wakened breathing in the dawntime house. I could hear it, faint and rasping, before I opened the door into the kitchen.

I wasn't surprised to see my mother sitting beside the fire. The curtains were still drawn and the light was off, but there was light enough from the range for me to see the grey in her dishevelled hair and the drawn greyness of her face. I knew without asking that she had been sitting there all night, waiting and watching. And praying. 'Go to bed, Mam.' I said. 'You look exhausted.'

She ignored what I said. She was sitting on the edge of the chair, her legs drawn together and crossed at the ankles, one hand nervously clutching the other in the lap of her navy skirt. 'Have you no idea at all,' she asked me, 'where Sadie might be?'

'Will you not go to bed, Mam,' I said again.

'What difference would it make?' she said. 'I couldn't sleep anyway until she was home.'

She was staring into the fire and I saw the dark streaks below her eyes and knew she had been crying. 'I'll get my coat,' I said.

When I came back, buttoning up my black coat, she was still studying the fire with vacant eyes. 'Don't waken your father.' Her whisper was urgent in the unlighted kitchen. 'We won't tell him what time she came in – he's as well off not to know some things.'

I opened the door of the lodge as gently as I could.

'Bless yourself going out, Michael.' I did as she told me, dipping my fingers in the shallow font and crossing myself with the holy water. As I eased the door shut I had a last glimpse of her, immobile, a grey-haired old woman by a dying fire.

I lifted my bike across the gravel, remembering how I had watched Nicholas Kerr do the same a few months previously. The dawn was brightening. Early birds sang in the High School trees and the air was heavy with an after-rain sweetness. I didn't want to think of Kerr laughing at my sister as he tiptoed across the drive with my bike on his shoulder.

My mother hadn't asked where I was going. I had no reason to head for the railway line – none, except that I had seen them there twice and I had no idea where else to look. Nicholas Kerr was bigger than me but there had been fear in his eyes when I snapped the bones of his fingers and I felt sure I could exploit the memory of that fear. This time, I told myself, pedalling downhill, I would break more than his miserable fingers. Yet, even as I promised myself to give Nicholas Kerr the hiding he deserved, I realised that I didn't want to fight him. If he and Sadie wanted to carry on, let them. Sadie would get hurt – a fellow like Kerr could have only one thing in mind for a girl like her – but she wouldn't listen. It was her problem, not mine. It wouldn't be long now until I was in college and my real life could begin. Ella had said so.

The path beside the railway line was mucky after the night of rain. Out on my right beyond the tracks and the boggy stretch of furze bushes, the sea was almost motionless, laden with grey mist. A lone gull, wheeling in the heavy air, squawked hoarsely and repetitively. The carriages on the far tracks loomed closer in the mist, a dark-green *caravanserai* waiting impassively for whatever travellers this desert track might offer up. Filmed-over windows stared back at me, sightless eyes blinded by cataracts of dribbled rain.

I discarded my bike, studying the long curving line of carriages, wondering where to begin. The blinds were pulled down on one compartment. Behind me, my bike, angled lazily against the wall, slipped to the ground. The bell jangled and the upended wheel turned crazily. I swore and righted the bike. I ducked between the wires, starting towards the compartment with the drawn blinds. My hurrying feet disturbed the bed of stones and I half-slipped, knocking my ankle against the railway track. I cursed aloud at the stinging pain. I didn't care if they heard me now. I wanted them to hear me, behind the cream-coloured blinds in the silent compartment.

My feet made no sound on the space between the two sets of tracks, spongy and topped with moss. I was under the blind-covered windows now, panting as if I had come a long distance. The windows were too high for me to reach. I hammered with my fists on the body of the carriage, and I shouted their names. 'Sadie! Nicholas! I know you're in there!'

Three times I hammered and shouted at them to come out. Only my raucous seagull companion answered, circling the silent carriages, scavenging in the dawn. 'If you don't come out,' I shouted, 'I'm coming in!'

Not even the seagull answered.

There were no doors on the near side. I stooped between two

carriages, dodging the iron couplings that hung down like grotesque umbilical cords. On the far side you could smell the docks, pungent on the wind at low tide. I tried all the doors, swinging up on to the wooden steps, shouting in frustration as I went. The last door in the carriage swung open to my impatient hand.

My feet pounded along the corridor. Even here, on the internal side, they had pulled down the blinds. I was frightened now. I knew they were here yet there was no answer, although I was making a racket that would waken the dead. 'It's no good hiding from me, Kerr!' I shouted the words angrily as I pushed and pulled at the door of the compartment. The glass-panelled doors refused to budge. In frustration I slapped with my palm at the silver handle and the doors opened, gliding soundlessly apart.

Nicholas was propped up in the corner of the long, upholstered seat. Sadie leaned back against him, wrapped in his arms. I wondered why her eyes were closed, why Nicholas was staring vacantly over my shoulder. 'Sadie?' I called her name timidly. 'Sadie – ?' I hung back, frightened, in the narrow doorway of the compartment. Her long hair was neatly brushed back from her face, as if someone had arranged it after she had fallen asleep. Nicholas's lower jaw hung slack; a fine dribble of spittle had run from the corner of his open mouth.

In the silence of the carriage, deeper than any silence I had ever known, I began to realise that I was, for the first time in my life, in the presence of death. I wanted to run but I forced myself into the compartment. Her hand was cold to my touch, as was his. Her right hand enclosed the fingers of his left, under her breast. Her hand looked small, gripping those large fingers, the fingers I had broken. She had died first, cherishing those broken bones, holding them close to her as she slipped away out of life.

I reached my hand out, as I had seen them do so often in

films, and I closed his eyes. With my handkerchief I cleaned the spit from his chin and dried his face. His skin was fine and white, unmarked by spots or the scars of acne. I tried, gently, to close his mouth, but his jaw was hard and cold, and I was afraid to press my hand harder against him.

Sadie's handbag was resting on the middle of the seat, a folded sheet of paper protruding from its open mouth. I opened the page and read it slowly, sitting back on my hunkers on the floor of the carriage. It was written in black ink in Sadie's hand.

We want to be together always.
We do not want to live in a world
where we cannot be together.
God forgive us.
Pray for us and for our baby.

Beside her signature, Nicholas had written his name in the same black ink. Even as his bulk wrapped her smaller body on the seat, so his signature dwarfed hers, overshadowing her neat writing with a sprawling, decorative flourish.

In a way, I wasn't surprised. It seemed as if I had known since waking in my room – it seemed ages ago now – that on this day the familiar would be made strange, what was unknown would become even stranger. It was not the strangeness that disturbed me, or wakened the tears in me as I sat back on my heels on the cold floor. Nor the blackness either, although my heart could hardly imagine a bleaker tableau than these two, their arms around each other in death, another life inside my sister snuffed out before it had even begun. But bleakest of all was the knowledge of their togetherness and of my own exclusion from it. They had touched each other's heart, shared each other's body. In the end, unwilling to live separate lives of shame and recrimination, they had shared a death.

The light was spreading over the sea and the railway, pushing through the blinds on the windows. It did not warm me, nor could it ever again warm these two. The sun poked its way around the edges of the blinds, glinting on the glass bottle that had rolled against the back of the seat. 'Forkan's Pharmacy' was written on the white paper gummed to the front of the flat bottle: when I opened it, a single capsule fell into my palm, a red-and-green capsule that had somehow escaped their despairing hands. I had seen enough films to know what it was.

I was still crying as I pushed the bottle and their last note into the pocket of my coat. Some of my tears were for my sister and this huge, handsome fellow whom I had so detested; some were for my mother, sitting by the fire in the lodge; most were for myself, for my aloneness. I saw how he had enfolded her in his arms and I wanted Ella in mine, together against the world. I wanted her close to me, her hair crushed against my chest, my life in her hands. Without her, life was nothing.

The phone rang.

I jumped, frightened by the harsh, jangling noise. The phone was on a small table with spindly legs in the hallway. In a moment I heard Mrs Willoughby's voice, high-pitched and nervous. I couldn't make out what she was saying. I didn't care. I was exhausted. The railway carriage with its voiceless passengers was still more real than the headmaster's wife talking on the phone on the other side of the door. At first I'd been interested, straining to follow the Rev's words as he dialled and talked, call after call – the police, the hospital, someone connected to the board of governors. I'd sat on the edge of the chair in the Willoughbys' sitting-room, trying to make sense of the one-sided conversations imperfectly heard from the hall. It was like a game, a diversion from the recollection of Nicholas's staring eyes and the spit dribbled on his chin. It couldn't work – the edge of terror in the Rev's voice ensured that: the terror and the occasional phrase flung clearly through the closed door. 'A frightful accident . . . one of our senior boys . . . the daughter of our caretaker.' Better to shut the words out but I couldn't stop my ears. 'Too soon to contact the boy's parents – we must wait for the doctor's report – no point in being unnecessarily alarmist, is there?' He couldn't keep the pleading alarm out of his voice.

Mrs Willoughby brought me tea and toast. A white china teapot with roses on its curved body. A silver toast-rack like in the films. Sadie would have liked them, she'd have enjoyed serving her guests in such style. Nicholas would never have seen her do it. They'd never have let him share a life with her. He'd never have wanted to, anyway. And yet he had chosen to share an end with her, his barely-healed fingers resting in hers. You could never really tell what anybody was going to do.

The big clock on the mantelpiece chimed the hour. I was startled to see it was eleven o'clock. The school had just been stirring to life when I'd come knocking on the door of the headmaster's house; Reverend Willoughby had been in his dressing-gown when he'd opened the door. The dark, patterned colours of his gown reminded me of the seat on which they sat, their arms entwined. He knew, sensed, that my calling at this hour must have something to do with Nicholas. What he didn't know about was Sadie. I watched his face fill with incredulity, with horror. He called for Mrs Willoughby, and we sat in the furniture-crammed sitting-room, dark and sunless, and once more I told my halting story.

The headmaster started to weep. His thin shoulders sagged

and his face crumpled in tears. They were ruined, he sobbed. What would become of them now, at their age, in the midst of such scandal and shame? Mrs Willoughby shushed him, told him to get a grip on himself, there were things he had to do. I wondered, watching the sobbing scarecrow figure, if I had not been mistaken in coming here rather than going to the lodge. Under his wife's urging, the sobbing subsided: you could see the thin shoulders feebly attempt to straighten back inside the dark stuff of the dressing-gown. When he knocked and entered the room later his face was freshly shaven – I could see where he had nicked the sagging flesh of his burgeoning gooseneck, a small splash of red above the whiteness of his dog-collar. Mrs Willoughby would bring me some tea, he told me, everything would be all right. His voice wobbled only a little as he advised me to try to rest.

In a moment I heard him on the phone. Throughout the morning the phone rang. So did the doorbell. Teachers from the school came and went. Wheels churned in the gravel. Through the lace-curtained window I watched the local minister from the Protestant church come and go in his Ford Prefect. The chairman of the board of governors came in a big car with shining chrome and a radio aerial. He left hurriedly, the heavy car ploughing waves through the grey gravel. The gardaí arrived in a black car: the uniformed guard remained at the wheel while the two plain-clothes detectives, Brylcreemed and wooden-faced, climbed slowly out, looking nervously about them. Reverend Willoughby did not invite them into his study on the far side of the hall: I could hear the exchange inside the front door.

'No,' I heard him say, 'I cannot allow it. The boy is too exhausted to make any kind of statement now. Besides, his parents must give their permission and he hasn't seen them yet.' I was glad there was no quaver in his voice, glad too when the detectives left a few minutes afterwards.

It was still only ten o'clock when the Reverend looked in to say that he was taking my parents in the car to the hospital. He left his question unsaid but I shook my head.

'No, sir,' I said. 'I can't . . . I mean, I'm not able . . .'

'It's all right, Michael.' Mrs Willoughby had materialised quietly by her husband's side. 'I'll explain to your parents, I'm sure they'll understand.'

They left together in the car. Mrs Willoughby returned alone, on foot, a few minutes later. I wondered what she could have said to my mother in the hurried interval to make her understand. My father might rant and my mother would weep but neither anger nor tears would ever bring them understanding. I couldn't help them. I didn't want to try. Perhaps they could help each other, as Mrs Willoughby had stiffened her husband's sagging spine when he first grappled with the news. They had grappled with much in their time. Photographs on the walls and propped up on the big dark sideboard told of a life before the High School – the pair of them young, she in short-sleeved floral dress and wide-brimmed sunhat, the Reverend in shorts and dog-collar, flanked by respectful black men who did not stand close enough to touch. There were group photographs of black schoolchildren, the Rev and his wife seated in the centre of the front row, pale and anaemic at the heart of blackness. They were, perhaps, no better off now, in the wake of scandal, than my own parents: they were too old, surely, and too fragile, with the High School closed, to set off once more for Africa?

Such distant shores were not for the old, the weak-spined, the thin-blooded. The world belonged to Ella and me. Only in death had Sadie and Nicholas been able to establish a union that would endure but for Ella and me it could be in the here and now. Her father and the rest of them would be afraid to scoff now, mindful of the cold bodies in the carriage: if nothing else, my sister's despairing end would serve as a warning to others that they must leave us alone, Ella and me: we had a right to our life.

I lay on the couch, remembering to keep my shoes off the dark leather. My body felt heavy with weariness but my head was light. I dozed, my mind wandering under an alien sun. Snared between waking and sleeping, I broke free to walk hand-in-hand with Ella under immense African skies of astonishing blue: little children chanted tables and rhymes and I watched their black faces blossom into smiles under Ella's coaxing words. In my half-waking I schemed and the Willoughby photographs swam before my tired mind but it was Ella and I who sat centre-stage for the mission-school camera.

Mrs Willoughby's voice reached me as from a great distance. 'You have a visitor, Michael.' I shook myself awake, got a glimpse of her sad, nervous face as she left the room.

'Oh, Michael! Michael!' Ella was standing in front of me. Her eyes were filmy, as if she had been crying. I got to my feet, struggling to form a question.

' Why . . . How did you get here?'

'It's all over the school, Michael.' She was fighting back tears now, her lovely eyes wet. 'My father is here. Most of the parents have already been told.'

Behind her, the clock chimed one: in a few hours the world had been taken apart.

'Dad's taking me home,' Ella said.

'He can't – he can't!'

She took my hand in hers. 'You're cold,' she whispered. 'They're saying that you found them, Michael – is it true?'

I couldn't meet her gaze. I looked beyond her to the African pictures on the wall. I wanted to reshape the world as I had dreamed and schemed it on the couch. 'Please, Ella.' I snuffled, whimpering, but I didn't care any longer. 'Don't let him take you away from me.'

'You know what my father is like, Michael.' She gave me a sad little smile. 'I had to threaten to make a scene before he'd agree to let me see you.'

I was momentarily puzzled. 'How did you know I was here?'

'The school is full of rumours, Michael.' Again, the small sad smile. 'Some of them not very nice.'

'What kind of rumours?' I asked angrily.

'You know what people are like, Michael – they believe the worst.'

'Let them!' I said fiercely. 'It doesn't matter what people think if you and I are together.'

She didn't answer. She came close and put her arms around me and I let her take my head in her hands and I felt her fingers in my hair and her shushing, soothing noises in my ear. In her nearness I could taste the hot winds of Africa, bound by neither class nor creed, free under skies of blue.

The door opened. Ella's father stood there, staring at us. 'Ella!' His voice was sharp.

She drew back from me, but only a little. 'You know I wanted to say goodbye alone, Dad.'

'Five minutes,' he said, tapping his watch. 'That's what we agreed.'

I met his gaze. He was shorter than me, but it was as if his eyes looked down from the eminence of years and position. 'I don't want Ella to go,' I said.

He stepped into the room then, closing the door behind him. 'What you want is no concern of mine or of my family.' He was measuring his words, a player in a courtroom drama. 'What happened here last night will leave a stain on this school that will never be wiped away. If the school were not already due to close, this incident would probably close it.'

'That's not my fault,' I protested. 'I didn't do anything wrong!'

'No,' he agreed, shaking his head of wispy hair, 'but the world is not concerned with such niceties. I bear you no ill-will, young man – in fact, I personally wish you well. I'm a democrat, after all. I simply don't wish Ella to pursue any kind of relationship with you. It's nothing personal, I assure you,' he finished, 'merely protective.'

I choked, wanting to hurl his sophistry back into his sheep's-head face.

'Don't,' Ella said quietly, squeezing my hand.

'I've told my daughter that she is to have no further contact with you – of any kind.'

'Dad!'

'And she has promised to respect my wishes.'

I looked, bewildered, from Ella to her father.

'Wait for me in the car, Dad,' she said. 'Please.'

'You have one minute, Ella,' her father said. He gave me a last look before leaving the room, closing the door firmly behind him.

'It's not true, is it?' I asked. 'Tell me it's not true.'

She didn't avoid my eyes. 'It's only till the end of college, Michael. I've made that clear to him.'

'But that's forever!' I sobbed. 'Another three or four years! You told me we could be together after we finished school!'

She reached for my hand, but I drew it angrily away. 'And I meant it, Michael,' she said quietly. 'But I also told you that I wouldn't lie to him again – and I won't. There's been enough lying – and look at how it ended.'

'And are we ended now?' I demanded. 'No contact for another three years while you're away in Dublin!'

'Is it such a long time?' Ella asked. 'Are you not able to wait a little while for me?' I couldn't answer her. My heart was a desert place that water could never reach. 'I have to go,' she whispered. I felt her fingers touch my face but I couldn't open my eyes for tears. 'You have to believe in us, Michael,' I heard her say, 'otherwise it's useless.' I heard the door open and close and I knew that she was gone.

I had forgotten it was Saturday. Small clusters of pupils still in school uniform were standing around in front of the school, voices raised in animated discussion. They fell silent as I approached. I felt their eyes upon me, but I looked straight ahead, making doggedly for the lodge. Behind me, the voices were raised again.

The fire was out in the lodge. Two cups, unrinsed, stood on the kitchen table. The sweeping brush was propped against a chair, discarded in mid-task. I didn't want to imagine the pain and bewilderment that had struck this house as surely as the avenging angel had laid waste the homes of the Pharaoh's Egypt. I knew what I had to do. I had known it as soon as the door had closed behind Ella in the headmaster's house. I had carried the knowledge with me on the short walk to the lodge, hugging it to myself like an unwanted secret. I stripped to the waist in the scullery and scrubbed myself with soap and cold water. The water numbed me; I started to shiver. The May sun shone weakly through the scullery window but I felt as if I would never again be warm, as if the whole world would be forever cold.

In my room I pulled on a clean vest and I took my good Sunday shirt out of the drawer. The shivering subsided but not even the heavy woollen jumper could take the cold out of my bones.

Sadie's duffle bag was hanging on a hook in the back hall. It still held a few of her old school books. My fingers shook as I removed the books. One fell open, revealing her neatly penned signature on the title page, and I dropped the book, startled, as if her eyes had suddenly opened in the silent carriage. I stuffed my other trousers and my spare shirt into the duffle bag along with my toothbrush, a vest, a few pairs of socks. The task soothed me, my hands moving mechanically, my mind closed against the day.

I bent over the bottom drawer and reached into the corner where I had hidden Ella's letters under some old notebooks. The letters were folded neatly, arranged in sequence. For a moment I fingered the letters, recalling the words and phrases which I had committed to my heart. And then – angrily – I stuffed them into the bag. The small blue volume of Yeats's poems lay in the same corner of the drawer. I dropped it, still angry, into the bag. There was nothing else I wanted. I looked around the room as if it had belonged to a stranger, as if someone else had sat at the small table all those nights, bent over Ovid and Shakespeare and geometry cuts. Maybe I wanted it to be someone else: in my cold heart I knew that I could not leave this room, this lodge, entirely behind me.

The loud knocking on the front door startled me. I stood stock-still, tensed, willing the caller to go away. It went on, louder than before. I heard the noise of the front door being opened, then I knew that it was Rosie who was calling my name. I looked quickly at the duffle bag, crammed to its mouth, staring back at me from my unmade bed.

Rosie called my name again and I shut the door of the bedroom and went through the back hall to meet him. His long, loping strides devoured the space between us, his great, flapping presence filling the room. 'I'm so sorry,' he said. 'More than I can say.' I could only nod my head. I had no words left in me, not even for Rosie. 'The mater told me,' he blurted on, 'when I got home from school. I came immediately – I got the car.'

Still no words would come.

'Is there anything I can do to help?' Rosie's cheeks had never been pale but they seemed pale now in our in our unlighted kitchen. 'It must be terrible for your parents . . . I mean, your poor sister. Michael, is there anything I can do?'

I found my voice then. 'It's all over,' I said. 'Ella is finished with me.'

He give me a strange look. 'Sadie . . . your sister, Michael.' Rosie's voice was puzzled. 'And poor Nicholas Kerr.'

'None of it matters now,' I said. 'Her father won't let her see me any more.'

'There are other things to think of now,' Rosie said gently. 'You'll have to help your parents through this – and I want to help, I'm your friend.'

'Why won't she see me?' I was angry, all my pain tumbling out of me. 'Am I not good enough for her? Is that it?'

Rosie laid a hand on my arm but I shook him off. 'You know the kind her father is,' he said earnestly. 'He's some kind of dinosaur left over from the stone age. The world is passing him by and he can't even see it. Ella knows it but she doesn't want to hurt him.'

'Three years – maybe four years – I can't bear it.'

'Of course you can.' His tone was cheerful. 'My cousin is lovely, Michael, but there are loads of other girls out there too, just dying to meet you.'

'Not for me,' I whispered, 'not for me.'

Rosie looked frightened now. 'It must have been awful for you.' There was an edge of wonder to his voice. 'Aunt Irene told mother on the phone that it was you who – who found them.'

I looked beyond him through the kitchen window. The sun was shining more brightly, the leaves on the big chestnut inside the gate radiant in the light. I shivered, remembering the mist curling around the carriages in the dawn.

Rosie must have noticed how I trembled. 'Come out home with me,' he said. 'You shouldn't be on your own now.'

'I'm going to lie down.' I hated myself, lying to him. 'I can't stay awake.'

'You're welcome to lie down in my place.'

I shook my head.

'You're sure I can't do anything to help?'

'There is one thing,' I said. 'I could use the loan of a few quid.'

Without hesitation he took the bulging wallet from the inside pocket of his sports jacket. From the mass of folded papers, leaflets and torn newspaper clippings which he collected and rarely discarded, Rosie took out two notes.

'How much?' he asked me. 'I have a twenty and a fiver.' I made no answer. 'OK,' Rosie said, 'take the lot; you're bound to have expenses at a time like this.' He brushed off my thanks, as if more embarrassed than myself by the exchange. 'It's three o'clock now,' he said, studying his watch, suddenly businesslike. 'I'll have the car and I'll come back for you at seven. I can take you to the hospital or . . . or wherever you have to go.'

We avoided each other's eyes.

'OK so,' Rosie said. Impulsively, he held out his hand. 'I'm really sorry, Michael.'

'Thanks,' I said.

'Till seven, then.'

I walked with him to the door and I watched him drive slowly through the gateway out on to the road. He turned briefly, smiling, his handsome face framed in the window of the car, his hand raised in farewell, then he was gone and out of sight. I didn't expect to see him ever again.

After he had gone I waited a few minutes, watching the alarm clock on the mantelpiece. At ten past three I slung the duffle bag on my shoulder and walked out of the lodge for the last time. The school was silent, the drive deserted. I hurried down the hill, fearful now lest I encounter the Reverend's car and my shocked parents. Nobody hailed me. The door of Billy's house was closed but I hurried past on the other side of the street. The unmarried mothers could be watching from the windows of the convent laundry but they were nothing to me. And yet I shivered, remembering how Sadie might have been confined among them. My fingers sought out her final note, pushed deep into my coat pocket: I had not told everything to Reverend Willoughby.

I could hear the train belching when I climbed the steps of the station, as if anxious to be on its way. I tried to cover my face at the ticket window, but the man inside barely lifted his balding head as he took Rosie's twenty-pound note and handed me back my change and a single ticket to London. 'By God, young fella, you took your time!' The ticket collector beamed at me as he punched my ticket with his little silver machine. 'You'd want to watch it or you'll be late for your wedding!'

He was laughing behind me as I sprinted along the platform towards an open door of the train. It was packed, mostly young men and women, with new hair-dos and brown suitcases. I had never met them but I knew these faces, had seen them all my life, coming and going with mongrel accents, flashing English fivers hard-won on the building sites and factories of London and Coventry and Birmingham. In his rare savage moments Rab would hold up this journey as the certain shameful reward for slackers in his English class. I looked at them, threading my way among them

295

along the corridor, and promised myself that I would never be one of them.

Along the length of the train, doors slammed. The guard's whistle blew, sharp and shrill. The engine belched louder, the great wheels clanked into life and the train pulled slowly out of the station. We gathered speed, and the footpath alongside us flashed by in a grey blur. I couldn't remember cycling back to the High after I had left them with eyes forever closed. I wondered, looking at the narrow path, too narrow by far for ambulance or car, how they had been carried back to town. The shunting track beside us was empty of carriages. Nobody could tell, watching the tracks slip behind us, what dreams had perished there in the innocent night.

Hours later, in another darkness, close to midnight, I stood on the deck of the Dún Laoghaire ferry, listening to the churning sound of the sea as we ploughed on towards Holyhead and London. I was too numb to feel the cold and I had no wish to join the drinking, raucous mob below deck. The darkness was welcome, a cloak to hide from me what I had been and what I yet might be. I took from my pocket the flat bottle and balanced it in my palm before hurling it into the night. In that immense sea it made no sound. I was afraid to open the little blue book, frightened lest my resolve fail me. Weeping, I tossed it into the sea.

I had left her letters last, so many that I could barely hold them in one hand. On top of them I laid Sadie's last letter. I raised my arm and opened my palm, and the sea-wind took them, carrying them out into the darkness above the waves. For a few moments I could see them, like lost gulls in the swirling air, searching for a place to land. Then there was only the darkness and the salty taste of the sea and my own tears.

TODAY

FIFTEEN

I can just see the roof of the High School from my window. It used to seem so . . . so grand in its high-windowed confidence, towering above the lodge. Yet its roof is only barely visible above the tops of these red-brick houses that cover the old rugby and hockey pitches. In the early mornings, before the house stirs to daily life (it's off-season, there's usually only a rare commercial traveller in, or sometimes the odd young couple on a fling who can't afford a hotel) I sometimes sit, sipping my first cup of tea, looking out the window. There's not much to see: a late-twentieth-century back garden that could be anywhere in any European city, shrubs and flowerbeds, red-and-green swings for the two children of the house, a tricycle discarded on the patch of winter lawn, waiting for the house to waken, waiting for spring to come. Beyond the garden, other homes, other fences. The hot tea steams up the window.

I was given the kettle, teapot and daily supplies after a week here, a sort of prize for fee-paying endurance. Sometimes I don't bother to wipe off the steam with my fingers and through the misted-up glass the 'executive-style' homes are seen only vaguely; they shimmer in the morning, disappearing into a mist which rings with the voices, loud and self-assured, of boys in rugger jerseys and girls in hockey kit. I find it oddly comforting, in a way I had neither expected nor wanted.

The Rackards have no idea that their off-season bonus – their quiet, well-spoken 'guest' from London – knew every blade of grass that once covered the site of this estate of houses. Not that Tom Rackard cares; at eight-forty every morning he's away to his middle-management job in the bank, son stowed safely in the back seat of the shining Japanese car, ready to be deposited for the day in the local primary school. Laura Rackard is another matter entirely, pretty, early thirties, upwardly mobile: 'We're at the stage where we have to take guests, the mortgage is enormous, but sometimes you wonder, they're not all like you, Michael.' She flirts a little but I have no wish to share in the intimacy that is offered. She doesn't believe I'm Irish. 'But you have such a lovely English accent,' she exclaims, 'almost like Prince Charles!'

I've given her to understand that I'm on sabbatical from my college in London. She's got it into her head that I spend my days in the local university library. I see no reason to correct my landlady's misapprehensions. She wouldn't be at all impressed if she knew of my visits to Billy's mother, in the terraced cottages down the hill.

Mrs Lally had been out washing the front window on that first morning. I hung back on the other side of the street, unsure of myself, not knowing why I had come here to stand on the once familiar hill, staring across at an old woman cleaning the window of the front room that housed the treasures of the house of Romanoff. Her squat body strained upwards towards the top of the window and she gave a last ineffectual shake of the yellow cloth at the unattainable corners before she subsided, grunting, on to her waddling hips. When she turned and saw me, she waved the duster like a flag and smiled cheerfully across the street. She might have been smiling at any stranger who caught her eye.

I moved slowly on up the hill. When I flung my brave words across the canteen at Palmer the previous day, I had given no thought to these final steps. *The Times* had marked the death of a pompous idiot who was the father of a girl whose memory I had tried, unsuccessfully, to bury for decades – that was all: the passing of a pretentious asshole who had once wounded a boy with a head full of poems and dreams and a beautiful girl. I had spent a lifetime trying to reinvent myself, yet a bland newspaper obituary could undo me in an instant: after all these years I was here, slowly climbing the hill, rounding the bend in the road, in sight of the old lodge.

The lodge was gone. The empty space where it had stood took my breath away – neither high walls nor dark green gates remained, just an empty space opening on to an unrestricted view of the old school. The ground was churned up by the heavy tracks of lorries and earth-moving machinery. What had been old and settled, sacramentally marked with the certainty of years and privilege, was new and raw and ugly. A builder's board was planted where the lodge had been, trumpeting of houses with *en suite* bathrooms and luxury apartments 'fit for gracious old-world living'. Beyond the old school building a bulldozer crawled across the broken earth and for a moment the sunny day was clouded with flying dust. From within the school came the sounds of hammering and electric drills, and a sudden loud crashing noise from the upper floor, and I had a vision of partitions crashing in the old dormitories, and Nicholas Kerr's trunk lying upside-down on the floor.

'We haven't anything ready for viewing yet.' The voice, friendly and apologetic, belonged to a shirt-sleeved fellow who had crunched his way across the rutted site to stand beside me. 'But you're welcome to take a look around inside if you like.'

'No thank you, I'm just looking.'

He was on to my accent at once. 'English? Or just been away for a long time?' His eyes were shrewd under the yellow hard hat.

'This used to be a school,' I said, ignoring his question.

'Boarding school, actually,' he said. 'One of our relics of oul' dacency.' His eyes were laughing, laying on the brogue. 'Jolly hockey sticks and all the rest of it. All gone but I'll say one thing for them – ' his voice had dropped confidentially ' – they had class, and you can't say that about many of my countrymen today.' He waited but I made no comment. 'Class.' He delivered the word reflectively. 'That's what we're trying to provide in these apartments – and in our houses too,' he added hastily, as if he might be accused of a sin of omission. 'You couldn't make a wiser investment in this town today and that's for sure.'

'I'm grateful to you for the advice.' I made a point of being polite to him. My mother would have narrowed her eyes and said he was 'on the make'.

I turned to go, but I couldn't keep the question from my lips. 'There was an old gate lodge – ?'

'To be sure there was.' He flung his arms expansively in the direction of the board that promised the glories of old-world living. 'Right there, rotten with damp and woodworm. It was the first thing that I got rid of – you'd wonder how anybody could have lived in it.'

It might have been worth it – just to see the astonishment in those shrewd eyes – to tell him that I knew exactly how people had lived in it. But I merely thanked him again and turned to go.

'You were at school here, weren't you?' You could hear the small triumph in his voice: I had forgotten how much we loved to live in one another's past here.

'Sort of,' I said over my shoulder.

It was a long day after that. I had slept badly the previous night in the small hotel near the railway station in Dublin, and the train journey west had tired me more than I had expected. Yet

I slogged onwards on foot, past the row of new houses flying their bed-and-breakfast pennants and deep into the sprawling estate which covered the old pitches. On one side a high wall marked the boundary of the smaller area which was earmarked for the latest phase of gracious living: on the other, the corrugated roof of the old stand in the sportsground told its own truth of that almost vanished world. I was unprepared for the echoes of schoolboy voices from beyond the stand, and I hurried past, sweating freely in the September sun.

I was even less prepared for the feelings that overwhelmed me when I stood at the wide-gated entrance to the cemetery, flanked by sloping lawns and beds of autumn flowers. Sadie was buried there, and my parents with her.

The abbot, sleek and plump in his belted soutane, had hovered solicitously beside my chair in his office as he told me of their deaths. When I'd applied to join the order I had told him the truth, that I'd had no contact with my family during the five years I had spent in England.

'You realise, Michael, that we had to make the usual enquiries about your family and your general fitness and so on in your home diocese.' I sat on the edge of the chair, waiting for the inevitable gesture of refusal from the sleek hands laced comfortably across his paunch. 'The authorities there have replied to us and I am pleased to say that reports of your character and education could not be higher. It's most gratifying to have a young man of your calibre wishing to join us here. I'm afraid, however, that I am the bearer of sad tidings regarding your parents. They passed away four years ago, within a month of each other.'

I was grateful for his gentleness and for his delicate refusal to pry into my absence of tears. I had cried myself out on the night ferry to Wales. In the crowded compartment of the mail-train from Holyhead I sat dry-eyed, trying to close my nostrils against the stench of stale drink and unwashed bodies. It was more difficult to close my mind upon the scene in that other railway carriage, in that other place . . . In that other *time*, I told myself, for already I saw it as a scene from a time and place I was leaving and to which I would not return. My companions in the compartment – a bunch of five friends from some village in County Mayo – were travelling *en masse* to promised jobs on a building site in London; only a little older than me, they were loud and friendly at first, offering me sandwiches and bottles of stout, but their good humour towards me changed to shoulder-shrugging indifference in the face of my sullen, monotone replies to their questions and their banter. I shut my eyes stubbornly and tried not to look at the fellow in the corner opposite me, slouched against the seat, while his hand played idly with the breast of the young girl who leaned against him. She was no older than Sadie but she was alive; she was not lying slumped against Nicholas in a carriage that reeked of the sweet stench of death.

At Euston station I hurried from the train without a word to any of them in the compartment. I was careful not to catch the eye of the young priest who stood, red-faced and bleary-eyed, outside the ticket-checker's barrier: I had heard of such priests, eager to help Irish emigrants find their feet on the foreign, sinful soil of London. I wanted no help. I sought only anonymity and a release from the pain of wanting her long, dark hair on my shoulder and her cool hand in mine.

The early morning streets of London held no release, afforded no hint of benediction. The long expanse of Euston Road stretched away in either direction, grey and almost deserted. I guessed it was about half past six in the morning. Less than twenty-four

304

hours had passed since I had walked out of the gate lodge for the last time, yet already a lifetime had passed.

Whether I turned left or right on Euston Road made no difference: in either direction lay only the unknown and the anonymity I craved. I hitched Sadie's duffle bag higher on my shoulder and swung right. I kept on walking until I reached Edgeware Road. The city was coming to life by then; there were cars and buses moving on the road. And I was tired. On a sidestreet off Edgeware Road I saw a sign in the window of a tall house advertising 'Bed-and-Breakfast. Hot and Cold. Weekly Rates'. The woman who answered the door had a cigarette in her mouth; she looked at me keenly before showing me the room; she looked at my money even more keenly when I paid her a week in advance.

I found a job that afternoon, as a porter in a department store on Oxford Street. It had the advantage of being close enough to walk from the bed and breakfast but I hated my green shop-coat and the endless carrying of shirt boxes and shoeboxes to the furnace in the basement. I had not traded one world for another simply to be another kind of porter, like my broken-nosed father.

It took one application form and two interviews to land a job in an insurance company. The pay wasn't much better than I'd been earning as a porter but I was determined to set myself on a different road. I bought a cheap suit which carried the bonus of a free polyester tie and I set about making my way up the ladder of the Worldwide General Assurance Company.

I shunned Kilburn and Camden Town and the other notorious Irish centres of London. I sought out no Irish papers, I gave up the practice of Sunday Mass. I worked on my accent, shaving it and refining it until it had shed its last trace of my home town. Once a week I went to the cinema with Carol, from the typing pool, a thin blonde in a short skirt with a left breast that felt surprisingly firm when she let me put my hand on it when we were closeted together in the shadows beside the tube station. She lived at home: not till three months later, on a Saturday afternoon, when my landlady was out, would she agree to come to bed in my digs. Gazing at her naked body, narrow-waisted and high breasted, I suddenly remembered Ella and my semen splashed all over Carol's flat white stomach. A month later she took me home to meet her parents, a miserable Sunday lunch in Essex with a silent mother and a tattooed father who told Irish jokes and laughed at my discomfort. In the months that followed, Carol talked ceaselessly about houses and loans and my bleak heart grew bleaker. She wept at first when I broke it off with her, then shouted and railed at me. I burrowed deeper into my cocoon and made sure I turned up on time for work every morning. The job was undemanding: every year I was advanced a clerical grade until, after five years, I was the supervisor of a small section that investigated potentially fraudulent claims.

By then I had a small flat off Baker Street. Young women wore Afghan coats and skirts so tiny that you could see their fannies when they sat down opposite you on the Underground. I avoided girls from the office, but 'swinging' London provided an endless supply of eager young females to warm my bed. I was going through a transparently bogus insurance claim one Friday afternoon when it suddenly occurred to me that I was a fraud myself. There was no obvious reason for this moment of epiphany: the office was its usual efficient self, the industrious silence punctuated by ringing phones and intermittent hoots of laughter occasioned by one of the more outrageous claims.

I went to Mass that Sunday morning for the first time since I had bought my ticket with Rosie's twenty-pound note. Nothing happened there either: no bells rang, no scales fell from my eyes, but I found some kind of comfort there, some element of relaxation. Three months later, having begun to attend Mass not just on Sundays but also mornings before work, I wrote to a monastery in the south-west, asking for details about joining. Two interviews with the abbot followed: there were long forms to be filled in.

Now the abbot was weighing my reaction to the news that my parents had been dead and buried for the last four years. 'What effect does this have,' I asked, 'on my application to join the order?'

None, he assured me, shaking my hand and welcoming me as a member of the family. But the look he gave me was long and searching.

I remembered it all now, standing outside the green railings of the cemetery, still unable to go in and stand at their grave.

I stayed for eight years with the order: a grim year in a novitiate that was ruled by bells and silence, followed by a year of basic philosophy in the order's own seminary. After that they had me marked for a different track: they sent me to university; kept me there, after taking my degree, to take my doctorate. I was a coming man, one of the new men who would inherit heaven on earth. After university I was being sent back to the mother house in the wooded countryside of the south-west, for a year of prayer and reflection before ordination.

The abbot was as urbane as ever when I told him I was leaving. They gave me a few pounds, a new suitcase and a one-way ticket to London. The abbot himself drove me to the railway station. Over the years I had come to know him as a member of one of England's oldest landed Catholic families, a pipe-smoking intellectual whose books had been prescribed reading for my university degree. 'Forgive me if I offer you a little advice, Michael – from a friend now, no longer your abbot.' We were standing on the pavement outside Exeter station. 'Take a little time to find out who you are and ignore the gospel injunction about not taking the time to bury your dead: go home and bury yours, and mourn them.'

A taxi pulled up, spilling out a business type who rushed into the station as if he had a fire in his trousers. The abbot laughed, looking after his fleeing figure: 'We spend so much time rushing to catch trains that we don't know where we're coming from, let alone where we're going to.'

Too many memories were crowding me, too fast, too furious. I turned away from the graveyard, heading back into town.

It was a different town. The Square was naked, its skirt of black railings torn away to expose a belly of scorched grass and low concrete walls. Back-packers in army surplus pushed sullenly past, their bearded faces bent over maps and guide books. I remembered that an article in the travel pages of *The Times* had described the town as 'a mecca for youth, the fastest-growing city in Europe.'

'Bollocks,' I said aloud, and a young girl with a chalk-white face and a stud in her nose turned to smile at me.

I checked into a hotel at the top of the Square before going back to the station to collect my bag. I ate dinner alone that night in a small café with check tablecloths and a fair-haired waitress whose shapely arse had been poured into a pair of Wranglers. I thought of my first year students back in the University of West London, my office door carefully opened wide against all possible charges of sexual harassment. Bad thoughts were another matter: like the poor, they were always with you.

I fiddled with my glass of lager on the check tablecloth. I figured I'd go back to my students and Palmer and Peggy the next day. Sodding Esmonde FitzArthur was dead and buried somewhere up in County Mayo: he certainly wasn't visiting this makebelieve

Mexican restaurant in one of the back streets of my old town. Neither was his daughter.

But I'm still here, three months later, on a December morning, watching as my tea fogs up the window of Laura Rackard's B & B, listening to the voices echoing from vanished fields. I blame Billy's mother for my being here still.

I had slept only fitfully on my first night – my only night – in the hotel on the Square. My room fronted on to the Square, smack in the firing line of the young pilgrims who had found at last their modern mecca: their drunken prayers and ribald hymns did not cease until well into the night. Occasional cars coughed by, grinding their way around the corners of the Square. Sleepless, I remembered the deserted streets through which I had stalked them in that other life.

There was time to kill the next morning before catching the eleven-thirty train back to Dublin. It was not impulse that drove me to Billy's house – I like to think that I am a creature of bells and regulated hours – rather, perhaps, a nagging curiosity to know what had happened. I had often teased my mother about her sentry-like observation of the comings and goings through the gates of the High School. I was, after all, the product of her genes: curiosity had to be satisfied.

The brass knocker gleamed with the sweat and proud polish of years. I had to knock a second time before I heard her slippered gait shuffling towards me in the hall. When she opened the door she looked up at me questioningly. Her hair was snow-white and I could see patches of her pink scalp through its white fuzziness. Her habitual smile, trusting as I remembered, transformed her round doughy face.

'Yes?'

'It's Michael,' I said, 'Michael O'Hara.'

Her mouth full, her face frozen in momentary disbelief. I saw her eyes measure my own lined face and the grey in my hair. Something like recognition dawned slowly in those disbelieving eyes. And then she began to weep. It was awful: great blobs of tears coursing down those puddingy cheeks, her round shoulders heaving as she sobbed. I reached out to touch her but was afraid to, and my hands just hovered there uselessly, terrified of her sobbing, wobbling body.

And then she laughed, a gasping snuffling laugh that splashed tears on to my jacket. 'Amn't I terrible?' Billy's mother said. 'Keeping you standing on the doorstep!'

She took me by the arm and led me inside, still laughing, still crying. We sat in the kitchen, bigger now, extended back into the small yard, crammed with expensive-looking cabinets and gadgets. 'The lads!' she said dismissively, when she caught me looking at the array of kitchen furniture. 'They're always changing things when they come, but they never stay.' She made a foray into the front room and came back, triumphant, with gold-rimmed bone china crockery that reminded me of Mrs Willoughby on the last day. 'I never get a chance to use the good stuff!' she exclaimed happily. 'And I haven't forgotten what you and Billy used to call my good dinner service!' Throughout the long morning of stories about her sons in America, it was the only reference she made to Billy.

I kept an eye on the clock at first but after half-eleven I didn't bother. There were other trains. The talk tumbled out of her, as if she had been too long without an audience. Some years the lads didn't come at all: they had families, jobs, even grandchildren. She was a great-grandmother, she said, pointing out the photograph of an infant cradled in the arms of a grey-haired old man. I had to look a second time before I recognised Billy's eldest brother. 'You'd think he was your brother, not your son,' I said gently.

'Wait till I tell him what you said!' she cried happily.

I made to leave but she waved me back to my chair. She made more tea and produced another set of china from the treasury in the front room. After she had poured fresh cups for us she fell silent. She worked her mouth in and out with the sucking noises of the aged. Her lips were scored with a hundred creases, like cuts on scorched paper. I could sense that she was trying to figure out how to speak of my past.

'I'd be telling a lie, Michael,' she began, 'if I didn't say that I couldn't understand what you did, leaving them like that. Your father couldn't speak with the shock and your mother was beside herself. It'd break your heart to see her beside the coffin that evening. You'd think the child was only sleeping in it and then they closed the lid on it and your mother just stood there like she was lost or not even alive herself.' She looked straight at me then, the withered mouth puckered. 'You should have been there, Michael. Your father was useless to her, like a baby. And on top of all that, your mother was frantic with worry about you. The poor woman didn't know if you were alive or dead. The guards were looking for you and your name was read out on the wireless. The only thing that consoled the poor woman was that the fella in the station remembered selling a ticket to London to a youngster who came rushing in at the last minute. It was all she had to hold on to. She used to pray for you every morning and night, that you were safe and sound, wherever you were.' She dropped her glance but I knew she was waiting for me to speak.

'I never meant to hurt anybody.' My voice sounded like a whisper. I had never once spoken of the events of that night and day to anybody since then. 'I was young,' I added lamely.

'Your mother and father were young too,' Billy's mother said, 'too young to lie down and die. Your father was gone within the year and your poor mother a few weeks later. It was like she was holding on till he was gone first, like she knew he couldn't manage without her. Your mother and myself were the one age,' she finished, with an odd girlish shake of her white head. 'She'd be eighty now, if the Lord had spared her.'

I could think of nothing to say.

'Have you been up to visit their grave, Michael?' My silence was answer enough. 'But you are going to visit them?' she persisted.

'Tomorrow,' I said, shamed by her loyalty. 'Tomorrow.'

And so I stayed a second night, this time in 'Journey's End', the unimaginatively named Rackard B&B.

Next morning I did not hesitate at the gates of the new cemetery (it had been 'new' ever since I had first heard of it as a boy). I followed Mrs Lally's directions, along the wide gravelled avenue, past the tall stone crosses with their attendant angels, down to the more modest memorials of recent times, in the shadow of the high limestone wall.

A black marble slab marked the place where they lay. The gold lettering glinted in the autumnal sunlight: John ('Jack') O'Hara, Elizabeth O'Hara, their beloved daughter, Sarah ('Sadie') aged 17 years. May they rest in peace. The provenance of the marble memorial was told in smaller italic letters sculpted into its base: *Erected in friendship and gratitude by their friends at the High School.*

My father, I thought, would sleep easier, confident that his allegiance had not gone unrewarded.

I turned away without attempting to pray. I had not prayed since I had left the order. Sometimes the words came into my head, like old rhymes remembered from school.

Without knowing why, I posted a note to Peggy asking her to let Palmer know that I might not be back for the start of term in October. By return I received, c/o 'Journey's End', a large manila envelope containing the university's pages of regulations governing illness and sick-pay. On the unsigned, accompanying compliment slip Peggy had written only two words: 'Why not?' I read the document carefully, paying particular attention to the clauses Peggy had marked with a yellow highlighter. When I had finished I carefully tore up the typed pages and disposed of them in a rubbish bin on the Square, at a safe remove from my landlady's wandering eyes.

By then I had acquired a quasi-residential status at 'Journey's End'. The university's name on the manila envelope had been noted; I had been conferred with my personal kettle, teapot and china cup. And I was calling to see Billy's mother every day. After a week it was assumed that I would call daily, towards five o'clock, after I had exhausted myself rediscovering – or perhaps discovering for the first time – my old town. Mrs Lally no longer asked when I was leaving, nor did I have any inclination to leave. I felt permanently tired, although I did little except walk, half-read a newspaper, call to see the old woman.

I hardly knew what I was doing, although I think now I do, sitting here at my window in the early morning. Slowly but surely I was chipping away at the walls I had built around my deepest heart and with equal slowness I was learning, to my dismay, that it housed only emptiness. The visits to Billy's mother in some way filled that void which I had hidden from myself: she has drawn me into another's life and, for once, I have neither run away nor raised my habitual walls.

One evening in mid-October – I had been here almost a month

at the time – Billy's mother invited me to have dinner with her. She was wearing a dark-blue dress with a white lace collar; she smiled happily when I thanked her and complimented her on the meal. It was no surprise when she took out the old chocolate box full of photographs.

Over the pictures she told me, for the first time, about Billy. His brothers, mindful of his youth and size, had found him work in the office of an Irish-American building contractor. He'd prospered; in a few years he was the boss's right-hand man. His mother beamed, passing me the photographs of the Billy I remembered: the mocking smile, the hair groomed, the world in his hands. He'd taken out American citizenship, married the daughter of an emigrant from County Kerry. He fell in with a bad lot then, his mother said: he must have done, or the drinking and the gambling would never have started. His brothers couldn't talk to him, nobody could. He stopped writing home. The older brothers responded evasively to her letters, her umpteen questions. The first she knew of what was going on came when the daughter of the County Kerry emigrant wrote to say that Billy was serving a jail sentence and she was divorcing him. His mother was vague about details; they let Billy out of prison after eight years.

'He's never come back to visit me since,' his mother said to me, fixing the tasselled lid on the chocolate box. 'He thinks I'd be ashamed of him and all I want is to see him.'

The following day I visited a doctor whose name I took from the phone book. He asked a few questions, wrote a few notes on an index card and scribbled a medical certificate for a week's leave due to exhaustion. I felt that my action in visiting the doctor was somehow connected with Billy and his mother but the connection eluded me, like a word that lingers just beyond the tip of your tongue. The only question the doctor asks now is how I'm enjoying my stay in the town. He writes the certificate without waiting for an answer. He has settled on backache as the cause of my continuing exhaustion; my latest cert covers me up to early in the New Year. I feel no guilt about taking the university's salary cheques – I was due a sabbatical anyway, but government cuts put paid to that.

Peggy sends me little gossipy notes from time to time; Palmer makes no comment when she presents him with my medical certificates but at departmental meetings he is loud in his praise of my temporary replacement, an earnest young theologian who dresses like a Mormon and extols the value of a ruggedly individualistic, self-help Christianity. She's trying to establish the marketplace rent, she says, for the boxes of books and records, the hi-fi and the pictures that she's been storing for me in her garage since I gave up my flat.

Billy's mother is going to ask me to come and live in her house. She hasn't asked me yet but she's shown me round the house, pointing out the many renovations that her sons have paid for – the wall-to-wall carpeting, the wall-to-wall tiles in the gleaming bathroom. We're going to have Christmas dinner together; none of the lads will be home and wouldn't it be madness for her to be sitting down alone to roast turkey and plum pudding? She'll probably ask me then, over the turkey and ham on the Romanoff treasures.

I think I know what answer I'm going to give her. I tell her about most things, when we sit in her kitchen with our cups of tea – what the man in the newsagent said, which café I drank coffee in, where my daily walk took me.

Yesterday I told her about Threadneedle Road and Rosie. It was raining when I stopped outside the house: new aluminium windows and a storm porch with sliding doors, but otherwise the same house, the same crescent tarmac drive where the car had stalled and Ella had climbed on the bar of my bike under her aunt's disapproving eyes. The woman who answered the door could have been a clone of my landlady; elegant in lemon sweatshirt and dark tracksuit bottoms, enamelled smile at the ready to answer my question. She was sorry but she'd never heard of the Roses; it must be a long time since they'd lived there, the people from whom she and her husband had bought the house seven years ago were called Murphy; they lived in Dublin, she thought, but she had no address for them. It didn't matter, I said, turning back down the road towards the prom in the drizzle.

Mrs Lally allowed herself a little smile when I told her about it, as if she knew more than I did. 'I used to be jealous of that lad,' she said, half laughing, 'when I'd see the two of ye going up and down the hill. I used to think it should be you and Billy, like it always was before he went off to America. I never forgot the lad's name. Your mother and myself used to think it was a disgrace that such a fine fellow had an old cissy name like Rosie. It just wasn't right.' Her mouth puckered, gathering the words, coming to the point. 'Wasn't his picture on the front of the *Tribune* years afterwards, beyond in Rome, being ordained a priest by the Holy Father himself.'

'Rosie?' I asked incredulously.

'Himself,' she said, 'the handsomest priest you could ever set eyes on, and his mother beside him as proud as punch, rubbing up against the Pope of Rome.'

I had to smile. If Rosie were going to be a priest – and he'd never mentioned it – where else would he be ordained but in Rome? I could imagine him introducing himself to the vicar of Christ on earth, assuring him of his support, perhaps offering a suggestion or two for improving the administration of the Vatican.

'He's out in South America or Africa or one of those places,' Mrs Lally said. 'He often has a letter to the paper in the *Tribune*, always looking for money for building churches or schools or something. He comes home now and again and it's always the same. You'll see his picture in the paper, good-looking as ever, and he'll be going on about the same stuff, building hospitals and the like. If you stay on here,' she finished, giving me a shrewd look, 'you're bound to meet him. He always turns up, looking for money.'

There's a little guile in the way she tells me things, feeding me a little information, doled out with a lighter hand than the enormous dinners she presents to me. It's her way of tempting me, luring me to the comforts of her lonely house with a diet of titbits from the past.

She has no need to tempt me. I feel welcome in her house. Each evening I look forward to our chinwag, our pot of tea, the comfortable silences. It won't be too difficult to decide what to do when she asks me to move into Billy's old room.

I haven't yet told her about my trip to Castlebar. I was here for two months before I was able to screw up courage enough to visit Ella's home town. It felt strange to be walking the streets of the town which had filled so many of my waking hours in the long-ago; a green square with a statue of some patriot, a straggling main street of pubs and small shops and fast-food joints. I felt vaguely cheated, making my way along that nondescript street; this was no fit territory for barefoot Yeatsian ladies bearing tall candles in their pale hands. I walked on, over a humpback bridge towards the far end of the town. Instinct or chance or whatever you want to call it had led me to her home: a fence of spiked grey railings, two tall stone gate-piers, a wooden plaque on one of them bearing the name, 'Grove House'. The house itself was set well back from the road, behind trim lawns, approached by a straight drive that was littered with the last leaves of November. It was smaller than I had expected, with a plain door and cramped upstairs windows that almost touched the blue slates. For all that, I gazed on it with hunger: hundreds of times my yearning finger had traced its name, 'Grove House', on the top of her sprawling letters, and I had fallen asleep with the name on my lips.

I had a glimpse of her that evening, about six o'clock, when she arrived back in her small black car. I watched from across the road as she turned into the drive, the dead leaves scattering before her. When she got out of the car and she faced briefly towards me, I feared that she must see me, standing there under the tree beside the bridge, but the moment passed and she reached into the back seat of the car. When she straightened she was holding her briefcase. I held my breath, drinking in the dark hair, still soft and long, framing that lovely face. Then she was gone and the door closed behind her. No lights were switched on in the front of the house. I waited for a long time but no other cars came. I checked into the dark hotel guarded by the stone rebel, and when I walked by Grove House at eleven o'clock that night, there was still only her small black car parked on the drive. The next morning, shortly after nine, I watched her leave alone to drive the short distance to her office. I'd spotted the brass plate on the tall stone building overlooking the green square: Esmonde FitzArthur, Solicitor, Commissioner for Oaths.

My journey back on the bus was thoughtful. It seemed that Ella lived alone but what was I to do? It's a question that occupies much of my time on these mornings by the window of 'Journey's End'. Sometimes I dream about it. Often I daydream about it. In my mind I can paint a picture of it.

It's evening when I walk up the drive, maybe springtime, but the trees are still spare and leafless against the western sky. There are lights in the windows of Grove House, as if she has been waiting for me for all these years. The curtains are not drawn and I pause for a moment to look at her through the small window-panes: she stands by the fireplace, one lovely hand resting on the marble mantelpiece, her head poised, as if she were listening to some music that I cannot hear, as I stand breathless in the night outside. Behind me, in the trees, a night bird stirs and the air is heavy with the rush of wings. I watch her turn towards the window, drawn by the noise in the darkening garden, and I look into those eyes that I loved for so long and she tosses the long dark hair that brushed my face on the long bicycle ride along the prom and Ella sees me, standing there in the yellow light, and her eyes crinkle up at me, blessing me with their smile. In my mind I can paint a picture of it.

After Christmas, or early in the New Year, I will stand in front of the plain door of Grove House and wait for her to open it. I've closed enough of them in my time. I plan to tell Billy's mother about it at Christmas but not until after I've accepted her invitation to move into Billy's room. Living there, being with that old woman, will be a kind of atonement for all I have done and left undone. It's a dream, but dreams don't come free and I have yet to pay the price of mine.

By the same author

Walking the Line: Scenes from an Army Childhood (autobiography)